THE LAW OF THE SEA

A NOVEL BY

DAVE GERARD

THE LAW OF THE SEA

ONE

The call came in around 10 a.m. on a Monday. I was drinking bad coffee and trying to clear a couple dozen emails from my inbox.

"I AM OF NIGERIA, HAVE FOUND GREAT TREASURE, MUCH MONEY, NEED ONLY FINANCING TO OBTAIN. PLEASE CONTACT ME PROVIDE BANK ACCOUNT INFORMATION. I WILL..."

I hit delete and scrolled on. There were a couple of emails from Bob Kruckemeyer with the subject line *re: motion to compel.* Kruckemeyer was a senior partner in the firm's class action division. He was a rainmaker and a noted asshole. He wanted a draft of a motion to compel by tomorrow. There was no need for a draft tomorrow, since the motion couldn't be filed for another month. But I put it at the top of my to-do list anyway.

I responded to a few inquiries on my contract case, deleted an email with the subject line "mid-level associate needed at Am-law 100 firm," and deleted another one explaining a boneheaded new IT policy that the firm was rolling out.

The phone rang. It wasn't an internal number. Lately, I had been getting a lot of spam robocalls asking if I wanted to sign up for free healthcare. After two rings, I picked it up.

"Jack Carver," I said into the receiver.

"Jack. Bob Kruckemeyer. How are you doing?"

I grimaced. Must be his cell. "Oh. Hello Mr. Kruckemeyer," I said. "I'm sorry I haven't responded to your email yet, I've been buried by—"

"Look, that's okay. Just get me a draft by tomorrow."

"I will," I said.

"Great," said Kruckemeyer. "But that's not why I'm calling. Listen, I need you to handle something for me. We've got a client, pro bono thing. I need you to take this."

"Sure, Mr. Kruckemeyer. I'd be happy to. Who's the client?"

"It's this legal aid clinic. We've committed to sending someone today. Jorgensen was going to go but she backed out. Had some kind of 'health' issue." Kruckemeyer grumbled at this.

"Okay," I said. "Is there a matter number for this or—"

"No, there's no matter number for this. Didn't I just say pro bono?"

I cursed at myself. "Right. Okay. I'll take care of it."

"Good. Should be pretty straightforward. The clinic is downtown. 2:30 p.m. You got that?"

"Yeah. 2:30 p.m. What day?"

"Today."

I paused. "Today?"

"Yes. So get down there and handle it." There was a click as he hung up the phone.

I sighed. No matter number. This meant whatever bullshit small-time assignment this was wouldn't be billable, and wouldn't count toward my quota. It was just extra work.

I got up and grabbed the suit that was hanging on the back of my office door. I always kept one on hand, just in case. As a litigator, you never knew when you might need to go to court. It wasn't often. But to tell you the truth, it made me feel like a superhero, costume at the ready, able to spring from a desk-bound paper clerk to man of action in a single bound.

In the bathroom, I looked at myself in the mirror as I put on my tie. I was six foot one with sandy hair. Thirty years old. I was probably handsomer a couple of years ago. Before the work and the stress and the late nights took their toll. But I still looked pretty good. My eyes were tired.

The tie was dark red. Conservative, in the old sense of the word. Unlikely to offend a judge or a juror or somebody's eighty-year-old grandfather who had fought in Vietnam. I finished the four-in-hand knot with a flourish, and then walked out the door.

The pro bono clinic was in an old, run-down building in downtown Houston. On the drive, I felt every crack in the asphalt in my old BMW coupe, which was rapidly attaining beater status. I grimaced each time I hit a pothole.

I parked at the clinic and went inside. The walls were an off-cream color, stained by the passage of time. At the front desk, a young woman smiled and said she would be right with me. There were a dozen people in the waiting area. Clients. The old and the downtrodden and the poor. I put on a smile and waved, and got a surprisingly warm reception. Maybe this wouldn't be so bad. Presently, I was ushered back to a conference room. There were a couple of other volunteers, and an older lawyer named Kevin, who worked for the clinic full time.

"We really appreciate your being here," Kevin said sincerely. "And so do our clients. These are people who can't afford a lawyer. We're just here to give them some basic legal advice. Nothing fancy. People come for things like landlord-tenant disputes, divorce papers, past-due bills, and things like that. We've got a manual here which covers some of the more common situations."

He passed out copies of a thick binder that had seen much use. I flipped through the pages. One volunteer, a nervous-looking man in his forties, raised his hand. "What if we don't know the answers?" he asked. "I practice trusts and estates mostly."

It was a good point. Law is a very specialized business. My specialty, for example, was commercial litigation. That meant I knew how to sue a business, or be sued by a business. But if you asked me to write a will, or draft a merger agreement, I'd be lost. I could figure it out. But you would be better off going to a specialist. Hell, even within commercial litigation there were dozens of different subspecialties.

"That's okay," said Kevin reassuringly. "We don't expect you to know everything. A lot of times all you need to do is provide a little common sense and understanding. Tell them what they need to look into, or whether they need to hire an attorney. Listen to them and do whatever you can to help. It is appreciated. And of course, don't hesitate to ask me if you have any questions."

After that, Kevin split us up and put us in separate rooms. I was placed in an old nineteen-sixties era office with a metal desk and Soviet-style green walls. I banged my knee twice trying to sit down. Eventually, I got myself situated. I placed a pen and a legal pad in front of me like a sword and shield, and waited for business.

My first client was an old lady who was having trouble getting her social security payments. They were being sent to an old address, and she didn't know how to update it. I found an FAQ online and printed out the change of address form. I helped her fill out the form, and told her where to mail it. She thanked me profusely, as if I had just performed a miracle.

My second client was a quarrelsome man in his early thirties who was having difficulty with his landlord. He hadn't paid rent in about a year, and the landlord was trying to evict him. I told him that, unfortunately, he didn't have many legal rights unless he paid rent. He kept saying that he was looking for a way to "lawyer" them (looking pointedly at me when he said it). He was disappointed when I told him it didn't work like that. Of course, there are ways to "lawyer" your way out of that kind of situation—you could file a bullshit lawsuit and tie the issue up in court for a while—but these methods are invariably more complicated and expensive than just paying rent.

A couple more people came in with legal issues through the afternoon, including another with a landlord-tenant question, one with a child custody issue I had no idea how to handle, and two people with questions that could be (and were) answered with a Google search. I was getting the hang of this.

At 5 p.m., Ashley Marcum walked in.

She was in her late twenties, with pale skin and long, dark hair. I could see the edge of a tattoo peeking out from under her sleeve. She had big eyes and carried a large purse over her shoulder.

"Hi," she said uncertainly, looking around as if she wasn't sure she was in the right place. I got up, slammed my knee on the metal desk, tried not to wince, and stammered out a greeting.

"Hi," I said. "Jack Carver." I reached out to shake her hand.

"Ashley Marcum," she replied.

"Please, take a seat," I said, wishing I'd worn a better suit. "What can I do for you?"

Ashley put her purse on the table and sat down. "I'm not exactly sure," she said. "I need to file a probate application. For my brother. David Marcum. He passed away."

"I'm sorry to hear that," I said, pausing for a moment. "What happened to him? If you don't mind me asking."

"No, I don't mind," she said. "But I don't know." She sounded frustrated. "We don't—we didn't—talk much. A couple of weeks ago, I got a package in the mail from him. I called him, but he didn't answer. His cell phone was dead."

I listened and scrawled some notes on my legal pad as she continued.

"All I know is that he was working for a company called Rockweiller Industries. I contacted them, and they told me he died. Some kind of accident. Since then, they've been giving me the runaround. First, they told me they didn't know how he died. Then they told me it was confidential. Now they say they can only talk to the executor of my brother's estate. That I need to file a probate case and get an executor appointed. I don't know how to do that. So I'm here." She shrugged helplessly.

I frowned at this. "That's odd," I said. "That they wouldn't tell you what happened to him. Is there a death certificate?"

"No."

"Did they say what kind of an accident it was?" I asked.

"No."

"Or where it happened?"

"No, they wouldn't tell me that either."

I didn't know what to make of this. "What did your brother send you in the mail?" I asked, more to buy time than anything else.

"Oh, I almost forgot," she said. "I have it here. This is the weirdest part." She reached into her purse and pulled out a big FedEx envelope that was torn at the sides and stopped up with tape. She pulled the tape off and upended it onto the table. Its contents spilled out in a rush.

It was gold. Thick, heavy gold coins. They weren't shiny, like the gold you imagine at Fort Knox, sitting in perfect, gleaming rows. These coins were discolored and blotchy, like birthmarks on a face. There were greenish-red-brown marks on them, as if they had rusted or tarred. It was as if layers of something was covering them so deeply that no amount of shine could get it out. They looked old, and out of place under the cheap fluorescent lights of the room.

I froze for a moment. I instinctively knew the coins were old and very valuable. I picked up one and studied it. It had some type of pattern on its face, but I couldn't make it out under all the grime. It looked like swirling lines. They reminded me of designs I'd seen at ancient Indian temples on a trip I once made to the remote regions of Rajasthan and Goa.

"Was your brother a coin collector?" I asked dubiously.

"Not that I know of. But..." she shrugged.

"Did he send you anything else?"

"No."

"Okay," I said, sitting back in my chair. I tried to think about what to do. As an attorney, you have to impart confidence, Kruckemeyer always said. Even if you don't always know what you're doing.

"I can help you file a probate case," I said. "That's pretty routine. We just open a file, inventory your brother's assets, and the court will appoint an executor." I wasn't a probate specialist. But I remembered that much from the bar exam.

"Who will the executor be?" she asked.

"Did your brother have a wife?" I asked.

"No."

"Kids?"

"No."

"Maybe your mother or father, then?"

She shook her head. "They both passed away when we were young."

"Oh. Okay. Well if your brother doesn't have any closer living relatives, then it would probably be you."

"That's fine. What do I have to do?"

"I can start the paperwork today, and we can try to get you in front of the judge in a week or two if you'd like."

"That would be great," she said, nodding at me. For a little too long. She had no mother or father to talk to about this. Or any close family besides a brother who was now dead. I realized suddenly that I might have been one of the first people she'd spoken to about it.

"I can also run a background check on your brother to see if I can turn up any more information," I added. Couldn't hurt.

"Yes. Thank you so much," she said.

I nodded. "Finally, I'd like to take one of these coins with me for examination. I may be able to tell you something about it. If we know where it's from, that might tell us something."

She hesitated for a second. No doubt questioning whether she should give the gold to a total stranger. But then she picked one up and gave it to me. People put too much trust in lawyers, I think. But in this case, it wasn't misplaced.

I didn't know what happened to Ashley's brother. Or how Rockweiller Industries was involved. But I did know how to find out where the coins were from. And on the way back to the office, I stopped to do just that.

TWO

I parked in the back of a run-down strip mall in midtown Houston and walked up a dirty stairwell to the second floor. I passed a dry cleaners, a Chinese restaurant, and an axe-throwing venue before arriving at a small office with bolted doors and no windows. A small sign in faded gold letters read: Dr. Richard Avoulay, Precious Metals Assayer. I rang the bell, and he buzzed me in.

Dr. Avoulay was a quiet, bookish man. He wore a white lab coat and round spectacles. I knew him from a divorce case I had been involved in the previous year. The firm didn't usually do divorces. But Kruckemeyer knew the husband, and he was rich. So we took it. We hired Dr. Avoulay to value the husband's antique coin collection.

At the close of the trial, the judge ordered the husband to turn over half of the coin collection to his soon-to-be ex-wife. The husband refused, telling the judge that he would rather go to hell. Then he proceeded to swallow a fistful of gold coins right there in open court. In the legal fracas that followed, the wife's attorney demanded disgorgement—that is, the return of the coins, by any means necessary. We refused, arguing that the husband had a Fourteenth Amendment right to control of his own body. We won. But the judge held the husband in contempt, fined him the value of the coins, and threw him in jail.

The gold was nonreactive, and sat peaceably in the husband's insides while the legal saga played out. Eventually they passed through, and the wife's attorney went after them again. She got them, albeit not cleanly.

I didn't blame the husband for what he did. She had cheated on him every day for a year.

Dr. Avoulay greeted me warmly. We made some small talk, and he invited me back to his lab. I had never been in the lab before. It was all metal walls and steel tables, a harsh contrast to the pleasant offices outside.

I withdrew an envelope from my pocket and took out the coin.

"What can you tell me about this?" I asked, offering it to him.

Dr. Avoulay put on a pair of gloves and took it. He scrutinized it with an expert eye and turned it over a few times, lightly brushing the tarnished surface.

"It's gold," he said. "Which you probably guessed. By the look and feel of it, I'd say it's high quality, maybe pure. It weighs nearly an ounce." He put the coin on a small scale to confirm the weight, which was accurate.

"What's it worth?" I asked.

"If this is pure, the value of the gold would be maybe fifteen hundred dollars. But this looks very old. If it's a collector's item, the historical value could be higher. Maybe two to three times that. Where did you get it?"

"A client," I said. I didn't want to disclose much at this point. "She inherited it, you could say. She doesn't know where it's from. There are a couple dozen of them."

Avoulay raised his eyebrows. "Museums or wealthy collectors might have coins like this," he said. "But look at how dirty it is. If it's an antique, it would have been cleaned and polished. This coin has been sitting somewhere undisturbed for a very long time."

"How long?" I asked.

"Decades at least. Maybe longer," he said.

This gave me pause. How could David Marcum have acquired gold coins that had been sitting somewhere for decades?

"I can perform an analysis, which may give us a clue as to the age and origin of the metal," Avoulay continued. "Assuming you want non-destructive methods, I can use specific gravity, neutron activation, or x-ray fluorescence, either wave-length dispersive or energy dispersive. In fact, if you have an hour to spare, I can probably do one of them right now."

I didn't know what all of that meant, but I trusted that he did. I also sensed an undercurrent of excitement in his voice. If Avoulay was that interested, so was I.

"Okay," I said. "I've got time. Let's do it."

I sat down in a corner and took out my laptop as Dr. Avoulay put on some goggles and busied himself with a set of metal contraptions.

"How's Bob Kruckemeyer?" he asked, as he inserted the gold into some kind of tray.

"Still saving the world, one billable hour at a time," I replied.

Avoulay chuckled. After that, he fell quiet as he became absorbed in his work. I opened up my laptop and answered a few emails.

Toward the end of the hour, Dr. Avoulay took off his gloves, returned the coin, and sat down. He looked unsatisfied.

"So?" I asked.

"Unfortunately, I can't tell the origin of the gold. I've never seen isotopes like this before. Most gold is mined from China, South Africa, the United States, Australia, and a handful of other countries. By looking at what isotopes occur in the gold, I can usually tell where it's from. But this gold is not from any of those places," he said.

I frowned. "So where is it from?"

"It could be from another country. A bigger lab might be able to tell you. But the really surprising thing is the age of the metal."

"The age? You said it was at least a couple of decades old, right?"

"Actually, it's much older than that. This gold coin is several hundred years old, at least. With more analysis, I could be precise. But if I were a betting man, Mr. Carver, I would say this coin is several centuries old."

"Centuries?" I said with a start.

"Yes. Gold has been around since the dawn of human civilization, of course, so there are much older samples. But this is rare nonetheless."

I sat for a moment, absorbing this information.

"I would recommend showing the coin to a numismatist," Avoulay continued. A numismatist, as I had learned during my last go-round with Dr. Avoulay, was a student and collector of coins. "Once this is cleaned, he or she may be able to recognize the markings on the coin. That could be the best way to determine its origin."

I thought about this. "Let's hold off on showing it to anyone else just now," I decided. "I'll ask the client about it."

Dr. Avoulay nodded. "Understood. Keep me posted. I'll be interested to hear what you find out."

"Me too," I said.

As I left Dr. Avoulay's office, I wondered. How had David Marcum gotten his hands on centuries-old, unidentified gold coins?

As I got back into my car, I took out my phone and emailed the firm's ace researcher, Lyle. I gave him David Marcum's date of birth and social security number, which Ashley had given me at the clinic. I asked him to run a background report and see what he could find. By the time I got back to the office, an answer was waiting for me.

Hey bud, read the email from Lyle. *Got your background report. Also managed to find a photo and an old resume. Take a look.*

Awesome, I wrote back. *Appreciate it. Thanks.*

No problem, came the instant reply. *I'm signing off but I'll check in with you tomorrow. Later.*

I opened the photo first. It was taken a few years ago, and showed David in the middle of two other people. He was handsome, with a fine-boned face and closely-cropped hair. He wore a devil-may-care smile and a black t-shirt that said "Fuck You, Houston's Awesome." I could see the resemblance to Ashley.

Next, I looked at the resume. David Marcum had attended college, and made good marks at a good school. But he had dropped out two or three years in. That was ten years ago, which would have made him around the same age as me. After that, he'd held a lot of different jobs. Sales, bartending, journalism, mechanics. Skilled in Microsoft Word, Excel, and a handful of other basic programs. Fluent in Spanish and Portuguese. Interests: football, yoga, European history, and scuba diving. A man of many talents.

The background report told a more troubling story. Marcum had several minor felony and misdemeanor charges on his record. Two DUI's. Public intoxication. Simple assault. Assault again. Reckless driving. There was nothing really major, like aggravated assault or armed robbery, but it was enough to give me pause. There were also a couple of outstanding judgments against the guy. Small things like unpaid rent, or other minor debts. I wondered again how Marcum had gotten the coins, uneasily this time.

There was nothing on his resume about Rockweiller Industries. But the company was easy enough to find online. Rockweiller was a multi-billion-dollar oil company, publicly traded on the New York Stock Exchange. It was headquartered in Houston and had lines of business all over the world. Oil and gas exploration, refining, pipelines, minerals, you name it. The company's website proudly displayed a picture of its founder, Kurt Rockweiller. He had been a titan of industry. I saw a picture of him from the 1930's. He looked tough. Like the kind of guy who would break a labor strike. Or fire your dad.

"Hey buddy," said a sly voice, interrupting my train of thought. I looked up. "What are you doing all dressed up today?" It was Harder.

T. Richard Harder III was an associate, like me. Harder stood about five-ten, with dark hair and a preppy expression. He was a year or two ahead of me at the firm. Harder had gone to an Ivy league school and thought pretty highly of himself. One of those people who like to refer to themselves as "type A." We called them gunners in law school. Always sitting at the front of the class, always raising their hand, always the first to throw you under the bus.

I swiveled my chair around and sat back, clasping my hands behind my head. "Had to go to a pro bono clinic today," I said casually. "Kruckemeyer asked me to cover it last minute. I've got to go to court this week on a case I picked up there." I said this like it was no big deal, but Harder wasn't fooled. He narrowed his eyes, jealous. Court was always a big deal, even in a pro bono case. I grinned.

"Pro bono, huh?" he said. "That probably won't make your 1099."

My expression soured. Harder was referring to my independent contractor status. You see, technically, I wasn't a regular employee at the firm. After law school, I had worked for a law firm for a few years. Then I had decided to hang my own shingle. Set my own hours, be my own boss, and all that. I rented office space and put out a press release that got about three hundred likes on Facebook.

Unfortunately, the likes didn't translate into clients. I managed to eke out a few cases, but no one was beating a path to my door. I shut down after less than a year, and took a job with HH&K (Holland, Haroldson, & Kruckemeyer). I was still trying to get LegalZoom to cancel my LLP fees, and they were being real assholes about it.

HH&K was an average, mid-sized law firm in Houston. There were a hundred just like us. We had some good lawyers, some bad lawyers, and a lot of mediocre lawyers. We weren't as glamorous or high paying as the big law firms in town, where everyone wanted to work (except those who actually worked there, who hated it). But we were a cut above the mom-and-pop shops that littered the billboards and benches.

As an independent contractor, I got paid the same as the other associates, and worked full time, so it wasn't like it made any difference that I was a contractor. It was just a tax thing for the firm. At least that's what they told me.

"Thanks, Dick," I said pointedly. This annoyed him. He preferred to be called "Richard," or "T. Richard," or "just Rich," although he couldn't get anyone behind that last one.

"Ah, don't be like that," said Harder, slapping me on the back. "I'm only joking. Tell me about the case!" He pulled up a chair and sat down, leaning forward expectantly.

Reluctantly at first, but then with increasing interest, I told him about the clinic, the girl, the death, and the gold. It was fun to get it all out. Even to Harder. He was a good audience, and suitably impressed.

"Is that what Kruckemeyer was yelling at you about earlier?" he asked. "The expenses?"

"Yeah. But he'll get over it." Kruckemeyer had given me grief over Dr. Avoulay's fee. He said it was a pro bono case, and I ought to have used a pro bono expert. As if those existed. But he calmed down after I reminded him that it was for charity and would make us look good. I also told him that Ashley had a bunch of gold coins. "Gold, eh?" he had mused. "In a pro bono case? Maybe we'll bill her after all. Don't need pro bono if you've got gold," he said with a chuckle.

Harder nodded. "So what happens now?"

"I fill out the paperwork to get her appointed independent executrix of the estate. Then I go to court to get it approved. After that, I'll call up Rockweiller and find out what happened to her brother."

"Sounds simple enough. Good luck. Let me know if you need any help."

"Will do."

The next morning, I got up early to look up probate procedures. To get Ashley appointed as executrix, I had to fill out some paperwork, give notice to creditors, and file a list of assets with the court. It was easy enough, and I got everything done by noon. The case was randomly assigned to the 375th district court. They had a general docket at 9:30 a.m. on Fridays. The Judge would deal with small matters like this, and I set it for hearing then.

After that, I turned back to Kruckemeyer's motion to compel. Then I knocked out a few things in my employment discrimination case. I left the office around six, worked out at the gym for an hour, and ordered a burger and fries for dinner. I cracked open a beer and settled down to watch some B-grade Netflix series called *The Dominator*. I went to sleep contented.

At some unknown hour of the night, I woke up to the sound of my phone vibrating insistently.

THREE

It took me a few moments to pass from sleep to wakefulness. I stared at the clock blearily. It was half-past three. My phone vibrated again. I grabbed at it blindly, trying to shut it up. Who was calling me at this hour?

I checked the phone and saw seven missed calls from Bob Kruckemeyer. That made me go cold all over. Kruckemeyer was demanding, but he wouldn't call this late, or this many times, except in an emergency. I bolted up straight in bed and called him back. He picked up right away.

"Jack," he said. "Where the hell have you been?"

"At home. Sleeping. What's going on?"

"Sleeping? Haven't you seen the filings in the Marcum case?"

I fell out of bed and stumbled my way to the kitchen table. I quickly opened up my laptop and pulled up the filing notifications. There was a notice, filed just after midnight, in the Marcum probate case. It said "Request for Temporary Restraining Order (TRO) and Emergency Injunctive Relief." It had been filed by Rockweiller Industries, and sought the immediate return of thirty-seven gold coins. It said that David Marcum had stolen the coins and illegally given them to his sister, Ashley Marcum.

"Jesus Christ," I said.

"What the hell did you do?" said Kruckemeyer. "Did you steal the coins? I thought you said she was going to pay our bill with those."

"I didn't steal the coins," I muttered.

"Dammit, Jack, what the hell have you gotten us into?"

I refrained from pointing out that it had in fact been Kruckemeyer who had sent me to the pro bono clinic, thereby getting us into this. "I don't know."

"Well you'd better figure it out. Fast. Look at the attorneys who filed this thing."

I scrolled down to the end of the filing where the attorneys' names appeared. It said Badden & Bock, New York, NY. I knew of them.

Badden & Bock was a big law firm out of New York with hundreds of attorneys. They were known for their corporate work on Wall Street, and also for their vicious litigation practice in high-stakes cases like securities fraud and antitrust. They hired the best law students out of Harvard, Yale, and Stanford, paid them huge salaries, and tried their best to work them to death. If they couldn't, that person would eventually be made partner and perpetuate the cycle.

"Badden and Bock," I said. "What are they doing mixed up in this?"

"Good question," said Kruckemeyer. "A better one is, when's the hearing?"

I looked for it. "It says tomorrow morning at eight a.m.," I said.

Kruckemeyer chuckled. "You sure about that, cowboy?"

I looked again. "Yes. Tomorrow morning. Wait. Oh God. It's already tomorrow. The hearing is today. In..." I checked my watch but didn't have it on. "In five hours? Is that even legal?"

"Heh. Nasty trick. They're trying to pull a fast one. File the TRO at midnight and get it heard before we can show up. They set it *ex parte.* But they didn't count on me burning the midnight oil. No sir."

Ex parte meant that they were going to try to do it without us. Usually, you have to have both sides present to get a court ruling on anything. *Ex parte* relief is reserved for extraordinary situations.

"How can they set this *ex parte* for this morning?" I asked. "Where's the emergency? There's no way this will work, right?"

"Eh. Depends on the judge. State court's a crapshoot. What court are we in?"

"The three seventy-fifth," I said.

"That's Judge Gleeson. He's okay. Older. Up for reelection this year, I think. He's no star, but he tries to do the right thing. Usually."

"Well the right thing is that you need an extraordinary situation to warrant an *ex parte* TRO. Right?"

"Right. Yeah. Look, can you do it?"

"What? Me, do this hearing? Against Badden and Bock? Are you crazy?"

"You wanted court time, didn't you? Well here it is. Just go in there and give it your best shot. It's pro bono. Not like any money is riding on this for us. I've got a client meeting at nine. I can't miss it."

"They filed a forty-page legal brief," I said. "How am I supposed to figure out what's going on and respond in the next four hours?"

"You can do it. I believe in you. Listen, just harp on irreparable harm and extraordinary remedy. Judge can't grant a TRO without that. I've got to go. Going to catch a little shut-eye. Go handle this. Keep me posted. And don't fuck it up." Then he hung up the phone.

I stared at Rockweiller's motion with dread. In addition to the forty pages, it also had fifteen attachments. I quelled a panic attack as I tried to figure out what to do. I decided I would just have to do my best. I called and texted Ashley, telling her that she needed to be in court first thing in the morning. I hoped she would get it in time. Then I sat down in the darkness and tried to make sense of things.

A few hours later, I was hurrying up the steps of the courthouse. I was exhausted, but had managed to stop for coffee on the way, which helped. I had been able to reach Ashley. She was waiting for me, sharply dressed despite the late notice. We hurried through security. These days, you had to take off your jacket, belt, and shoes to get into the courthouse, like a TSA line at the airport.

"How did they know about the coins?" Ashley asked me as I put my shoes back on. "I didn't tell anyone."

"Kruckemeyer thinks they were tracking the probate filings. I had to list the coins as assets of your brother's estate. They could have been watching the filings for any mention of David Marcum."

"But how can they just set a hearing like this at midnight? Don't they have to give us time to prepare if they're accusing my brother of stealing? It seems so unfair."

"It is. And it's not supposed to work like this. But unfortunately, sometimes it does."

"What are the chances that they win?"

"In theory, small. They are supposed to have to show an extraordinary need to get a temporary restraining order, which they don't have. But I don't know. State court in Texas is a rodeo."

"Okay," she said. Ashley wore a look of calm concern. Overall, I thought she was handling the situation well. Better than me.

We took the elevator up to the eighteenth floor. This took a while, because the elevators were slow and half of them were out of service. But when we arrived and opened the door to the 375th, the courtroom was empty.

"Shit," I muttered, fumbling with my phone to check that I had the court right. "Are we in the wrong place?"

"No. Look." Ashley pointed to a notice posted on the door. It was a handwritten note saying that the 375th district court had temporarily moved to the 234th, and the 234th had temporarily moved to the 188th. These mix-ups were the result of flooding from a recent hurricane, which forced the courts to share space.

I cursed and ran to the directory. I traced my finger down the list, looking for the 234th. It was on the thirteenth floor. I checked my watch.

"The elevator is going to take too long," I said. "Come on. We'll take the stairs."

We rushed down five flights of stairs and arrived at the 234th. Breathing hard, I straightened my tie, pushed open the doors to the courtroom, and walked in. It was a few minutes after eight.

Normally, the courtroom would have been peopled with lawyers sitting around and waiting for the judge to call their case. But today, it was almost empty. They must have sealed the hearing. The only lawyers there were three figures in dark suits, sitting at the right-hand counsel table and eyeing me coldly. Badden & Bock.

Judge Gleeson was already on his bench, reading some papers. He frowned down at me as I walked in. The atmosphere was tense.

"You're late, counselor," he snapped. Not a good start.

"I apologize, Your Honor," I said. "This TRO was filed at midnight, and there was a courtroom change at the last minute, and—"

The Judge waved this away brusquely and turned to the Badden & Bock attorneys.

Their leader stood up and addressed the judge. He was a tall man who looked to be in his late forties. He was impeccably dressed and had an intense, unpleasant look on his face. "Zachary Bock, Your Honor, for Rockweiller Industries," he said in a deep baritone. "And these are my colleagues, L. Lucius Quinto and Kathleen Loudamire." He gestured toward the other two, who stood up in turn.

They were younger, about my age. Associates, probably. Lucius Quinto was tall and handsome and looked like he had played lacrosse at boarding school. Loudamire was short and heavy, with a forced rictus of a grin on her face that looked to be hiding deeper issues.

"Your Honor," Bock said, "Ms. Ashley Marcum is in possession of extremely valuable and sensitive property belonging to Rockweiller Industries. We are seeking a temporary restraining order and immediate return of the property, as well as damages, sanctions, and other penalties against Ms. Marcum and her attorney."

"What?" I spluttered. "Your Honor—"

"Counselor," the Judge said sharply, "please don't interrupt until Mr. Bock is finished."

Loudamire and Quinto smirked at me from across the room. What the hell was going on here?

Bock held up a sheaf of papers and continued. "I have with me sworn affidavits attesting that the several dozen gold coins in Ms. Marcum's possession in fact belong to Rockweiller Industries," he declared. "They were stolen by her brother, David Marcum. I also have records, if the Court wishes to see them."

Quinto dashed forward and handed the records to the Judge, as if he was scoring a goal. Then he stalked over to me and gave me a dog-eared copy. I thanked him, but he only looked at me with distaste.

"In addition," Bock continued, "I have Mr. Stanley Stuttgardt, a corporate representative of Rockweiller Industries, to testify about the matter."

A nondescript, middle-aged man stood up. He was dressed in a gray suit and stodgy black shoes.

Judge Gleeson appraised him for a moment. "Very well," said the Judge. "I will hear his testimony."

Bock nodded to Stuttgardt, who walked up to the witness stand and sat down.

The court reporter faced him. "Please raise your right hand," she said. "Do you swear to tell the truth, the whole truth, and nothing but the truth, so help you God?"

"I do," said Stuttgardt.

"Mr. Bock, you may proceed," the Judge said. Bock walked to the witness stand and faced Stuttgardt.

"Please state your name for the record, sir," he said.

"Stanley Stuttgardt."

"Mr. Stuttgardt, what is your job title?"

"Executive Vice President for Rockweiller Industries."

"How long have you been working for Rockweiller Industries?"

"About ten years."

"Are you knowledgeable regarding the operations and records of Rockweiller Industries?"

"I am."

I half listened as Bock went through the preliminaries and established Stuttgardt's familiarity with the records. I used the time to quickly flip through the documents they had handed me. There were several affidavits (sworn statements) which did no more than list the name and title of a Rockweiller employee and say that, to their personal knowledge, the gold coins belonged to Rockweiller Industries.

Then I turned to the records, which were some type of corporate logs or property forms. They were heavily redacted. The only thing that wasn't blacked out was the fact that thirty-seven gold coins of indeterminate origin allegedly belonged to Rockweiller Industries.

Eventually, Bock got to the point. "Mr. Stuttgardt," Bock said, "who do these coins belong to?"

"Rockweiller Industries."

"And who stole them?" Bock continued.

"David Marcum," Stuttgardt replied. I felt Ashley tighten up beside me.

"How do you know that?"

"Based on my conversations with witnesses and review of relevant documents."

"Could you identify the coins if you had them in front of you?"

"Yes."

Bock turned to the Judge. "Your Honor," he said, "If Mr. Carver has the coins, I would request that he display them to Mr. Stuttgardt."

The Judge looked at me. "Counselor?" he said.

Ashley looked at me questioningly. I saw the bulge in her purse and nodded. She took out the envelope with the coins and handed it to me. I walked to the table in the center of the room and carefully emptied the coins onto on to it. They sat there heavily, looking almost reddish in the dim courtroom light. Even with all the grime and the bad lighting it was obvious what they were. The Judge craned his neck over the bench to see, captivated. Bock said something to him.

"Eh?" said the Judge, distracted.

"I said, may we proceed, Your Honor?" said Bock.

"Yes. Ahem. Proceed."

"Mr. Stuttgardt, do you recognize these coins?" Bock questioned.

Stuttgardt spent a few minutes examining them, and counted them too.

"Yes," he said.

"Do these coins belong to Rockweiller Industries?"

"They do."

"Are they the ones that were stolen by David Marcum?"

"They appear to be. But...one is missing." Bock frowned. This was off script. "I count thirty-six coins here," said Stuttgardt. "But I believe there were thirty-seven."

I felt my face flush. I reached into my pocket and dug out the coin that I had given to Dr. Avoulay. "My apologies, Your Honor," I said. "I forgot that I had one of the coins."

I thought about trying to explain, but decided to shut up. I placed the coin on the table with the others. Everyone glared at me, including the court reporter. I felt damned.

"Your Honor," Bock announced, "The evidence establishes that these coins belong to Rockweiller Industries. The Court should order their immediate return to prevent further harm to Rockweiller's interests."

"Very well," said the Judge. Then he addressed me. "Any cross-examination, counselor?" he asked.

My heart was racing as I stood up. It was game time. "Yes, Your Honor," I said shakily. Stanley Stuttgardt faced me politely.

"Good morning," I said.

"Good morning," he replied.

"Mr. Stuttgardt," I began, deciding to take a chance, "did Rockweiller Industries report the theft of these gold coins to the police?"

Stuttgardt paused for a moment. He looked at Bock. Bock gazed back at him, his face impassive. "No, we did not," said Stuttgardt.

"Why not?"

"Because the existence of the coins is a secret. Any public reports about them could be...damaging to the company's interests."

"The *existence* of the coins is a secret?" I repeated. I looked sideways at the Judge. His interest was piqued.

"Yes," said Stuttgardt.

"Why?" I asked.

"I can't disclose that information."

"Ah. You can't disclose it. I see. Where are the coins from?"

"That's confidential."

"Uh huh. How did David Marcum steal them?"

"I'm afraid that's confidential as well."

"When did he steal them? Who saw him steal them? Why did he do it?"

Stuttgardt grimaced. "Regrettably, on the advice of our attorneys, all of that is confidential as well."

"I see." I clasped my hands behind my back and paced around the room, as if I was thinking. "So let me get this straight," I said, furrowing my brow. "You're telling the Judge that David Marcum stole these coins. But you can't tell him when, where, why, or how, and you don't have a single witness here who saw him do it. Do I have that right?"

Stuttgardt didn't answer. The Judge stared at him, clearly troubled.

I walked back to my table and I flipped through the documents. I was buying some time, thinking about what to ask next. Ashley flashed me a smile. I smiled back, taking confidence from her. Then I turned to Stuttgardt once more.

"Mr. Stuttgardt, do you know that David Marcum was killed while in the employ of Rockweiller Industries?" I said.

This seemed to take the Judge aback. They hadn't told him about that. Stuttgardt hedged. "I am aware that he is deceased. I am not aware of the...particulars of the situation."

"Uh huh. And do you know that Rockweiller won't tell us how he died?"

Stuttgardt fidgeted, clearly uncomfortable. "As I said, that information is confidential."

"Right. So instead of telling us how he died, you're here trying to take his sister's property. The last thing he left her. Isn't that right?"

"I..." Stuttgardt trailed off. I was rolling now. I turned back ready to hit him with another question.

But Bock wasn't about to let me build any momentum. "Objection!" he said, jumping to his feet. "Irrelevant. This hearing isn't about David Marcum's death. It's about the coins."

The Judge frowned at him uncertainly.

"Your Honor," I protested, "It is totally relevant. How can Rockweiller try to take these coins from my client without even telling us how he got them, or what happened to her brother?" The Judge turned back to Bock for an answer.

Instead of speaking, Bock reached his hand back smoothly. Kathleen Loudamire slapped a remote control into his palm. Then Lucius Quinto clicked on a screen that I hadn't even realized was there. He loaded up a PowerPoint presentation. It had thirty slides.

"Your Honor," said Bock formally, "Rockweiller deeply regrets the death of David Marcum, even though it bears no liability for it. But, be that as it may, *that is not the subject of this hearing*. Mr. Carver may make inquiries through the proper channels, and if necessary, file a lawsuit regarding Mr. Marcum's death. Indeed, he has already opened a probate case regarding the matter.

"The sole issue before the Court today is the stolen property that belongs to Rockweiller Industries. I've prepared a presentation with supporting authorities to explain the law regarding ultra-sensitive commercial matters. If you will indulge me."

The Judge nodded, and Bock then launched into a lengthy legal argument, spending about thirty minutes walking through his presentation. He talked about other judges that had went his way, and court opinions that said what he wanted them to. By the end of it, I was damn near persuaded, and I could see the Judge was getting there too. Somehow, Bock had changed the conversation, and the basic unfairness of the situation seemed to fade away.

At the close of the presentation, the Judge turned back to me for a rebuttal. I did my best to make a few points that I had jotted down. But I couldn't respond to Bock's well-prepared legal argument on the spot. I asked the Judge for more time so I could put together a real response. There was no harm in letting us hold on to the coins for a few more days, I said. But I saw on the Judge's face that it wasn't enough.

At the close of my rebuttal, Bock turned back to the Judge. "Your Honor, in light of the evidence that the coins belong to Rockweiller Industries, and the lack of any evidence to the contrary, I move that the coins be returned to Rockweiller Industries immediately. If there is further dispute, the coins can be given back. But at this time, the preponderance of the evidence shows that they belong to my client."

The Judge nodded. "I agree. The coins are hereby ordered to be returned to Rockweiller Industries." I cursed under my breath.

"Thank you, Your Honor," said Bock. "Now, I would like to turn to the matter of sanctions and attorney's fees—"

"No," said the Judge. "I'm not going to entertain a motion for sanctions or fees. Mr. Bock, Mr. Carver, thank you for your argument. That will be all. Have a pleasant day." Judge Gleeson banged his gavel and departed the bench.

I stood there, dumbfounded, as Bock & Co. gathered their things. Quinto and Loudamire smirked at me on their way out. Bock didn't even deign to give me a glance.

Two hours later, I was back in the office, sprawled out in my chair. I was exhausted. I sighed and picked up a small globe that I kept on my desk. I had bought it after Harder gave me flak for not having any decorations in my office. It had cost me ten dollars from Target. I spun the globe idly as I dwelled on the hearing.

I had gotten rolled. I tried to think of what I could have done differently. Asked better questions. Objected to the evidence. Had better legal arguments. Figured out a way to jam up the hearing and give me more time to prepare.

Ashley had taken it well. She thought we had been sandbagged, and that I had done a great job under the circumstances. Usually, it was supposed to be the lawyer propping up the client after a loss. But I was grateful. I knew I was going to get an earful from Kruckemeyer, and knowing that Ashley appreciated my efforts felt good.

I turned to my computer and looked up Zachary Bock, the lead attorney from the hearing. There were a number of articles, awards, and publications mentioning him. He was listed in Super Lawyers and some other prestigious directories. There was a recent profile about him in a legal magazine. I clicked on it.

> Coming in at number seven on our up-and-coming list of New York super litigators is Zachary Bock, of Badden & Bock, LLP, the New York megafirm known for its high-stakes Wall Street work. Mr. Bock is a scion of the Bock family, the grandson of founder Cornelius Bock, who started the firm in the early 1930s. But don't think he got into the firm on his connections. According to Mr. Bock, his father was the black sheep of the family.
>
> That didn't stop Zachary Bock, who is back at the firm that bears his name with a vengeance. Mr. Bock went to Harvard Law School and clerked for the

> Second Circuit Court of Appeals in New York. After accepting a job offer at Badden & Bock, Mr. Bock quickly made partner, and has been making his way up the ranks ever since.
>
> Colleagues say Mr. Bock is a workaholic and a brutal opponent, someone you want at your back and not on the other side of a case. The word at the firm is he's a rising star, tapped for executive management in the future.

I also looked up Bock's associates, Lucius Quinto and Kathleen Loudamire. They were stars too. They had studied at Harvard and Yale, respectively, and received top marks and coveted honors like law review, moot court, and mock trial. They had both clerked for federal judges for a year after law school, which was a mark of distinction. Loudamire was on the chess team. To my amusement, Quinto actually did play lacrosse.

I felt better after reading about my opponents. There was no shame in being beaten by a super litigator. I just wished that Kruckemeyer had been there, or someone else who knew what they were doing. Then we might have had a fighting chance.

I was idly scrolling through a list of Quinto's lacrosse tournament victories when my door blew open, revealing the grinning faces of Harder and Vijay.

"How'd your hearing go?" asked Vijay. Vijay Gagnasetti was an associate too, around the same year as Harder and me. Vijay was tall and well muscled and played a lot of sports. He was a cool guy. He was an independent contractor, like me, but no one doubted he would be full-time soon.

"Not well, I hear," said Harder, smiling broadly. He waved a piece of paper at me, which turned out to be a signed copy of the TRO.

"It could have gone better," I said, snatching the TRO from him. "How did you get that?"

"Could have gone better?" Harder said incredulously, ignoring my question.

"That sounds like an understatement to me, Rich," Vijay remarked.

"I'll say. How do you even lose a TRO like that?" said Harder.

"Yeah, bro," echoed Vijay. "How do you even lose that? My ninety-year-old grandma could have won it. And she's not even a lawyer. As a matter of fact, she's dead. But she still would have won."

"Nice," I muttered.

"But seriously," said Harder. "You realize that Kruckemeyer's going to kill you, right?"

I flipped him the bird and we went at it for a while longer. But our rough camaraderie was interrupted when Kruckemeyer himself walked in, holding up a paper of his own.

Bob Kruckemeyer was sixty years old. He had a thick mane of hair that he dyed reddish-blond, and big shoulders from his days playing college football. The shoulders were stooped now, but he still had an imposing presence. In his moods, Kruckemeyer alternated between crotchety old man and boyish good humor. For some reason, he was currently in the latter.

"Oh ho," he said with a chuckle. "What's this? Are you giving our star litigator here a hard time?"

"Just a little bit, Mr. Kruckemeyer," said Harder, grinning at me and waiting for the inevitable. But Kruckemeyer didn't look angry. In fact, he was smiling.

"Now, now," Kruckemeyer said. "He did a good job. In fact, he did a great job. Badden & Bock just faxed over a settlement offer. It seems that our boy's performance shook them up. They're waving the white flag."

"A settlement offer?" I said, sitting up straight.

"That's right."

"How much?"

"A quarter million dollars."

"Holy shit!" I said. Harder and Vijay's mouths fell open.

"Didn't I say you could do it?" said Kruckemeyer. "Must have been my sage tutelage."

"Must have been," I said, taking the paper in disbelief. There it was:

> In consideration for a mutual release of all claims between the Estate of David Marcum ("the Estate") and Rockweiller Industries, Inc. ("Rockweiller"), Rockweiller hereby offers the sum of two hundred and fifty thousand dollars ($250,000) to the Estate. This offer will remain open for one week from today.

There was a bunch of boilerplate, and it was signed by Zachary Bock.

"Wow," I said. I was shocked to see these kinds of numbers in a pro bono case. "What do we do now?"

"Now you call up your client and present the offer. Give her the good news. Nice work, Jack. You did good," Kruckemeyer said.

I accepted Harder's grudging congratulations and a backslap from Vijay that nearly knocked me out of my chair. Then I called Ashley, basking in the feeling of victory. Moments ago I had felt like a loser. But now, I felt like my loss had really been a win. I'd showed my mettle to Badden & Bock, and now they wanted to settle. Ashley picked up right away.

"Hey, Ashley. It's Jack Carver. Listen. I've got some good news."

"Hey, Jack. What's up?"

"Badden and Bock made us a settlement offer. They want to settle all claims against the company by your brother's estate."

"Why? I thought they were winning."

"I thought so too. But it's quite a sum."

"How much?"

"Two hundred and fifty thousand dollars."

"I'm sorry, what?" she said. I repeated the figure again.

"Did you say *two hundred and fifty thousand dollars?*" she said incredulously.

"I did," I said, grinning into the phone. "Kruckemeyer thinks the hearing didn't go so well for them after all."

"What's the catch?"

"There is no catch. Of course, all of the Estate's claims against Rockweiller would go away in the settlement."

"Who would get the money?"

"Well, since your father and mother are no longer with us, and David didn't have any next of kin…I guess you would."

There was silence at the end of the line as she tried to process that. "I don't know what to say," she said finally. "That's more money than I make in years."

"It's a lot," I agreed.

"Would they have to tell us what happened to him?"

"I don't know. The offer doesn't specify."

"Can we find out?"

"Of course."

We talked a little more about the details. I said I would talk to Badden & Bock and let her know what they said.

"You know, I wasn't sure about the legal aid clinic," she confessed to me as we said goodbye. "I didn't know if anyone would be able to help me. Or if anyone would even care. But you did."

I tried to find something to say, but all I could come up with was, "Of course. Just doing my job."

"Really, Jack," she said sincerely. "Until you came along, I couldn't make those guys give me the time of day. I'm really grateful."

"You're welcome," I said, touched. Something caught in my throat. I cleared it and promised to call her soon. After we hung up, I just stared at the wall for a while, smiling faintly. It's not often you get to help people like that in my line of work. Corporations are people too, I guess. But somehow, this felt different.

FOUR

After the settlement offer, we sent a letter to Badden & Bock, demanding to know what had happened to David Marcum as a condition of any settlement. We asked for a reply within a week. But the week came and went, and there was no answer.

In the meantime, Ashley suggested we investigate the one lead we had: the return address on the envelope with the coins. She thought that might give us a clue about where her brother had gone, and what he was doing. Oddly enough, the return address was listed as a scuba diving resort in Key West, Florida called Aqua Ray. So I said hell yes, we should investigate.

I convinced Kruckemeyer that we might learn something useful. Maybe find a witness, or someone who remembered David Marcum. The more we knew, the more leverage we would have in settlement negotiations, I reasoned. This argument appealed to Kruckemeyer, and he signed off. Thus it was that I got an all-expenses paid trip to Key West, to the unending envy of Harder and Vijay. I was also keen to spend more time with Ashley, although I didn't mention that part.

Ashley and I flew into Key West in the afternoon. I had always wanted to fly into Miami and then drive the highways that crisscrossed the Florida Keys until they reached Key West, the bleeding edge of the United States, connected to the mainland by a thread of asphalt, a mere ninety miles from communist Cuba, where a Castro still reigned. But it was a longer drive than I thought, and it wasn't billable. So we flew straight there.

I watched the beautiful skyline of Miami fly by through the windows. I had been to Miami once. It had felt like a different world. Of blue and white towers by the sea, where everyone was good looking and rich didn't seem to have to work. Good life if you can get it. We landed in Key West and checked into a hotel. We strolled around the island for a little while, enjoying the sand and the sea air as the afternoon faded into evening.

Early the next morning, I put on jeans and a casual blue button down with some medium-nice shoes. I didn't want to roll up to a diving resort in a suit. But I didn't want to wear shorts and a t-shirt either, since this trip was ostensibly business, and I was (ostensibly) a lawyer. I met Ashley for breakfast around half past seven. She was dressed more casually than I was. She eyed my outfit without comment, leaving me wondering. After breakfast, we called an Uber and headed to the diving resort.

Aqua Ray wasn't really a resort, actually. It was more of a local spot. People went there to live the Key West lifestyle. Lots of sun, lots of water, little money. I had read reviews of the place online. Most of them were bad, with tourists complaining about the poor service, run-down facilities, and contemptuous treatment by the locals. But the "most helpful" review gave it five stars and said: "this is the original Key West dive shop. If you don't live here, don't come here. Each and every one-star review warms my heart because the more of them there are, the less of you I see. F$&K TOURISTS." It was signed SeaLubber65.

After we arrived, we walked through a thick cluster of palm trees and under a faded wooden sign. On the left, there was a dive counter, with rows of well-used scuba tanks and wetsuits behind it. On the right, there was a bar, and a couple of old guys were sitting around drinking beer and smoking. The sign above the bar said "Krueger's."

We got some looks as we walked up to the bar. Interest for Ashley, disinterest for me. The bartender was a whale of a man with a big old belly and badly dyed blond hair. He had a handlebar mustache and looked like Hulk Hogan gone to fat. He was shirtless, and his body was deeply tanned and tattooed all over. I guessed he was one of the true locals. He stared at me as I walked up to the bar.

"Good morning," I began. "I'm hoping you can help me. I'm looking for information about someone named David Marcum." He grunted at me and continued to polish a glass he was working on. "I'm an attorney," I persisted. "I'm representing the estate. If you could just—"

"Fuck off," he said, turning away from me. One of the guys at the bar snickered. He was thin, with long hair and sunglasses. He was obviously stoned.

Ashley gave me a look and walked up to the bar. She put on a winsome smile and called out to the bartender again. "Excuse me, sir," she said warmly. "Hi. I'm sorry about that. Do you think we can get a couple of beers? One for this gentleman too," she said, pointing to the stoner. Ashley nudged me and I put some bills on the table. She coaxed the bartender back and he grudgingly poured us the drinks.

Ashley said she was sorry to bother him, and this wasn't official or anything, but she was David Marcum's sister, and he had passed away recently, and we needed help finding out what happened. She explained that he had listed a return address here and was hoping someone knew him.

"Holy hell. Dave's dead?" said the bartender with a start. He turned to the thin man sitting at the bar. "Did you know that, Jared?"

"Nope," said Jared.

"Shit," the bartender said. "What happened? He get into an accident or something?"

"That's the thing," Ashley said. "We don't know. We really have no idea. I've been trying to find out." I heard the frustration spill through in her voice.

"I'm sorry," the bartender said sincerely. "I really am. The name's Trevor Thompson. I was a friend of your brother's." He stretched out his hand and Ashley shook it. He shook my hand too, albeit reluctantly. "Sit down," he said. "You're his sister. I can see it. What can I tell you? How can I help?"

We sat down and told him that David had gone missing some time ago, although we left out details like the gold coins and the connection to Rockweiller Industries. We asked what David had been doing at Aqua Ray, and whether Trevor knew anything about his disappearance.

"Anything you could tell us about David would be helpful," I said.

Trevor nodded. "Dave came out here maybe a year ago," he said, remembering. "He walked right up to that counter there and said he wanted to go diving." Trevor jerked a thumb toward the scuba equipment. "Jared here was working the counter, and he told Dave there was a Speedo in the back he could sell him. We all laughed about that, and I even spat out my beer. You remember that, Jared?"

Jared nodded evenly, and Trevor continued. "We all expected him to tuck his tail between his legs and ask for another. But Dave, that sassy little bastard, he says 'I'm here to scuba dive, but I'll whip your sorry ass at skin diving any day of the week.' So we go oh-ho, and they get to doing it, and then next thing you know he takes Jared in a free-dive competition, eighty feet deep with no gear or mask. You have to be good and also crazy to do a thing like that. Kid had lead in his balls."

Jared nodded again, acknowledging this fact. "After that," Trevor continued, "Dave stayed here, and they gave him a diving instructor job. Everyone liked him, the tourists and the locals both, and this ain't an easy crowd to please." Trevor nodded in the general direction of the dive counter. "He did some guided dives. Spent time hanging out with the local yokels. Chased women. Did some treasure hunting. Just lived that easy Key West life."

"Treasure hunting?" I interjected.

"Yeah. Some of these guys like to dive and search for old treasure. You know, gold in wrecks and that sort of thing. It's like a pastime."

"They ever find anything?"

"Sometimes. We've all pulled a few coins from the seabed. Silver, copper, a few gold. Jared found one the other day, actually. I'm keeping it for him as collateral on his bar tab." Trevor reached behind the counter and slapped down a gold coin on the bar. He grinned at Jared, who flipped him off.

But Ashley and I didn't even notice. We were staring fixedly at the dirty gold coin that Thompson had put down on the bar. It looked just like the gold coins that Marcum had had. Ashley and I exchanged glances. I realized that my mouth was hanging open and closed it.

"Where did you find that?" I asked Jared. Jared shrugged silently. Trevor spoke for him. "He found it diving, probably. They're worth a hell of a lot once you polish them up."

"David had some of those in his possession when he died," I said, deciding to tell him that much. "He had a couple dozen, actually. They looked just like that."

Thompson raised his eyebrows at this. "Couple dozen, huh? Bastard was holding out on us. That's a lot. I've almost never seen anyone find more than a couple, and I've been here a long time. Everybody hears stories about treasure, it sounds romantic, they think they're going to be the next Mel Fisher. But it ain't so easy."

"Mel Fisher?" I queried.

"You never heard of Mel Fisher?" Thompson chuckled and poured himself a beer from the tap. "He's a legend in these parts. Him and his crew found a wreck, back the seventies. The *Atocha*. Spanish galleon. Biggest find of all time, and him just a Florida treasure hunter. He spent years looking for it, never gave up. His son died one day, out in a dive accident, but he kept going."

"Today's going to be the day," Jared intoned softly.

"That's right," said Trevor. "That was his motto. Today's going to be the day. Every day. And one day, it was."

"Amen, brother," said Jared with a blissful smile. "A hundred million dollars of treasure, right here on the coast."

"A hundred million dollars, huh?" I said, amused. I looked at Ashley, who had the same reaction. She suppressed a smile.

"Oh yeah," said Trevor, oblivious. "But after that, the government tried to take it from him. They tried to say it was theirs because the water was Florida property."

"Fucking deep state," hissed Jared.

"Fisher fought for ten years," continued Trevor, "with lawyers, and eventually, the judges sided with him. You can probably go read the case, what with you being a lawyer and all. See for yourself. Yeah, people here, they all dream of being Mel Fisher."

"The man," Jared said.

"Right," I said. "What about people here? Any finds?"

"A few here and there. This guy Baker found a whole chest once, years back. Rotted, totally buried in the sand. The current must have pulled it up close to the surface, and he hit it with a metal detector. Got a whole load of silver for his trouble. That was a sweet day."

"What did they look like?"

"Looked just like that," he said, pointing at the gold coin.

"Did they have any markings on them?"

"That depends. Ones I've seen, they'll have Roman numerals, or Spanish, or some faces on them sometimes. Most of the gold here is from the Spanish ships, see, that used to go between America and Europe.

"What about more serious finds?"

Trevor shook his head. "The shoreline has been searched to hell and back. The serious finds are all offshore. You need boats, equipment. Money. The guys here aren't serious guys."

"What about David?" I asked. "Did he ever find anything?"

Thompson thought about that for a minute. "I'll tell you, he found something once. There's this wreck we all dive sometimes, the *USS Cargoland*. Done it a million times. Dave got curious about it, and he looked up the ship in a book. You remember that, Jared?" Jared nodded.

"He went to the library and looked it up in a book. A book!" Thompson shook his head, as if amazed that someone would read. "He found a register, an inventory of the ship. And the layout. He looked it up, measured it against the wreck, and found something that we all missed. A hidden compartment. There was something in there, buried behind an aft door, just under the sand. Nothing too valuable, mind you. More of a keepsake. But it was something. You could tell he had the mind for that sort of thing."

"Yeah," said Jared the stoner. "He was sharp."

Thompson went on, "Dave also did some contract work as a diver. We all pick up small jobs here and there, repair, salvage, that sort of thing. He was quick and good at it, so it wasn't hard for him to get work."

"Did he ever work for a company called Rockweiller Industries?" I asked.

"Don't know," said Thompson, scratching his head. "Rockweiller's an oil company, isn't it?"

"Yes."

"Could be. Oil companies hire commercial divers to install rigs, fix underwater pipelines, that sort of thing. ROV's took a lot of the market, but there's still things you need a man to do."

"ROV's?" I interjected.

"Remotely Operated Vehicles," Thompson said. "They're like underwater drones. You operate them from the surface. But you can't send a machine to do a man's work, can you Jared?"

Jared shook his head. "No, sir."

"Damn right. Anyway, commercial diving can be dangerous, but it's good work if you can get it. Dave was a good diver. I wouldn't be surprised if he worked for a company like Rockweiller, but I just don't know."

After we'd finished talking to Thompson, we paid our tab and prepared to leave. But before that, Thompson offered to take us on a scuba dive, compliments of the house. It was the least he could do for Dave's sister, he said. I was hesitant, and asked whether we didn't need a license to do that. Thompson said yes, but we could do an exploratory dive where he'd teach us the basics and take us underwater for thirty minutes or so. I was reluctant. As a lawyer, you're trained to think about the downsides of every situation. It's not a positive state of mind, really.

But then Ashley told me to stop being a pussy, which sent Thompson and Jared into howls of laughter. It took me aback. It was a joke, but her tone of voice was crude, even cruel. I thought about her brother, and wondered for a moment what was beneath her winsome smile. But after that, I had to do it. Some people say they never give into peer pressure, but I'm not so pure as all that.

So Trevor took us down to the beach and showed us how to put on masks, fins, and a scuba tank, and breathe through the regulator that supplied us with air. Ashley looked stunning in a dark bikini, and I saw a few more tattoos across her back and shoulders while I pretended not to look. After about a half hour of practice with the equipment, Trevor said we were ready to go, ignoring my protestations about needing more practice.

The dive was fantastic. One of the great experiences of my life. The clear blue waters of Key West had some of the best diving anywhere. We saw schools of brightly colored fish, sea urchins, and reefs filled with every kind of plant and animal life. Everything was vivid, as if my eyes had been supercharged into a brilliant HDR display. Ashley and I swam around excitedly, pointing things out to each other, talking with bad hand signs and trying to not to laugh. For all of his bluster, Trevor proved a watchful guide. He led us slowly to some of the best sights while keeping a close eye on us to make sure we were alright.

I experienced a feeling of serenity underwater. It was like being in a sensory deprivation tank, or floating weightlessly through space. Everything was enveloped in a deep quiet. The only sounds I heard were the bubbles flowing steadily out of my regulator. I floated around, enjoying the moment. The pressure of the water around me seemed to free me from the pressures and cares of the world above.

After a time, we splashed back to the surface. Ashley and I yelled happily at each other. We implored Trevor to take us on one more dive, and he agreed, beaming to see how much we liked it. This time, we went out on a small dive boat, to what Trevor said was one of his favorite spots. It turned out to be a wall of coral that you could float down and enjoy at your leisure, almost like the side of a cliff, but underwater. The coral was fantastic, and we swam around and up and down, gazing at it.

When I looked down, I felt a sense of vertigo. The wall was sheer, and extended farther than the eye could see. It faded into a murky darkness where the rays of the sun ended. I felt cold water emanating from down there, and wondered how deep it went. It gave me a thrill, as if I was standing on the edge of an abyss.

I looked up, and suddenly saw that the figures of Thompson and Ashley were far above me. I hadn't realized how deep I'd gone. I felt a twinge of panic. But Thompson noticed, and immediately swam down and brought me up gently.

Thompson later told me that the wall went down nearly a thousand feet. He wouldn't take most divers more than a hundred feet down, if that. To go deeper, you needed special training, and even special gas mixtures to breathe. Diving at that depth came with all sorts of dangers that could injure or even kill an experienced diver. Nitrogen narcosis. The bends. I didn't know what they were, but they sounded ominous. Thompson had been down as far as two hundred feet once. Word was that Jared Diamond had been deeper, and maybe David Marcum too.

After the second dive, we headed back to Aqua Ray. We took off our heavy scuba tanks and dried off on the beach, soaking up the last rays of the Key West sun. I was exhausted, in a good way. The bar was closing, and almost everyone had left.

We changed back into our clothes. Thompson gave us his cell phone number and told us to call if there was anything else he could do.

"Thank you for your help," Ashley said sincerely. "And for the dives. They were amazing." I nodded my agreement, beaming from ear to ear.

"Yeah. No problem, girl. And when you find out what happened to Dave, let us know. We all liked your brother, you know?"

"We will," Ashley said firmly.

As we left Aqua Ray, the setting sun casting a faint reddish hue into the sky, I looked back once. Trevor Thompson was facing away from me, behind the bar. I saw his broad back as he reached up and grabbed a liquor bottle from the top shelf. There was a big tattoo in faded green ink across his shoulders. It said "SeaLubber65."

Back at the hotel that evening, I looked up the Mel Fisher case that Thompson had mentioned. I was curious to see whether there was any truth to the tale. Surprisingly, there was. Mel Fisher had actually found the wreck of an old Spanish galleon called the *Nuestra Señora de Atocha*, and the government had tried to take it away from him. The case was a complicated, multi-year saga that made its way through various judgments and appeals. It even landed in the U.S. Supreme Court at one point.

The Supreme Court opinion was typically dry and boring. But the opinion below, by the Fifth Circuit Court of Appeals, was more interesting. It was styled *Treasure Salvors, Inc. v. Unidentified Wrecked and Abandoned Sailing Vessel*, 569 F.2d 330 (5th Cir. 1978). I printed out a copy at the hotel's business center. Then I went up to my room and made myself a cup of hot tea. I sat outside on the balcony facing the ocean, and read.

> This action evokes all the romance and danger of the buccaneering days in the West Indies. It is rooted in an ancient tragedy of imperial Spain, and embraces a modern tragedy as well. The case also presents the story of a triumph, a story in which the daring and determination of the colonial settlers are mirrored by contemporary treasure seekers.
>
> In late summer of 1622 a fleet of Spanish galleons, heavily laden with bullion exploited from the mines of the New World, set sail for Spain. Spain, at this period in her history, was embroiled in the vicious religious conflicts of the Thirty Years' War and desperately needed American bullion to finance her costly military adventures. As the fleet entered the Straits of Florida, seeking the strongest current of the Gulf Stream, it was met by a hurricane which drove it into the reef-laced waters off the Florida Keys. A number of vessels went down, including the richest galleon

> in the fleet, *Nuestra Senora de Atocha.* Five hundred fifty persons perished . . . . A later hurricane shattered the *Atocha* and buried her beneath the sands.
>
> For well over three centuries the wreck of the *Atocha* lay undisturbed beneath the wide shoal west of the Marquesas Keys, islets named after the reef where the Marquis of Cadereita camped while supervising unsuccessful salvage operations. Then, in 1971, after an arduous search aided by survivors' accounts of the 1622 wrecks, and an expenditure of more than $2 million, plaintiffs located the *Atocha.* Plaintiffs have retrieved gold, silver, artifacts, and armament valued at $6 million. Their costs have included four lives, among them the son and daughter-in-law of Melvin Fisher, plaintiffs' president and leader of the expedition.

I spent a half hour reading through the whole opinion, fascinated. I looked the up the judge who wrote it. His name was Walter Pettus Gewin. He was appointed to the Fifth Circuit Court of Appeals in 1961 by John F. Kennedy. He could have been a novelist, I thought.

As it happened, the Fifth Circuit was the federal appeals with jurisdiction over Texas too. There were thirteen federal appeals courts in the country. The Fifth Circuit used to cover Florida as well, until Florida split off into the Eleventh Circuit in 1981. Judge Gewin had died that same year.

I sorted through the convoluted legal history of the case. In 1971, Fisher made a deal with the State of Florida. He agreed to give Florida one-quarter of the proceeds from the *Atocha* in exchange for salvage rights. This was based on the understanding that the *Atocha* was in Florida waters. But in 1975, the U.S. Supreme Court ruled that Florida didn't have rights to those waters. So Fisher didn't pay them. They fought about this in court for several years. Fisher won.

But after Florida got knocked out, the federal government jumped in. The government claimed it had rights to the *Atocha* under the Antiquities Act, which makes all historic objects and sites "monuments of the United States." The court rejected this argument, finding that the Antiquities Act didn't apply outside the territorial waters of the United States, where the *Atocha* was found.

After losing that one, the government tried to argue that it owned the treasure as the "successor to the prerogative rights of the King of England." That didn't make any sense, since the ship was Spanish, not British. But the government came up with the harebrained scheme that, because in ancient England, abandoned property belonged to the Crown, and because the successor to the Crown in America was the federal government, ergo the abandoned property of the *Atocha* belonged to the federal government.

Needless to say, Judge Gewin called the government out on this tortured logic (in a more measured way than I would have) and ruled for Fisher. Later, U.S. Supreme Court declared Fisher the final winner in 1982. I tried to imagine what Fisher had gone through. The years of searching, the millions of dollars spent, the loss of his son, all capped off by years of litigation against the government. I didn't think I would have had the wherewithal to stand it.

Judge Gewin described the *Atocha* as holding "a treasure worthy of Midas: 160 gold bullion pieces, 900 silver ingots, over 250,000 silver coins, 600 copper planks, 350 chests of indigo, and 25 tons of tobacco."

Buried somewhere in a footnote, the court fixed the modern-day value of the treasure: 450 million dollars. I blinked when I read it, thinking it must be a typo. But it wasn't. I looked it up online, and came up with the same figure. Thompson and Diamond had been right. In fact, they had understated it.

I put down the opinion and went inside. I felt relaxed. I left the balcony doors open wide and fell face first into bed. I listened to the sound of the palm trees swaying in the wind, and the warm ocean breeze blowing through the window. I fell asleep dreaming of lost seas and Spanish gold.

FIVE

The next week at the office, I put aside the mysteries of the Marcum case to focus on more mundane matters. Kruckemeyer was complaining that I was spending too much time on vacation in Florida and not enough time billing hours. So I took care of a few things in the class action suit, and then pulled up the file on the employment discrimination case I had been neglecting.

The plaintiff in this case claimed that he was fired from a Mongolian barbeque restaurant because he was Mongolian. The trouble with his claim was that the owner of the restaurant, as well as most of the staff, were Mongolian as well. The real reason the guy had been fired (within weeks of being hired) was that he had shown up late, drunk, and/or high on several occasions, received five customer complaints in the space of a single day, and then, in the final straw, had been caught pissing in the mung-bean soup.

The guy wasn't going to win the case. Any jury would laugh him out of court. But it could easily take several years, and tens of thousands of dollars, to get the case all the way to a trial. An employment discrimination case usually presents a "fact issue"— legal jargon for "he said, she said"—which requires a jury to resolve. A judge won't usually toss it out early on a motion. The owner of the Genghis's Golden Grill didn't understand how he could be sued over this, and why he had to pay us all of this money to defend it. But that's America for you.

I opened a letter that I had received from the opposing attorney. It was accompanied by a thick set of discovery requests.

> Dear Mr. Carver:
>
> Please find attached my client Mr. Altantsetseg Batu-Bayarmaa's first discovery requests. As you know, we are entitled to responses within thirty days pursuant to the rules of civil procedure.
>
> Do not even think about objecting to these discovery requests. Mr. Batu-Bayarmaa's entire life was overturned by your client's salacious actions in terminating him solely because of his race. Accordingly, we will accept nothing less than full and fulsome responses to each and every document request, interrogatory, and request for admission. If you do not provide this, we will not hesitate to seek a court order, and also seek attorney's fees, costs, sanctions, and any other available options at our disposal...

This went on at some length, and then went on to list the settlement demand: 500 thousand dollars. When I read this, I nearly choked. The letter was signed with a flourish by attorney H. Hubert Thung.

A lot of times, you'll find that the character of an attorney matches that of his client. This case was true to form. I looked up Thung online. He was a young guy, probably not more than twenty-six years old, who had no idea what he was doing. He fancied himself a crusader for justice, and since, as far as I could tell, he didn't have any other cases, he was going ham on this one.

I took the letter over to Kruckemeyer's office and sat down in a huff. He spent a few minutes reading the letter while I stewed.

"Salacious," Kruckemeyer said with a frown. "Is that even the right word?"

"No," I said. He finished reading the letter and gave it back to me.

"How can he ask for that much money?" I burst out. "The guy worked there for three weeks and made fifteen hundred dollars. Now he wants half a million. It's outrageous!"

Kruckemeyer chuckled. "Now, now. Settle down. This is the usual game. A bit on the high side, but it's the oldest trick in the book."

"How do you mean?"

Kruckemeyer waved his hand. "Plaintiff's attorney starts out with a big number. A ridiculous number. You know it, I know it, everybody knows it. But now, you've got five hundred thousand dollars stewing around in your head. The client's got that stewing around in his head. So later on, when we talk real settlement, maybe ten thousand dollars, it doesn't sound so bad. See? You ask for the store, maybe you get a piece of it. The psychologists call it 'anchoring.'"

"Huh," I said, surprised to hear Kruckemeyer quote psychology. He was a wily old fox.

"Screw that," I decided. "We should give him nothing."

"Heh. I hate to tell you, but we will probably have to give him something. And worse, we'll only be able to give it to him after we spend some coin fighting this Thung guy. Now. What are they asking for?"

I handed him the discovery requests that came with the letter. They sought every document under the sun. There were also interrogatories, which were written questions that we had to answer under oath. Finally, there were some requests for admission. That's where the attorney makes a statement and asks if it's true or not. There were about sixty of them, and I could already see they were chickenshit:

Admit that you wrongfully terminated Altantsetseg Batu-Bayarmaa.

Admit that you do not *not* have a policy of employment discrimination.

Admit that no witnesses saw Altantsetseg Batu-Bayarmaa urinate in the mung-bean soup."

Kruckemeyer chuckled at these. "Okay, Jack. You know the drill. Object and respond. Then figure out what documents we actually need to give them."

"Should we try to give them something reasonable? Or take a hard line and say no?"

"Eh. Sounds like this Thung guy is real Viet Cong. He's going to drag us to court no matter what we do. So may as well say screw 'em. Go hard. But not too hard, I don't want the judge to sanction us. Gotta walk the line. Okay?"

I sighed. "Okay."

"Good. Now, how's the class action case coming? I think we're going to need to tee up a seventh motion to compel. Let me fill you in on the details..."

Toward the end of the week, as I was finishing up on the discovery requests, I walked by the conference room. I stopped when I saw what was going on inside. The partners were all in there, yelling at each other.

I wandered over to Vijay's office, which had a partial view. The conference room was paneled in glass, so you could see what was happening inside. I could make out muted shouting, although I couldn't hear what was being said. Harder was in Vijay's office pretending to discuss a case. He mimed showing a stack of documents as Vijay nodded in mock concentration. But they were really just watching the show.

"What are they yelling about?" I asked.

"Dunno," said Harder. "Some type of conflict."

He meant a conflict of interest. A conflict is when representing one client could hurt another client. For example, you can't represent someone in a lawsuit and then turn around and sue them in the same lawsuit. The ethical rules prohibit it, and lawyers can get disqualified for doing it. That example is obvious, but most conflicts are more subtle.

The argument continued for a while, and then Kruckemeyer pointed a finger straight through the glass at us. He pressed the intercom and an assistant appeared. Kruckemeyer said something to her, and a moment later she walked out and approached us.

"Shit," whispered Harder. Then, more loudly, he said "I think we need to cross-check the responsive documents so we can validate our assumptions..." But he quieted down as the assistant ignored him and walked up to me.

"Mr. Kruckemeyer would like to see you in the conference room," she told me in a hushed voice.

"*Ooooh*," said Harder and Vijay together, like schoolgirls.

"Shut up," I said, and went.

Kruckemeyer beckoned me in and bade me take a seat. I did so, feeling uncomfortable. I knew most of the partners, at least in passing. But this meeting was above my pay grade.

I quickly picked up on what was going on. It was the Marcum case. We had run a conflicts check on Rockweiller Industries and discovered that a partner at the firm, Carl Wurlheiser, had done some work for them a few years back. So now the partners had to decide whether we could take the case. Wurlheiser and Kruckemeyer seemed to be the primary antagonists, judging by the direction and volatility of their hand gestures.

"She needs our help, Carl," Kruckemeyer was saying. "We already said we'd take the case. We can't back out now and leave her to the wolves."

"Don't play the sympathy card with me," retorted Wurlheiser. "You should have run a conflicts check earlier," he said. "You knew about Rockweiller's involvement from day one." Wurlheiser was a skinny man in his mid-forties with a pinched face and horn-rimmed glasses. He did contracts and drafting work. I didn't like him.

"So what, Carl, we shouldn't give legal advice at a pro bono clinic without a two-day waiting period?" said Kruckemeyer.

"I don't make the ethical rules," said Wurlheiser.

I chimed in at this point. "I didn't realize the case was going to be adverse to Rockweiller," I said. "She came in to ask for help probating a will. After I found out, I ran it through conflicts as soon as I could."

Kruckemeyer seized on this. "You see? We didn't know, Carl. What's the problem here?"

"The problem is that they are one of my clients," Wurlheiser shot back.

Kruckemeyer slammed his fist down on the table. "Dammit, Carl, you haven't done any work for them in a year. And they weren't even sending you much back then. It was a couple hundred thousand dollars, that's it. And it has nothing to do with a wrongful death case. There's no conflict here."

"Just because I haven't got work from them in a while doesn't mean I won't get it in the future," argued Wurlheiser. "If you sue them, we never will."

"In the future? Come on. I heard you lost that account after you got drunk and hit on their new assistant general counsel at a bar association mixer. Stephanie Rivera, was it?"

Wurlheiser turned red. "That's completely untrue! There was a transition. She wanted to work with her own people."

"Right. A transition."

"I'm not going to sit here and listen to this!"

"Fine, fine. But look, we can't just leave this Ashley Marcum character to herself now. We've agreed to take on this pro bono case. We've got a duty—"

"Bullshit! You just want a payday."

"Well so do you! And look at the economics of this. It's a death case. There's already a settlement offer on the table. Anything we get is shared among the firm."

The partners nodded at this. The bottom line. Wurlheiser shook his head, seeing that he was losing.

Kruckemeyer turned to another partner who had been observing the discussion. "What do you think, John?" he asked. The room quieted respectfully.

John Remington was a legendary litigator in his late fifties. He was one of those old- school lawyers, a veteran of a hundred trials, which didn't happen anymore. He was also supposedly brilliant, able to muster the most complex legal arguments and maneuvers while also being relatable to a jury, which was rare. I'd seen him a few times, even shaken hands with him once. He was very quiet and down to earth, for all his reputation. He wasn't a formal leader at the firm, but the partners all respected his judgment.

"I don't think it's a good idea," said Remington quietly. "There's a potential conflict. We could end up in litigation about it later."

"Come on," said Kruckemeyer. "This is going to be a one-and-done settlement. Guy dies, company pays, insurer indemnifies. That's it. It has nothing to do with the work we were doing for Rockweiller. They've already made an offer."

But Remington just shook his head. "I'm against it."

Kruckemeyer turned to me. "Jack," he said. "Tell them what happened." He swirled his hand at me, as if trying to coax the story out. I gave the partners an abbreviated version of my trip to the pro bono clinic, my meeting with Ashley, the gold coins, and the TRO hearing against Rockweiller.

"Hang on," said Remington, interrupting me at that point. "You're telling me that Rockweiller filed an *ex parte* temporary restraining order to get back a bunch of coins?"

"Yes," I said.

"Who were their attorneys?"

"Badden and Bock. From New York."

Remington sat back and frowned. "That's unusual. I know who Rockweiller uses for local matters in Houston. It's not Badden and Bock. The fact that they brought in their heavy hitters from New York on some nickel-and-dime case suggests there's more here than meets the eye."

"What do you think it means, John?" asked Kruckemeyer.

"I don't know," said Remington. "But I was already suspicious when you told me they offered to settle before we even made a demand."

"Why?" I interjected. "It's a death case, right? So they're going to pay something."

"Yes," agreed Remington. "But Rockweiller Industries is known to be litigious. I have seen them litigate slip-and-falls to the hilt to avoid paying a cent. It's very unusual for them to offer a settlement this early."

"Well that's great news," said Kruckemeyer. "We may be sitting on a winner here. More reason to take the case. What do you say, John?"

But Remington just shook his head again. "No. This means it might be a good case. But it doesn't mean we should take it. I'm still against it."

"Fine," said Kruckemeyer. "We've heard the arguments. Let's vote. Who wants to keep this multimillion-dollar case we got for Ms. Marcum, who needs our help?"

Although Remington had spoken against it, his observations had convinced the partners there was gold in them hills, so to speak. A majority of hands went up. An assistant was called in to prepare a letter of representation to the Estate of David Marcum, and a letter of termination to Rockweiller Industries.

SIX

Several weeks passed after the conflicts meeting. The negotiations with Rockweiller had stalled. They refused to tell us what happened to David Marcum, and we rejected their settlement offer. We exchanged a few emails and phone calls after that but got nowhere.

In the meantime, we signed Ashley up as a paying client. The case had come from the pro bono clinic, so we wouldn't charge for our work to date. But if we took the case forward, we had to. A suit like this, against a company like Rockweiller, was too costly to take on for free. So we agreed on the standard contingency fee, which was forty percent of any recovery.

Forty percent sounds like a lot. But lawyers take a risk on contingency cases. Some of them pan out, and some don't. And the client doesn't pay anything unless they win. Without the lawyer, the client would get nothing. I thought the contingent fee was a pretty good system. It aligned the interests of lawyer and client. The lawyer had a strong motivation to win, and not to run up unnecessary costs. In the past, it used to be that lawyers would take a third of the recovery.

But now, with increased litigation costs and time to trial, it was more often forty percent.

Eventually, Kruckemeyer decided to up the ante. We threatened to file suit against Rockweiller if they wouldn't make a deal. In response, Badden & Bock sent a letter. They sent it by regular mail, certified mail, email, and hand-delivery, in case we hadn't gotten the other three. This is what it said:

> Re: Settlement Communication – Confidential Pursuant To Texas Rule of Evidence 408
>
> Dear Mr. Kruckemeyer:
>
> We are in receipt of your communication indicating that you plan to file a lawsuit on behalf of David Marcum's Estate.
>
> Be advised that if you reject our settlement offer and file suit, the company will respond with the maximum available resources at its disposal. The discovery phase of the case will take years. Rockweiller Industries will interview and depose every available witness, including Ashley Marcum and any of David Marcum's friends, family, or acquaintances with any involvement in the matter whatsoever. Rockweiller will assert counterclaims and seek recoupment of its attorney's fees, which will be substantial. Rockweiller would fully intend to take the case to trial, and, even in the unlikely event of an adverse verdict, would vigorously appeal the result.

The letter then launched into a ten-page diatribe about the dire legal, financial, and moral consequences of any lawsuit against Rockweiller Industries. Bock cited case law, jury verdicts, and median time-to-trial statistics in various jurisdictions. It was an imposing document. It closed with the following:

In an effort to avoid further dispute, we are willing to offer your client $300,000 to settle all potential claims against the company. As I have said in our previous correspondence, Rockweiller cannot and will not disclose further information about Mr. Marcum's death due to the sensitivity of ongoing commercial matters.

This offer is non-negotiable and will remain open for forty-eight hours. Rockweiller Industries will not make it again.

Sincerely,

Zachary Bock

The letter worried me, and it scared the hell out of Ashley. Kruckemeyer just said "hmm," but I could tell he was concerned as well.

The next day, as we were thinking about what to do, my phone rang. It was my assistant. She said that John Remington wanted to see me.

I grabbed a legal pad and headed up the stairs. This was a rare occasion. Remington was a lone wolf. He usually only worked with junior partners or above, and none of the associates knew him very well. I didn't know why he wanted to see me, but I guessed it was about the Marcum case.

Remington's office was in a corner on the floor above mine. It was quiet, with none of the raucous back-and-forth of associates, paralegals, and secretaries like on my floor. Remington was on the phone, but he motioned me inside. I sat down and looked around.

The office was big, with a good view. There were two shelves crammed with books, with everything from legal treatises to history to fiction to random topics I had never heard of. There were signed sports memorabilia here and there, some family photos, and various trinkets and ornaments scattered around. Trophies from cases won, I guessed. There was also an antique hunting rifle hanging above Remington, behind the desk. Legend had it that he kept it primed and loaded at all times.

Remington wore a suit and tie, like he did every day. He didn't believe in business casual. The only distinguishing feature of his wardrobe was a pair of black cowboy boots, well-worn and chased with silver. These were kicked up on his desk. The boots would look outlandish on almost anyone else. But somehow, he pulled it off.

After a few minutes, Remington hung up the phone and turned to me. "So," he said. "I hear you're having trouble with Rockweiller Industries."

I nodded.

"What's the issue?" he asked.

I handed him the letter from Bock and explained the negotiations. Remington quickly scanned through the letter. After page two, he crumpled it up and casually threw it into the trash.

"The usual nonsense," he said. "They're bluffing."

"How do you know?" I asked.

Remington gave a wry smile. "Because I've been through this rodeo a time or two. The letter looks threatening. But in reality, the longer the letter, the more scared they are. See how they only raised their settlement offer by fifty thousand, to make it look like they're at their maximum. The truth is, they're nowhere near it."

"But how do we get them to tell us what happened to David Marcum? Kruckemeyer doesn't want to file a lawsuit. He thinks Rockweiller will go scorched-earth if we do."

Remington nodded. "Yes. They probably will. And there are some political considerations at play too."

"How do you mean?"

Remington crossed his boots on the desk and then explained. "From our side, there won't be any conflicts issue if we settle. Even though Kruckemeyer won the vote, some of the partners are uneasy. If there's no lawsuit, there's no problem. And of course, we won't have to do any work if we settle.

"From Rockweiller's side, there are good reasons to settle before a suit too. Once a lawsuit is filed, everything is out in the open. Rockweiller is a public company, which means it will be news. A lawsuit also triggers certain insurance and reporting requirements that they don't want to deal with."

"Oh," I said. "I didn't know all that."

"I wouldn't expect you to."

"Right. So what now?"

Remington sat back and looked out the window for a while, thinking through the situation. Then he turned back to me. "How do you file a lawsuit without filing a lawsuit?" he asked.

I frowned as I contemplated this riddle.

"Here's what you're going to do."

"A pre-suit deposition?" Harder asked me. "What's that?"

He was sitting in my office and quizzing me on my meeting with Remington.

"It's where you take a deposition before you even file a lawsuit," I said.

A deposition is like a formal witness interview. It's taken under oath. But only the lawyers are there, not the judge or jury. Depositions are a primary fact-finding tool in civil cases. They are used to find out what a witness will say before trial. Usually, they happen around the midpoint of a case.

"Holy shit," said Harder. "I didn't even know you could do that. How?"

"Rule 202, Texas Rules of Civil Procedure," I said nonchalantly, as if I did it all the time. "Technically, it's supposed to be used to investigate a potential claim or suit. But we're going to use it to file a lawsuit without actually filing a lawsuit."

"Awesome," said Harder.

"Yeah. Plus it's a surprise tactic," I added. "You depose their witness before they get a chance to get their story straight. Usually, depositions happen months or even years into the case. By that time, everyone has reviewed the documents, figured out their legal positions, and prepped their witnesses to the nines. So you get whatever story they want you to get. But in a pre-suit deposition, you jump the gun and get the witness even before day one." I explained all of this as if it had been my idea, and Remington hadn't relayed it to me word-for-word.

"Dude," said Harder, awed.

"Dude!" echoed Vijay from down the hall.

"That's amazing," said Harder. "None of this was your idea though, right?"

"Don't you have work to do, or something?" I asked.

"Alright, alright. Whatever, bigshot," Harder said.

"Later," I said, grinning at him.

A week later, I was at the courthouse for my next dust-up with Badden & Bock. I had my pre-suit deposition request in hand. It listed the topics I wanted to ask about. The death of David Marcum; David Marcum's employment with the company; and the gold coins that David Marcum had sent to Ashley. I also had requests for Marcum's personnel file, as well as any written investigations into his death.

Badden & Bock filed a considerable opposition to my pre-suit deposition request. It was the usual perfectly formatted document with hordes of legal authorities. They argued the court had no jurisdiction, no venue, and that there was no good reason to order a pre-suit deposition at all. After reading through all of it, I was worried they might be right. I had sent Remington their brief, but he hadn't responded.

Unlike last time, the courtroom contained an assortment of lawyers, milling around and waiting their turn. The bailiff was dozing off at his station, and the clerk was typing away at her computer. I walked over to the docket sheet where the case list was posted. It was the usual smorgasbord of discovery motions, pleas, and other legal issues. I saw my case, *In Re: David Marcum*, near the middle. Good. I sat down in the back benches to wait my turn, and observed the proceedings.

Judge Gleeson was sitting up on the bench, looking bored. Two attorneys stood in front of him at the podium. They were too dignified to jostle, but it was clear that they both wanted the podium. They looked like two airline passengers passively-aggressively fighting over an armrest. Gleeson looked at them. "Does one of you want to go first?" he asked dubiously.

The nature of the dispute soon became clear. The first lawyer was trying to get some documents. The second lawyer said he hadn't got proper notice because the request was emailed to him, not mailed to him. The first lawyer pointed out that he had got the request anyway, so what did it matter. The second lawyer didn't deny this, but kept going on about due process, and how his client hadn't got any, and how this was America and he was entitled to justice. Judge Gleeson heard about twenty minutes of this and then ordered him to turn over the documents.

These discovery fights seem past the point of absurdity. But it's easy to say that as the observer, or as the judge. When you're the lawyer, it's different. Lawyers are good at making the other guy look like the asshole. And sometimes, if you put up enough bullshit, and write big enough briefs, and act indignant in court, it's hard to tell who's right and who's wrong. Everybody gets tarred, even when there's only one person doing the tarring. And it's difficult for a state-employed judge to figure it out in his nine-to-five. So sometimes the judge gets it wrong. And assholes keep filing motions.

Shortly before the end of the hour, the courtroom door opened, and Bock & Co. walked in. They caused a stir. I heard "Badden & Bock" and "New York lawyers" whispered around the courtroom. It was obvious that they were not the usual ham-and-eggers, as Grisham calls them, that take up space in the southern state courts. A few minutes later, Judge Gleeson called our case, and I walked to the front.

Bock spoke first. "Zachary Bock, Your Honor, for pre-suit defendant Rockweiller Industries. It is a pleasure to see you again. I'm sure you remember my colleagues, L. Lucius Quinto and Kathleen Loudamire." They waved, and Judge Gleeson nodded, probably not remembering them at all.

"I trust that the Court has reviewed our response to the Plaintiff's motion for pre-suit deposition and cross-motion for protection that was filed last night," Bock said.

"I did," said Judge Gleeson dryly. "All fifty pages of it."

"We have several extra copies, should the court desire it." He motioned to Quinto, who sprung forward with a thick binder in hand.

The Judge waved it away. "I've got a copy here. Thank you."

"In that case, Your Honor, I'd like to start with jurisdiction, if the Court will indulge—"

"Excuse me, Your Honor," I said. It came out as a squeak. I cleared my throat. Dammit. "I believe that as the movant—"

Bock glared at me. "Excuse me. I'd like to finish my statement."

But the Judge interrupted him. "Counselor," said Judge Gleeson, "this young man is the movant, so at least here in Texas—" he said this with a light emphasis—"that means he goes first." This drew a couple of laughs from the gallery. He had an audience this time.

"Of course," Bock said smoothly. He turned to me.

I gathered my papers and began my practiced statement. "As Your Honor knows, we are requesting a pre-suit deposition regarding the circumstances of David Marcum's death while in the employ of Rockweiller Industries. If we determine that there is cause to sue, we will do so. If not, we will withdraw the petition. This method will put the least burden on the parties and the Court while providing us with the opportunity to learn what we need to know." I explained the circumstances and legal issues in a little more depth, and then thanked the Judge for his time. It was a little rote, but I wasn't expecting this to be a big deal.

Zachary Bock listened to this as if he could barely contain himself. As soon as I'd finished, he jumped up. "May I respond, Your Honor?"

"Please."

Bock motioned to Loudamire, who instantly activated a PowerPoint on the screen that had been set up for him. I had a sinking feeling of *de ja vu.*

Bock walked through twenty slides of the PowerPoint with aplomb. He explained that there was absolutely no cause for a pre-suit deposition, and that it would pose an undue and intolerable burden for his client. He argued that the Court had no jurisdiction, because Rockweiller Industries was not headquartered in Texas and none of the events had occurred in Texas. He also argued that the venue was improper, and that there was no possible cause for a lawsuit to go forward anyway. He probably talked for about thirty minutes, passionately and intensely.

After Bock had completed his argument, the Judge turned to me. "What do you have to say to that, young man?"

"I—" I stammered. I felt caught flat-footed. This was quickly turning into a repeat of the last time.

At that moment, the courtroom door swung open, and John Remington walked in. He was wearing a gray suit and holding a large, well-worn briefcase. He was wearing his black cowboy boots, and the heels clicked noticeably on the hardwood floors, drawing everyone's attention. Remington walked up to the counsel table, put down the briefcase, and stood next to me, waiting as if carved out of wood.

"Mr. Remington," said Judge Gleeson, acknowledging him. The Judge looked at him with an expression that I couldn't read. They were of an age.

"Your Honor," Remington replied formally. "I apologize for my late arrival. I had believed this would be a routine issue and didn't anticipate substantive legal argument."

"Well," said the Judge, gesturing at Bock and his PowerPoint.

"If you would permit me to shed some additional light on what my colleague has no doubt ably expressed," he said, gesturing at me. The Judge nodded. "Very well," he said.

"David Marcum was killed while within the employ of Rockweiller Industries," said Remington. "We want to know whether Rockweiller had anything to do with it. Rule 202 allows a plaintiff to 'investigate a potential claim or suit' with a pre-suit deposition. That's what we're doing here, plain and simple. If there's something there, we'll file a lawsuit. If not, we won't, and we'll save everyone a lot of time and money."

This seemed to make sense to the Judge, who turned to Bock. Bock looked shocked. "Your Honor, the pre-suit plaintiff has not responded to any of our substantive arguments with respect to jurisdiction, venue, undue burden, or the propriety of this suit at all." Bock's associates looked suitably outraged as well. The Judge turned back to Remington.

"Respectfully, I believe that Mr. Bock is missing the point regarding jurisdiction," Remington responded. "We are not asserting personal jurisdiction. We are asserting jurisdiction *in rem.*"

My jaw dropped. *In rem* was an obscure, ancient basis for jurisdiction. Literally it meant "power against the thing" in Latin. *In rem* jurisdiction meant that the Court had power over the case because it had power over a physical piece of property. But *in rem* jurisdiction was the subject of dusty old court cases from the 1800s. You read about them in law school. But I'd never actually seen it used. Bock's eyes near bulged out of his head.

Remington continued. "For example, the Texas Supreme Court has upheld jurisdiction on an *in rem* basis over an oil tanker that was docked in the port of Houston, regardless of the location of the defendant's headquarters. That reasoning is equally applicable here. With respect to venue, as Your Honor knows, where venue isn't proper in any other county, it is proper in the county in which the plaintiff resided at the time of the accrual of the cause of action. Texas Civil Practice & Remedies Code section fifteen-point-oh-oh-two-four. And finally, with respect to the undue burden argument, we're asking for two sets of documents, and six hours with a corporate witness. I don't think that's too much to ask in a death case."

Zachary Bock was livid, and the associates stared, shocked that someone had actually read their brief. Bock started to say something. But the Judge brushed him off.

"That makes sense to me," he said. "Motion granted. The pre-suit deposition is ordered." He scrawled his signature on the order and handed it to Remington.

"Your Honor," said Bock, "I must protest. At a minimum, we require additional time to file an emergency petition for appeal—"

But the Judge waved him away. "File your appeal if you want, but I doubt you'll get it. It's just a pre-suit deposition. Put up a witness, Mr. Bock. Thank you." Remington thanked the Judge, picked up his briefcase, and walked out.

I caught up to Remington outside the courthouse.

"That was amazing!" I said.

Remington smiled. "That was close."

"Close?" I repeated. "That didn't look close at all."

"That's because I know Judge Gleeson, and I know he didn't read any of the papers that Bock filed last night. Their brief was actually very good. We're on thin ice with respect to jurisdiction and the propriety of a pre-suit deposition at all. Which is why I came in late and made it look like no big deal."

I was suitably awed. "What do we do now?" I asked.

"We take the deposition. Not too soon, because I don't want them to complain about unreasonable notice. But not too late, because I don't want them to get up to any mischief, like file a writ of mandamus." A writ of mandamus was where you filed an emergency appeal in the middle of a case instead of at the end. It was rare.

"They won't be able to get mandamus on this though, will they?" I asked.

"Probably not. But I'd rather not give them time to try. Set the deposition for ten days from now. That should be about right. Even if they file something, the court of appeals won't get to it by then."

"Okay. Is there some way I can help you prepare?" I asked Remington.

"No. I'm not taking the deposition. You are."

"Me?" I said, feeling a sudden thrill. Like the TRO hearing, this was exciting, but also daunting. Usually, partners handled important depositions. I hadn't done many before. And the ones I had done were on smaller, inconsequential matters.

"Uh, okay," I said. "Great. Do you... have any thoughts? On topics for the deposition? Or what I should ask?"

"Whatever you want. That's the beauty of a deposition. You get six hours, and they have to tell you anything you want to know. Go get 'em."

Anything I wanted to know. I thought of all the questions I had about this case. About David Marcum. About Rockweiller Industries. About the coins. They were all going to be answered, and everything would become clear.

"Thank you!" I yelled at Remington as he walked off toward some other building nearby. He didn't turn. But he raised a hand, acknowledging me. Sometimes, the law is a beautiful thing.

SEVEN

As Remington predicted, Bock & Co. sought an emergency stay in the court of appeals. They also filed a motion for reconsideration with Judge Gleeson. A motion for reconsideration is where you ask the judge to change his mind. Judges hate motions for reconsideration, and they are usually a waste of time.

Neither of these methods proved successful. So Rockweiller grudgingly agreed to present Stanley Stuttgardt, corporate representative, for deposition, to answer any and all questions we might have about David Marcum's death. A few days before the deposition, they coughed up the records we had asked for. I tore them open, eager to see what they would say.

The first document they sent was David Marcum's employment file. It turned out that Marcum had worked for Rockweiller as a commercial diver, just like Trevor Thompson had thought. The job description said he did undersea installation and repair work on offshore oil and gas platforms. He only worked there for about five months. He was paid as an independent contractor, like me. But other than his address, social security number, and date of birth, there was little information in the file.

The strange part of the records, though, were the dates. They said that Marcum had worked for Rockweiller three years ago. I flipped through the rest of the file but didn't find anything more recent.

I called Ashley. "Hey, Jack," she said. "I was just thinking about you."

"Jinx," I said. She laughed, just a little, and I smiled, just a little.

"What's up?" she asked.

"We got the employment records from Rockweiller."

"And?"

"And...they don't make sense. They say that your brother worked for Rockweiller as a commercial diver, like Trevor thought. But here's the thing: it was three years ago."

"Three years? But I thought he was working for them when he died."

"I thought so too." But then I wondered. Had they actually said that? Or had we just assumed it?

"Is there anything more recent?" Ashley asked.

"No."

"What else do the records say?"

"Not much," I said, flipping through them. "There's a job description and some payment information. Some boilerplate HR stuff. He wasn't an employee, so I guess they didn't have a full file. They're basically just tax documents."

"Do they say where he was working? Or what project he was on?"

"No."

"How much did he get paid?"

I scanned through the file. There was a little box that said wages. It read *$156,000,000.* I stopped and read it again. That couldn't be right.

"Hang on," I muttered. "I must be reading this wrong."

"What is it?"

"It says he made a hundred and fifty-six million dollars. Somehow I don't think five months of scuba diving would be that lucrative."

"What? No."

I looked through the rest of the records. But the number repeated in several other places. Then I noticed a little symbol that appeared next to the dollar sign. It said "$COL."

I frowned into the phone. "What's COL?" I asked, mostly to myself. I started to look it up.

"COL? It stands for Colombian peso. It's the national currency of Colombia."

I stopped. "Colombia? Like the country? How did you know that?"

"My dad was from Brazil. He had some family in Colombia. I've visited many times."

"Oh. I didn't know that."

"Yeah. My dad moved to the U.S. when he was twenty-five. He got a green card and then citizenship eventually. I was born here, but we grew up speaking Spanish and Portuguese."

"Wow."

"Yeah. I come off as a basic white girl, I know."

"I see. Okay. So, Colombian peso. Let's see if that checks out."

I pulled out a calculator and steeled myself to do math. I hated math. If I'd been any good at it, I would have been working on Wall Street.

"The exchange rate is about thirty-eight hundred Colombian pesos to one dollar...that means he made...about forty-one thousand dollars. Does that sound right?"

"Over five months?" she asked. "That's pretty good."

I looked up the average salary of a commercial scuba diver. It could go up to about a hundred thousand dollars a year. So if Marcum was a good diver, 41,000 dollars for five months' work was in the ballpark. "It fits," I said.

"So he was being paid in Colombian pesos, for a dive job a few years ago," said Ashley.

"Right."

"Meaning he was working in Colombia."

"That would be the logical extrapolation."

"Why?"

I shrugged over the phone. "I guess Rockweiller has operations in Colombia. I don't know."

"But this doesn't explain what he was doing for them lately, does it? Was that in Colombia too? Why isn't it listed in the records?"

"Good questions," I said. "And I don't know the answers. But we're going to ask all about it at the deposition."

"I can't wait."

"Me neither."

After I hung up with Ashley, I did some research into Rockweiller's operations. Sure enough, they did oil and gas work in Colombia. They owned offshore natural gas platforms in the Chuchupa gas field, just off the northern coast. Rockweiller had partnered with Colombia's state-owned company, Ecopetrol, to develop the field. I bet that was where Marcum had worked.

Interestingly, a press release mentioned a potential new gas field off the coast of Cartagena, Colombia. I searched for more information about it online but found only rumors and innuendo. One newspaper editorial railed against the idea of developing any new gas field near Cartagena, which was one of Colombia's oldest and most beautiful cities, if in fact a field was there.

I also read Rockweiller's 10-K report, which is the annual report that public companies have to file. It was a treasure trove of information about the company's operations. The 10-K warned of risks that Rockweiller ran in Colombia, including that new oil and gas finds might not pan out.

The report also warned of more immediate risks. Oil and gas pipelines were a favorite target of guerilla groups. One of the big Colombian pipelines, the 480-mile Caño Limón-Coveñas, had been bombed over one thousand times during its lifetime. The guerillas also took hostages sometimes, and would ransom them back. The report also listed "political risks," parlance for the propensity of South American governments to nationalize and seize foreign assets in times of economic trouble. An edgy place, to be sure.

And then, on a lark, and for no apparent reason, I typed in "treasure wreck Colombia" into the search bar. I guess I was bored, and tired of research. I was daydreaming about the *Atocha*, or Ashley Marcum, or maybe both. I hit enter, idly curious what I would find.

I blinked few times when I saw the results. Then I refreshed the page, thinking I must have messed up the search. But I hadn't.

On the very first page, there were a slew of results about a treasure ship in Colombia. And these weren't just regular search results, either. They were *news* reports. All of this was recent, or at least ongoing.

"'Holy Grail' of Spanish Treasure Galleons Found Off Colombia," one article said. "Shipwreck Worth Billions Discovered Near Cartagena," proclaimed another. "300-Year-Old Galleon Rumored To Be Worth $17 Billion."

My mind reeled. *Seventeen billion?* I thought. That was impossible.

I looked up to see if anyone was nearby. Seeing that the coast was clear, I closed my office door and began to read.

The articles were about a sixty-four-gun Spanish warship named the *San Jose* that had sunk off the coast of Cartagena, Colombia in 1708. The *San Jose* had been part of a Spanish fleet that was hauling several years' worth of taxes and profits from the Spanish colonies to the Crown. The money was to be used to fund the War of the Spanish Succession, a bloody, thirteen-year affair in which France, England, and the Netherlands vied for control of the Spanish throne.

But the *San Jose* never made it home. A British Commodore named Charles Wager caught the fleet off the coast of Colombia in a daring raid, which later became known as Wager's Action. Wager blasted the *San Jose* to smithereens with cannon, killing most of the six hundred people aboard. The bulk of the fleet escaped and made it back to Spain, including the *San Jose*'s sister ship, the *San Joaquin*. From the *San Joaquin*'s inventory, experts were able to deduce the value of the *San Jose.*

The *San Jose* had been carrying gold, silver, and emeralds worth somewhere between one and seventeen billion, depending on who you asked. I didn't know how it was valued. Or whether it was true. But all of the articles agreed that it was worth more than any ship that had been found before.

Unsurprisingly, a legal battle raged over who owned the *San Jose*. The saga read like a cautionary tale about making deals with foreign governments.

According to reports, a group of American investors called the Sea Search Armada (SSA) said they found the *San Jose* in 1981. They said it took them years and millions of dollars to do it. SSA found the wreck at a depth of one kilometer on the Colombian continental shelf. They were able to identify the ship by its unique bronze cannon, which were engraved with dolphins. The wreck was said to lie somewhere near the Rosario islands, just off the coast of Cartagena.

After it found the wreck, SSA said they cut a deal with the Colombian government. SSA would salvage the wreck in exchange for a third of the treasure. But Colombia reneged on the deal. The Colombian parliament passed a law that retroactively reduced SSA's share to five percent.

Not about to take it lying down, SSA sued the Colombian government in the Colombian courts. Over the next twenty years, SSA won a series of legal battles and appeals, culminating in a 2007 ruling from the Supreme Court of Colombia in their favor. I thought that would be the end of it.

But somehow, the Colombian government still refused to give SSA rights to the ship. It seemed like a blatant abuse of power to me. But there wasn't much you could do if a whole country decided to screw you. SSA had tried to sue Colombia in the U.S. too, but was thrown out because they waited too long to file suit.[1] I doubted a U.S. court could have done much about it anyway.

The case sparked news interest around 2018. But none of the articles answered an important question to me—why did Colombia have any rights to the ship at all? The *San Jose* was

[1] *Sea Search Armada v. Republic of Colombia*, 821 F. Supp. 2d 268 (D.D.C. 2011).

a Spanish warship, not a Colombian one. And the gold and silver it carried came from Bolivia and Peru. Back then, these were colonies of Spain, taken by the Spanish conquistadores in their endless quest for territory and treasure. Colombia was involved only insofar as the ship sank in its waters. But possession is nine-tenths of the law, as they say. Maybe that's as true today as it was in 1708.

For the second time, I had found a link between the Marcum case and one of these ancient treasure wrecks. I thought again about the gold coins David Marcum had. There was no way they could be from a ship like that, I told myself. The whole notion was so fanciful it didn't even deserve a thought. But the idea wouldn't easily leave my mind.

I resolved to ask about it at the deposition. It was probably nothing. But like Remington said, I could ask whatever I wanted. So why not satisfy my curiosity?

Treasure. Oil. Blood. Money. I wondered if this had anything to do with David Marcum. Or was I following a gilded rabbit hole down to nowhere?

EIGHT

The deposition was set for the following morning. I had finished my preparation and was reasonably confident that I was ready. I wanted to go home and get some sleep. But first, I had to attend the annual bar association's Judicial Honors Gala.

HH&K, like all good law firms, made an effort to attend fundraisers for judges, and donate to their election campaigns. Attendance was often delegated to younger lawyers like me. Judge Gleeson was one of the judges being honored. So Kruckemeyer told me that I'd better damn well show up and shake his hand.

The gala was held at one of Houston's marquee country clubs. It was evening when I arrived. I had gotten my car detailed, and it gleamed as I pulled up, the dents and scrapes hidden by the darkness. I tipped the valet five bucks and walked up a marble staircase to the entrance.

"Champagne?" a waiter asked me, offering up a small flute as I walked in. I thanked him and accepted it. I walked up to a table in front and found my name tag, which was handed to me by a young woman with a smile. Then I entered the ballroom.

I sipped my champagne while I looked around to get my bearings. The ballroom was big, with room for a couple hundred people. Crystal chandeliers cast a soft yellow light around the room, the type of glow that makes everyone look better. Well-dressed couples and groups were talking in a mellow hum, and a string quartet played tasteful music at the far end of the room. Waiters walked around with appetizers, and there was a bar at either end. About half of the men wore tuxedos, and the other half suits. I didn't have a tux, so I'd worn a dark suit with an evening tie.

I saw someone making their way toward me, double-fisting drinks. It was Harder, wearing a tuxedo. He held out one of the drinks, a whiskey on the rocks. I glanced around quickly and then quaffed my champagne in a single gulp. Then I took the whiskey. Harder and I clinked glasses.

"Decent of you, old boy," I said, sipping it appreciatively. "Meet any of the judges yet?"

"I said hello to Wright and Whittaker," said Harder. "Talked up the firm a little bit. I told them about some of the initiatives we're rolling out. The new associate mentorship program, the pro bono stuff, and all that. They seemed really excited."

"I'll bet," I said.

"I want to say hi to Judge Tolliver too," Harder went on. "Him and my dad go way back. One time I had this case in his court, and he just loved my argument..."

Harder started to drone on about some brilliant thing he had done. I tuned him out, listening just enough to nod and offer the odd "nice" or "oh really?" at the right moments.

Meanwhile, I sipped my whiskey and looked around the room. I spotted the judges, older figures surrounded by clusters of people listening to them respectfully. They seemed a little awkward. Judges aren't politicians. They don't have the easy, practiced grace with which a congressman asks for coin. But they do have to get elected, and fundraising is a part of that.

In Texas, like in many states, judges are elected. Their campaigns are funded primarily by lawyers—the same lawyers that later appear in front of these judges. Ostensibly, lawyers donate to ensure a strong judiciary. That benefits everyone. But they also donate in a subtle attempt to influence the outcomes of cases. It's never overt; a judge won't rule your way because you give him money. But when the lawyer who funded a judge's entire election campaign shows up in court, you can imagine that creates certain pressures.

In the 1980s, there was a case called *Pennzoil v. Texaco*, which ended in a ten-billion-dollar jury verdict, one of the biggest of all time. The lawyer for Pennzoil, an infamous Texas trial lawyer named Joe Jamail, made a ten-thousand-dollar donation to the judge's reelection campaign just two days after he was appointed to the case. And both sides later donated hundreds of thousands of dollars to the justices of the Texas Supreme Court during the eventual appeal. None of this was illegal, or even uncommon. But there are a lot of subtle ways that a judge can influence a case, and you have to be realistic about these things.

"Are you even listening to me?" Harder asked, to which I replied "hmm?" which evidently was the wrong thing to say.

"I don't know why I even bother to tell you these things," he huffed.

But my attention was focused on something else. I had caught sight of Judge Gleeson, the judge in our case. He was surrounded by a knot of well-wishers, including some younger attorneys.

Gleeson was an even-keeled, older judge. He was not a star, nor a dunce. He had been around a while and knew his business. He was receiving an award tonight. Thankfully, we had been supporting this event for years, so our donation and well-wishes would not look like anything untoward. My job was to shake hands with Gleeson, mention the firm, and not say anything stupid. Kruckemeyer was especially adamant about that last part.

I was about to walk over there, but then stopped. I recognized two of the lawyers talking to Judge Gleeson. Kathleen Loudamire and L. Lucius Quinto. Quinto was listening intently with a frown above his chiseled jaw line, while Loudamire stood awkwardly and giggled.

"Get a load of that," I said to Harder, gesturing with my glass.

"What?" said Harder, still annoyed with me.

"Badden and Bock," I said. "Those are the two associates from the court hearing."

"Oh really?" said Harder. "Aren't they from New York?"

"Yeah. The firm has a Houston office too, but their flagship is in New York. That's where those two work."

"What are they doing at this shindig?"

"I think they're here to meet the Judge," I said.

"What, in that pro bono case of yours?" scoffed Harder.

"It's not pro bono anymore."

"Whatever. I doubt they came down from New York to just to attend some Texas state judges' party, no matter how important your little case is."

"Probably not."

"They're wearing nice suits. How much do you think they make?"

"You know how much they make."

Salary was standard at the biggest law firms in New York. It started at over two hundred thousand dollars a year now. Plus bonus. If Loudamire and Quinto were a few years in, they probably made three or four hundred thousand dollars a year, easy. Everyone knew it, including (and especially) Harder.

"Yeah," said Harder, envious.

"Hey, why didn't you go work there?" I asked him, as if the thought had just occurred to me. "You went to Cornell or something, right?"

I knew full well that Harder had interviewed for those big firm jobs after law school, but struck out. He was still bitter about it.

"Asshole."

I clapped him on the back. "Ah, come on now. Think of the positive. If you worked there, you'd be an even bigger douchebag."

"Appreciate it," he said sourly.

"Anytime."

Just then, we saw a young woman walking up to us, waving excitedly. She had short blond hair that bobbed up and down as she came. Her outfit wasn't particularly fashionable. It looked like it had been lifted from her mother's closet a decade ago.

"Ugh," muttered Harder. "It's Cindy. New associate at the firm. I've been assigned to be her mentor."

"I thought you were all about the mentor program?"

"Yeah, yeah. She's a strange one, though. I know some people who went to law school with her..."

Harder shut up and put on a fake smile as she approached. "Hey, Cindy!" he said.

"Hey Richard!" she replied.

"Glad you could make it."

"I'm so excited to be here! This is amazing. I've never been invited to one of these things before."

"This is Jack Carver," said Harder, introducing me.

I reached out to shake her hand. There was something oblivious about her, but I liked her immediately all the same. Her smile was genuine, and her eyes were guileless.

"*The* Jack Carver?" she said. "Richard was talking about you earlier. He said you joined the firm relatively recently too. From some small Podunk shop, I think he said. Isn't that right Richard?"

Harder was making motions to try and cut off this line of conversation.

"Absolutely," I said, turning to Harder. "Podunk and Podunk. You've got a good memory, Dick."

"Dick?" Cindy said.

"Yes. We like to call him Dick around the office. Among friends. He prefers it," I added.

"I do not," he said, elbowing me in the ribs.

"Harder!" I yelled.

"First time I've heard that one," Harder muttered. But Cindy spluttered with laughter. At least someone appreciated my sense of humor.

"You going to go say hi to Judge Gleeson?" Harder asked me, an edge in his voice.

I contemplated this for a moment. "You know, I think I will," I said, putting down my drink and straightening my tie.

"This should be interesting," said Harder. "I'm coming."

I shrugged. "Suit yourself," I said. I made my way toward the knot of people in front of Judge Gleeson. Harder and Cindy followed. I felt a bit apprehensive, since the Badden &

Bock associates were there. But I wasn't afraid of them. They spotted me and said something to each other.

"Judge Gleeson," I said, putting on a big smile as I approached. "Jack Carver, with Holland, Haroldson, and Kruckemeyer. Congratulations on the honor."

Judge Gleeson shook my hand. I thought I saw a flash of recognition in his eyes. He may have remembered me from the hearing, although it would be impolitic to mention it.

"Mr. Carver," he said. "Hello. How do you do?"

Harder lunged forward and introduced himself as well. "T. Richard Harder," he said. "The third." Harder pumped Judge Gleeson's hand for all he was worth. "Chair of pro bono and associate development efforts at HH&K. A real pleasure."

"Nice to meet you, Mr. Harder. Lyle Gleeson. Thank you for supporting our event."

"Absolutely. It's so great to be here. So great," Harder said.

I interjected. "And this is Cindy..." I paused expectantly for her last name. But Cindy just smiled blandly, not getting it. There was an awkward pause. I recovered by making some comment about the judiciary's charity work, which had been described in a little booklet they'd passed around earlier. Judge Gleeson demurred. We made a bit more small talk, and then I made ready to leave, before I could say something stupid. But he stopped me.

"Have you met these young lawyers, Mr. Carver?" Gleeson said, indicating Quinto and Loudamire. "They're from New York, I believe." His voice was neutral, but I thought I saw a sardonic glint in his eye. I couldn't tell if he recognized them from the hearing or not. Frankly, they had done little more than hold Bock's jockstrap. "Perhaps you could make them feel welcome," he said to me.

"Of course," I said, turning to Quinto and Loudamire. Judge Gleeson bid us a good evening and walked off to another knot of well-wishers.

"Well, well," said Loudamire in her nasally, high-pitched voice. Who even says that, aside from villains in bad movies?

"Kathleen," I said. "You're looking well." I greeted Lucius Quinto too, and he introduced three of the local Badden & Bock associates, insufferable-looking young white men from Houston. Their names were Chad Waller, Derek Doniger, and Cornelius Adipose, a real gem of a guy whose cleft chin was raised at a near forty-five-degree angle as he looked down on me.

"Chad went to Penn, and clerked for Judge Rawlings," Quinto said. "Derek went to Georgetown, and clerked for Judge Ollison. And Cornelius went to Stanford, and clerked for Judge Flynn on the Fifth Circuit Court of Appeals."

What Quinto was saying was that all of them had gone to Ivy League schools, and all of them had clerked for federal judges, which was a mark of prestige. Top law students competed to serve with federal judges for a year or two after graduation. The law clerks attended court hearings, did legal research, drafted judicial orders, and advised the judge how to rule. It was an invaluable way to gain experience and connections, and to see how law worked from the inside.

"Wow," Harder said admiringly. "The Fifth Circuit. Very prestigious post."

"Thank you," deigned Cornelius Adipose.

Harder turned to me. "Where did you clerk again, Jack?" he asked nonchalantly.

I forced a smile. "I didn't. Wanted to get right to work, you know?" In reality, I hadn't had a prayer at landing one of those spots. But all of them murmured their fake understanding, as if they understood the siren song of capital all too well.

Harder clapped me on the back. "He's good, though. One day soon maybe the firm will even promote him from independent contractor to full time employee. Eh, Jack?" Waller and Doniger snickered. My smile froze in place. I wanted to throttle Harder.

"What about you, Richard?" Loudamire asked. "Did you clerk?"

"No. But I did attend Cornell for law school," he added quickly.

"Good school," Quinto said, favoring him with a nod.

"Thank you," said Harder. "It was a great experience."

"We take a couple of Cornell grads each year, don't we?" Quinto said with a sideways glance at Loudamire.

"We do," she confirmed. Quinto smiled handsomely and sipped at his drink.

"So," said Chad Waller, or Derek Doniger, I couldn't remember which. "I hear you and Kathleen are facing off tomorrow." He was smirking.

"We are," I said.

"Do they let associates take depositions at your firm?" Cornelius Adipose asked, puzzled. "I would have thought a partner would handle it, for an important matter. I assume Zachary is handling it from our end?" he asked Loudamire. She nodded.

"Our firm likes to make sure associates get hands-on experience," I told him. "So they're not just highly paid paper-pushers, you know?"

"I see," said Adipose. "How does your client feel about that?"

"Quite well, thank you," I said

"What firm are you guys with?" Cindy interjected.

"Badden & Bock."

"Oh, wow!" she said. "That's a great firm. You guys must be really good." I scowled at her, annoyed. They demurred.

"Badden and Bock was on today's donation list for the event," Cindy continued. "A platinum level donor to Judge Gleeson. That's fifty thousand dollars minimum, isn't it?"

"Something like that," said Quinto, exchanging glances with Loudamire. I frowned. I hadn't known about that.

"Isn't it sort of weird to make a donation when you have a case pending in front of the judge?" Cindy asked, puzzled. "Are you allowed to do that?"

They stiffened up. "Of course," said Quinto. "It's standard practice to support the judiciary. That's what this event is all about. Obviously, our firm adheres to all of the ethical rules."

"Hang on," I said incredulously. "You guys gave fifty thousand dollars to Judge Gleeson? Tonight?"

"I don't know the details," said Quinto. "You'd have to talk to our pro bono committee about that." Loudamire smirked.

I had a bad feeling about this. But there was nothing I could do about it just then. So I traded a few more barbed pleasantries with Quinto and Loudamire and then made my exit. I had done my job and wanted to get a good night's sleep. Loudamire and Quinto would both be there tomorrow, and I resolved to wipe the smirks off their faces. Cindy and Harder stayed, and continued chatting to the Badden & Bock associates as I walked away.

When I got home, I took off my suit and tie and sank down onto the couch. My apartment was dark and cool. It was a loft, with exposed brick walls and pipes. The kind of place that lets people know you're chic. The interior had been redone with warm hardwood floors. It would look great if I had the wherewithal to decorate it. No matter. I was a minimalist, I told myself.

I checked the time. The deposition was coming up in less than twelve hours. But I was too amped up to sleep. So I switched on an episode of *The Dominator* to take my mind off things.

The Dominator had started as one of those scripted wrestling shows where they decide who wins and loses each match. The titular character, The Dominator, was a real wrestler. He had been a UFC fighter before he snagged the lead on the show. The series was pitched as a way to bring back the glory days of the WWF.

Unfortunately, the ratings for season one were dismal. In season two, the producers decided to write off The Dominator, who wasn't connecting with audiences. So The Dominator was set to lose a bout to The Subjugator, who would then replace him as the lead character, perhaps improving the show's prospects before it got cancelled.

But instead of going down, The Dominator went off the rails. He smashed The Subjugator, seriously injuring him in the process. This shocked the producers, who were ready to fire him. But the footage leaked onto the internet, and people went wild. The ratings jumped, and the producers couldn't fire The Dominator anymore. They had to keep him on. But they never knew when he was going to follow the script and when he was going to fight for real. This heady mix of staged performance and reality TV delighted fans, and the show had built up a small cult following. Rumor was that the producers were going to hire a real wrestler, someone from the UFC, who would finally take down The Dominator whether he liked it or not. I was hooked.

I checked my email, a reflexive habit in the modern legal world. Oddly, there was a new email from Bock & Co. They must have sent it just now. I checked the time. It was eleven thirty.

"Dear Mr. Carver," the email said. "Please find attached a privilege log, detailing records that Rockweiller has withheld from tomorrow's deposition. Best regards, Kathleen Loudamire." I frowned as I opened it.

A privilege log is a list of documents that are being withheld under the attorney-client privilege. The privilege lets you keep emails with your attorneys confidential. But you still have to acknowledge they exist. So, when the other side asks for documents, you list them on what's called a privilege log. It's a simple chart that includes the name of the document, the date, who wrote it, and a brief description of why it it's confidential. Privilege logs are one of the most boring things in the legal field. And that's saying something.

This was a short privilege log. I had seen ones that spanned thousands of entries in bigger cases. No doubt Bock & Co. had sent it late, so I wouldn't have a chance to look at it before tomorrow. I grinned. They hadn't counted on me burning the midnight oil, I thought.

I scanned the log. There were emails between Badden & Bock, Stanley Stuttgardt, John Cartwright (the general counsel of Rockweiller Industries) and others with subject lines like "Re: David Marcum" and "Investigatory finding."

Most of these emails were dated just months ago. I wondered again why they hadn't given us any more recent employment records.

There was one person on the privilege log who didn't have a Rockweiller or Badden & Bock email address. His name was Lloyd Gunthum. He had a simple gmail address. All of the others were easy to look up by their company bios and LinkedIn pages. But I couldn't turn up anything about Lloyd Gunthum online. Just like David Marcum, I thought. I made a note to ask about Gunthum at the deposition.

Finally, there was one document title that was blacked out. Redacted. That was odd. Usually, you could redact parts of documents that were privileged, but not the title. The name of the document itself must be privileged. That was unusual, and I made a note to ask about that as well. I wrapped up my review and sent the documents to our researcher Lyle so he could save them. After that, I got ready for bed.

About fifteen minutes later, Lyle called me on my cell.

"Hey bud," he said.

"Hey Lyle," I said, glancing at the time. It was past midnight. "Working late?"

"Yeah. I'm calling about these documents you asked me to upload. You've got that deposition tomorrow, right?"

"Right."

"There's something I thought you should know."

"What's that?"

"You know that redacted entry in the privilege log? The one with the title blacked out?"

"Yes."

"Get this. When I converted the file for storage, I noticed they didn't redact it properly. Somebody didn't scrub the metadata. That means we can see what's under the redaction."

I felt goosebumps prickle up my arms.

"Bush league mistake," I said. I'd seen this happen before. First year attorneys would try to redact PDF's manually, not realizing that the metadata would be unaffected.

"Exactly."

"What does it say?"

"Take a look."

Lyle sent me the converted file. I opened it. Where the redaction had been, the text was now readable. The entry was dated a few months ago. This is what it said:

Author: K. Loudamire.

Type: Microsoft Word file.

Title: Memorandum Regarding Marcum Incident, and Liability for Death in Extraterritorial Jurisdiction.

The next morning, I got up at the crack of dawn. I was exhilarated. Today was the day. At long last, we would learn what happened to David Marcum. Ashley was going to be at the deposition too, and I told her to meet me there.

I picked out a bold tie. It was pink with white stripes and an edgy texture. It set off my navy suit nicely. There would be no judge at the deposition, and I didn't really care what Bock & Co. thought of me. I wanted to look young and sharp, and show some flair. Maybe I spent too much time thinking about my ties. But you'd be surprised at how lawyers agonize over neckwear, the only splash of color in an otherwise conformist wardrobe.

I ate breakfast, gathered my materials, and got ready to go. The deposition was set for 10:30.

Then, just as I was heading out the door, I got an email notification. An order from Judge Gleeson in the Marcum case. I put down my stuff and downloaded the order.

> On this day came to be heard Rockweiller Industries, Inc's Motion for Reconsideration. Having considered the arguments and the applicable law, the Court has determined that it requires further argument on the propriety of a pre-suit deposition. According-

ly, for the time being, the Court hereby GRANTS Rockweiller's Motion for Reconsideration, and QUASHES the deposition of its corporate representative. The Court will hear further argument in one month's time.

Jude Frank R. Gleeson.

NINE

I raged about it to Remington a few days later. "How can they just donate fifty thousand dollars and get their motion granted the next day? Is that how justice works around here?"

I was in Remington's office, pacing around in agitation. Cindy and Harder were there too, sunk into two big leather chairs. They had never been in there before, and gazed around with interest at the bulging bookshelves and the antique hunting rifle slung up on the wall.

After Badden & Bock's stunt with the Judge, Remington told Kruckemeyer that there was no point in "pussyfooting around" anymore, and that we ought to file the lawsuit. He also suggested that we staff up the case, which meant adding more associates. We would need it to handle the legal firepower that Badden & Bock would throw at us.

Kruckemeyer grumbled, but agreed. Because the case was on contingency, the firm was fronting the expenses until an eventual payout. This meant the money was coming out of Kruckemeyer and the other partners' pockets, which he was not happy about.

I suggested adding Cindy, and Kruckemeyer suggested Harder, who I suspected didn't have enough to do. Remington took them both. It was agreed that Remington would be lead counsel on the case, and Kruckemeyer would be the originating partner. That meant Remington would do most of the work, and Kruckemeyer would collect most of the money, which suited both of them.

"If I can just say, sir," Harder had said to Remington when we first walked in, "I'm thrilled to have the opportunity to work with you. I've heard a lot of incredible things, and I'm pumped. Super pumped." Harder had put on a suit and tie for the occasion. He'd even shined his shoes. Gunner.

Remington regarded Harder without comment for a few beats. Just as it started to get pleasantly awkward, Cindy broke the silence in her guileless fashion.

"Jack may be ranting, but he has a point. I know that judicial donations are legal. But this one seems pretty blatant." I frowned at her, taking exception to the word "ranting."

Remington nodded. "It was pretty on the nose," he agreed.

"I bet they were worried about what the corporate rep would say when I deposed him," I said with a hint of bravado. Harder scoffed.

"Maybe," Remington said neutrally. "But it doesn't make a whole lot of sense. We're going to get the deposition anyway. Once we file a lawsuit, we can depose anyone we want. The best this did was to delay it for several months."

"But who pays fifty thousand dollars just to stall?" asked Cindy.

"Exactly," said Remington. "And more importantly, what did they pay fifty thousand dollars to stall *for*? The only explanation I can think of is that there's something time-sensitive going on here."

"Like what?" Cindy asked.

"I don't know. But I intend to find out."

"What about the death memo?" I asked. I had told Remington about the privilege log, and the redacted entry Lyle had uncovered. I felt sure it was the smoking gun. "Is there a way we can get our hands on it? It may tell us everything we want to know."

But Remington was not sanguine about the prospect. "I doubt it," he said flatly. "We could challenge the privilege, but I don't see us winning that fight."

"Why? The memo obviously has relevant information," I argued. "How can they withhold it? It doesn't seem fair."

"The law isn't always fair," Remington said patiently. "But there's a purpose behind the attorney-client privilege. It gives people breathing room to talk to their lawyers. We balance the need for fair discovery of the facts with protections for lawyer-client advice. Imagine if you had to turn over all of your conversations with your lawyers. No one would ever talk to one again, lest anything they say be used against them. That would be no good."

"Right," I said sheepishly. I guess I had read that somewhere in law school.

"We'll get the story anyway, Jack. They won't be able to hide the witnesses. Or the facts. Just the legal advice. I know the memo has a sexy title and you want to read it. But we're just going to have to do this the old-fashioned way."

I nodded. "The old-fashioned way. Got it."

Remington reached into his desk and pulled out a copper tin. He took something out of it and slipped it into his mouth. It was chewing tobacco, I noticed with a start. He put the tin back in the drawer and then steepled his hands in front of him on the desk.

"Now. The primary thing I am concerned about right now is Judge Gleeson. After this chicanery with the deposition, I don't have a lot of confidence in him. And this may be a sign of worse to come. I don't want to be fighting an uphill battle the whole case." We nodded in agreement.

"We could file a motion for recusal," Harder suggested. "Surely a donation this flagrant would get some traction. If we win, we can get him booted off the case. If we lose, at least we would preserve our objection for the record." This was actually not a bad idea. I had thought about it myself.

But Remington shook his head. "No. We're not going to do that. Going after the judge is a dangerous game. If we lose, he'll be against us for the rest of the case. And the other judges won't look kindly on us, no matter how good our reasons. So we're going to try another tactic."

"What tactic?"

"We're going to file in federal court."

Our eyes widened as we considered this idea.

Federal court was a whole different ballgame. Thus far, the case was in state court, like most cases are. The federal courts only hear cases about federal law, or big lawsuits involving people or companies from different states. They were designed to provide impartial hearings in those kinds of situations.

The Founding Fathers imagined that a company from, say, Pennsylvania, might get a raw deal from a jury in Virginia, who might prefer their own guy or gal to some big out-of-state corporation. As much as I'd like to think it's different today, it isn't. You get whip-smart trial lawyers stirring up juries against the evils of foreign corporations. They donate to the judges, who stay out of the way. I've learned the hard way that you can get hometowned in the twenty-first century just as hard as the eighteenth.

But federal courts are different. Federal judges serve for life. They can't be removed except by impeachment, just like the President. This means that federal judges have no fear of election cycles or public opinion, and are free to rule as the law requires. They also tend to be better qualified, get paid more, and have law clerks to help them. All of this translates to better decisions. Or I thought so, anyway. Some people criticized federal judges as unelected rogue actors with too much power. Usually, those are the people on the losing end of the case.

Cindy looked puzzled. "I don't understand," she said. "How can we get into federal court? I thought they only hear cases about federal law, or between people from different states. We're representing a Texas guy suing a Texas company."

"We were," said Remington. "Until something that Jack discovered."

"Me?" I said.

"Yes, you. Tell me. What does the federal diversity jurisdiction statute say?" Remington asked. His voice took on a Socratic tone, like a law school professor's.

Law schools traditionally used the Socratic method to teach law. This calls for a dialogue between teacher and student to stimulate critical thinking. I can't say whether it did that or not. But it did make people pay attention in class. Law students were terrified of being called on by the professor, which happened at random. So they paid close attention to the reading, lest they be embarrassed in front of their peers. The Socratic method also helped accustom students to public speaking. It was tough, but effective.

"Uh. I didn't bring my civil procedure book with me," I hemmed. Harder took out his phone and started Googling.

Remington sighed. "Put that away. Twenty-eight U.S.C. Section thirteen-thirty-two grants federal courts 'original jurisdiction of all civil actions where the matter in controversy exceeds the sum or value of seventy-five thousand dollars, exclusive of interest and costs,' and is between 'citizens of different States.'"

"You had that memorized?" said Cindy, surprised.

"I have read it many times. Now. What does 'citizens of different states' mean?"

"It means what it says," Harder theorized. "You know. Citizens from...different states. Of the Union."

"Nice one, Matlock," I said.

"Shut up."

"For federal jurisdictional purposes," Remington said, ignoring our squabble, "a person is a citizen of a state if he or she resides there and evinces an intent to remain. Jack, what did you find out about where David Marcum lived?"

I screwed up my face, trying to figure out where he was going with this. "He grew up in Houston. He had an apartment in Montrose. Then he stopped paying the bills."

"And where was he during the last year of his life?" Remington prompted.

"The last year...he was in Key West. He stayed at Aqua Ray..." It hit me. "Of course! He lived in Florida!"

"And if he's a Florida resident," said Cindy, snatching up my train of thought, "and Rockweiller is a Houston company, then it's a civil action between citizens of different states. So we can get into federal court!"

Remington smiled broadly. "Exactly. There may be some other ways to get in too. But this ought to do the trick."

Harder spoke up. "I hate to be a wet noodle, but wouldn't we rather be in state court for this? That's usually better for plaintiffs like us, right?"

"That's a fair stereotype," Remington agreed. "But in this case, we're already at a disadvantage with Judge Gleeson. Badden & Bock won't be able to bully a federal judge the same way. And a federal judge won't put up with the type of nasty tactics I'd expect to see from them in this case. So in the long run, I think we'll be better off. That's also one reason I suggested we file the pre-suit deposition. We had a chance to see what judge we'd draw, and how that would play out. We did that. Now we get to do a little forum shopping."

Our jaws dropped at this master-level strategy. "That's brilliant!" said Cindy.

"That will depend what judge we draw in federal court," Remington cautioned. "But I think almost any judge would be preferable to Judge Gleeson in this instance."

"Excellent," I said. Harder nodded in agreement.

"Good," said Remington. "Now, here's what I want you all to do. Write this down." We took out our legal pads and stood ready.

"First, prepare the federal lawsuit," he instructed. "I want to file this week. Rockweiller is trying to stall this thing, which means we want to ram it forward.

"Second, serve discovery requests. I want every email or scrap of paper that has anything to do with David Marcum. And I want deposition notices for anyone and everyone you can think of." We jotted this down.

"Third," Remington continued, "contact Marcum's bank, his cell phone company, his internet service provider, etc. Get his records. If we have those, we'll be able to follow the trail of his life from day-to-day. Maybe we can see where it stopped. Ashley should be able to get the records as executrix of the estate." I wrote that down. I hadn't thought of that. Genius.

"Fourth, prepare a motion to get the coins back from Rockweiller. We should be able to get them for inspection, if nothing else.

"Lastly, do some old-fashioned detective work. Call anyone you can think of who might know what happened to Marcum. His friends, past employers, acquaintances, girlfriends, anyone. Someone somewhere has got to know something, and I want to know what it is."

"Got it," I said, writing all of that down. "Anything else?"

"No. Go get it done."

Cindy chattered excitedly as we left Remington's office and headed back down to our floor.

"That was incredible!" she said. "He knows everything!"

"Seems like it," I said.

"Should we sit down in the conference room and divvy this all up?" Harder suggested.

"Sure," I said.

After a bathroom break, we set up in one of the smaller conference rooms. Harder and I waited in silence for a moment while Cindy got a cup of tea and a muffin. Presently, she sat down with her legal pad at the ready.

I started to speak, but Harder interrupted me. "Okay," he began. "So here's what I'm thinking. I'll handle the depositions and prepare to question Rockweiller's people. Cindy, you do the jurisdictional research and start drafting discovery requests. I'd also like to see a draft of the motion to get the coins for inspection."

I looked at Harder incredulously, but he pretended not to notice. Cindy scribbled down his orders, but eyed me uncertainly. She was aware of the tension, even in her typically oblivious state.

"Jack, you draft the lawsuit," Harder instructed. "You can also handle the background sleuthing. You know the case and the client best, so I think you're the best bet for that important task. Meanwhile, I'll put together a task list in a Google spreadsheet, so we can all edit—"

"Are you fucking serious?" I interrupted him.

"About the spreadsheet?" Harder said, as if he didn't understand. "We can use a different program if you prefer. We don't have to use Goo—"

"Fuck Google. You don't give the orders here, Harder. It's my case."

"Actually, it's Kruckemeyer's case. And Remington is running it."

"It's my case," I repeated. "I brought it in. Ashley's my client. You were brought on to help me. Not the other way around."

"Technically, the *estate* of David Marcum is the client," Harder said snootily. "Not Ashley. And I'm the senior associate. Naturally, I'll manage the task allocation. That's firm policy. I don't see why this has to be an issue. I'm just trying to find the best way for us to collaborate and leverage our resources on key tasks, that's all."

"Leverage this," I said, getting up and giving him the middle finger. Not the classiest reaction, maybe, but it was heartfelt.

I stormed out of the room, furious at Harder's bullshit. I went back to my office. It took me a while to cool down. But eventually, I got back to work. An email popped up from Harder with his "task list" in a Google doc. He asked me for the case file number. I ignored him.

But Harder had cc'd Kruckemeyer on the email, and presently Kruckemeyer wrote back and approved of the task list. "Good job," he wrote. "Looks like you have this sorted out. Good job Richard. Good job Jack. Let's get it done."

I smoldered. But there wasn't much I could do about it just then. I wasn't about to run to Remington about Harder's bush league power play. He would probably tell me to shut up and figure it out. Whatever. I would sort this out later. For the time being, I opened up a new Word document and began drafting the lawsuit.

That evening, I met Ashley for dinner. We went to Sushi King, a hole-in-the wall restaurant with a solid B+ rating and a good happy hour. It was pretty bare bones. But it was popular, mostly for the three-dollar spicy tuna rolls and two-dollar sake bombs. I had offered to take Ashley somewhere fancier, but she declined.

We ordered a couple of Sapporo beers and some edamame, shishito peppers, and baked mussels to start. Then we settled on a dragon roll, a couple of spicy tuna rolls, and the eponymous King Roll for the entrees.

"Why'd you pick this place?" I asked, sliding a baked mussel into my mouth. "Not that it's bad. But we could have gone anywhere. Oichi Omakase, if you wanted. Kruckemeyer would have picked up the tab." Oichi Omakase was the best Japanese place in town. It was just down the street. I had been there once, on someone else's dime. It was incredible.

"Yeah, I know," she said. "But I don't usually go for fancy places. Unless I get dragged there on a date. And I could eat these spicy tuna rolls all day." She rolled her eyes to the ceiling as she put another one in her mouth.

"They are good," I agreed, stacking a heap of wasabi onto one. "A date, huh? Does that mean you're single?" I said nonchalantly. Or tried to.

"I am."

"Good to know," I said.

"Yep." She ate another spicy tuna roll and regarded me in silence for a moment.

"Not that it matters," I added. "Lawyer-client relationship, and all. You know."

"Right." She picked up another spicy tuna roll and then smiled at me provocatively. My breath caught for a second.

"Any news on the case?" she asked, switching tracks.

"Yeah," I said, relaxing as we returned to more familiar ground. "We're getting ready to file in federal court." I told her about Remington's strategy and our plan of action. She was duly impressed. I didn't mention my squabble with Harder. She didn't need to hear about that.

"What does Remington think about the coins?" she asked.

I shrugged. "Not much. He's more focused on your brother's death."

She nodded, spearing the last spicy tuna roll with a chopstick. "What do *you* think about the coins?" she said after a little while.

The King Roll arrived then, and I used that as an excuse not to answer. But as the King Roll ran out, the question was still there. I thought about the *Atocha*, and the coin we had seen at Aqua Ray. I thought about the *San Jose*, and Rockweiller's operations in Colombia.

"I don't know," I said.

"What if they were from a ship like the *Atocha*?" Ashley asked, voicing the question I hadn't dared to ask. She looked at me, trying to gauge my reaction.

I picked at my plate. "I didn't mention this," I said finally. "But I read about a big find in Colombia. A recent one. Near Cartagena, actually."

"The *San Jose.* I know."

"You know?" I said, surprised. "How?"

"I can use Google too," she said dryly. "Even though I'm not a lawyer."

"Oh," I said, embarrassed. "Duh. Sorry."

She waved it away. "What if Rockweiller and my brother somehow got tangled up in something like that?"

"I can't say I haven't thought about it," I admitted. "But I just don't think it's realistic. Rockweiller is an oil company. If anything, it was probably some new oil or gas find."

"But what about the *San Jose*? And the fact that my brother was in Colombia? And that their offices just happen to be near Cartagena?"

I shook my head. "Coincidence. Rockweiller has a lot of offices around the world. The fact that they're there, and so was your brother, and we read this news article about the *San Jose...*" I spread my hands.

"You're probably right." She finished the King Roll and cleared the rest of her plate. "Suppose we wanted to know more, though. Just hypothetically. What would we do?"

I shrugged. "Serve discovery. They're going to have to tell us eventually."

"Will they?" she asked doubtfully. "They've done a pretty good job of shutting everything down so far."

"Yes," I admitted. "But now we're filing a federal lawsuit. And Remington is involved. Somehow, I don't think they're going to be able to stop him."

"Maybe you're right."

We finished the remainder of our food and drink. Our server brought the check. It was fifty bucks. What a steal.

After dinner, I walked Ashley to her car. Then I said goodnight and walked back to mine, which was parked some distance away. On the way back, I walked past Oichi Omakase, and stopped for a moment to peer inside.

The window was frosted, but I could see the warm, mellow atmosphere within. It was lit by candles and Japanese lanterns. Everyone seemed to be either good looking or rich, or both. I sighed and began to walk away when something caught my eye.

It was Harder. I pressed closer to the window to get a better look. He was sitting at a table inside with two others. I recognized them as Lucius Quinto and Cornelius Adipose, two of the associates from Badden & Bock. They were drinking and laughing, and seemed to be concentrating intently on what Harder was saying. What was he doing there? I wondered.

I thought about brazenly walking in to find out. But I decided against it. I would ask Harder about it later. For the time being, I set my curiosity aside and walked away.

As I got back into my car and drove home, I thought about Ashley's question. About how to find out more. As it happened, there was another way. To find out about treasure wrecks, and whether they could possibly have anything to do with her brother, Rockweiller, or this case.

We could hire an expert.

TEN

After we filed the federal lawsuit, the litigation began in earnest. Bock & Co. were furious at our bait and switch. They castigated us for "flagrant forum shopping" and "barefaced abuse of the judicial process," whatever that meant. I found this ironic after their timely "donation" to Judge Gleeson. But howl as they might, they couldn't do anything about it. Judge Gleeson had no power to stop the federal suit. And privately, I guessed he was happy to have the matter off his hands.

The federal judge who drew our case was named Nathaniel L. Graves. He sat in Galveston, a small beach town about an hour south of Houston. Galveston and Houston were part of the same judicial district, and sometimes cases were assigned between them. I didn't know much about Judge Graves. But when I told Remington, he shook his head and grinned. "Oh, boy," he said. "Strap in." I didn't know what to make of that, but I had too much on my plate to worry about it just then.

Per Remington's plan, we served a horde of discovery requests on Rockweiller, noticed depositions, and filed a motion to get the coins back. Bock & Co. fought back, objecting, moving to quash, and generally being obstructive in every way they could. Remington said this was because we were putting the screws on them. This legal scuffling took place over the weeks and months after we filed suit, and Cindy, Harder, and I all worked overtime responding to their challenges.

Between the Marcum case and trying to keep up with my other matters, I hardly had a moment to myself. Finally, I managed to steal a free afternoon by telling Kruckemeyer I was taking a "mental health day." This confused him for just long enough for me to make my escape.

I used the day to seek out my expert.

When lawyers need to know about a certain subject, they hire an expert. In a financial case, for example, they might hire an accounting expert. In a medical case, a drug expert. And so on. The expert would help the lawyer understand the subject and explain it to a jury, if it came to that. Expert witnesses were often criticized as hired guns who would say anything the lawyers wanted them to. But right now, I just needed information.

As luck would have it, one of the world's foremost experts in maritime archaeology was currently on a teaching fellowship in San Marcos, Texas. I called his office to make an appointment, and headed down the next day.

San Marcos was a new city, built on the river. The university boasted Spanish-style architecture, with cream stucco walls and red adobe tiled roofs. College students walked lazily between classes and napped in the shade. I consulted a large campus map to see where I was going. Eventually, after some wrong turns and students who waved me in vague directions, I made my way to the office of Professor Jacob A. Schnizzel. I knocked on the door and stepped inside.

I had expected a maritime archaeologist to be a rugged, seafaring type of guy. Tall, with a sailor's tan and an air of the sea about him. Schnizzel was none of these things. Instead, he proved to be a short, fast-talking Jewish guy from Brooklyn. He wore jeans and a rumpled white shirt with a coffee stain down the front.

Schnizzel's office was a mess. There were textbooks and academic paraphernalia strewn everywhere. Most of the books seemed to be about computer science. There were a few about C and C++, as well as a beauty called "Java with Java," which featured some nerd drinking a steaming cup of coffee and giving the would-be reader a thumbs up. Belatedly, I noticed a sign on the door that said "Jacob Schnizzel, Professor of Computer Science." Did I have the wrong guy?

Schnizzel jumped up and shook my hand energetically. "Jack Carver, I presume. My assistant tells me you need an expert. I do lots of cases out of New York and Florida, but I haven't had any in Texas. Some people say I wouldn't come off well to a Texas jury. But what do they know?" He blew off this fanciful notion with a wave of his hand. "So. What's the case about? Software dispute? Breach of intellectual property agreement? Trade secrets? I do it all." He rubbed his hands together excitedly.

I hesitated. Maybe I did have the wrong guy. "Actually, I'm not looking for a computer science expert," I said.

"Oh no?"

"No. Sorry. Is it possible I have the wrong Jacob Schnizzel?"

Schnizzel scratched his head. "There are a few hundred of us in New York City. But I doubt nearly that many in San Marcos."

"No. Well you see, I was actually looking for a Professor Jacob Schnizzel, expert in maritime archaeology."

Schnizzel's eyes lit up. "Maritime archaeology!" he almost shouted. "Well, why didn't you say so! That's what you need an expert for? Fantastic. I've been waiting for this kind of case. It's not a field that sees much litigation. How exciting."

With a generous amount of gesticulation, Schnizzel explained that while his day job was computer science, his passion was maritime archaeology. In his spare time, he had become one of the world's leading experts on the subject. Looking around his office more closely, I saw a collection of artifacts and relics from another time. A beaten bronze battleship. A beautiful white-sailed galleon, looking for all the world like a blooming flower. An antique globe, which looked considerably more authentic than the one I had bought for ten dollars from Target.

"It's not like I'm a world-class expert in maritime archaeology the same way as in computer science," he said modestly. "But I do alright. Anyway. Enough about me. What can I do you for?"

"For now, I'm just looking for some preliminary opinions," I said cautiously.

"Go on."

"If tell you about the case, will you keep it confidential?"

"Of course. Think of this like an initial consultation with a lawyer. If I can help you, we'll move forward. If not, I won't divulge anything I learn."

"Great. You don't do any work for Rockweiller Industries, do you?" I added, thinking about conflicts.

"No. I don't think I ever have."

"Great."

I filled Schnizzel in on David Marcum's death, the gold coins, and the lawsuit against Rockweiller Industries. I also mentioned Mel Fisher's *Atocha*, which he was familiar with, and what we had learned at Aqua Ray.

"Hmm," said Schnizzel, furrowing his brow. "Do you have any of the coins with you?"

"No," I said, cursing myself for losing them to Bock. "We're trying to get them back. I took one to an assayer, though. He said it was pure gold and had been sitting undisturbed somewhere for a long time."

"Did the coins have any writing or markings on them?"

"I think so. But they were covered with dirt or something, and I couldn't make it out."

Schnizzel considered this. "What you're describing does sound like the type of coin you'd find in a wreck. But that may be wishful thinking. You could also find them in any number of other places. They could have been owned by a collector, or uncovered at an estate sale. They could be from a museum. A couple of years ago, some kids stole a four-pound silver bar right out of the maritime museum in Florida." I stirred uneasily, reflecting once more on David Marcum's background.

"Supposing it was a wreck, though," I said. "What are the chances it's from a new find?"

"A new find?" Schnizzel scratched his head. "It's possible. People find notable wrecks every few years. Some contain gold or silver in the quantities you're describing."

Schnizzel got up and poured himself a cup of coffee from a huge pot brewing on his desk. He offered me some, but I declined and took water instead.

"How many of these wrecks are out there?" I asked.

Schnizzel took a sip of his coffee. "Nobody knows. Some say there could be as many as three million shipwrecks still undiscovered, and that the value of all the treasure they contain could exceed sixty billion dollars."

I choked on my water. "What?"

Schnizzel grinned at me. "Now you see why my elective is so popular."

"How is that possible? Where do they all come from?"

"Well. They come from several millennia of failed seafaring travel. But the most famous wrecks—like the *Atocha*—date back to around the Age of Discovery."

Schnizzel took another sip of coffee and regaled me. "The Age of Discovery was the period roughly from the fifteenth through seventeenth centuries," he explained. "When Spain and Portugal set out to explore and conquer the world between them. After Columbus discovered America, and Cortés conquered the Aztec Empire, the New World became a massive source of bullion for Spain. She would seize silver from the mines of Bolivia, and gold from the bowels of Peru, and ship it back to the Old World to fund the endless European wars.

"The fortunes Spain took from these places were staggering. She became the richest and most powerful nation in the world on the backs of these countries. All of this wealth was sent back to the Old World in colossal treasure fleets, on galleons so bloated with gold and silver that they could barely float. But crossing the ocean in those days was a dangerous business. One-third of the ships sank, mostly in storms, sometimes in naval battles or pirate raids. Hence all of the shipwrecks.

"Modern-day treasure hunters employ sophisticated techniques like side-scan sonar and remotely operated vehicles—ROV's—to find and recover these wrecks. By combining new technology with old nautical records, they have been able to salvage wrecks that have lain undiscovered for centuries. And these aren't just mom-and-pop shops either. Many of them are experienced outfits backed by well-capitalized investors. There are even some publicly traded companies in the business. Take Odyssey Marine Exploration, for example. It's traded on the NASDAQ. It's a treasure hunting company. Or at least, it used to be."

"But—sixty billion?" I said, still in disbelief. "Surely that figure is exaggerated."

"Maybe," Schnizzel admitted. "The number was put forth by a well-known treasure hunter. Treasure hunters are optimistic by nature. They have a vested interest in inflating the amount of wealth out there. It helps them finance more expeditions. And a lot of the value is historical. People will pay more for ancient coins and artifacts than the metal alone is worth. So, is there sixty billion dollars' worth of treasure out there? I don't know. But is there a lot of it? Certainly."

I thought about this as Schnizzel got up and poured himself another cup of coffee. He sat back down and gulped it with relish, swirling it around the mug as if it were a fine wine.

"What are the chances that the coins we're dealing with are from a wreck like Mel Fisher's *Atocha*?" I asked finally.

Schnizzel chuckled. "The *Atocha*? Unlikely. That was a once-in-a-century find. You don't see wrecks like that every day. No, no."

"But there are wrecks of that magnitude still out there?" I persisted.

"Certainly. There are many of them. You've got the *Merchant Royal*, for example," he said, ticking it off on his fingers. "That was a British ship that sank in 1641 with a hundred thousand pounds of gold on board. There's the *Cinco Chagas*. A Portuguese carrack that sank in 1594 after a naval battle with the British. It was rumored to have cargo worth a billion in diamonds and gems. There's *La Trinite.* Part of the lost French fleet of 1565. And those are just a handful. There are many more. But the odds of finding any one of them is low."

"Where are most of these wrecks discovered?"

"You can find them all over the world. But perhaps the most famous ones appear—or should I say disappeared—on the routes that Spain and Portugal used during their golden age, centuries ago."

"What about near Cartagena, Colombia?" I asked, taking a stab in the dark.

"Oh, sure. Cartagena was a big port for the Spanish Main in its heyday. The English privateer Sir Francis Drake, better known to the Spanish as *El Draque*, sacked Cartagena twice, including in 1586, when he lit the city on fire for a month until the inhabitants paid him a king's ransom to leave."

I raised my eyebrows. Talk about scorched earth. I could almost hear Kruckemeyer chuckling in my head. "*El Draque*, eh?" he would muse. "Could use a fellow with that kind of spirit at this law firm."

"What do you know about the *San Jose*?" I asked.

"Ha! You know more about this than you let on, don't you? The *San Jose*! What a find. What do you want to know?"

"Well," I said carefully, "Rockweiller has offices in Cartagena."

"Ah. You're wondering if Rockweiller has some connection to the *San Jose*, or to some other wreck in the area."

"I know it's thin, but...yes."

Schnizzel scratched his head. "I haven't heard of any new finds near Cartagena lately. And I don't see how Rockweiller could be involved with the *San Jose*. It's already been found. There's a legal dispute about it, I know. I heard that Colombia was trying to hire a new company to salvage it. Maybe it's Rockweiller? That's the only thing I can think of."

Rockweiller hired to salvage the wreck? That was an interesting idea. It would fit with the secrecy of the whole thing. If Marcum had taken the coins from the *San Jose*...what would Rockweiller have done?

"To be candid, though," Schnizzel said, "it seems unlikely. Occam's razor and whatnot."

I must have looked puzzled, so he explained. "Occam's razor is the principle that the simplest explanation for something is usually the true one. Rockweiller is an oil & gas company. Ergo, if they found something, it's more likely to be oil or gas than some treasure wreck." I nodded, thinking of the rumors I'd read about a new gas field near Cartagena.

"And even if it was a treasure ship, they don't always turn out the way you think," he cautioned. "Take the Tobermory Galleon, for instance. That was a Spanish ship that sank off the west coast of Scotland centuries ago. There was rumored to be fabled wealth aboard. Over the centuries, various Earls of Argyll tried to raise the wreck, and fought with the Stuart kings over the salvage rights. But if one of these earls had read the records in the Spanish archives, they would have known that there never was any treasure on the ship in the first place."

Schnizzel stopped to check his watch, and then jumped to his feet when he saw the time. "I've got to get to my next class. Come on, I'll walk you out." He grabbed his bookbag and we headed out the door.

Out on the quad, the day was sunny, and the air was rich with the smell of grass and flowers. We strolled along a bright stone walkway, interspersed here and there with shade from the trees.

"I have to ask," I said. "What are you doing in San Marcos? It seems a rather...landlocked destination, considering your interests."

"Ha! True. There's not much maritime archaeology to be found in the San Marcos River. That's a bit of a story," Schnizzel said.

Schnizzel had been born and raised in New York City. He got his computer science degree at Columbia University, and taught there for ten years. From there, he moved to Miami, planning to live and teach by the beach. There he met another professor. She was one of those big-haired blondes from Texas. They fell in love and were soon married. When she got an offer to teach back in her hometown of San Marcos, Schnizzel followed. Unfortunately, soon after they arrived in Texas, she had started an affair with the local football coach. Now they were getting divorced.

"The fucking football coach," Schnizzel muttered, clearly still bitter about it. "That's what happens when you move to Texas."

"I'm sorry to hear that," I said, genuinely feeling for the guy.

"Bah," he said, waving his hand. "Ancient history. Anyway, I kind of like it here. It's a nice change from the bustle of Miami and New York. I may just stick around after I finish my term. Well. I'm glad you came to see me. Let me know what else I can do to help. And if you get your hands on those coins, bring them to me! I'll tell you where they're from."

I promised to do that, and we parted ways.

ELEVEN

It was a few months into discovery that we got our first big break in the case. The answer came in the form of paper rather than gold.

In response to our discovery requests, Badden & Bock document dumped us. The document dump is a time-honored tradition in civil litigation. You give the other side so many documents that they can't tell the good from the garbage. It used to be that lawyers would dump rooms full of boxes on each other, and make the other side spend days or weeks reviewing paper files. Now that everything was electronic, it was worse.

In the old days, the name of the game was trial by ambush. Old lawyers still reminisce fondly about whipping out a red-hot document and making an unsuspecting witness shit himself right there on the stand. No more. In the 1980s, the rules of civil procedure were amended to allow for more discovery. Now, everyone knows everything that anyone is going to say before they say it. In theory, this makes trials more fair. In practice, it also makes them more expensive. You wouldn't believe how many documents there are in the average case, and how much it costs to review and fight about them.

When Badden & Bock finally sent us the documents we asked for, I opened the index, eager to see what they said. I pulled up the file count.

It said 1.4 million.

I checked and then re-checked it to make sure I wasn't seeing things. Then I slumped back in my chair, dismayed. How Rockweiller had gotten to 1.4 million documents about David Marcum was beyond me. I doubted the guy had two emails to rub together. But we had asked for all documents, and I guess we got them.

Initially, I was excited about the sandbox of material they had given us. I was sure there must be something useful in there. So Cindy, Harder, and I searched through the documents over the next couple of days. We looked for key terms like Marcum, death, oil rig, scuba diving, coins, gold, COL, Gunthum, and others.

But soon enough, it became clear that there was almost nothing useful about David Marcum in them. Most of the documents were irrelevant emails, reports, newsletters, and the other day-to-day electronic correspondence of a corporation. The documents we wanted were either hidden away among the garbage, or not there at all. We wouldn't know which until we started going through them the hard way.

So we put together a document review plan. Or rather, Harder did. He made a show of "creating protocols" and "leveraging technology" to maximize efficiency. These buzzwords might have impressed a luddite like Kruckemeyer. But in reality, they didn't mean much. After all the "leveraging" was said and done, we were still left with about half a million documents that someone needed to eyeball.

So Cindy and I sat in front of our computers for eight, ten, sometimes twelve hours a day, clicking through the documents one by one, the blue light of the monitors burning into our eyes, and the cheap blaze of a fluorescent sun shining down from above, day after day.

Early on, Harder tried to micromanage us. He sent about ten emails a day trying to get "buy-in" from "the team" (i.e., Cindy and me). We ignored him, and pretty soon he joined us in the review. He didn't have much else to do anyway. Our enmity faded amid the stultifying monotony of the documents.

And then, finally, Cindy caught our first break.

I was experimenting with some yellow glasses to filter out the harsh blue light of the monitors when she called. The glasses worked, but also made me look like an idiot. Consumed with this existential tension between form and function, my review rate plummeted, because I kept looking up to make sure that no one saw me.

I took off the glasses as I picked up the phone. "You know you can just come down here. You're like three offices away," I told her.

"I think I found something," she said, ignoring my jibe. I heard an undercurrent of excitement in her voice for the first time in what felt like months.

"What is it?"

"I was looking through Rockweiller's insurance certificates," Cindy explained. "You remember how we asked for those?"

"Yeah." Insurance was important because it would tell us how much coverage Rockweiller had in case of an accident. That often ended up being the most that a company would pay to settle a case. If an insurance company was eating it all anyway, it was no skin off their back. "What did you find?" I asked.

"Well, they dumped about two hundred different policies on us. For every line of business they have. It took me a while, but I read through all of them."

"You read through two hundred different insurance policies?" I asked incredulously. Insurance policies were among the most boring types of documents in existence.

"It was only a couple thousand pages. Excluding the appendices. Anyway, the important one is a commercial general liability policy for ten million dollars."

"A fat sum."

"Yeah. The policy names some additional insureds, including David Marcum and Lloyd Gunthum."

I frowned. "Lloyd Gunthum. Why does that name sound familiar?"

"Because he was on the privilege log."

That jolted my memory. Gunthum was one of the people on the privileged communications at Rockweiller. Including the death memo. "Right."

"Now, here's where it gets interesting," Cindy said. "You see, it's not a Rockweiller insurance policy."

"What do you mean?" I said, puzzled.

"It's owned by another company. Called Excel Resources."

"Never heard of them."

"Neither had I. But I looked them up. Guess who owns a majority stake?"

"Who?"

"Rockweiller Industries. I found it on their ten-K. You gave me the idea when you looked up that Colombia stuff."

"Ninja."

"Thanks. Here's the kicker: I think Marcum was actually working for Excel Resources, not Rockweiller Industries, when he disappeared. That would explain why we haven't seen any documents about him."

I sat bolt upright in my chair. "Of course," I said, thinking about it. "If he wasn't technically working for Rockweiller, that would explain why they have no recent employment records."

"Exactly. To test my theory, I ran searches for Excel Resources. And it worked. I'm finally finding stuff about David Marcum."

"What sort of stuff? And hang on. Why didn't we find these when we searched for his name? They should have come up."

"I have a theory about that too. A lot of the Excel Resources documents were hand-scanned in. From paper copies. They didn't OCR well. I think that's why our searches didn't pick them up."

OCR stood for Optical Character Recognition. That was what scanned text to make it computer readable. It wasn't always perfect, especially when documents were badly scanned. I was immediately suspicious. I wouldn't have put it past Bock & Co. to do that intentionally. "I just started going through these," said Cindy. "But they look promising."

"Brilliant! You're amazing, Cindy!"

"I try," she said, and I could hear her beaming into the phone.

Sure enough, Cindy's insight yielded fruit, and we slowly started to piece together what David Marcum had been doing for Rockweiller and Excel Resources.

Marcum had worked for Excel in the months leading up to his disappearance, as Cindy had suspected. He was a diver, and he was paid as an independent contractor. In U.S. dollars this time, not Colombian pesos. The records said nothing about where he worked.

But we did learn that he was working on a ship. Marcum's name appeared on things like ship's logs, food requisitions, and inspection checklists. From this, we were able glean that he was onboard a ship called the Excelsior, a seventy-meter vessel fitted for salvage and recovery operations. The Excelsior carried enough food, water, and supplies to sustain a crew for a journey of several weeks.

Lloyd Gunthum was the captain of the ship—the same man who appeared on the privilege log. Gunthum owned a large stake in Excel Resources, in partnership with Rockweiller. The crew of the Excelsior were: Thomas Barber, Michelle Kauller, Richard Layes, Jeremy Riker, Carl Ruthers, Jason Dubino, and David Marcum. They were sailors, divers, and equipment operators. We had their pictures and personnel files, and I scrutinized their faces, wondering if any of them knew what happened to David Marcum.

The Excelsior carried scuba equipment for everyone aboard, including wetsuits, masks, fins, weights, tanks, and an air compressor. The ship also had a remotely operated vehicle (ROV) to reach depths that divers could not plumb. Finally, it carried a number of search tools, including a magnetometer and a side-scan sonar. I knew from Schnizzel that these were the tools that treasure hunters used to hunt deep-sea wrecks. But I also knew they were used in modern-day salvage as well, so it might not mean anything. Still, my interest was piqued.

Of Excel Resources itself, we didn't learn much. We knew it was a deep-sea search and recovery outfit, but that was about it. Lloyd Gunthum was a mystery too. He didn't have a social media presence, and we couldn't find anything about him online.

Finally, try as we might, we couldn't find out anything about what the Excelsior was doing, where it had been, or how David Marcum had died. That information was all missing or redacted as "ultrasensitive." Badden & Bock shouldn't have been able to do that. But unsurprisingly, they had.

I kept waiting for Bock & Co. to slip up, like they had with the privilege log. Out of 1.4 million documents, I figured someone must have screwed up somewhere, and we would get a glimpse of what was really going on. But there was no chink in Badden & Bock's armor this time, and the truth remained as elusive as ever.

At 10 a.m. on Friday, I grabbed a couple of heavy binders and lugged them over to Kruckemeyer's office.

We had set up a weekly meeting to keep track of the case. Remington hated meetings, and rarely attended. So it was usually just Kruckemeyer, Cindy, Harder, and me. We would sit down, talk about the documents, strategize, and shoot the shit.

The door to Kruckemeyer's office was closed when I arrived. I sat down outside. Inside, I spied someone through the glass door. It was David Wurlheiser. Wurlheiser was talking animatedly, and Kruckemeyer seemed to be listening and nodding reluctantly. Eventually, Wurlheiser got up and stormed out. He didn't bother to look at me, but stalked off and disappeared into the elevator. I walked into Kruckemeyer's office. Kruckemeyer motioned me to sit down. He looked tired.

"What was that all about?" I asked, jerking my thumb toward Wurlheiser.

Kruckemeyer sighed and pinched the bridge of his nose. "David is on me about the conflict again. We got a letter from Rockweiller Industries, demanding that we recuse. On account of the prior work. It's bullshit. But David is named in the letter, so he's feeling it. He's a contracts guy, not a trial lawyer. He's not used to this kind of pressure."

Kruckemeyer slid the letter across the desk. It was long. I skimmed it and saw allegations like breach of fiduciary duty, misuse of confidential information, and abrogation of the lawyer-client privilege.

"We're not going to recuse, are we?" I asked, concerned.

"Pshhaw. Recuse? Me?" Kruckemeyer scoffed. "You know I'm a stone-cold litigator, Jack. My panties are made of sterner stuff than David's. No. We'll recuse once we stick it to them, and not a day before. Don't you worry about that. Now. On to other stuff. How's my Mongolian barbeque case? Is it heating up?" He chuckled. It was about the fifth time he'd made that joke. But I laughed dutifully and described the skirmishing between myself and H. Hubert Thung, which he always enjoyed.

"Where are Cindy and Harder?" I asked, checking my watch. It was ten past the hour. They were usually here by now.

"They're in some ethics seminar," he said dismissively.

Lawyers had to do a certain amount of Continuing Legal Education (CLEs) every year. These were seminars where you learned about a variety of legal topics. Most of them were useless. But it didn't matter, because no one paid attention anyway. At best, CLEs were an opportunity to socialize with lawyers you hadn't seen in a while. But after the pandemic, a lot of the CLEs went virtual. So even that benefit was gone. I guessed that about one in ten people actively listened to a

CLE online, as opposed to having it on in the background whilst shopping on Amazon.

The hardest CLEs to find were the ethics ones, of which you had to do one or two every year. These taught you the tough stuff, like don't steal from your client, or lie to the judge, or be an asshole. Most lawyers were pretty good about the first two. I had done the ethics seminar that Cindy and Harder were in. Total snooze fest. It was about conflicts, actually. I had picked up a few nuggets about imputed conflicts and firm associations. So that was something.

To my surprise, as I opened the key documents binder and began to update Kruckemeyer, Remington showed up. So I caught them both up on the case. I went over our document review progress, explaining what methods we were using, what we had found, and how it all fit with our theory of the case. I showed them the key documents, and they questioned me about some of them. Remington was particularly interested in scuba diving equipment, for some reason. I promised to send him more on that.

At some point, I remarked on the unfairness of the document dump, and how it was bullshit that we had to review so many documents while Rockweiller just lolled around and laughed.

Kruckemeyer chuckled at this. "They may be lolling now. But they weren't lolling before, I guarantee. I bet those guys reviewed every email before it went out the door."

"You can't be serious," I protested. "That would have taken forever!"

Kruckemeyer shrugged. "They've got the manpower. They put an army of grunts like you on this, no offense, and bill by the hour." Remington nodded in agreement.

"That doesn't seem very efficient," I said.

"Oh sure it is. They're making a killing."

"I meant for the client. Rockweiller."

"Oh. No, they're getting screwed. But that's what litigation is about."

"But why do they put up with it? Aren't they in charge?"

Kruckemeyer waved his hand dismissively. "Pshhaw. Client's not in charge. Rockweiller's got some milquetoast in-house counsel on the job. Couldn't litigate his way out of a paper bag. He's scared shitless that if they produce one wrong document, it'll wreck the whole case. Waive privilege or some other apocalypse. So they tell the lawyers to look at everything. Which Badden and Bock are happy to do."

"Wow," I said.

Remington nodded. "I might have put a finer point on it, but Bob is right. Bock is the one driving this train. And he's not concerned about efficiency. Now don't get me wrong—there's a case to be made for reviewing all of the documents. That way, you know exactly what's going on, and you don't turn over the wrong thing. Could it be done more efficiently? Oh, yeah. But there's no incentive. The lawyers get paid by the hour. If they're more efficient, they lose money."

"But you'd think the in-house lawyers would know this," I said.

"They do. But they come from the same law firms that they later farm out work to. It's the way they know to do business. That's the system," Remington said.

"Good work if you can get it," said Kruckemeyer. "Unfortunately, we're on contingency here. We don't get paid by the hour. So we don't get to stuff that peacock. Got to use our heads, like your girl Cindy did." He sighed. "Goddamn David Wurlheiser. If he had more game maybe we'd be on the defense side of this. Think of the billings," he said dreamily.

"Is there anything else?" Remington asked as we wrapped up. I took a deep breath. "There is one more thing."

For a while now, I had been debating whether to tell Remington and Kruckemeyer about my treasure wreck theory. I hadn't said anything so far. It seemed too far-fetched to be true. But after talking with Schnizzel, and learning what I had about the coins, the *Atocha* and *San Jose* cases, as well as Rockweiller's presence in Colombia and the equipment aboard the Excelsior, I decided to say something. I would give them the facts and let them draw their own conclusions. If they thought it warranted further investigation, they would say so. If not, I would let it go.

So I laid out everything I had learned as best I could in a neutral, measured tone. As I heard myself say it out loud, I thought I made a pretty compelling case.

"What if Rockweiller found one of these ancient wrecks?" I concluded, trying to suppress my excitement. "It would explain the secrecy surrounding the case. It would explain why Rockweiller hired Badden & Bock to get the coins back. And it would explain why they're fighting so hard to conceal what happened to David Marcum. I know it's a long shot," I admitted, my heart beating faster. "But do you think it's possible?" I waited for an answer, poised on the edge of my seat.

Remington and Kruckemeyer looked at each other for a long while, considering this.

Then they burst into laughter. Kruckemeyer slapped his knee and cackled so hard I thought his dentures would fall out. Remington rarely laughed, but now he almost fell out of his chair. After a minute or so they calmed down and wiped the tears from their eyes.

"Golly," said Remington, still chuckling. "I needed that. That is one tall tale. But let's stick to the facts of the case, alright?"

"That's right, Jack," said Kruckemeyer with mock severity. "Stick to the facts. We're here to figure out what happened to David Marcum. Not Blackbeard. Okay?"

The mention of Blackbeard sent Remington into peals of laughter again. Kruckemeyer grinned. "What? What'd I say?"

Kruckemeyer got up and gently patted me on the shoulder. "Good stuff," he said. "But a little less time digging for buried treasure, a little more time billing hours, eh? Good man."

Remington and Kruckemeyer might have blown me off. But Harder and Vijay showed considerably more interest the next morning. Kruckemeyer had probably told them about it, and they came into my office with wide eyes and hushed voices. So I told them all about the Florida trip, the cases, and what I knew about the coins. They proved to be an attentive audience.

"You're saying these ships are worth hundreds of millions of dollars?" said Harder incredulously. I pulled up the *Atocha* court case and showed him where it said so.

"Dude. How is that possible?" he asked.

"Dude," agreed Vijay.

"And that was in the eighties," I added. "It would be worth even more today."

"What would you even do with all of that money?" Harder wondered.

"Lot of cocaine," said Vijay.

"Shut up," said Harder. Vijay shrugged, unapologetic.

Harder leaned toward me intently. "Is there any chance your girl's coins could be from that kind of situation?" he asked in a low voice. He and Vijay looked at me expectantly.

"I don't know," I said cautiously. "I mean, it's possible."

"The odds are against, obviously," Harder said.

"Right. Obviously. But it's possible." I nodded. They got it.

"Wow," whispered Vijay. "Imagine that." We all sat back and imagined it. The staggering amount of wealth in those ships. What it would be like to have that much money. What we would do with it all. I could scarcely conceive of it.

"There's only one thing you'd have to watch out for," Harder said thoughtfully.

"What's that?" I asked.

Harder and Vijay reached into their pockets and donned a pair of eyepatches and paper mache swords.

"Pirates!" they yelled together. Then they pranced around my office, laughing hysterically and whacking me with their swords while yelling "yar" and "argh" and suchlike. Eventually I told them to fuck off, at which point they collapsed on the floor in gales of laughter and then left me alone.

It was in a sullen mood that I went back to my document review.

After we had mined the Excel Resources documents for all they were worth, it was time to confront Badden & Bock. At Kruckemeyer's direction, I prepared a letter demanding that Rockweiller produce all documents they had withheld about the Excelsior and David Marcum's death. We knew they wouldn't do it. But it was a necessary opening shot in the court fight that was coming.

We also served deposition notices for the Excelsior's captain and crew. No matter how many documents Rockweiller hid from us, they couldn't hide their people. I was sure someone on the crew knew what had happened to David Marcum. And they were going to have to tell us under oath, like it or not.

Badden & Bock wasn't going to give this up without a fight. We would have to go to court and take it, in front of this Judge Graves, whoever he was. So we began marshalling our arguments, and a court date was set.

The last thing to come out of the Rockweiller documents was a master list of all current and former employees of the company. It was a gigantic spreadsheet with tens of thousands of names that listed dates and places of employment for people around the globe. I doubted Rockweiller had intended to give it to us. It probably got caught up in the shuffle.

Initially, I didn't think much of it. But in fact, this spreadsheet was destined to lead me on my most exotic adventure yet, a place that had featured in my thoughts and dreams for some time now: Cartagena, Colombia.

For one reason the firm knew of, and one they did not.

TWELVE

Ashley and I flew into Cartagena on the redeye. There were no direct routes, and our plane made two stopovers on the way. I spent the night trying to sleep under a pair of airline blinders, crammed in the middle seat and bent over my tray table like the hunchback of Notre Dame.

But my mood lifted as the city came into view. Cartagena was a seaside resort town, but it had a historic feel to it. The city was built in old stone and bright colors, and there were red and yellow and blue roofs as far as the eye could see.

We arrived in the morning and checked into our hotel. It had a stylish, boutique feel. I had found it on Yelp, which listed it as a top spot for romantic getaways. I glanced over at Ashley to see if it made any impression. It did not, as far as I could tell. We sat down in the hotel restaurant for breakfast, and I ordered a traditional Colombian dish called *arepas*, a type of cornbread pancake served with eggs and beans.

"You got the list?" Ashley said, all business.

I nodded and pulled out a folder containing names and addresses. I handed it to her.

From the master employee list that Rockweiller had given us, we had identified all of their employees in Colombia.

Then, we'd narrowed that down to the dates that Marcum worked for them. Finally, we culled the list to include former employees only. We couldn't talk to current employees without going through Badden & Bock. And I doubted they would be accommodating. But former employees were fair game. So we planned to interview these select people and see if any of them remembered David Marcum.

The job would have been easier by phone. That would have saved us the trouble of trekking around Colombia to track these people down. But the master list didn't have phone numbers, and our trace programs were next to useless here.

The list did have addresses, however, the better to send these people paychecks. So we were going to do some old-school, door-to-door canvassing. Remington liked old-school, and said people were more likely to talk to us in person, anyway. He also said they were more likely to talk to Ashley than me. Combined with her knowledge of the language and the country, this made her an indispensable asset on the trip. Harder had tried to score this plum travel assignment, but was rebuffed. Kruckemeyer said he was needed at command and control. Ha.

Our food arrived. I ate with gusto while Ashley plotted our route. Then we rented a car and began.

There were about two dozen names on our list. It proved to be slow going. Traffic was bad, and the streets were rough. Ashley drove with grim determination around roadblocks and potholes while I navigated. Some of the neighborhoods were nice. Others were ungentrified. I thought we were going to be carjacked at least twice. But we never were.

At each address, we would park the car and Ashley would walk up, smile, and inquire. Many of the people were not home, and others had moved away. We talked to a few former employees, but none of them remembered David Marcum.

It was late afternoon when finally, we hit pay dirt. The man's name was Vasco de Valencia. He wasn't home. But his wife was, and she directed us to his place of business at a manufacturing plant a few miles away. We drove there and asked for him. After a short while, a pleasant-looking man came out to greet us.

"Vasco de Valencia?" Ashley inquired.

"Yes," he said politely. "I am Vasco de Valencia. What can I do for you?"

"You worked for Rockweiller Industries a few years ago?"

"Yes." There was a hint of wariness in his voice.

"Do you remember someone named David Marcum?"

"Dave. Yes, I remember. What about him?"

Ashley and I exchanged hopeful glances. De Valencia's English was good, so I decided to take the lead.

"Mr. de Valencia, I'm sorry to tell you that David Marcum passed away."

"Dave died?" said de Valencia, dismayed. "What happened? He was a young man."

"That's what we'd like to talk to you about. My name is Jack Carver. I'm an attorney from the United States. I'm investigating his death. This is Ashley Marcum, David's sister."

"I am sorry for your loss," he told her sincerely, shaking her hand.

"Thank you," she said. "Anything you could tell us would be helpful."

"Of course. What do you want to know?"

"How did you know David?" I asked.

"From Rockweiller Industries. We both worked there a couple of years ago. On a gas rig. I did installation. Dave, he was a diver. He go underwater, place parts. Good man. Everybody like him." Ashley smiled wistfully.

"How long did he work there?" I asked.

"Half a year, maybe."

I nodded. This lined up with the records. "Did he leave after the installation was finished?"

"No. He got fired."

This took me aback. There was nothing in the file about that. "Fired? For what?"

De Valencia laughed. "For getting into trouble with the supervisor, Rozato."

"What kind of trouble?"

"Rozato, he was a strict boss," de Valencia explained. "Not good to work for. We all scared of him, except for Dave. Dave would sit on the platform after dives, drink a *cerveza*, smoke a cigarette. Rozato was not happy with this."

Ashley shook her head. "Classic Dave," she said under her breath.

"So he had a falling out with Rozato?" I asked.

De Valencia nodded. "Rozato hate Dave. But he couldn't fire him. Too good at diving. So Dave keep drinking *cerveza* and smoking cigarettes and laughing at Rozato. Later, another diver came to the project. Older guy."

"Do you remember his name?"

De Valencia thought for a while. "Gunther, maybe?"

"Gunthum?" I said with a start. "Lloyd Gunthum?"

"Yes," de Valencia said. "Gunthum. That's right."

That was interesting. The name kept coming up. "You're sure? Could you describe him?" I asked.

"Yes. He was maybe fifty. American. Experienced guy. He was in the army, I think."

"How do you know?"

"Just a feeling. I was in the army. I know."

"So Gunthum came to work with David Marcum? Why?"

De Valencia shrugged. "I don't know. Maybe they needed two divers. Maybe Rozato got tired of Dave."

"Did Dave and Gunthum get along?"

"Yes, they get along good. I see them go for drinks sometimes, at a bar on the *playa* after work."

"How long did they work together for?"

"Not long. Maybe a couple weeks. Then, Dave got fired." De Valencia smiled as he recalled the incident.

"One day, Dave was standing on the platform after lunch, drinking *cerveza*. He turns and starts pissing off the side.

"Rozato, he is on the lower platform. He starts yelling at Dave to put his dick away and get back to work. Dave pretends not to hear him, and he turns to the side. His piss gets real close to Rozato. He piss far, Dave.

"The piss is getting closer and closer to Rozato. Rozato yells and moves away. Then, Rozato slip and fall off the edge of the platform, into the water. Big splash. Everyone laughs.

"Dave, he throw a life preserver and a *cerveza* down to Rozato and he say 'Hey *chochito*, live a little, eh?' Rozato fires him right there from the water. Dave, he just shrugs and say, 'You can't fire me, I quit.'"

I laughed along with Valencia as he finished the tale. Ashley was less amused.

"After that," de Valencia went on, "Dave get his stuff and say goodbye. We all sad to see him go. Except Rozato."

"Did you ever see him after that?" I asked.

De Valencia shook his head. "No."

"And the other guy, Gunthum?"

"Gunthum stay on to finish the project. Took a couple more months. No problems. Job done, then he left. I continue working on the platform for a while, maybe another few months. Then my contract ended."

"Did Dave ever work with Rockweiller again after that?"

"I don't know," he said.

I nodded. I looked at Ashley to see if there was anything else.

"Did Rockweiller ever have any problems with safety?" Ashley asked. "Accidents. Injuries. That sort of thing."

De Valencia thought about it. "No," he said, shaking his head. "Some minor stuff. I think someone got killed once, a few years back. But that's the business. I never heard Rockweiller had a bad safety record or something like that."

"Okay," I said. "Thank you for your time. We appreciate it."

"No problem. I'm sorry for Dave. I hope you find out what happened."

"Thank you," Ashley said. After that, we got back into the car and left.

I was troubled as we drove to our next stop. As much as I loved de Valencia's story about Marcum, it was clear that Marcum had a rebellious streak. I thought back to his background report. It wasn't hard to imagine him nicking a few gold coins from a company like Rockweiller Industries. Especially if they had fired him.

I didn't share this concern with Ashley. No client wants to hear about her brother's failings. And she knew them already. But I wondered what a jury would think. That's what this would come down to, in the end.

For the time being, I put the issue out of my mind. There was nothing I could do about it. As Kruckemeyer liked to say, you couldn't put your client on a pedestal. It didn't mean we weren't right.

Ashley and I drove to some other places before dark, but didn't have any more luck. The next day, we tackled the second half of our list. We managed to speak to two more former employees. But neither of them had worked with David Marcum.

One of them remembered Marcum's name, though. A man named Julio Jimenez. He had worked as a security guard on a rig just off the coast. He said the rig had a small office with some personnel records in it. Jimenez had never met David Marcum, but recalled the name from the file. He didn't know any more than that. We thanked him and left, and then went back to the hotel for the evening.

We had finished our list early, and we still had one more day in Cartagena. I knew just what to do with it.

The next morning, we woke up early and drove to a private airfield.

Before the trip, I had consulted Schnizzel about notable treasure wrecks near Cartagena. He had highlighted a few: the *Nuestra Senora de Tarragona*, the *San Felipe*, the *Los Tres Reyes*, and a pair of unidentified Spanish galleons that sunk in the area. And then there was the biggest find of all—the *San Jose*.

The *San Jose* had lain heavily on my mind in the days leading up to our trip. Although it had already been found, it hadn't been salvaged. And Rockweiller might have been hired to do it. The Colombian government was secretive about the whole thing, so there was no way for me to know. But if there was work going on, there was a good chance the site would be active.

My plan was to charter a plane and fly over the sites of each of these wrecks to see if I could spot any unusual activity. If one of the wrecks had been found, perhaps there would be ships and salvage operations in the area. Schnizzel had given me the coordinates for each of the wrecks. Or rather, the coordinates where they were generally believed to be. Schnizzel had even managed to find the actual coordinates for the *San Jose*, although they were top secret.

I hadn't shared my fly-by scheme with anyone at the firm. I knew what they would say. Even the normally enthusiastic Schnizzel was dubious about it. But Ashley was game, and we decided to go for it. I have to say that I was also enamored with the idea of flying over the ocean in search of lost treasure, like a pilot in search of Shangri-La. That may have influenced my plan. If we found something, I would tell Remington and Kruckemeyer. If not, I would keep my mouth shut and eat the expense.

Since I was funding the flight personally, I picked the cheapest one available. The result was a young pilot who had just gotten his flying license. He was advertising flights on the Colombian equivalent of Craigslist. We met him at the airfield, which turned out to be a flight school. He barely looked old enough to shave. But he seemed nice enough, and one of the older instructors told me he was an ace.

With that recommendation, we ascended into the skies in a Cessna 172, a tiny plane that has been around in largely the same form since the 1960s.

I had this majestic idea of what flying in a small aircraft would be like. I imagined soaring above the clouds, and reigning over the earth like an eagle. I had even toyed with the idea of getting a flight license myself. But the Cessna was nothing like that. It felt more like flying in a tin can. It was loud, and we had to wear headphones to be able to hear each other.

I gave the pilot the list of longitudes and latitudes that Schnizzel had plotted out for us. He had no idea what they signified, but was content to plug the numbers into his GPS and cruise toward them on my dime.

Despite the noise and the feeling that I was thousands of feet in the air in a can of Bumblebee tuna, I enjoyed the experience. The view was brilliant, and we were engulfed from all sides in blue – the dark blue of the water and the bright azure of the skies. The sun beat down on us warmly and illuminated the land and water beneath us. Ashley was captivated. I caught her grinning from ear to ear. I smiled to myself. The trip might have been worth it just for that.

The first coordinates that we passed over were Schnizzel's best guess at where the *Nuestra Senora de Tarragona* had sunk. The *Tarragona* was a five-hundred-ton galleon that hit a reef and sank mere leagues from Cartagena in 1564. Its cargo was never recovered. According to historical accounts, the merchants had been so angry about the loss that they murdered the ship's captain in port. We crisscrossed the area at low altitude, but saw no signs of activity.

The next coordinates were those of the *San Felipe*, which sank in 1572. The ship somehow caught fire and blew up a few hours out from harbor, probably from all the gunpowder aboard. Both the *Tarragona* and the *San Felipe* would be worth millions, Schnizzel had assured me. But there was no sign of activity there either, except for a small fishing boat making its way across the shimmering blue expanse.

The third set of coordinates were for the *Los Tres Reyes*, which sank in 1634 with about 1.5 million pesos aboard. It would be worth far more than that today. But there was nothing there, either. Nor did we find anything at the coordinates for a pair of two unidentified Spanish galleons that were destroyed in 1669 by fire ships of Henry Morgan, one of the most notorious pirates of the day.

The final set of coordinates were those of the *San Jose*. My breathing quickened as we approached the spot.

Unlike the other ships, we knew the *San Jose* was here. At these very coordinates, a kilometer below the surface, on the edge of the continental shelf. Somewhere down there were the remains of six hundred people, sixty-four guns, and enough gold and silver to see me through a thousand lifetimes. I strained my eyes, gazing down at the sea, hoping to see something. Anything.

But though we crissed and crossed the waters above the site, there was nothing but calm blue waters. I directed the pilot to circle the area, and we spent the remainder of our flight time straining to see a hint of activity. But we found nothing.

That evening, Ashley and I dined at a picturesque restaurant by the sea. We ate ceviche and other Colombian delicacies on the deck and watched the sun set over the ocean. Although we hadn't learned as much as I'd hoped, Vasco de Valencia's information had made the trip worthwhile. Ashley and I chatted about the flight we took, and the people that we met. She mentioned that David Marcum had known how to fly, though he didn't have a formal license. A friend had taught him illegally in the deserts of New Mexico, Ashley said. I wasn't surprised.

As our dessert arrived, I saw that Ashley had her eyes fixed on a small island, just offshore.

"I wonder what that is?" she said, pointing at it. The island was connected to the mainland by a narrow causeway.

"Funny you should ask," I said. "That's an offshore oil facility. Owned and operated by none other than Rockweiller Industries."

"You're kidding me!"

"Nope. I read about it in their 10-K."

"Is that why you brought me here? For the view?"

"Yes," I said, laughing. "But not that view. That's actually a tiny man-made island, you know. Apparently, it was cheaper than constructing a platform. That's the place where the security guard worked. The one we talked to. Julio Jimenez."

We gazed out at the island. It looked hazy in the setting sun. There was an air of mystery about it, the long bridge fading into shadow, disappearing into an artificial island in the sea.

We made conversation as the waiters came and cleared away our plates. But Ashley was distracted. She kept looking at the island. After dinner, I paid the bill and we went outside to call a cab. But she stopped me.

"Wait," she said, gesturing toward the island. "Let's go a little closer." I shrugged, and we walked toward the long causeway that began on the beach. It was farther away than it appeared, and it took us a while to get there. Once we arrived, we walked around it, studying the entrance. It was fully dark now, but there was a full moon, which cast a soft, silvery light.

The mouth of the causeway was protected by barbed wire. On closer inspection, we saw that a narrow highway, paved with concrete, led to the island. The entrance was deserted. A thick padlock barred any trespass. There were "keep out" signs that even I could read.

Ashley eyed the fence and flexed it with her fingers.

"Don't even think about it," I warned. "This is private property. There's no way to climb that, anyway. It's fifteen feet of barbed wire. And the whole place is in plain view of the town."

Ashley didn't answer. She picked her way down to the water, and I followed. We looked out at the island. Lit faintly in the distance, we saw no obvious signs of life. But it was hard to tell. It was dark, and the island was at least a half mile offshore.

"What if we could get there?" Ashley asked, her eyes bright in the moonlight.

"We can't," I said flatly.

"Not over the fence. I mean by the water. We could go directly to the island. There's no fence there."

She was right. The island itself wasn't fenced in. We had seen that before it got dark. It relied on the water to keep people away.

"Are you crazy?" I said. "What do you want to do, swim out there? Even if we could, there's bound to be security. What would we even do over there?"

Her eyes didn't waver at all. "Jimenez said they keep records there. Remember? Personnel files. We could find out what they're holding back from us. About my brother. You know they haven't given us everything."

"No," I agreed. "But this isn't an Indiana Jones movie. We can't just go barging into Rockweiller's private island to root around for files. It's illegal. And it could seriously compromise our case if they found out."

Her lip curled. "Man up," she said, her face taking on a harsher cast. "David would have done this in a heartbeat. I'll find us a boat. This will be a ten-minute ride, max. I'm tired of Rockweiller's bullshit. Let's do it."

I was startled by the tone of her voice. I protested vehemently, but there was no stopping her. She said that she was going with or without me, and unless I wanted to tie her up or turn her in, I'd better get on board or shove off.

An hour later, we were on a small fishing boat with an old diesel motor, bearing toward the island. The boat's owner was a nervous-looking fisherman named Alfonso Curacao. Ashley had approached a few fishermen at the wharf as they were tying up their boats for the day. With her fluent Spanish and easy charm, it didn't take her long to find a ride. At her direction, I shoved pesos into Curacao's hands until he agreed to take us. She didn't tell him where we were going.

Once Curacao figured out our destination, he had second thoughts. He tried to talk Ashley out of it. But he was no more successful than I was. Ashley just responded in a calming, cheerful manner, as if she didn't know what all the fuss was about. Curacao kept going, albeit with increasing wariness.

As the small island grew nearer, we were struck by how beautiful it was. It seemed like a miniature tropical paradise, with palm trees all over. There was a compound in the middle, and a small dock by the western end. It felt like one of those mini-planets I'd seen in cartoons as a kid, where you could circumnavigate the globe in a few moments, and gravity somehow worked to keep you glued to the ground.

Ashley told Curacao to dock near a thick cluster of palm trees. As we approached, she jumped out of the boat into knee-deep water. When Curacao protested, she came back at him sharply, and said something to the effect of, he'd better be there when we got back, or else. With a last look at the distant shoreline, I rolled up my pants, took off my shoes, and jumped in after Ashley.

We quickly waded to shore. I shook the water off and put my shoes back on. Then we peered through the palm trees toward the center of the island.

The compound in the middle of the island turned out to be a small shack, made of concrete, with a metal door in the front. A single floodlight cast a harsh glare over the scene. There was a sign somewhere that said *Industrias de Rockweiller, Entrada Prohibida*, in big red letters. But the place seemed deserted. I couldn't see any cameras, despite my best efforts to find them.

Ashley picked her way around the island, circling the edges. I followed her. There appeared to be nothing else there besides this small building and oil equipment everywhere else. After walking the whole island, we returned to the shack. Ashley looked at me. Then, without another word, she walked boldly toward the shack. I held my breath and followed. When we reached it, we were surprised to find that it the door wasn't locked. Ashley took a deep breath, turned the handle, and opened it.

Sitting right there, hunched over and reading an old paperback novel, was a Colombian security guard in a faded blue uniform. His eyes went wide with shock when he saw us. Both he and Ashley froze, their mouths open as they stared at each other.

Shit, I thought. *Shit, shit shit.* There was a handgun on the guard's hip, and a phone on the wall. If he picked up either of those things, we were done. My heart started to pound. Ashley remained stock still. Her lips moved as if to say something, but nothing came out. All of her bravado was gone.

So I walked forward. I'm no action hero, but I can step up when the time comes. I wasn't very good at deception. The only thing I could think to do was tell the truth.

"*Hola*!" I said, putting on my biggest lawyer smile. "I'm an attorney from the United States. *Un abogado*. I apologize for dropping by unexpectedly. We anticipated arriving earlier, but our flight was delayed. I'm here to obtain some corporate records for Rockweiller Industries."

The guard's hand was half lifted, whether at the gun or the phone I couldn't say, but my words stayed him for a moment.

"*Registros*?" he said in heavily accented English. "For corporation? *No hablo ingles muy bueno*."

"*Si. Registros.* You're doing just fine. Corporate records, that's correct." I fished into my pocket and took out the subpoenas we had served on Rockweiller. They looked very official, if somewhat crumpled, and ordered the production of all sorts of documents and records—including those related to David Marcum.

The guard hesitated.

"We're seeking the records described in these subpoenas," I said authoritatively, handing him the documents. "They relate to a former employee named David Marcum, who may have worked in this general vicinity several years ago. Perhaps you recognize the name?"

I kept on talking as he leafed through the papers. I kept up a steady flow of five-dollar words, hoping to brazen it out.

The man was completely off guard. He had no idea what to do with this unexpected American attorney who had appeared near midnight with these very official-looking document requests. Ashley was looking at me in amazement. I held my breath. The guard held the papers, quite obviously not knowing what they said, and at a complete loss as to what to do with them.

"You see how these are addressed to Rockweiller's corporate counsel," I said, pointing at the heading. "We're looking for the records described below, in requests for production numbers one through fourteen. You follow?" I put the slightest bit of impatience into my voice, as if I was starting to be disappointed with his lack of response.

The guard mumbled something. At that point, Ashley unfroze. She jumped in and smiled and started talking to the guard in Spanish. She seemed to be explaining and apologizing, all the while turning on her natural charm. It was working. They went back and forth for a while, and I saw the guard relax. Then he turned to me.

"Identificación?" he asked.

I reached into my pocket and pulled out my actual business card, which said: Jack Carver, Attorney at Law, Holland, Haroldson, & Kruckemeyer. The guard turned it over a few times in his hands, and then, under the pressure of silence, he buckled, handed back the card, and turned toward a small file cabinet behind him. My heart was thrilling in my chest, and Ashley looked at me with crazy wide eyes.

After a minute, the guard pulled out a manila folder labelled "Marcum" and gave it to us. We laid it out on the table and opened it. The guard said something apologetically to Ashley. Then he went over to the phone and picked it up. I tensed, but there was nothing we could do.

He dialed a number and let it ring. Despite my apprehension, it seemed that no one was monitoring the line this late at night. After some time, he shrugged and hung up. I nodded reassuringly to him as Ashley looked through the records.

"So?" I asked quietly. "What do you see?"

"I'll be damned," she said, surprised.

"What is it?"

She showed me the records. They were the same ones that Rockweiller had given us for the pre-suit deposition. They showed that David Marcum had been employed by Rockweiller several years ago as a commercial diver, for about five months, and that he was paid a total 156 million COL.

"Huh. That's just what we already knew."

Ashley blinked. "Maybe they actually did give us all of the records," she said, equally at a loss. We leafed through the rest of the papers, but there was nothing else in the small file that we didn't already have.

The guard was eyeing us warily. I turned back to him with a smile. "Great," I said. "*Muy bueno.* That's what we needed to know." There was a small copier in the shack, and in my most brazen act yet, I had gall to ask the guard to make me copies. I didn't want to leave emptyhanded, which I felt would look suspicious.

The guard obliged. After we were done, we thanked him and prepared to leave. There was still an air of tension in the room.

Ashley looked at me pointedly. She motioned to my pocket. It took a minute, but I got the hint. I took out my wallet and withdrew a fat stack of Colombian pesos.

"Appreciate your help, *amigo*," I said, handing them to the guard.

At this, he relaxed, and finally smiled for the first time in this surreal encounter. I suppose that was the way it worked down here.

"Good night," I said.

"Buenas noches," replied the guard.

Ashley waved goodbye as well and stepped out of the shack. We walked calmly, and I tried to hide the shaking in my arms and legs. As soon as we were out of view, we broke into a dead run toward the cluster of palm trees that was hiding our boat.

My heart was pumping with adrenaline. I kept waiting for the guard to burst out and try to stop us, but he didn't.

Curacao was still there, waiting for us. We jumped into the boat, ignoring his urgent recriminations. Ashley told him to get the hell out of there as fast as he could. Curacao gunned the engine and we sped away from the island, and toward the shore.

"That was fucking amazing," Ashley told me, as we stood there in the moonlight, her hair waving in the wind, the ocean spray kicking up all around us. She was breathing hard. And she was looking at me a different light now. There was admiration in her eyes. Or maybe something else.

"You were great too," I said. "Teamwork."

Back on the shore, I doubled the money we'd given to Curacao. He thanked us and bid us good night, no doubt wishing he'd never met these *gringos*, despite the payday. After that, we walked back to the hotel and went to bed.

I lay awake for a little while, staring at the ceiling. I thought about the surreal encounter we'd just had. About the treasure flight that morning. About Ashley, and the way she had looked at me, and whether I should have done something before the night had ended. But I was tired, and I soon fell asleep. The next morning, we woke up early and caught a flight back to Texas.

THIRTEEN

Dear Mr. Carver,

Pursuant to your subpoena, please find enclosed David Marcum's banking records for the last five years. We trust this will assist with your claim.

Sincerely,

Travis Scott

Senior Counsel, Bank of America

I grinned as I tore open the package. I had been waiting for these.

Early in the case, we had contacted David Marcum's bank, his cell phone company, his internet service provider, and others to get records. With his bank and cell phone records, we would be able to trace what he was doing, where he was going, and who he was talking to. With his internet search history, we would almost be able to tell what he was thinking. By then, the court had appointed Ashley as executrix of the estate, and she called to get the records some time ago.

Unfortunately, it wasn't that easy. The first problem was that we didn't have a death certificate. Companies like Apple or Google would defend their users' privacy to the death, and sometimes beyond. It was hard enough to get records when you *did* have a death certificate. Without one, it was almost impossible. I tried to explain that we couldn't get a death certificate until we knew how he died, but we couldn't know how he died unless we got the records. But they were not interested in my catch-22, and politely told me to pound sand.

I asked Remington about it, and he told me to subpoena them. In a civil case, an attorney can subpoena just about anyone he or she wants and make them give up information about the case.

So we subpoenaed everyone we could think of, including David's email provider, his apartment complex, his Amazon account, and more. I even subpoenaed his dry-cleaner, on the off chance that his shirt choices might tell us something about where he had gone. A slew of responses came back over the next few weeks and months. Some of the companies fought us, and we had to threaten them with all manner of legal action if they didn't comply. Eventually, most of them agreed to cooperate.

Unfortunately, what we got was not very useful. That was because of the second problem, which Ashley had warned me about: David was a privacy nut. He was one of those conspiracy theorists who thought the government spied on everything he did. He had no social media, used burner phones, and refused to call or text except on an encrypted messaging app called Signal.

Signal stored virtually no data about its users. It erased conversations after a certain period of time. The last time that David had wished Ashley a happy birthday, the message had disappeared six minutes later. The government hated Signal, which could be used by terrorists, protestors, Edward Snowden, or the average American who didn't want the government spying on their conversations. So although we sent a subpoena to Signal, we were not surprised when it came back empty handed.

Our subpoena to David's email provider was equally unhelpful. David used ProtonMail, an encrypted email service based in Geneva. It was founded by a team of scientists who met at the CERN research facility. Our subpoena to Switzerland was met with a brusque communique, written in Swiss, which, when decoded via the auspices of Google Translate, told us to eat shit. Remington said that we could try to serve Letters Rogatory under the Hague Convention for something or other, but that it probably wasn't worth the trouble.

Luckily, some of the other companies were easier to persuade. We caught a break with Bank of America. I served them with a flurry of record requests, and hit upon the notion of subpoenaing their high-ranking executives, including their CEO, to testify under oath. I probably couldn't have actually made them testify. But rather than fight about it, they caved and agreed to let us see the records.

I picked up the phone and called Ashley. "I've got the bank records. Opening them as we speak. You want in?"

"Yes! I'll come by this afternoon before work. Don't peek without me."

"See you then."

The records were a welcome respite from everything else that was going on. It was three weeks after our return from Colombia. After we had gotten back, I had fessed up to Remington about our little excursion to Rockweiller's island, and about my treasure hunting flight.

Remington had been furious. He asked whether I was an imbecile, or whether I really thought I could go around breaking into private property like some gumshoe in a detective novel. He said that when Rockweiller found out—when, not if, because they surely would—this could seriously jeopardize not only my legal career but also our credibility with the judge, and therefore our ability to prosecute the case. Then he yelled at me for chasing fairy tales when we had a dead man on our hands and no clue how he had died. If I wanted to be a treasure hunter, I ought to take a vacation and do it on my own time, he said.

I hung my head and apologized profusely. I think Remington felt bad for me, because after that he let it go and didn't bring it up again. I should have told Kruckemeyer at the same time, because when I did, I got a second tongue-lashing, this one so loud that half the office heard. Thereafter, I was relegated to document review for the next couple of weeks, which I did with my head down and no complaints.

It was a good thing I'd come clean about it, though, because Rockweiller did find out. A week after my return, Badden & Bock filed a motion for sanctions, ethical censure, and disbarment with our new judge. The motion recounted my trespass, complete with video footage and an affidavit from the guard. I guess there had been cameras after all.

Rockweiller's motion chilled me to the marrow. It put me in the worst possible light. I didn't sleep for days after reading it. Remington thought disbarment was unlikely. But as to the rest, he admitted he didn't know. Cindy and Harder responded to the motion, because I was in no condition to do it. They put their backs into it, which further eased my ill-feeling toward Harder.

Remington himself put the finishing touches on our brief. I almost felt good about the final draft. But I knew that, because of me, we were going into our first hearing in front of Judge Graves on the back foot. Instead of the hearing being about Rockweiller's discovery tactics, it was also going to be about me. It was set for one week's time, and I was scared half to death over it.

I put all of that aside for the moment and turned to the records we had gotten from Bank of America. A few hours later, Ashley and I were posted up in a conference room with a sheaf of papers spread out in front of us. We had David's bank records for the last five years, including credit and debit card statements.

From the bank statements, we traced David's spending over the last couple of years. Two years ago, he had been living in Houston. He paid 1,200 dollars a month in rent for a small apartment in Montrose. Montrose was a quaint, hipster neighborhood with a lot of bars, restaurants, and tattoo parlors. Most of Marcum's daily charges were typical living expenses like groceries, gas, food, and drinks. And most were within twenty miles of Montrose. David had also traveled to a handful of places in the last year. Credit card activity showed that he'd flown to Colorado in the winter (to ski) California in the summer (to surf) and Mexico once, although those days were mostly done with cash. Marcum kept his monthly expenditures impressively low, and his only streaming subscription was HBO, which I thought showed class.

About a year ago, his rent payments stopped, but the other expenses continued. I matched up the dates with a lawsuit against him for unpaid rent.

Then, about seven or eight months ago, David had moved to Key West, Florida. We saw the same type of charges at coffee shops, bars, etc., but now at different locations in Key West. This would have been during his time at Aqua Ray.

We also noticed withdrawals, weeks or months apart, for hundreds of dollars at a time. Altogether, these added up to thousands of dollars over the course of about six months. David had used cash to buy things he didn't want to attract attention to. It was part of the whole privacy, conspiracy theory mentality. So it was possible that the very records we most wanted to see weren't in these statements at all.

Two months ago, all activity cut off. The final charge was for $8.77 at Pollo Tropical, a Caribbean fast-food chain in Florida. After that, it was blank. We scanned backward, looking for anything unusual.

"There," Ashley said suddenly, stabbing her fingers at the sheet.

I looked. And there it was. Two flights, bought several months apart, on American Airlines. One of them was a couple months before his disappearance. The other one, mere weeks before.

The charges didn't say where he was flying to. But from the prices, I was sure they were international. The first flight cost about thirteen hundred dollars. The second one was closer to eighteen hundred. It didn't cost that much to fly anywhere in the U.S., except maybe first class. I tried to guess where he was going based on the fares, but I couldn't. The price seemed a little high for Colombia. But I wasn't sure.

Luckily, I knew just how to find out. The next day, Cindy and I drew up subpoenas to American Airlines. We demanded a response within fourteen days, and I set a calendar notification to tell us when the day came. Then we hired a process server to send them out. I had done enough of these subpoenas by now to know what I was doing. I'd probably have to fight a little with American Airlines, but they would give it up.

Harder also had the idiotic idea to try and subpoena the Transportation Security Administration, in case American Airlines wouldn't play ball. I thought this was a waste of paper. A gnat had a better chance at taking down a human being than we did at getting the attention of a government behemoth like the TSA. But it was easier to serve the subpoena than to argue with Harder, so I did it to shut him up.

Once we got David Marcum's flight records, we would know where he had gone during the last few weeks of his life. And I had a feeling that wherever it was, that was where he had disappeared.

But before that, I would have to face my fate before Judge Nathaniel Graves in Galveston, Texas.

FOURTEEN

The federal courthouse in Galveston was built in the 1930s in the Art Deco style. I thought it looked like a cinderblock with windows. The courthouse shared space with the post office, and ran what business you'd expect from a sleepy beach town an hour south of Houston.

The federal judge in this courthouse was anything but sleepy, though. The Honorable Nathaniel L. Graves had strong opinions and dispensed justice with a heavy hand. As the lone federal judge in Galveston, he was essentially the lord of all he surveyed, and acted like it. Graves was famous for dragging warring litigants into court, telling them what he thought their cases were worth, and forcing them to settle. Later, the lawyers would grudgingly admit that the settlements were fair and saved them years of litigation. But never to their clients, and never in public. Graves also had a brilliant legal mind, and his sharp and often humorous opinions were read by judges around the state.

Graves was well-liked in the Galveston community. He raised sums for local charities and leaned on lawyers to donate, which invariably they did. He appointed lawyers to handle criminal cases for those who couldn't pay. Graves was not afraid to take on powerful interests, either. He had once presided over a corruption case involving half a dozen local officials accused of embezzling funds. When party heavyweights visited him privately and suggested that he lay off, he hauled them into open court, clapped them in irons, and told them that he would lay off "when I get impeached by Congress and convicted by two-thirds of the U.S. Senate—and not a goddamn day before!"

So it was with trepidation that any lawyer filed into the United States District Court for the Southern District of Texas, Galveston Division. Especially me.

I arrived in Galveston early, and spent the extra time driving down Seawall Boulevard, enjoying the salty tang of the sea air. The weather was overcast. I watched the seagulls wheel and caw as the gray surf of the Gulf pounded sand into muddied water below. I parked for a few minutes and just stood by the ocean, letting the rhythmic sound of the waves soothe my anxieties.

An hour later, Remington and I walked into the courtroom. Judge Graves was sitting on his high bench as we walked in. He had a big face and a jutting jaw under a thick mop of hair that was shot through with gray. Graves was flanked by his law clerks and staff. He was sitting there as calm as you please, reviewing some papers through his thick reading glasses.

One of the young law clerks stood up, straight as a spear, and called out loudly. "The United States District Court for the Southern District of Texas, Galveston Division, is now in session. God save these United States and this Honorable Court!" He said it with such gusto that it echoed around the chamber once he had finished. Then he sat down, satisfied.

The other clerk called the case number, and the proceedings began.

Graves looked up. "Good morning, counselors," he boomed. "You may be seated. I see that this case was re-filed from state court, and that there are a number of outstanding discovery issues."

"That is correct, Your Honor," said Bock with his trademark arrogance.

"Very well," said Judge Graves. "Why don't we deal with those issues now."

"I'm afraid those issues aren't ripe for decision yet," Bock demurred. "We haven't yet had the Rule 26 scheduling conference. That means that the plaintiff's discovery issues cannot be addressed for another thirty days at least." Loudamire and Quinto shook their heads sorrowfully at this thorny bit of procedure that was preventing the wheels of justice from turning.

It was a ploy. Under Federal Rule of Civil Procedure 26, attorneys are supposed to meet for a "conference" before serving any discovery requests. I had tried to set up such a conference about five times. But Loudamire kept dodging my calls or claiming that they were "otherwise occupied." I glared at her. She smirked.

"Well," said Judge Graves, "we'll call this a Rule 16 scheduling conference then, so we can get it out of the way."

"Your Honor, unfortunately, I must object. This was not formally noticed as a Rule 16 conference. Accordingly—"

"Accordingly what, Mr. Bock?," said Graves, interrupting Bock mid-sentence. "Shall we reconvene in thirty days, and waste everyone's time, in order to be in compliance with the letter of the Rule?"

Bock shrugged as if to say, I didn't draft the Federal Rules of Civil Procedure.

Remington stood up and spoke in a monotone voice. "As Your Honor knows, Rule 16 also gives the Court discretion to hear discovery matters prior to a Rule 26 conference if it deems it appropriate."

"Indeed so. How do you say to that, Mr. Bock?" Graves asked.

Bock hedged. "Technically yes, Your Honor. But that discretion should not be applied here. If you've read pages sixteen through twenty of our brief—"

"I have read pages sixteen through twenty of your brief, Mr. Bock," Graves said, "and I am not persuaded. So we will take up this issue now. Understood?"

"Yes, Your Honor."

Loudamire's smirk withered, and now it was me suppressing a grin. I liked this judge.

"Good," said Graves. "First, I see that there is a dispute over the res. A set of ancient gold coins, if it can be believed. I verily shiver with excitement. Now, explain to me why the plaintiff shouldn't have a chance to analyze them."

I knew what was coming. Bock reached his hand back, and Quinto slapped the PowerPoint remote into his hand like a football. The courtroom's screen powered on, and I saw Bock's latest masterpiece load. It had forty-four slides.

But Graves was not interested. "Mr. Bock, I would like an answer, and not in the form of a PowerPoint presentation. I have read the briefs and assure you that I am familiar with the issues. Spending another hour with the same arguments, gussied up with what I have no doubt are pretty graphics and animations, will not assist me in making a decision. So why don't you simply explain to me, in your own words, why the plaintiff shouldn't have a chance to analyze the coins."

Bock spluttered but eventually spit out an answer. "Because, Your Honor, the coins are ours. Judge Gleeson of the three hundred seventy-fifth District Court in Houston, Texas already said so."

"No he didn't," Graves said. "He merely awarded the coins to Rockweiller on a temporary basis pending trial. There was no final ruling on the merits, isn't that correct?"

"That's technically correct, Your Honor, but implicit in that ruling is—"

"There's nothing implicit about that ruling, Mr. Bock. It seems to me that we have a bona fide dispute about who owns those coins. The plaintiff wants a chance to analyze them. Why shouldn't they get to?"

"Because, Your Honor, the coins were stolen. This would allow them to benefit from the fruits of their ill-gotten labor."

"But aren't you putting the cart before the horse?"

"No, Your Honor. In addition, there's a significant flight risk. We believe that Ashley Marcum may take the coins and run."

Graves raised his eyebrows. "A flight risk? Where is she going to go? Will she decamp to Treasure Island, to bury the coins with Long John Silver?" He turned to Remington. "Mr. Remington, is your client going to run away with the coins?"

Remington looked back at him levelly. "No, Your Honor."

Graves turned back to Bock. "There you have it, Mr. Bock. Mr. Remington is an upstanding lawyer in this jurisdiction. He says his client will not run away with the coins. Further, I will order him to post a bond with the Court in an amount equal to the value of the coins. Good?"

Remington grimaced. He didn't want to put up a bond. But he nodded. "That's good with me, Your Honor."

"Good. Issue solved." Bock sputtered a few more objections but Graves cut him off. "Let's move on. Now. Your motion for protective order. You don't want depositions to happen for privilege reasons. Is that correct?"

"That's correct, your Honor."

"It is my understanding that the young man, David Marcum, died while in the employ of Rockweiller Industries. Is that correct?"

"Technically, not exactly, but more or less, that is the situation, yes."

"And you're saying that they can't take the depositions of the crew, who may know what happened, because of privilege?"

"Yes, Your Honor," Bock said without the slightest hint of remorse.

"So how are they supposed to figure out how he died?"

Bock shrugged, as if this was a grand problem and he welcomed any and all solutions. "The information is privileged, Your Honor. As we've argued extensively in our briefs—"

"Mr. Bock," said Graves matter-of-factly. "That is complete horseshit."

"Excuse me, Your Honor?" said Bock, aghast.

Graves' face took on a chilling expression. He pointed a finger at Bock. "I don't know what kind of bullshit you get away with in New York, or what wool you pulled over Judge Gleeson's eyes. But I can assure you that it's not going to fly here. I know damn well that the attorney-client privilege doesn't shield the basic facts of what happened to this young man."

Graves continued as Bock stared at him, shocked. "I am going to give you the benefit of the doubt this one and only time. Do not try to pull cute legal maneuvers with me. The next time I see a frivolous argument, I will sanction you. Is that clear, Mr. Bock?"

"It is," Bock said in a strangled voice.

"Good. I like to sort these things out early on so you know how things stand. That's the beauty of a Rule Sixteen conference, don't you think? Put up your witnesses for deposition."

Bock nodded weakly.

"Good," said Graves. "Is there anything else?" Bock leaned over to confer with Quinto and Loudamire for a moment.

"Yes, Your Honor," he said, recovering his poise. "There is the matter of our motion for sanctions." My stomach turned over and the grin melted off my face. Judge Graves looked at me thoughtfully. Remington had told me to look penitent and let him handle this. Neither of us knew how this would turn out.

Bock continued. "Attorney Jack Carver broke into private property, used artifice to trick a guard, and stole records belonging to Rockweiller Industries. I request that the Court sanction Mr. Carver appropriately, including but not limited to censure and disqualification from this case." Bock finished with a note of brutal finality. He looked at me. There was no hint of pity in his dark eyes.

Judge Graves' thick eyebrows drew down into a frown as he stared at me. I quailed. My heart was beating overtime. I wished this could just be over with.

Abruptly, Judge Graves began to laugh. "Artifice, indeed!" he boomed in his deep bass voice. "Mr. Carver, you are quite the swashbuckler. A caper in Colombia. A moonlit masquerade on a mysterious island. An old federal judge like me cannot partake in these hijinks, I'm afraid. But I surely relished reading about your exploit."

Bock was flabbergasted, as was I. "So you're not going to sanction him?" Bock said, his voice rising an octave.

"For what?" Judge Graves asked. "A sanction requires that Rockweiller Industries suffer some prejudice. He didn't take anything, or find out anything he didn't already know. There was no property damage. He didn't lie to the guard, technically. No harm no foul, wouldn't you say, Mr. Bock?"

Bock spluttered at this, protesting about violation of the law, and private property, and of ethical standards among members of the bar. Graves let him talk for a while before cutting him off.

Then he turned back to me, his voice somber once more. "Young man," he said. "My amusement masks what is, as Mr. Bock quite rightly points out, a serious breach of ethics, illegal trespass, and attempt to steal information from Rockweiller Industries. In view of your youth, and the fact that no harm was done, I am going to let you off. This time. But be warned. The next time I see even the slightest bit of questionable behavior, I will not hesitate to sanction you, suspend you from practicing law before this Court, and throw you in jail. Is that clear?"

I swallowed. "It's clear."

"Good!" said Judge Graves, in good humor again. "In addition, I will grant Rockweiller Industries' motion for protective order with regard to ultrasensitive information. But do not abuse this privilege, Mr. Bock," he warned, curdling Bock's smile before it began. "Thank you for your time, counselors. We are adjourned." He banged his gavel, and that was that.

FIFTEEN

A week after the hearing, Rockweiller grudgingly turned over the coins. They sent them in a Brinks truck, sporting armed guards with rifles and flak jackets. The guards looked at me sourly as I signed for them. I didn't care. I thought Bock was being a tad melodramatic about the whole thing. I immediately telephoned Professor Schnizzel, who bid me to bring them to San Marcos at my earliest convenience. He and I had been in periodic contact about the case since our last meeting, and he was excited to see the coins.

The drive from Houston to San Marcos took a couple of hours. Most people think of Texas as a desert, made of dust and tumbleweeds and the Marlboro man, staring a thousand yards away from a faded billboard on the side of the road. But that's west Texas. East and central Texas are quite green. The highways wind their way through some handsome farmland and ranchland, sparsely tended, with old fences and odd houses by the side of the road. If you put on some country music, and drive a little faster than you should, you can reach a Zen-like state, with the sun and the road and the sunbaked sky all blending together into the present moment, and the hours slip by like fingers on a sundial. A tank of gas is cheaper than a therapist, and in my experience, the open road can be just as good.

Ashley tagged along for the drive. She had never been to San Marcos before and wanted to meet the great Professor Jacob Schnizzel. The weather was so hot we could see shimmers on the asphalt, and stores and houses miraged into focus as we drove by. We gassed up once on the way and got coffee and kolaches, and saved the receipts.

As we drove, I found myself dwelling on the court hearing. I wasn't sure who had won. We had gotten the coins and the depositions. And I didn't get sanctioned. But Bock got his ultrasensitive order, and I knew he would use that to hide whatever they'd found. I was also sure that my "swashbuckling" in Colombia had influenced Judge Graves' decision. Ashley took the blame for that squarely, and apologized for putting me up to it. But I was frustrated nonetheless. Every time we seemed on the verge of discovering something, it got yanked away.

I held a glimmer of hope that Schnizzel would be able to tell us the secrets of the coins, and that we would finally learn what had happened to David Marcum at the depositions, set to take place in just a few days.

Once we arrived in San Marcos, we made our way across campus toward Schnizzel's office. Schnizzel was holding office hours when we got there. He was surrounded by a mob of students and was yelling and gesticulating wildly with an erasable marker. After a few minutes, the crowd dispersed, chatting amongst themselves about anything and everything but computer science. Schnizzel beckoned us in and sat down tiredly.

"Gen-Z," he muttered. "There's no work ethic anymore. It's all Tik-Tok and Instagram." I agreed. Must be getting old.

Ashley smiled and extended a hand. "Professor Schnizzel! I'm Ashley Marcum. So pleased to finally meet you."

Schnizzel jumped up from his chair, noticing her for the first time. "Ms. Marcum! Of course. Jack's told me all about you. Delighted to meet you. Simply delighted."

"I am delighted as well," Ashley said.

Schnizzel wasted no time eyeing the big briefcase I had brought. "So," he said, rubbing his hands together. "You got the coins. How about that. Sometimes I wondered if you ever would. Or if they really even existed. It all feels so unreal sometimes, don't you think? Just a bunch of words on legal paper. But there's nothing like solid gold to make things feel true."

I put the briefcase on Schnizzel's desk. It was banded with metal and secured with a built-in combination lock. Bock had given us an even nicer briefcase. But Remington had me take it to a specialist, who found that it contained a tracking device. I was furious and wanted to tell Judge Graves about it. But Remington said this wasn't the time, and that I should just throw it away and get a new one. I toyed with the idea of floating the briefcase down the Buffalo Bayou, to see if Loudamire would chase it all the way to Louisiana. But, mindful of Judge Graves' proscription against hijinks, I didn't.

I entered the combination to the briefcase. The lock snapped up, and I opened it to reveal its contents.

The inside glowed with a soft golden light. The first time I had seen the coins, they were marred beyond recognition. But now they had been polished to a high sheen. They looked entirely different. Like the most exquisite pieces in the world. We stared at them for a long while. There's something mesmerizing about gold, which has fascinated humanity since the dawn of time.

Schnizzel reached in reverently and scooped up a handful of coins. He let them waterfall through his fingers. Then he picked one up and examined it carefully.

His eyes widened in astonishment.

"I don't believe this," he muttered.

"What?" I asked. "Do you know where they're from?"

Schnizzel picked up a few more coins, examining them and evidently coming to the same conclusion. "Yes, I know where they're from," he said distractedly. "An amateur coin collector with five sales on e-bay would know where these are from. You've had me looking in entirely the wrong part of the world."

Ashley and I stared at each other in bewilderment. Without saying another word, Schnizzel ransacked his desk and produced a big canvas tube, which he unrolled to reveal a map of the ancient world. He weighed down the corners of the map with a mug of coffee, a C++ book, a bronze battleship figurine, and a Pez dispenser, the age of whose Pez I didn't care to guess. Some coffee sloshed onto the map, unnoticed.

"This is going to require a history lesson," Schnizzel said. He stabbed a finger at the continent of the Americas. "In 1492, Christopher Columbus discovered the New World. Sailed the ocean blue, yada yada. Within a year or two, reports of his discovery filtered back to Europe. You can imagine the shockwaves this caused, the discovery of a new continent at the edge of the known world."

Schnizzel moved his finger and pointed to Europe. "After receiving the news, Spain acted quickly. She wanted to secure rights to this new world. And she wanted to secure them before Portugal, then her great maritime rival for control of the seas.

"King Ferdinand and Queen Isabella of Spain petitioned the Pope to support their claims to the New World. The Pope, Alexander VI, was a Spaniard. Predictably, he issued a papal bull in favor of Spain. He set a line of demarcation and declared that everything west of this line—including the entire New World—belonged to Spain." Schnizzel took the whiteboard marker and slashed a black line straight down the map, just east of the Americas.

"He just...declared ownership of the world?" Ashley asked dubiously. "Can you do that? What about the people living there?"

"What about them? In those days, they were considered savages, fit only to be exploited by Europe."

"That's terrible."

"Indeed. But that's colonialism for you." Schnizzel jabbed the map again. "No other European power accepted the Spanish Pope's decree, which would have given Spain control over the New World. King John II of Portugal was especially incensed, because it interfered with Portugal's rights in the region."

"I don't blame him," I said. "A Spanish Pope? Sounds like an inside job."

"Is it so different today?" Schnizzel queried. "Don't presidents appoint supreme court justices with the aim that they will do what the president wants?"

"Come on," I scoffed. "That's a bit of an exaggeration, don't you think? Sure, the President appoints justices who share his or her views. But after they're appointed, the President doesn't have a say. They do what they think is right."

"Really? What about *Bush v. Gore*?"

He was talking about the election case of 2000, in which the five conservative justices of the Supreme Court voted to give the presidency to Bush, and the four liberal justices voted to give it to Gore. Ashley raised her eyebrows. I started to say something, but stopped.

"In any case," Schnizzel continued, "in 1494, Spain and Portugal made a deal, and signed the Treaty of Tordesillas. This treaty affirmed the line of demarcation, but moved it a little to the west. The result was that Spain and Portugal split the world between them. Roughly speaking, Spain got the Western half of the world, and Portugal the East." Schnizzel drew another line straight down the map, a little ways east of the other one, that cut through a chunk of Brazil.

"The Treaty of Tordesillas was ratified by the new Pope, Julius II. Some years later, a Portuguese explorer named Pedro Álvares Cabral discovered and laid claim to what is modern-day Brazil. That's why everyone in Brazil speaks Portuguese, while the rest of South America speaks Spanish."

"This is all fascinating, believe me," said Ashley. "But what does it have to do with the coins?"

"Ah!" said Schnizzel triumphantly, like a professor who has finally been asked the question he has been waiting for. "The relevance is this. Under the Treaty of Tordesillas, this entire half of the world—" he gestured at most of the western hemisphere—"belonged to Spain. But the other half"—now he gestured to the east—"belonged to the Portuguese.

"These coins," he continued, "are not from Colombia. In fact, they are not from South America at all."

"Then where are they from?" I cried.

"Why, they are from Asia."

"Asia?" I repeated stupidly. I tried to orient myself to this new development. Were we looking in entirely the wrong place? What did that mean?

"But how would my brother get coins from Asia?" Ashley asked. "He's never been there, as far as I know. And everything we've seen so far points to Florida or South America. Asia's not even on our radar. Right, Jack?"

"Right," I muttered, dazed.

"Even so," said Schnizzel. "The coins are from Asia. Look at the markings. They are very distinctive. Any wreck expert worth his salt would know these, although an assayer might not. I may even have an idea of where in Asia they are from. Although I will need some time to confirm."

I nodded. The Judge had given us thirty days with the coins, so Schnizzel could take his time. I looked closely at the flowing lines and shapes that had so reminded me of Indian temples in Goa. I wasn't far off.

As Schnizzel walked us out, he chattered on about the coins and the Portuguese Empire and where they might be from. But I barely heard him. I was still trying to process the import of this news. What on earth did it mean?

We shook hands and prepared to leave. Schnizzel was going on vacation for a week or two, he said, but he would see what he could do beforehand.

Just as we began to walk away, I heard a voice call from our left. "Hey Schnizzel!" came a gruff baritone. "How's it hanging!"

I turned and saw a beefy man in his late forties, sporting a crew cut and an athletic tee. He wore sunglasses that were tethered to the back of his thick red neck by Croakies.

"Fuck you, Cal," Schnizzel yelled back at him.

"Now, now," the man said, grinning cheerfully. "No hard feelings! Have a super day!" He waved at us and power-walked away.

I stared at his departing back. "Is that..."

"Yes," Schnizzel said darkly. "The football coach. Un-fucking believable, these people. Sometimes I feel like I'm living in Talladega Nights."

Ashley looked perplexed, but was savvy enough not to comment.

"Thank you for your help, Professor Schnizzel," she said with a smile. "It's been enlightening."

"Of course. I'll let you know as soon as I know more," he promised.

It was only a few days later, as I was stewing on the meaning of the Asia connection, that Schnizzel's hypothesis got another boost. At exactly 5 p.m. the day before the depositions, we finally got our subpoena returns from American Airlines.

It took longer than it should have. Bock & Co. had mounted a frivolous legal challenge to try and block us. They had no grounds to do it, and the Judge wrote that their objections bordered on bad faith. But these machinations did no more than delay us for a little while.

I opened the records. And finally, *finally*, I knew where David Marcum had gone.

Both of the tickets were round trip. On the first flight, the records showed that Marcum flew there and back. On the second flight, he flew there. But there was no record of him ever boarding the return flight.

That meant that David Marcum never came back from the second trip. Wherever he went, that was likely where he had died.

The destination for both flights was the same: Kuala Lumpur, Malaysia.

SIXTEEN

At last, the day of deposition dawned. I waited for a last-minute motion to quash, or an email announcing that the witnesses had up and moved to Timbuktu. But none came. At the appointed hour, Harder and I traversed the hot pavements of Houston to the downtown offices of Badden & Bock.

It was sweltering outside, and the heat hit me like a blow. Texas is hot in the summer, and the effect was magnified here in Houston, a sprawling, white-hot concrete jungle, peopled by corporations and the servants of corporations, hurrying to and fro in starched white shirts and checkered ties, choking on the fashion of another time, another place.

I was in a bad mood. I had barely slept the night before. After learning about David Marcum's trip to Malaysia, I spent the night scouring Rockweiller's documents for anything to do with the place, hoping to learn something, anything, before the deposition.

There were over ten thousand documents with the word Malaysia in them. Most of them were duplicates or other garbage I was able to filter out. But even so, it took me hours to sort through it all. I sat there well past dark, and then well past midnight, drinking coffee to keep going. Eventually, around 3 a.m., I had seen everything that was there. It wasn't much.

The only real things of interest I found were a pair of consulting contracts that Excel Resources had for unspecified services to be performed in Malaysia. The contracts didn't say what Excel paid these companies for, or how much. The first contract was with a company called Southeast Asia Salvage. The second was with a foundation affiliated with someone named Suharto. That was the same name as the former president of Indonesia, who hogged all the search results. This meant I could find little about Suharto or the other company online. I didn't know what to make of these contracts, so I tagged them and set them aside for later. I got home at about 5 a.m., and slept a measly two hours until seven. That partly accounted for my bad temperament this morning.

But the real thorn in my gut was that I wouldn't be taking the depositions today. Harder would.

Harder had been pushing Kruckemeyer for the depositions for months now, arguing that he was the senior associate and should get to do them. Remington was out of pocket on some big coal trial in West Virginia. And I didn't have a lot of juice after the Cartagena incident. So Harder won out. I was relegated to "second-chairing" the depositions, as Kruckemeyer sympathetically put it, which was not a thing. But I tried to set aside my resentment as we approached Badden & Bock's offices. We needed to present a united front to Rockweiller. And to Ashley, who would be there as well.

When we arrived at the offices, I looked up in surprise. I had expected Badden & Bock to be in some brand-new, steel and glass tower. But instead, they were in an older, almost iconic Houston building.

The building was fifty stories of tan brown stone. It rose up into three distinct pyramidal roofs, each higher than the last. The pyramids were ridged, and they looked almost like steps, or Legos, building their way toward the sky. This gave the building a blurred, indistinct look from afar, like graphics in an old video game.

I gazed up at the façade as we approached. The design was baroque, inspired by 17th-century Dutch architecture. It was clad in red Swedish granite, highlighted with copper obelisks. I knew all of this from an architecture tour I had taken once. At sunset, the tower turned blood red, giving it an almost sinister aspect. The sharp-ridged pyramids added to the effect, and made it look like some kind of supervillain's lair. The tower was built by oil money in the 1980s, like much of Houston was. I was impressed with Badden & Bock's choice of offices in spite of myself. I thought it showed class and a respect for the city's history.

We entered an imposing lobby and took the elevator to the fiftieth floor. A pretty young assistant manned the front desk. She barely acknowledged us. Harder and I sat down to wait for Ashley. We didn't look at each other. Harder fumbled with his notes, looking stiff and nervous. I didn't care.

Ashley arrived a few minutes later. She was dressed in business casual, and looked stunning. I swallowed hard. Harder had the same reaction. It didn't help.

Harder got up to introduce himself. He put on a fake smile and held out his hand. "You must be Ashley Marcum," he said. "I've heard so much about you. Richard T. Harder III. Senior associate. I'll be taking the depositions."

"Hi there," she said, shaking his hand. She looked at me quizzically.

"This is Harder," I said neutrally. "He is going to be taking the depositions."

"Oh," she said, observing me closely but not saying any more.

"I'm the senior associate," Harder added, to make sure she was aware. "We thought that the more experienced person should be doing this. No offense to Jack, of course, who's been doing a tremendous job." This would have been condescending if it had come from someone with any actual authority. I suppressed the urge to choke him.

"Ah," said Ashley.

"Plus, I'm the guy you call when you need to play hardball," Harder said with a wink. This was disastrous, and it backfired spectacularly, as he seemed to realize a moment later. I guffawed, and Harder turned red. But Ashley just smiled her winsome bartender's smile at him. He continued to chat her up as the assistant showed us to the conference room. I tuned him out as we entered.

The conference room was impressive. It took up a full side of the fiftieth floor. Out of the wall-to-wall windows, I could see the city spread out below in a panorama, miles of concrete and highways on a flat-baked plain as far as the eye could see. Smokestacks and oil wells rose darkly in the distance.

Bock & Co. were already there. Bock himself sat at the head of the table, wearing his trademark arrogance. Quinto and Loudamire sat next to him, wearing knock-offs of the same expression. Lined up on the side of the table were the deponents. I recognized their faces from the personnel files: Thomas Barber, Michelle Kauller, Richard Layes, Carl Ruthers, and Jason Dubino. Lloyd Gunthum wasn't available, and we had agreed to depose him at a later date. I frowned. There was someone else missing, but his name eluded me. Besides the witnesses, there was a court reporter (older, female, great nails) and a videographer (young, male, bearded).

The atmosphere was tense from the moment we walked in. I didn't do anything to make it less so. In Texas, attorneys are usually cordial to each other. Although Houston has its share of firebrands, attorneys know they are part of the same community, and that the way they treat each other will get out. But the same wasn't true of attorneys like Badden & Bock, who made unpleasantness a weapon in their arsenal. We exchanged greetings coldly. But I sensed the slightest bit of warmth between Harder and Quinto. That made me think back to Oichi Omakase. I wondered again what he had been doing there.

Harder almost tripped over his chair as we sat down. Then he fumbled with his microphone. The videographer had to help him clip it to his shirt. It was obvious that he hadn't done this many times before. He apologized and tried to crack a joke, but no one laughed. Eventually, he settled down and got started.

The first witness was Thomas J. Barber. Barber was hairy, overweight, and sweating profusely. His neck folds spilled out of a too-tight white shirt. The videographer turned on the camera, and Barber stated his name for the record. Then the court reporter swore him in. "Please raise your right hand. Do you swear to tell the truth, the whole truth, and nothing but the truth, so help you God?"

"I do," said Barber. And with that, Harder began. "Would you please state your name for the record, sir?" he asked.

"Objection!" came a nasally voice. Both of us blinked in surprise and turned our heads. It was Loudamire.

Harder looked at her uncertainly. "Come again?" he said.

"I object."

"To his name? Why?"

"Because it's cumulative. The witness has already stated his name on the record. It's a complete waste of the witness' and everyone else's time to ask again."

I stared at her incredulously. I had expected them to be obstructive. But this? I saw Bock and Quinto smirking from the sidelines.

"Okay..." said Harder, trying not to pick a fight. "I'll stipulate that the witness' name is in the record. Let's move on. Mr. Barber, have you had your deposition taken before?"

"No, sir."

"Do you understand the procedures?"

"Yes, sir."

"If you don't understand a question, will you let me know?"

"Yes, sir."

Harder continued in this vein for a little while, laying out the ground rules for the deposition. Starting with the basics helped begin a rhythm of question and answer with the witness. When done right, it made the deposition flow.

"Do you understand that you are under oath today, the same as if you were in front of a judge or jury?" Harder asked, completing the standard introduction.

"Objection," Loudamire said nastily. "Harassing. The witness already knows he is under oath. Your question implies that he would violate that oath, which is harassing and totally inappropriate." Harder opened his mouth to argue with her.

I knew what they were doing. Harder was a rookie. So they were putting pressure on him. It's not easy to take a deposition with an attorney in your face like that. You shrink back from hard questions, or don't probe deep enough, afraid of the pushback. It's a nasty tactic, and totally improper. But short of complaining to the judge, there's not much you can do about it.

To his credit, Harder gamely fought down Loudamire's objections and stuck to his question. Eventually, he dragged it out of Barber that he understood he was under oath. Harder then asked if there was any reason that Barber couldn't testify truthfully today. Barber paused. For too long, I thought. He looked at Bock. Finally, he said "no."

Harder gave him a strange look, but didn't press the point. "Very well," he said. And then, finally, we got some information.

"When did you first meet David Marcum?" Harder asked.

"About six months ago," said Barber.

"How did you meet him?"

"We were on the same boat. The Excelsior."

"You worked together?"

"Yes, sir."

"And that was the first time you met him?"

"Yes, sir."

"How long were you on the ship together?"

"Couple of weeks. Maybe three or four."

"Was it contiguous?"

Barber's face screwed up in confusion. "Contigu-what?" he said.

"Consecutive. Was it all at once."

"Oh. No. Well, mostly. He flew in and out. He was on the ship once for a while, left, then came back."

"Where was the ship?"

"Objection!" Loudamire shrilled. "Calls for ultrasensitive information." I looked carefully at Bock. I knew the ship must have been in Malaysia, judging from Marcum's flight records. That also lined up with what Barber had said about two flights. But Bock's face didn't give anything away, and I couldn't tell if he knew that we knew.

"What did Marcum do on the ship?" asked Harder.

"He was a diver."

"What was he hired to dive for?"

"Objection!" said Loudamire. Her face assumed a condescending look. "Perhaps counsel was not aware that the court entered an ultrasensitive protective order in this case. If counsel attempts to violate the protective order again, we reserve our right to move for sanctions."

Harder gritted his teeth and moved on. This was what I was afraid of. As much as I enjoyed watching Loudamire be a prick to Harder, it wasn't good for our case. It wasn't really Harder's fault, though. If they refused to let Barber answer the questions, there wasn't much we could do about it just then.

"Who hired David Marcum?" asked Harder. Barber looked at Loudamire and braced himself for another objection. But none came, and he answered.

"I think it was Lloyd."

"That would be Lloyd Gunthum?"

"Yes, sir."

"He's the captain and owner of the Excelsior?"

"That's right."

"How did Mr. Gunthum know David Marcum?"

"They worked together in the past, I think. I'm not sure."

"Who else was on the ship with David Marcum?"

Barber jerked his thumb toward the other witnesses, who were all sitting quietly and observing. "This lot. And Jeremy Riker." That was it, I thought. Riker. The missing crew member.

"Where's Jeremy Riker?"

Loudamire shrieked another objection and Barber's mouth snapped shut.

I looked over at Ashley. I could see she was frustrated. So was I. They were blocking even basic questions about their witnesses. I doubted that Riker's whereabouts were ultra-sensitive. But Harder didn't push back, and just moved on. He continued with background questions for the next thirty minutes or so. He covered what ground he could, shying away from controversial topics. I started to get concerned. We would need more than this. But finally, Harder flipped a page in his outline, steeled himself, and got to the meat of it.

"How did David Marcum die?" he asked. I watched Barber carefully. I caught myself holding my breath. This was what we were here for. Out of the corner of my eye, I saw Ashley tense up as we awaited the answer.

But Loudamire cut Barber off before he could say anything. "Objection!" she said. "Calls for privileged and ultra-sensitive information." I looked up incredulously. This was the same stunt they had pulled at the TRO hearing. They were trying cover up David Marcum's death with privilege. Exactly what Judge Graves had warned them not to do. But here they were, playing the same old games. I saw the anger written plain on Ashley's face.

I'd had enough. I was in a black mood to begin with. I was fed up with Badden & Bock, fed up with Harder, and fed up with the whole damn legal system, which seemed like little more than a vehicle for expensive assholes to abuse people.

I slammed my fist down on the table, startling everyone. "That's it," I said. "This is bullshit. You know damn well that's not protected information. You're abusing the attorney-client privilege. This is exactly what Judge Graves told you not to do. I am putting you on notice that you are now in violation of a federal court order from the Southern District of Texas."

I turned to Bock and pointed my finger in his face. "If I hear one more dogshit objection from her, or you, or anyone else, I swear to God I will pick up this telephone and get Judge Graves on the line right now. And he's going to sanction you, and your client, and you, and you." I pointed at Loudamire and Barber, who paled. Then I picked up the phone that was sitting in the middle of the table, daring them to try me. "How do you want to play this?" I demanded.

Bock opened his mouth in surprise, which quickly turned to outrage. Then we got into a screaming match. He yelled about my foul language, and I yelled about his complete disrespect for the rule of law. Eventually, he caved and agreed to let Barber answer the question. He wasn't scared of me. But he was scared of Judge Graves. Good. Harder seemed a little shocked by my outburst. So did Ashley. But I caught the faintest hint of a smile on her face.

After the shouting had subsided, Harder cleared his throat and asked the question again. "What happened to David Marcum?" he said. I glared at Loudamire, daring her to object. She kept her mouth shut this time.

Barber took a deep breath. "He died in a scuba diving accident." I exhaled subconsciously. Out of the corner of my eye, I saw Ashley do the same.

"When did this happen?" Harder asked.

"Toward the end of our voyage."

"Do you remember what time of day it was?"

"Yes. It was the afternoon."

"Can you tell me, in your own words, what happened?"

Barber nodded. "We were diving," he explained. "Working on something underwater. I think I'm not allowed to say what. But we went down in shifts. Usually twos, sometimes threes. But David Marcum dived alone. Usually, you go with someone. It's good practice. You take a diving buddy, in case things go bad. But we didn't know Marcum that well, and he wanted to go solo. He seemed to know what he was doing, and Lloyd gave the okay. So we didn't question."

Ashley nodded absently to herself. That sounded like her brother. I looked at Barber carefully. His narrative sounded rehearsed. But that wasn't unusual, I knew. Bock & Co. would have taken him through the story many times.

"That day," Barber continued, "Marcum was gone longer than he should have been."

"How long?"

"I don't know exactly. But it was a few hours."

"How long would he normally be down on a dive?"

"Thirty or forty minutes. Then he'd surface. That's standard length."

"When did you notice he was gone?"

"Around the one or two-hour mark. Like I said, he was going solo, so we didn't keep track perfectly. But around then, someone said 'Hey, where's Dave.'"

"Who said that?"

"I don't remember."

"And then what happened?"

"We all went out to look for him. Everybody grabbed tanks and got in the water. Even Lloyd. We looked for hours. I didn't feel good about it. If he hadn't surfaced by then, he never would, I thought. But we kept looking, long past dark."

"Did you find any trace of him?"

"No."

"What did you do after that?"

"We put down anchor. Dubino worked the ROV straight through the night, to see if he could find anything that way. Nothing. The next day, we got into the water again and looked. But we didn't find anything."

"You found no trace of him?"

"No."

Harder paused for a moment, thinking about what to ask next. He reviewed some notes.

"Did you like David Marcum?" he said after a moment.

Barber seemed caught off guard by the question. "Yeah," he said. The answer sounded genuine. I saw a flicker of some emotion cross his face. But I couldn't place it.

"What do you think happened to him?" Harder asked.

Barber shrugged. "I don't know. I guess he ran out of air, or went too deep, or got tangled up in something. Scuba diving can be dangerous. That's why you don't go it alone."

"Did you continue to search for him after that?" Harder asked.

"After the second day, we called it off. We didn't think there was any chance we'd find him after he'd been gone that long. We stayed in the area and continued our work. We kept an eye out, of course. But we never saw him again."

Harder paused and scribbled something on his pad.

So that was it, I thought. A scuba diving accident. That was what we had suspected all along. But it felt unsatisfying, somehow. After all this time, I had expected more. I watched Ashley's expression. She looked calm.

"Where did this accident happen?" Harder asked after a while.

"Objection," said Loudamire. But not as loudly this time. "Calls for ultrasensitive information."

"What was Excel Resources searching for?"

"Same objection."

"Did you find anything down there?"

"Objection, ultrasensitive information, privilege."

"Do you recall a set of gold coins that David Marcum had?"

"Same objection."

This continued for some time. Loudamire objected to any questions about the where, what, or why Rockweiller was doing. There was nothing we could do about that now except preserve our objections for the record. To get more information, we would need to convince Judge Graves to reconsider his ruling on ultrasensitive information.

At the end of an hour and a half, Harder finished with Barber, and we took a recess. Bock & Co. kindly provided us with a small office down the hall to palaver in. We went in and closed the door. Ashley sat down in a chair. She looked drained, somehow. Deflated. But I also saw that she was breathing more easily. Almost as if she were relaxed. Maybe that's what she had needed. Just to know.

Harder let out a deep breath. "Well," he said. "There it is."

"There it is," I agreed. I turned to Ashley. "How are you feeling?"

She shrugged tiredly. "I don't know. I guess I thought there would be more to it."

I nodded. "I know what you mean."

We talked about the deposition a little bit and discussed what to do about the ultrasensitive stuff. But mostly we just sat and processed what we had heard. After about fifteen minutes, we went back into the conference room to question the other crew members.

Harder deposed the remaining crew members one after the other: Michelle Kauller, Richard Layes, Carl Ruthers, and Jason Dubino. Each of them told the same story. Loudamire kept the deposition within bounds by objecting whenever Harder strayed into ultrasensitive territory. Harder spent about an hour in total with each witness. We didn't learn much new. I checked the time frequently and tried not to yawn.

Toward the end of the day, Harder did something brilliant.

It was on the last witness. Layes or Dubino. I couldn't remember which, as they had all blended together by then. Harder took him through the same line of inquiry that he had used with the other witnesses. It was anticlimactic, since we'd all seen this play out several times now, including Layes or Dubino (whichever it was) himself. I yawned and half-listened to the familiar sequence of questions.

"What is your occupation?"

"Scuba diver."

"What were you doing on the Excelsior on the day in question?"

"Scuba diving."

"How long have you been doing scuba diving?"

"'Bout twenty years."

"Are you good at it?"

"I reckon."

"When did you start working for Excel Resources?"

"'Bout five years ago."

"What do you do for them?"

"Scuba diving."

This went on for a while. Then Harder asked another question, in the exact same tone of voice, without varying his pitch or pace at all.

"Did you find anything besides the gold coins?"

Layes/Dubino answered before he could think about it. "Some artifacts. The bronze lions. The can—"

I froze. Out of the corner of my eye, I saw Bock and Quinto freeze too. I had to rewind the scene in my head to make sure it had actually happened. It took a few moments for Layes/Dubino to process what he'd just said. It was like watching someone get shot and then keep going a few more steps before collapsing. I saw an expression of horror dawn on Loudamire's face. She opened her mouth to spout an objection, but it was too late.

"Objection!" screamed Loudamire. "Objection! Calls for privileged and ultrasensitive information. Violation of protective order!"

"What did you say?" Harder asked Layes/Dubino, ignoring her.

"Nothing." He was visibly shaking.

"Did you say lions?"

"No."

"No?" Harder asked incredulously. He turned to the court reporter. "Madam court reporter, would you please read back what the witness just said—"

"Objection!" said Bock, breaking in. "Objection. Totally improper. This...Mr. Harder, this is despicable. To try and trick a witness into answering a question that you know is off limits. I guarantee that the Judge will hear about this. This is a sanctionable offense!"

"What, asking a question, or telling the truth?" Harder shot back.

This devolved into a four-way shouting match between Harder, Bock, Loudamire, and myself. Layes/Dubino sat there sweating while we fought it out. In the end, Bock and Loudamire wouldn't let Harder ask the question again, or ask any more follow up questions. Their position was that Layes/Dubino had never said it. They called off the deposition, saying they were going to go to the Judge for sanctions. After that, we stormed out of Badden & Bock's offices and back onto the street. As we walked toward the parking lot, the tall Houston tower faded behind us, turning crimson in the light of the setting sun.

A few days later, we reported to Remington's office. Kruckemeyer was there too. We had sent them a summary of the depositions, as well as the videotapes. Remington had the video of Thomas Barber's deposition up on a screen as we walked in. He did not look happy.

"Who the hell taught you to take a deposition?" Remington demanded as soon as we walked in. "Bob, did you do this?" he said, rounding on Kruckemeyer. Kruckemeyer grimaced and shook his head.

Harder was nonplussed. "I'm sorry," he said uncertainly. "But I'm not sure what I did wrong."

"Not sure what you did wrong?" Remington repeated, his voice going up an octave. "I'm not sure what you did right. For starters, why in God's name did you let all of the witnesses sit in on each other's testimony? Why didn't you invoke the Rule?"

The Rule, as it is known, requires other witnesses to leave the room when someone is testifying. The point of the Rule is so witnesses can't hear each other's testimony, and then tailor theirs to match it. Frankly, I hadn't thought about the Rule either. But I wasn't about to bring that up.

"The ah...the Rule," Harder stammered. "I guess I didn't think about it."

"You didn't think about it. Do you think you might have gotten different testimony if you hadn't let every Tom, Dick, and Harry sit there and watch the show?"

"I guess…I guess I might have."

"You're damn right you might have. If you'd taken them separately, there might have been inconsistencies that could tell us something."

"Right. I should have done that. I'm sorry."

"And more fundamentally, Richard, you didn't get any details. Who are these people? What did they do before Excel Resources? Have they ever been convicted of a crime? How much are they paid? What is their relationship to Lloyd Gunthum? What is their relationship with Rockweiller Industries? Have they ever talked to anyone else about David Marcum?"

"Right. I see."

"And what about the accident, for Christ's sake? What kind of scuba gear did they use? How deep did they go? Was there any history of malfunctioning equipment? Had there been accidents before? Were the safety logs maintained? Did they come back with Marcum's gear missing? Did they report the accident? Why or why not? What search parameters did they use to try and find him?" Remington continued to fire off questions while Harder hung his head lower and lower.

"You get up to seven hours for each deposition, Richard," Remington said. "Seven hours. Do you know why? It's so you can nail down the details. It's all in the details. That's where you find the little discrepancies. The ones that unravel things. You took what, one or two hours with each witness? It's inexcusable. You let them bully you into cutting it short. This is why I don't let associates take depositions."

Harder was devastated. He looked like he was about to cry. Even I felt bad for him by that point. Remington saw this and relented. He sat down in his chair and let out an explosive breath. "I'm sorry, Richard. I don't mean to be so hard on you. This is a skill that takes time to learn. You'll get there."

Harder nodded. "I'm sorry, sir. Can we take their depositions again and use the rest of the time?" he asked hopefully.

"No. That's not how it works. It's one and done." We sat for a minute to absorb this.

"Luckily for us," Remington continued, "the primary actor, this Lloyd Gunthum character, wasn't there. So we'll get one more shot at this through him."

"We can also go after Jeremy Riker," I added. "He was on the ship, but they didn't put him up for deposition. I don't know why." I made a note to ask Badden & Bock why Riker wasn't there, and ask Lyle to find out what he could about the guy. "And at least we learned something, right?" I said in Harder's defense. "We know what happened to David Marcum. That was the whole point. I mean, we suspected he might have died in a scuba diving accident. But now we know." Harder nodded his agreement.

"Oh, we learned something alright," said Remington. "I watched the videos of each and every one of these witnesses, Jack. And I'll tell you one thing for certain: they're lying."

SEVENTEEN

A week after the deposition, I got a call from Jacob Schnizzel, who was back from vacation.

"Professor Schnizzel," I said, cheered. "How was your trip?"

"Fantastic," he said. "It was fantastic. I went to Miami. My old stomping grounds."

"Get a tan?"

He chuckled mirthlessly. "A tan? Me? No, sir. Not with one hundred SPF sunblock. No skin cancer for me."

I filled Schnizzel in on the latest developments. He was thrilled to hear that Marcum had flown to Malaysia. This validated his theory about what part of the world we were dealing with. And the flight to Kuala Lumpur narrowed his focus considerably. He started rattling off the names of famous ships in the area. The *Sao Paulo*, the *Dourado*, the *Ceylon*, the *Serrao*...

I also told him about the deposition. When he heard about Dubino's slip up, he immediately seized on something.

"Can-something, you say?" he interrupted me. "He said 'can-' before he was cut off? Could he have been saying 'cannon?'"

I blinked, thinking back to the deposition. "Maybe," I said slowly. "Hang on." I pulled up the video and found the spot. Then I played the audio out loud. We heard Dubino say "can—"

"Cannon!" Schnizzel exclaimed. "He was going to say cannon!"

"You might be right," I admitted.

"If they found a cannon, then they found a wreck," he said confidently.

"You think so?"

"Oh, yes. Cannon are the primary way by which archaeologists identify ancient wrecks. They register strongly on magnetometers, so you can pick them up at a distance. And by looking at the style of the cannon, you can tell what time and place the ship was from. Cannon are very distinctive. The *San Jose*, for example, was identified by the unique dolphin engravings etched into its cannon."

"Wow," I said in wonder. "You really think they found a wreck?"

"I do." He could barely contain his excitement. "We may have a new find on our hands, Jack. This is phenomenal. To think that you may have been right all along...incredible. Did the witness say anything else?"

"Oh, yeah. That's actually what I wanted to ask you about. He said something about bronze lions."

There was silence on the other end of the line. I continued talking, describing how obstructive Badden & Bock had been, and how I had lit them up and saved the day. I also threw some shade at Harder, which was a little mean-spirited, and I regretted it.

"What did you say?" Schnizzel said, interrupting me.

"About what?"

"About lions. I must have been daydreaming. For some reason I thought you said bronze lions."

"Yes, I did. Dubino said they found bronze lions with the coins and the 'can-' whatever. Harder got it out of him pretty cleverly, actually. I thought the lions might indicate a wreck. Maybe some kind of old artifact."

Schnizzel didn't answer for the longest time. I checked my phone, thinking he must have hung up. "Hello?" I said. "Professor?"

"Bronze lions," he muttered finally. "No. No, that would be impossible." He seemed distracted, as if talking more to himself than to me.

"Come again?"

"Never mind. Forget I said anything."

I shrugged. Whatever. "Okay. So. What do we do now? How do we find out which wreck it could be? And more importantly, how do I convince Kruckemeyer and Remington that I'm not delusional, and that this is a real possibility?

"You're on your own with that second part. That's your battle. As far as which wreck...did you check the documents? Surely there's got to be *something* in there. That would link Rockweiller to a wreck."

Did I check the documents. Ha. "You'd think so," I said. "But no. Believe me, I've looked. I read every document with the word 'Malaysia' in it. The only thing that came up were two consulting contracts. Southeast Asia Salvage, and some other one. I don't remember. And receipts from a Malaysian food truck. A Rockweiller executive used to eat Golden Nuggets and Singapore Noodles for lunch there every day."

"Did you say Southeast Asia Salvage?" Schnizzel said.

"That's right. Why? Have you heard of them?"

"Maybe. Listen. What was the name of the other company?" he asked. There was a strange urgency in his voice. "Do you remember?"

"The other company..." I screwed up my face, trying to think of it. "It was some foundation. Soo-something. Soo... hang on."

"Suharto."

"Yes," I said, surprised. "Suharto. That was it. How did you know?"

Schnizzel said something, but he was too soft, and I couldn't hear him. "Pardon?" I said. But he just kept whispering it over and over. Eventually I made it out. "*Oh my God.*" I tried to get more out of him, but he just kept saying it over and over again. I heard something break on the other end of the line.

"Professor Schnizzel?" I said, concerned. "Are you okay?"

"Yes. I just dropped something. Hang on. I need to sit down for this." He sounded unsteady.

"What the hell is going on?"

He breathed quickly into the phone. Hyperventilating. I heard him take a few deep breaths to calm down. Finally, he spoke.

"There was a ship," he told me. "That sank near Malaysia. A very famous ship. It was said to have bronze lions aboard. And..." he trailed off.

"What ship?" I said impatiently. "Was it one of the ones on your list?"

"No. It's not on the list. Too implausible. Impossible, really. And yet..."

"And yet what?" I said, exasperated. "Spit it out already! What's the ship?"

Eventually, after some more coaxing, Schnizzel finally told me name of the ship. I looked it up. I saw who had sailed it, and when, and how it sank. And what it was said to be worth.

It completely blew my mind.

Two days later, I called a special meeting in Remington's office. It was well past dark by the time we gathered. Remington was annoyed. He didn't like meetings, and had a lot to do. But his annoyance faded into curiosity when he saw that Schnizzel had driven down for the occasion, and that he carried a quantity of books and maps under his arm. Cindy, Harder, and Kruckemeyer were there too. I'd even called in Lyle, who gave me thumbs-up as he sat down.

Schnizzel and I had worked madly for two days straight trying to confirm the insane theory we had come up with. I alternated between feeling delusional and feeling that I had finally found the answer we had been searching for all this time. I had stayed up all night thinking about how to convince Remington and the others to buy into it. I was running on adrenaline and Red Bull and nothing else. Even now, I wasn't certain whether this was a dream. I had the coin briefcase with me. Its heavy handle felt reassuringly solid in my hand.

"Looks like we've got the whole gang here," remarked Kruckemeyer. "I hope this is billable."

Ashley was the last to arrive. "Sorry I'm late," she said hurriedly as she sat down.

"Not at all," said Remington. He stood up to greet her. A big silver belt buckle flashed as he moved. I realized this was the first time they had met. Remington introduced himself courteously, turning on the charm he usually reserved for juries and no one else.

"It's a pleasure to finally meet you, Ashley. I'm John Remington. Jack's told me a lot about you. We're very fortunate to have you as a client." Ashley responded in kind, clearly taken by his cowboy charm. I could swear she even blushed.

"Okay, Jack," said Remington, sitting back down in his chair. "You called us all here for a reason. What's so important?"

I waited for everyone to quiet down and give me their full attention. Then I spoke. "We think we know what Rockweiller found," I said simply.

"Really?" said Remington. There was an edge to his voice.

"Really," I said.

I stood up slowly and opened the briefcase for all to see. Then I deliberately upended it, scattering the coins across the floor. They sank into the heavy carpet like so many overripe golden leeches. Everyone stared, captivated. I could be a showman too.

"Let's go over what we know about these coins," I said, putting on the most confident expression I could muster. "From the beginning, we've known these coins have something to do with David Marcum's death." This much was fair, and I saw agreement around the room.

"We know the coins originated in Southeast Asia, around the sixteenth century. We know this from dating techniques, and from the markings on the coins." Schnizzel nodded, confirming this. "From the flight records we obtained," I continued, "we also know that David Marcum was in Kuala Lumpur, Malaysia when he disappeared. With this information, Professor Schnizzel began to research where the coins might have come from."

I had to step cautiously for this next part. I was conscious of how my theories had been received in the past. "One possibility that Professor Schnizzel considered," I said carefully, "was that the coins came from a shipwreck. Lloyd Gunthum and Excel Resources are in the salvage business, after all." I saw the skepticism on Remington and Kruckemeyer's faces, but I bulled forward.

"Now. Here's the inflection point," I said. I opened my laptop, and pulled up the video of Jason Dubino's deposition. My heart was beating faster. "Last week, Richard deposed the crew of the Excelsior. One of the crew members, Jason Dubino, let slip that they had found something with the coins. What he was saying, we believe, was 'cannon.'"

I played the video of Dubino saying "can—" at the deposition. I saw Remington and Kruckemeyer consider it. It was plausible.

"As Professor Schnizzel will tell you," I said, "cannon are the primary means by which archaeologists identify old shipwrecks. If Rockweiller really found a cannon at the site, then there's a good chance that's what it is."

Remington regarded me dubiously. "Okay," he said finally, folding his arms across his chest. "Fine. I get that the coins are significant. And I know that Excel Resources is in the salvage business. So let's assume, for the sake of argument, that Dubino really said cannon. That this theory is true, and not just some lark. How do you figure out what wreck it is?"

"Well that's the thing," I said. "We think we already know."

Now I had their full attention. I nodded to Schnizzel, who unrolled one of the maps he had brought. He spread it across the floor. Everyone leaned over to look.

"Professor Schnizzel was able to identify a number of wrecks within a few hundred miles of Kuala Lumpur, Malaysia," I explained. "If that's where David Marcum flew, we reasoned that the site must be close by. We also limited our search to high-value wrecks, the kind that would interest Rockweiller Industries. These are the targets that we found." I placed a gold coin on each of a half-dozen places on the map.

"From the documents, I gleaned a few other pieces of the puzzle." Cindy and Harder frowned at this. I hadn't told them about the contracts. "Excel Resources entered into two consulting contracts, for services to be performed in Malaysia. One was with a company called Southeast Asia Salvage. The other was with a foundation that belonged to Suharto, the former President of Indonesia."

I passed out copies of the contracts. Cindy and Harder flipped through them. I saw Remington and Kruckemeyer wondering what the hell the former President of Indonesia had to do with this.

"These two companies had something in common," I said. "They both searched extensively for a certain shipwreck located in Southeast Asia. A shipwreck within striking distance of Kuala Lumpur. Both of these companies spent many years, and many millions of dollars, in pursuit of this wreck. Both failed, like all those that came before them. And there were many."

Everyone was spellbound now. Whether they believed me or not, I had their attention.

"The ship they sought was one of the most famous that was ever lost," I said. "In fact, many would say that it was the most famous treasure ship that sank anywhere, at any time, in history." I saw them draw in a collective breath.

"This ship had a few distinctive pieces of cargo," I continued. "These were described many centuries ago, when the ship was lost. There was a jeweled bracelet, which was said to protect its wearer from harm. There was a table of pure gold, made to serve a queen."

I paused and looked at Harder. "The last notable objects were a set of lions, cast in bronze."

"Bronze lions?" Harder repeated uncertainly. "You mean... you're talking about what Dubino said. At the deposition."

"Exactly."

"And you think this ship...the one with the bronze lions... that's what they found?"

"We do."

"So?" Cindy interjected, bursting with anticipation. "What ship was it? Tell us already!"

"The ship," I said, "was called the *Flor de la Mar*."

The *Flor de la Mar* was a Portuguese carrack that sank approximately five hundred years ago. It went down in a place called the Strait of Malacca, which was a waterway off the northern coast of Sumatra. The *Flor de la Mar* was the flagship of a famed Portuguese conqueror named Alfonso de Albuquerque.

In 1511, Albuquerque had sacked a city-state called Malacca, which was then the richest city in all Asia. It was the crown jewel of the Malaccan Sultanate, and the port of call for many trading vessels in the region. Albuquerque had spent ten years plundering Southeast Asia, and the conquest of Malacca was the capstone of his voyage.

Albuquerque was a ruthless man, and the sack of Malacca was terrible. Thousands perished, and from then on, the city was ruled by the Portuguese for the next several hundred years. After he conquered Malacca, Albuquerque loaded his fleet with the fabled wealth of the Sultan's palace and the richest merchants of the city. Albuquerque's ships carried a fabulous sum of gold and jewels and other plunder, and the *Flor de la Mar* held the cream of the crop. It was said to have been the richest treasure ever gathered in the history of the empire.

Albuquerque set sail from Malacca, intending to return to Portugal. During his long sojourn in Asia, Albuquerque had fallen out of favor with King Don Manuel. Albuquerque's enemies at court had poisoned the King against him. The fortune and fame he had amassed in Asia had fast eclipsed that of anyone else, and they were jealous.

These enemies whispered that Albuquerque plotted to usurp the King's rule and declare himself a sovereign in Asia. This was not an unusual charge against admirals and viceroys of the time, all of them ambitious men who held great power at long distance from the Crown. From half a world away, Albuquerque could do little to assuage the King's fears. But by bringing him the unsurpassed treasures of Malacca, Albuquerque hoped to silence his enemies and win himself back into the King's good graces.

Flor de la Mar meant "Flower of the Sea" in Portuguese. The ship was worthy of the name, and its great white sails bloomed like a flower of the ocean. But although the ship was grand, it was also old, and had sustained damage over the long voyages.

Soon after Albuquerque set sail, a terrible storm hit his fleet. The storm caught the ships in the Strait of Malacca, between Malaysia and Indonesia. The fleet scattered, and the *Flor de la Mar* foundered on some treacherous shoals and sank. Albuquerque himself made a harrowing escape from the *Flor de la Mar* on a makeshift raft, and managed to make it to one of the other ships, the *Trinidad.* But *Flor de la Mar*, along with its cargo and everyone aboard, was irrevocably lost.

Everyone sat in silence for a long while after I relayed this tale. Remington and Kruckemeyer exchanged a long look. But there was no laughter this time.

Schnizzel stood up and addressed the room with unaccustomed seriousness. "Gentlemen and ladies," he said. "If—and I do say if—we are right, the magnitude of this find cannot be overstated. The *Flor de la Mar* is widely considered to be the greatest treasure ship that sank. Ever." He emphasized it to make sure we understood. "There has never been another like it. It can only be compared with fortunes that border on fable, like El Dorado, or Montezuma. The Borgias. This ship would instantly make its finder one of the richest persons in the world."

There was silence for a while. I waited to see who would speak first. Finally, Remington did. "Show us where this ship went down," he said.

Schnizzel crouched down by the map on the floor. "According to historical sources," Schnizzel explained, "the *Flor de la Mar* sank off the coast of Sumatra. The exact location is a matter of some dispute. But it is believed to be somewhere in this general area." He pointed to the northern part of the Strait of Malacca, bordered by Malaysia to the north and the island of Sumatra, a part of Indonesia, to the south.

"Who owns the Strait of Malacca?" Cindy asked curiously. It was a good question.

"Unclear," said Schnizzel. "The Strait is bordered by Malaysia, Indonesia, and Singapore. Each of them have claimed jurisdiction over it at various times."

"That's why all the secrecy in this case," I explained. "If anyone knew Rockweiller had found this, they'd have about five countries after them in a heartbeat."

Kruckemeyer grunted. "That's one hell of a rodeo."

"Indeed," said Schnizzel. "The Strait of Malacca is also one of the world's busiest shipping lanes. It has been since ancient times. More than a quarter of the entire world's oil and trade passes through there annually."

"Holy...smokes," said Harder, with a glance at Ashley.

"Yes. A hundred thousand ships sail through the Strait every year. It's fraught with geopolitical tension. There are accidents, stand-offs, piracy, you name it. Quite the hotspot."

There was silence for a while as we all contemplated this. Kruckemeyer looked thoughtful. Remington pinched the bridge of his nose and sighed.

"What do you think, John?" Kruckemeyer asked him.

"I don't know what to think," he admitted.

Kruckemeyer nodded. "I know what you mean. I'm not sure whether Jack's crazy, or whether this is crazy enough to be true."

"Maybe if we show this to Judge Graves, he'll reconsider his ruling on ultrasensitive information," I suggested. "Then we could find out for sure."

Remington shook his head. "No. If we show him this, Judge Graves will throw us in the loony bin. Maybe we can tease it out in discovery given enough time. I don't know. But there's a quicker way to skin this cat. It just depends how sure we are that Jack's cockamamie theory is right."

He sat for a while longer, meditating on it. Finally, he turned to Ashley. "Well, Ms. Marcum," he said with a smile. "You've heard the theory, and you've heard the evidence. What do you think? Are you willing to bet that Jack and Professor Schnizzel are right? That Rockweiller Industries has found the wreck of the famous *Flor de la Mar*, and that's what your brother got mixed up with?"

"Yes," Ashley said without hesitation. "I trust Jack and Professor Schnizzel. I believe them."

Remington nodded. He seemed to come to a resolution. "Then we're decided," he said.

Remington turned to me. "I want you to call Badden & Bock tomorrow and set up a settlement conference. Tell them to bring someone with authority to resolve the case. We'll do the same." Kruckemeyer nodded slowly, seeming to understand.

"A settlement meeting?" I asked, confused. "Why?" Remington ignored my question.

"You think it's true, then?" Schnizzel asked him.

Remington regarded him skeptically. "Let me ask you something, Professor."

"Sure."

"You're telling me that Rockweiller found an ancient Portuguese galleon. One of the richest vessels of all time."

"Carrack, actually," Schnizzel corrected. "But yes."

"Whatever. And people have been looking for this ship for five hundred years."

"Right. Since it sank in 1511."

"And you're sure that it sank here, in the Strait of Malacca." He pointed at the map.

"Of that, I'm quite sure."

"Okay. Assuming I buy all that, answer me this: how exactly does the *Flor de la Mar*, one of the greatest treasure ships of all time, stay hidden for five hundred years, in one of the busiest shipping lanes in the world? And how did Rockweiller find it now?"

"How, indeed?" said Schnizzel.

EIGHTEEN

At high noon exactly one week later, we walked into Badden & Bock's lair in downtown Houston.

I didn't know why Remington wanted a settlement meeting. The conventional wisdom was that it was better to let the other side ask for a settlement. That put you in a stronger negotiating position. Basically, whoever asked first was saying "uncle." But I didn't know if Remington held by the conventional wisdom.

The assistant up front was all smiles this time as she led us to a private room with a beautiful sandalwood conference table. It was festooned with food and drink. There were finger sandwiches, pastries, fruit, and Fiji water bottles piled high on a side table. I poured coffee and mixed it with cream and sugar. I took a sip. It was excellent. Cindy loaded up a plate with sandwiches and pastries while Schnizzel and Ashley chatted amiably about the university in San Marcos. Ashley was considering going back to school there. Remington just sat quietly, waiting, as if carved out of wood.

Presently, Bock & Co. filed into the conference room. Bock, Quinto, and Loudamire were all there. With them was a bland-looking man in his early fifties with gray hair and a tired expression. I recognized him as John Cartwright, general counsel for Rockweiller Industries. There was also a younger blonde woman. Assistant general counsel Stephanie Rivera. Finally, there were a pair of men with golf tans and confident expressions. They wore blazers with their shirts open at the neck. Rockweiller executives, I guessed.

Introductions were made. Then Bock waited for us to begin. But Remington just sat there calmly. He didn't look as if he would say anything in a thousand years.

Bock cleared his throat and assumed his typically adversarial expression. He nodded to Loudamire, who handed out copies of a glossy folder entitled "Settlement Discussions – Privileged & Confidential." I opened it and flipped through the contents. There was a lengthy typewritten part describing possible outcomes, risks, and acceptable negotiating parameters, followed by a bunch of graphs and charts. I didn't see a number anywhere.

Bock clasped his hands together and addressed Remington. "I appreciate you reaching out to discuss settlement," he began. "This document is intended to suggest a framework for negotiations. By engaging in such negotiations, we do not intend to imply an admission of liability. However, we believe this will aid in setting out the ways and means by which a settlement might be reached."

The others nodded sagely. I doubted that any of them had read it, with the possible exception of whatever poor associate had put it together. Probably Loudamire, judging by her wrinkled suit and lethargic expression.

"As you can see," Bock continued, "we've considered the nature of the unfortunate accident that befell Mr. Marcum. We've also considered the risks associated with litigation in this jurisdiction. We have taken into account the insurance coverage available. Further, we have estimated the size and probability of an adverse jury verdict, as well as the probability of likely outcomes on appeal. This is based on all available data. Page five contains a detailed itemization of—"

"Cut the shit, Bock," Remington said evenly.

Their whole side of the table took a shocked step back.

"Excuse me?" said Bock, flabbergasted.

Remington paused to let the moment settle. "I know what this is about," he said quietly. I felt the tension rise. I caught myself holding my breath.

"I don't follow," said Bock.

"I know what your client found," said Remington. "That caused this whole mess."

"I don't know what you're talking about," Bock replied coolly.

Remington nodded. "Right. When's the last time you went to Malaysia, Bock?" he asked. I saw him flick an eye toward Cartwright and Rivera, gauging their reactions. They both froze. The executives glanced at each other with a look of disquiet.

But Bock just stared back impassively. "I don't know what you mean."

"No?" Remington said. "I'm talking about the salvage business. I'm talking about Excel Resources. I'm talking about what Lloyd Gunthum found, in a place called the Strait of Malacca. Ever heard of it?"

Now there was an unmistakable reaction. Cartwright had gone completely rigid. He was staring at Remington, the color drained from his face. Stephanie Rivera whispered something urgently in his ear. I felt like we were playing Marco Polo, and getting closer.

My heart was beating faster. It felt almost dreamlike. I waited for Remington to say it. To come out with my delusional theory, and for everyone to stop for a moment, and then look at each other and laugh at me, like they all had when I proposed this crazy idea to begin with.

"I don't know what you're talking about," said Bock, his face still giving away nothing. "Excel Resources engages in salvage operations. That's public knowledge. I don't see the relevance."

"I'm talking about a certain ship that sank in that area," said Remington. "A very old ship. Historic, one might even call it. Does that ring a bell?" The whispers from Rivera and the executives grew louder.

"No," said Bock.

Remington paused for a moment, and then leaned forward and just came out with it. "No? What about the *Flor de la Mar*?"

Quinto choked on his coffee, spilling it everywhere. John Cartwright went white as a ghost. The executives' eyes almost blew out of their skulls. Loudamire ran out of the room and slammed the door, and Stephanie Rivera hissed something at Bock. He told her to shut up, but I heard it. "*How the fuck did he know that?*" she said.

Remington took in their reactions and smiled humorlessly. "You know, when Jack first told me about his theory, I laughed him off. Buried treasure? I said. Yeah, right. If you believe that, I've got a bridge to sell you in Brooklyn. I knew that you all were hiding something. But I figured it was an oil find. Some of that black Texas gold. But no. This is the real thing."

Bock finally spoke. It was clearly an effort. "Obviously, I don't know what you're talking about," he said, his jaws grinding together. But the jig was up. We all knew it.

Remington nodded. "Right," he said. "Well, here's what we're going to do." Remington pushed aside Bock's fancy settlement folder, untouched, and clasped his hands before him.

"You're going to cut your bullshit privilege assertions and give me unrestricted access to all documents and witnesses involved in David Marcum's death. You're going to tell me what really happened, and exactly how the *Flor de la Mar* was discovered. Then, we're going to negotiate a reasonable settlement with all of the facts in front of us.

"If you don't," continued Remington, "I will amend our lawsuit to include the *Flor de la Mar*. A lawsuit needs to have all of the operative facts, wouldn't you agree?" Bock looked like he was about to choke.

"If I do that," said Remington, "my guess is that Portugal, Malaysia, and half of Southeast Asia may have something to say about it. They may ask, for instance, why you haven't reported the find of the *Flor de la Mar* pursuant to national and international law. They may also ask what you intend to do with it. That could cause considerable embarrassment to Rockweiller Industries," Remington said, glancing contemptuously at the executives. "Particularly given the company's sensitive international relationships."

Remington paused for a moment to let this sink in. Then he sat back, clasped his hands behind his head, and kicked his black boots up on Badden & Bock's fancy sandalwood conference table. "We can do this easy or hard," he said. "It's really up to you."

Bock snapped out of it, trying to recover. "Even assuming that, uh, what you say is true, and of course, uh, uh, we absolutely deny these allegations, there is no way we would simply agree to such a course of action—"

Remington ignored him and addressed John Cartwright directly. "You've got forty-eight hours to turn over all relevant documents and get me times to meet with the witnesses. You know where to find me."

With that, he got up and walked out the door. We followed him. On the way out, I glanced into one of the offices along the far wall. Through the blinds, I saw Loudamire. She was sitting alone in the corner, sobbing.

We were bursting with excitement as we followed Remington into the elevator. He signaled us to be quiet until we had left the building. His policy was never to talk until he'd left enemy territory, so to speak. Just to be safe.

We exited back out onto the hot street. The lunch crowd of lawyers and businesspeople in their blue and white starched shirts seemed like so many drones, oblivious to the momentous event that had just transpired fifty floors above their heads.

Cindy and I couldn't contain it anymore. We started yelling and high-fiving each other, about how we had totally owned Bock & Co., and how the executives had basically fallen out of their chairs, and did-you-see-Quinto's-tie-fold-into-his-coffee-cup, and everything else. Some of the businesspeople looked up in surprise as they walked by, wondering what was going on. Ashley and Schnizzel were ecstatic. Remington finally allowed himself a smile.

"So what happens now?" Ashley asked breathlessly.

"Now," said Remington, "they show us their cards, tell us what happened to your brother, and settle the case."

"Are you serious? How much are they going to pay?"

Remington shrugged. "Ten million, easy. That's the single-incident limit on their insurance policy."

"*Ten million*, did you say?" Ashley repeated incredulously. "And they're going to tell us everything?"

Remington nodded. "Yes. And that's assuming this was just a simple accident, which I find suspect. If there was something else going on, it will be higher."

"Oh my God," she said. "Just like that?"

"Just like that," Remington confirmed. "These guys are in the middle of a serious international incident. If that's really the *Flor de la Mar* they found, then they are looking at billions of dollars at stake. If word of this gets out, they'll be up shit creek without a paddle, if you'll pardon my French. Add that to whatever happened to David Marcum, and we have enormous leverage over them right now. Bock may not like it, but Cartwright will see it. That's one reason I wanted him there today."

"And the other?"

Remington chortled. "Did you see their faces? That wasn't a settlement meeting. That was a show. I wanted to see whether we were right or not. That's why I asked Jack to make sure they brought someone from the company. Bock has a pretty good poker face, but those other guys were like open books." He shook his head. "If we'd been wrong, I'd have looked as dumb as a rock. Like Jack did when he first told us this idea. But I don't mind looking the fool now and again if I have to."

"Thanks," I muttered.

"I can't believe this," Ashley said. Neither could I. I shook my head to try and clear the sense of unreality.

"It's not over yet," Remington cautioned. "But I'd say we're in a good place."

"When do you think they'll call?"

"Within forty-eight hours," he said confidently.

Forty-eight hours, I thought. In forty-eight hours, we would know everything, and the end of the case would finally be at hand.

NINETEEN

I was sitting in my office, idly doing research, when the case notification came in.

I felt relaxed for the first time in months. Ashley, Cindy, Harder, and I had stayed out late last night, enjoying unlimited sake and sushi at Sushi King, courtesy of Bob Kruckemeyer. We had laughed at Loudamire and Quinto, conjured wild theories about the *Flor de la Mar,* and speculated on what Ashley would do with her newfound riches. We also talked in more sober tones about her brother, and what we would learn when Rockweiller finally showed us their cards. But overall, the mood was festive. Harder and I went at each other mercilessly, and Cindy and Ashley choked on their sake bombs in laughter.

The next morning, I woke up pleasantly hung over. Now it was early afternoon. I sat back, kicked my feet up on my desk, and let out a contented sigh.

The partners were well pleased with me. Kruckemeyer said that it took guts to stick to something that sounded so stupid, even after a lot of people told me so. Remington went so far as to give me the extraordinary compliment of "good job." Other partners dropped by my office too, offering congratulations on a job well done. I picked up my ten-dollar globe and spun it, wondering if I would get a bonus out of this, and whether I should use it to buy a nicer globe.

I heard my email ping. Usually, I had the sound turned off. Otherwise I felt like a squirrel, jerking to and fro every time someone sent me a message, which was usually not worth the kilobytes it was printed on. But I was watching YouTube videos, so the sound was on. I clicked over to see what it was.

It was a case alert for Rockweiller Industries. My stomach tightened. I had set up a case notification on them a few months ago. It informed me every time Rockweiller sued or was sued. Most of the lawsuits were routine stuff; slip-and-fall at a refinery, a breach of contract with a pipeline operator, a wrongful termination, and so on. But this one looked different.

It was a federal lawsuit that Rockweiller had just filed in the Southern District of Florida, Miami Division. It was styled *Rockweiller Industries, Inc. v. Unidentified Shipwrecked Vessel.* My mouth went dry. I quickly downloaded the complaint and read it.

> Rockweiller Industries Inc. ("Rockweiller") files this Verified Complaint *in rem* against an Unidentified Shipwrecked Vessel ("Vessel"), its apparel, tackle, appurtenances, and cargo, the coordinates of which will be kept secret due to the extreme sensitivity of the matter. Rockweiller attaches the sworn statement of Lloyd Gunthum, attesting that the facts herein are true and correct.
>
> The Court has admiralty and maritime jurisdiction within the meaning of Rule 9(h) of the Federal Rules of Civil Procedure and Supplemental Admi-

> ralty Rules C and D. Further, the Court has original jurisdiction over this matter pursuant to 28 U.S.C. §§ 1331 and 1333. In addition, the Court has *in personam* jurisdiction as well as constructive quasi *in rem* jurisdiction over the Vessel.

I skimmed through the legalese, looking for the meat of it. And then on page seven, I saw it:

> Rockweiller believes that the Vessel which is the subject of this verified complaint is the remains of a Portuguese carrack originating in the sixteenth century. The name of the Vessel is believed to be the *Flor de la Mar*.
>
> Rockweiller has deposited with the U.S. Marshal several gold coins and a bronze lion recovered from the site for the symbolic arrest of the wreck. Rockweiller asserts a salvage award claim pursuant to the law of salvage and a possessory ownership claim pursuant to the law of finds. Rockweiller hereby requests that the Court award Rockweiller title to the wreck, and for all further relief to which it may be justly entitled.

The lawsuit was signed by Zachary Bock, of Badden & Bock, New York, NY. I sagged back into my chair.

They had called our bluff. Not only had they refused to settle, but they had struck first and filed a lawsuit of their own. In one blow, we had lost our leverage, and the knife we had against their throats was gone.

I didn't understand. This got them out of the frying pan with us. But it put them in a much bigger fire. Or so I thought.

I called Remington. He picked up immediately.

"They filed a lawsuit," I stammered, not expecting him to answer the phone. "Rockweiller Industries…the *Flor de la Mar*. I just got the notification a few minutes ago."

"I know," he said tersely. "I'm reading it now."

"Oh. You are?"

"Yes."

"What are they doing?" I blurted out. "I thought they had to keep this from going public."

"So did I," said Remington. "I'm as surprised as you are. And I hate surprises. What is even more inexplicable is where they filed it."

"What do you mean?"

"The Southern District of Florida. As you know, the Eleventh Circuit issued a ruling several years back that basically guts their entire case. As far as I can tell, what they've done is legal suicide."

The Eleventh Circuit was the federal appeals court in Florida. When the Eleventh Circuit made a decision, all of the federal judges in Florida had to follow it. This was called precedent, or *stare decisis*. It's the same principle that makes all courts do what the U.S. Supreme Court says.

"Right," I said. "Obviously." Actually, I had no idea what ruling he was talking about. But I didn't want to look stupid, so I kept my mouth shut. "What do we do now?" I asked.

"I don't know. I need to think about it. I'll be in touch." Then he hung up.

The *Flor de la Mar* lawsuit caused a sensation in the press. The Sun-Sentinel, the Tampa Bay Times, and the Miami Herald all picked it up. Then the internet got wind of it, and the soon the story was trending on national and social media. "Billion-Dollar Shipwreck Discovered," proclaimed one headline. "Sunken Treasure Found After 500 Years: Case To Be Heard in Miami" said another. "Portuguese Powerball: Winning Ticket Sold."

On television, the talking heads began to weigh in. The networks reached out to every pseudo-expert with half a clue about shipwrecks and put them on TV. Schnizzel was furious. He said they were all hacks and was bursting to go on the air and "show them what a real maritime archaeologist can do." But Remington told him to wait, and that he would get his chance.

A byproduct of this "expert" speculation was that the value of the *Flor de la Mar* increased every day. It started out as "billions," which was likely true. But the media kept bidding it up. The news anchors would play a game of chicken with the experts, daring them to go higher. A reporter would say, in hushed tones, "do you think it could be worth more?" and the expert would say, with gravitas, "it's possible." This phenomenon echoed across the networks, and whichever expert went the highest was the most in demand. Soon, the reasonable experts were eclipsed by those who were less so.

This frenzy reached new heights after someone unearthed an issue of Skin Diver Magazine from March 1992. The cover story was about the *Flor de la Mar*, and the headline proclaimed "$80 Billion Treasure Wreck Lost and Found."

The fact that a magazine had printed it decades ago made it gospel, and this became the *de facto* value of the *Flor de la Mar*. Anchoring, I thought, remembering Kruckemeyer's technique. The news pointed out that this was equivalent to one-quarter of the value of all of the gold in Fort Knox. Some of the more aggressive experts started to bid up the number even higher, until it was flirting with a hundred billion dollars.

It was insanity. As valuable as the ship was, it wasn't worth that much. But just how much it really was worth, nobody knew.

After watching the news all day, I was in a funk. I called Cindy. "Are you following this?" I said.

"Yep."

"Can you believe it?"

"Nope."

I told her what Remington had said about the Eleventh Circuit. "I didn't want to ask him about it. But what do you think he means?"

"It's obvious. Haven't you read the *Odyssey Marine* case?"

"Not lately." Meaning, not ever.

"That's probably what he's talking about. Read it. I'm going to lunch."

"Cindy!" I said, exasperated.

"I'm hungry!" she exclaimed.

I relented, and told her to come see me as soon as she got back. I didn't feel like doing research just then, so I called Schnizzel. I mentioned the *Odyssey Marine* case, and he recognized it instantly.

"Oh, yes," he said. "I'm quite familiar." I was annoyed. Was I the only one who didn't know about this case? "I should be," he added with a chuckle. "I testified in it."

"What?" I said with a start.

"Yes. I was an expert witness for Odyssey Marine. Although I don't know what your boss is talking about. That's legal stuff. Above my pay grade. But I'll tell you about the case, and maybe you'll figure it out.

"In 2007, a company called Odyssey Marine Exploration discovered a shipwreck a hundred miles off the coast of Gibraltar. Near Spain. They were searching for the *Merchant Royal*, one of the most famous and elusive wrecks out there.

"After some years, they found a ship. But it wasn't the *Merchant Royal.* Instead, it proved to be a thirty-six gun Spanish frigate called the *Nuestra Señora de las Mercedes*. It went down off the coast of Gibraltar in 1804."

"Was this *Mercedes* a big find?"

"Quite. According to court papers, the *Mercedes* contained silver specie worth over six hundred million dollars in today's terms."

"Jesus."

"Indeed. I believe it was the richest haul ever documented. The *San Jose*, off the coast of Colombia, is said to be bigger. But that's theoretical. Until it's actually dredged up, you never know."

"And the *Mercedes*—did Odyssey actually recover any of it?"

"Oh, yes. The company flew seventeen tons of silver on a private plane from Gibraltar to an undisclosed location in Florida. Then, they filed a claim for ownership of the wreck in U.S. federal court."

"Did they get it?"

"Well. Let's just say that's when things got interesting." I leaned into the phone, eager to hear more. But it was not to be. "Shit, look at the time," said Schnizzel. "I've got to get to class. But read the opinion. We'll talk later." I opened my mouth to protest, but there was a click, and Schnizzel was gone. I would have to read the thing myself.

There were a bunch of legal opinions in the case. I downloaded the first one I found.

> This action between Odyssey Marine Exploration and the Kingdom of Spain adjudicates the right to possession and ownership of more than

> $600,000,000.00 in silver specie. This action presented from the outset not merely the dicey prospects of a damages action; this action presented a claim to ownership by a party holding-in-hand an enormous, historic trove of treasure, holding-in-hand riches "beyond the dreams of avarice." A contest for $600 million—winner take all—is plenty sufficient to endanger any boundary, to awaken any frailty, and to excite any temptation.
>
> Observing this contest evokes an ageless insight on money: She is the sovereign queen of all delights; For her, the lawyer pleads and the soldier fights.[2]

I read, and began to piece together the history of the case. After Odyssey Marine filed for ownership of the *Mercedes* in Florida court, Spain intervened in the case. Intervention is where someone else with an interest in a case joins the lawsuit. Spain had an interest in the *Mercedes*, so she intervened and told the Florida court that the *Mercedes* belonged to her, not to Odyssey, which had dredged up the ship, stolen her silver, and disturbed the bones of Spanish sailors long at rest. Odyssey countered that the *Mercedes* had been lost and abandoned for centuries, and never would have been found if not for Odyssey's efforts.

So the Florida court had to decide whether to give the ship to the owner or the finder. The key to the whole thing was sovereign immunity. Sovereign immunity is the legal doctrine that makes the property of one country immune from prosecution in the courts of another. It's recognized in one

---

[2] *Odyssey Marine Exploration, Inc. v. Unidentified Shipwrecked Vessel*, 79 F.Supp.2d 1270 (M.D. Fla. 2013) (citing Richard Barnfield, *The Encomion of Lady Pecunia* (1598)).

form or another by most courts around the world. It helps keep the peace.

It's complicated, but the law of sovereign immunity in the U.S. basically works like this: if the *Mercedes* was acting in a "sovereign capacity," like a warship, then she was immune, and belonged to Spain. If she was acting in a "commercial capacity," like a merchant ship, then she was not immune, and belonged to Odyssey.

To answer this question, the court had to delve into the geopolitics of 19th-century Spain. It made for fascinating reading. I closed my door, blocked out the present, and stepped back into the past.

In the late 18th century, Spain and Britain fought as allies against France. This was the heady era of the French Revolution, after the French rose up and beheaded their King, Louis XVI. The other European monarchs were terrified that they would get the same. So they banded together and set out to crush the Revolution in its cradle. But this proved more difficult than they had anticipated. A French general named Napoleon Bonaparte rose to power, and led the armies of France to throw back every nation ranged against them.

In 1796, Spain switched sides. She signed the Treaty of Ildefonso, secretly promising to support France against Britain. Then, in 1802, Britain signed the Treaty of Amiens with Napoleon. Amiens brought a short-lived peace to these eternal adversaries, and to all Europe.

Spain used the peace of Amiens to collect money from her viceroyalties around the world. The *Mercedes* was ordered to Peru by the ruthless Spanish Generalissimo Manuel Godoy, who was nicknamed "the sausage maker." There, the *Mercedes* was to pick up silver bullion and then return to Spain.

The *Mercedes* took on an enormous amount of silver in Peru, as well as other cargo like copper, tin, Church funds, military payroll, and even tree husks. It also took money from private citizens, to be shipped across the sea. In all, the *Mercedes* was loaded with approximately 900,000 silver pesos, and sailed with a fleet of three other ships back to Spain.

But on the way home, the fleet was intercepted by a British naval squadron. Evidently, the British knew that Spain was secretly supporting France under the Treaty of Ildefonso. And they didn't believe the peace with Napoleon would last. So they ordered the Spanish fleet to port.

The Spanish refused, and the British opened fire. At the outset of the battle, the British landed a single shot to the *Mercedes*' powder magazine, destroying the entire ship in a single spectacular explosion and killing all of the hundreds of people aboard. The other Spanish ships surrendered immediately. Later, Spain declared war against Britain, and entered the Napoleonic Wars on the side of France.

The upshot of all that history was this: even though Britain and Spain weren't technically at war when the *Mercedes* sank, the *Mercedes* was acting in a military, sovereign capacity when she went down. That meant the ship was entitled to sovereign immunity and belonged to Spain.

Odyssey had one last card to play. And it was a clever one. Odyssey argued that even if the *Mercedes* herself was sovereign property, her cargo—six hundred million dollars' worth of silver—was not. Transporting money was something that merchants did, not sovereigns, Odyssey argued.

But the court said no. It declared that the ship and her cargo were one and the same under the law. It looked to some other laws, called the Sunken Military Craft Act and the Abandoned Shipwreck Act. The court reasoned that these laws were similar, if not identical. So the court extrapolated their logic to say that the *Mercedes* and her cargo were inseparable.

Besides resolving Odyssey's claim, this also allowed the court to deftly sidestep perhaps the most delicate question in the case—which had to do with Peru.

You see, the silver aboard the *Mercedes* had been taken from the mines of Peru. Peru was then a colony of Spain. Spain conscripted the indigenous natives and forced them to work in the silver mines under harsh conditions. Some twenty years after the *Mercedes* sank, Peru declared its independence from Spain.

So Peru intervened in the modern *Odyssey Marine* case, and argued that it had a patrimonial right to the silver. Peru argued that Spain couldn't say with a straight face that Odyssey had stolen its silver, when Spain had stolen that very silver from Peru in the first place.

The court said some nice words about Peru, but in the end, it sided with Spain. By ruling that the ship and its cargo were one and the same, the court was able to dodge the delicate question of who was right and wrong in the colonial age, hundreds of years ago. The court said it had no jurisdiction, and dismissed the case based on sovereign immunity. But it nonetheless ordered the silver returned to Spain.

After that, to add insult to injury, the court made Odyssey pay Spain a million dollars in attorney's fees for bad faith litigation. The court said that Odyssey had concealed the identity of the wreck to keep Spain in the dark. Nowadays, Odyssey didn't do much treasure hunting anymore. It wasn't hard to see why.

The case left a bad taste in my mouth. It didn't seem fair. The treasure never would have been found if not for Odyssey. And the silver had originally belonged to Peru. I thought each of them should have gotten a share at least. But as Remington was wont to say, the law isn't always fair.

The Eleventh Circuit's opinion in *Odyssey Marine* didn't have the flair of Judge Gewin's opinion in the *Atocha* case. But it was thorough and well written, and had an understated solidity that I liked. I looked up the judge who wrote it. Her name was Susan Black. She was the first woman to be appointed to the Eleventh Circuit Court of Appeals.

By the time Cindy returned from lunch, I had figured it out. I knew what Remington meant when he said it was crazy for Rockweiller to have filed the case in Florida. Cindy sat down in my office, and I explained it to her myself.

"In *Odyssey Marine*, the court ruled in favor Spain, and against Odyssey," I said. "They gave everything to the owner of the ship, and nothing to the finder."

"Right," said Cindy.

"If the Florida court in the *Flor de la Mar* case follows that ruling, then it would give the whole ship to Portugal, and nothing to Rockweiller."

"Yes."

"*Odyssey Marine* was decided by the Eleventh Circuit. So if it's binding precedent in Florida..."

"Which it is."

"...Then the outcome in the *Flor de la Mar* case has to be the same. Which means if Portugal intervenes—as it surely will—the court will give the *Flor de la Mar* and everything in it to Portugal, with nothing to Rockweiller."

"Exactly."

I sat back and tried to make sense of this. "Anywhere else, they would have had a shot," I said wonderingly. "They could have filed in New York. Or Washington D.C. Hell, they could have filed in Texas. None of those courts are bound by the Eleventh Circuit. It could come out differently."

"Yep."

"But they filed in Florida."

"Mmhm."

"But why? It doesn't make any sense. Don't they know this?"

"I'm sure they do. Bock & Co. may be assholes, but they're not stupid."

"No. So what game are they playing?"

"I have no idea," she said.

Soon enough, the reason that Rockweiller had filed in Florida became clear. It emerged in the news over the next several days. I saw it on MNN, the Maritime News Network, a show in the high seven-thousands (channels, that is) that reported exclusively on maritime news. This might be anything from the movement of the U.S. Seventh Fleet in the Pacific to tracking the progress of a container ship, complete with hours-long footage and running commentary.

The main anchor on MNN was Rufus Rockaway. He looked like a character from a bad 80s sitcom. Rockaway had a big red afro that he wore above turtleneck sweaters and green suit jackets, even though he lived in Florida. There was also a part-time anchor named Katie Tyler. She was an older blond lady who seemed normal by comparison. Tyler was patched in from a different location, so they had split-screens when they talked.

MNN had been reporting on the case non-stop for the last couple of days. I had begun to keep them on in the background on a small TV I had in my office. I wanted to stay up to date on any new developments. I also found them entertaining, in a guilty sort of way.

A few days after the story broke, I saw Rufus Rockaway flashing pictures of Queen Isabella and King Ferdinand of Spain across the television. Notwithstanding that this was the wrong country, and the wrong time period, I sensed something was up, and switched on the sound to listen.

"...a deal with Portugal. Sounds like a treaty of eternal friendship to me, doesn't it Katie?" Rockaway was saying.

"It sure does, Rufus, it sure does." "Let's just hope this treaty lasts longer than my last marriage, Katie," said Rufus, chuckling at his own joke.

Katie chuckled right back and made an *oh stop!* motion across the screen.

"Do you think they exchanged friendship bracelets, Katie?" Rufus asked.

"They probably exchanged binding legal documents, Rufus," said Katie.

"Oh, you!" replied Rufus. He flipped his hair in that signature way that he had.

"Well, if this deal holds up, it seems like Portugal and Rockweiller Industries will both be big winners from the *Flor de la Mar*..."

I muted the TV and pulled up the real news online. There were a number of reports that Portugal had made a deal with Rockweiller on the *Flor de la Mar*. One local Florida paper ran the headline "Deal of the (Sixteenth) Century?" and reported on a statement from Portugal. It was a fluff piece from the Portuguese Ministry of Foreign Affairs.

> In acknowledgement of the ground-breaking work that Rockweiller Industries has done in locating this long-lost relic of Portuguese history, and the work

> they will continue to do in salvaging and restoring the *Flor de la Mar*, the nation of Portugal has entered into a mutually beneficial agreement with Rockweiller Industries...all historical items of Portuguese ownership will be retained by Portugal, with the remainder of the cargo to be shared between Portugal and Rockweiller Industries pursuant to an agreement, the details of which are confidential...

The financial papers reported a jump in Rockweiller's stock as the market tried to price in the value of the find. Even though Rockweiller was a big company, a piece of the *Flor de la Mar* could put a boost in its revenue numbers for years, one analyst said.

I called Cindy. "Are you seeing this?" I asked.

"You're not watching MNN again, are you?"

"No," I lied. "Have you seen the reports about the deal with Portugal?"

"Yep."

"That's why they filed in Florida," I said heavily. "Because Portugal is on their side."

"Yep."

"So Portugal gets ownership under the Eleventh Circuit ruling. And Rockweiller gets ownership under a contract with Portugal."

"It would seem so."

It would seem so, indeed. We'd been outfoxed.

That evening, I ordered Chinese food. The remains of yesterday's dinner (the same thing) were still sitting on my counter, with chopsticks sticking out the top. I wondered why I ate Chinese food with chopsticks when no one was watching, when it was easier with a fork. Lacking answers, I slumped down on the couch and flipped on an episode of *The Dominator*.

Later that night, I called Ashley. She usually finished her shift at the bar this time on weekdays. She picked up after a couple of rings.

"Hello?"

"Hey. It's me."

"Hey." There was a pleasant moment of silence.

"You know, you're the only person that calls me," she said. "You and this one weird cousin. Everyone else texts."

"Well. I'm your lawyer. I figure I should call. Plus if I give you legal updates by text message they will end up as Exhibit A in a malpractice suit someday." She laughed.

I told her about the developments. She had heard about the lawsuit, and we took a moment to marvel at the fact that we were right. The *Flor de la Mar* was real, and Rockweiller had found it. Then I explained Rockweiller's legal maneuver, and what it meant for our case. That we had lost our leverage and would have to go back to doing things the old-fashioned way.

Ashley took it in stride. "That's okay," she said. "I never expected this to be easy. We'll get it eventually. I trust you."

Although Ashley didn't seem to need consoling, I did. The next day, I made my way to Kruckemeyer's office. I slumped into one of his chairs, deflated. Kruckemeyer pulled himself away from an email he was typing, annoyed. But when he saw my expression, he became sympathetic.

"You alright there, Jack?" he asked gently.

"I guess," I said, dejected. He nodded.

"Look, I know we were on the edge of a big win here. And it got ripped away. I'm sorry about that. I've been there. You've just got to roll with the punches."

"I know."

"Don't feel so bad. You did a good job. Figured all this stuff out before anyone else did. Hell. And remember, we still got a real case. All this treasure stuff, that's not what this is about." He waved his hand. "It's about your boy. David Marcum. Kid got killed. And we need to find out who done it."

"You're right," I said, nodding resolutely. "We do."

"That's it," he said. "Get after it. Put that clever brain of yours to work." I got up, feeling just a little bit better about things. Kruckemeyer saw it and nodded approvingly. He turned back to his screen as I headed out the door. "Oh, and one more thing," he said. "We've got a motion for summary judgment coming up in the class action case. Going to need a draft from you soonest."

After that, things slowly got back to normal. I went back to work on my other cases. The summary judgment brief was a lot of work. Summary judgment is when you ask the judge to toss out a case. A lot of times, it's the turning point in a lawsuit. If we won, the class action would be over. If we lost, the client would pay a lot of money to settle. Otherwise, they would have to face a jury. An insurance company would rather be staring down the barrel of a loaded gun than do that. So I began the grueling amount of legal research that was required to write a fifty-page insurance class action brief.

I also fought with H. Hubert Thung over piddling discovery matters in the Mongolian barbeque case. Thung was a tool. But compared to Badden & Bock, dealing with him was peanuts. Thung kept asking me to "meet and confer," but I had no interest in spending an afternoon with him. So I played the same tricks that Bock & Co. had used on me. Thung wasn't sharp enough to catch on, and I was able to delay as weeks stretched into months.

Meanwhile, I followed the *Flor de la Mar* case from the sidelines. But MNN was on in my office less and less. I felt sad as I watched the world marvel at a ship whose secret was no longer mine. No one made the connection between the *Flor de la Mar* and our little lawsuit in Texas. There were no calls asking about David Marcum. But although the world might not care, I did, and I was determined to find out what had happened to him.

Since the *Flor de la Mar* went public, it was hard to get Badden & Bock to respond to my inquiries. They seemed to have little interest in the Marcum case now. They barely answered my discovery letters, and when they did, it was with none of their usual vitriol. Absurdly, I felt sad. As if they had moved on. We were small fish now that the *Flor de la Mar* was out of the bag, I guessed. They had bigger things to do.

Nonetheless, I was determined to make them play ball, whether they wanted to or not. The first thing we needed to do was line up the deposition of Lloyd Gunthum. Gunthum was the key player in this. Remington was going to take his deposition personally. I had confidence he would be able to get the truth.

I started working up an in-depth deposition outline for Remington. He didn't need it. But I needed to do it. I pulled every single document related to Lloyd Gunthum or the Excelsior. I analyzed and summarized them and sent the important ones to Remington. He would write back with questions and more document requests, and I went back to the files and answered them. I learned a lot about deposition prep from this, so the time was well spent.

For some reason, Remington was keenly interested in the Excelsior's scuba records. The ship had come back with one less set of scuba gear than it set out with. Marcum's set. The ship also came back with five missing weight belts. But that didn't seem significant. Other than that, the logs all checked out. Maybe Remington thought there was an equipment malfunction. I sent him everything we had, and even asked Lyle to order some books on scuba diving. Remington somehow found time to read the books and mark them up with questions.

In the meantime, Cindy and I dutifully plugged away at the Rockweiller documents for a couple of hours each day. I also thought about privilege. The death memo had never left my mind, and I felt certain that the answers were in there. But Remington said that Judge Graves would never waive privilege unless we could prove they were lying. And I didn't know how to do that.

It was maybe two months after the *Flor de la Mar* went public that I got a phone call from an unknown number. "Jack Carver," I said, picking up the phone.

"Mr. Carver," came a raspy voice at the other end. "This is Jeremy Riker. I believe you are looking for information about David Marcum."

TWENTY

I flew into London in the early evening. I had been there once, on a layover. It had been cold and rainy then, just like it was now. I left the airport and looked around for a place to eat. I spied a McDonalds, glanced around guiltily, and went inside. I didn't have the time to figure out London cuisine just then. So I ordered two Big Macs and wolfed them on the sidewalk. Then I pulled up the address of the place I was going.

Jeremy Riker was the last crew member aboard the Excelsior. He no longer worked for Rockweiller, which was why he didn't appear at the depositions. This meant that we could talk to him without Badden & Bock around. Lyle had found several numbers for him, and we had been trying to track him down. But we hadn't been able to reach him. Until now.

After the *Flor de la Mar* became public, Riker had finally called me back and said he had information about David Marcum. He hadn't been on the Excelsior when Marcum had died. He'd left the company shortly before that. But he knew something about it. He was willing to part with this knowledge in exchange for cash.

Riker refused to talk on the phone, afraid it would be tapped. It was the kind of attitude I'd come to expect from anyone involved in this case. We dickered a little, and then I got together fifteen thousand dollars in cash and a plane ticket to London. I spent nine hours drinking Budweiser and watching Hugh Grant movies all the way across the Atlantic. (Scratch that, I spent the time reading case files and making deposition notes).

I met Riker at a bar called Popinjay's. The name evoked a cheerful establishment, but the place was anything but. Instead, it was a battered old building that looked like it was built before both world wars. I entered through a back alley and pushed my way through a sour, unwashed set of customers to the bar.

Inside, my eyes searched the room and met those of a weathered-looking man sitting in a booth. He wore a black leather jacket and had a sardonic cast to his face. He signaled me with a raise of his drink. I walked over and sat down.

"Thanks for agreeing to see me, Mr. Riker," I said.

"Got the cash?" he asked harshly. I handed him a thick envelope. He looked inside, and quickly ruffled through the stack of hundred-dollar bills. Then he smiled, raised his glass, and took a deep swallow.

"To your health," he said. "I have to respect a man who flies nine hours for a beer."

"Eighteen hours," I corrected him. "If you count the way back."

"Well. The least I can do is buy." He flagged down the waitress. I started to ask her if they had any American beers, but I caught Riker and the waitress's expressions and just asked for whatever Riker was having. It was sour and warm, like what I imagined alcoholic piss might taste like.

"What do you want to know?" Riker asked.

"Whatever you can tell me about David Marcum, Lloyd Gunthum, and Rockweiller Industries," I said. "Or Excel Resources. I'm not sure of the difference."

Riker took a sip of his beer. "Excel Resources is Lloyd Gunthum's outfit," he said. "Rockweiller took a majority stake some years ago. Gunthum was doing some oil and gas work for Rockweiller, primarily in South America. Commercial diving, pipeline work, that sort of thing. He had a side business in search and recovery too. Usually contracts to recover vessels, or equipment that had sunk in some accident or other. But Gunthum also had an interest in these older ships. The treasure wrecks."

"Why?"

Riker shrugged. "Partly it was business. Gunthum made a find many years ago, I heard. A big one. Once you get a taste, it's hard to forget. And there's something romantic about it, don't you think?" he grinned mockingly at me.

"Maybe. From what I know about him, Gunthum doesn't seem like the type," I said. Riker shrugged.

"What did Gunthum find all those years ago?" I asked.

"I don't know. He's pretty secretive. Most people in that business are. You say too much, someone else will try to take what you find. And there are all sorts of government rights tied up in those things. You heard of those *maricon* Spaniards who took the *Mercedes* from Odyssey Marine. The U.S. tried to do the same to Mel Fisher over the *Atocha.* So why would anyone tell Spain or Portugal if they found another galleon? So many of the finds go unreported. Someone finds one, they salvage it quietly, sell the proceeds over time. That's probably what Gunthum did with his first find."

"But not with the *Flor de la Mar*," I said.

"No," Riker allowed. "That one was too big. And in too prominent of a place. There was no way for them to do it without attracting attention."

"Right. Okay. Let's go back to Lloyd Gunthum. How did he interest Rockweiller in his little enterprise?"

"Gunthum had been working with Rockweiller for some time in South America. He pitched a partnership for salvage operations. Rockweiller would take a majority stake in the business. They would provide the capital, he would provide the expertise. This was not some big corporate deal cooked up in the boardroom, you understand. More likely it was with one of Rockweiller's local execs in South America. They probably knew Gunthum, gave him a few million dollars and some rope, and let him see what he could do. To a company of that size, it wouldn't even be a blip on the radar."

"How do you know all this stuff?"

"I worked with him for a long time."

"Why'd you leave?"

"We had a falling out." He didn't seem interested in elaborating, so I didn't ask.

"How did Gunthum do with Excel Resources?" I said.

"He did well. Gunthum is sharp. He used to be in the special forces, you know. Afghanistan. Yemen. Specialized in search and rescue operations, and killings, I heard. He knows how to make a plan, and he knows how to execute. Most guys, they can do one or the other. But not both."

"How does he look for these ancient wrecks?"

"He would look at old historical records, maps, accounts. He had an eye for them. Then he would use sonar and magnetometers to search likely areas. Gunthum is better at it than most."

"What about the *Flor de la Mar*?"

"What about it?"

"How did he find that one?"

Riker looked at me as if he didn't understand. "The *Flor de la Mar*?"

"Yes. The ship I'm here about," I said impatiently. "How did he find it?"

Riker continued to look perplexed. "You don't know how he found it?" he asked.

I stared at him, wondering what he was talking about. "How would I know how he found it?"

Riker frowned at me. "But then...why are you here?"

I spread my hands, confused. "If you don't know, I get it," I said. "But Rockweiller won't tell us. We don't understand how they found it. That's what I'm trying to figure out."

Riker stared at me in confusion for a moment, and then realization sparked in his eyes. He started to laugh. It was a low, harsh laugh, but pretty soon he couldn't control himself. He coughed and almost choked on his beer. Some people looked at us from the next table over.

"What's so funny?" I hissed at him.

"You don't know," he said, trying to stop coughing. "You don't even know that. Wow. They must be doing a better job in this case than I thought."

"What are you talking about?"

Riker finally got control of himself. He leaned over to me and spoke in a low voice.

"Gunthum didn't find the *Flor de la Mar*," he whispered.

"I don't follow."

"Rockweiller didn't either."

"Then who did?" I asked, puzzled.

Gunthum leaned even closer. I could smell the stale beer on his breath. "David Marcum. He's the one that found the *Flor de la Mar*."

I gaped at him, trying to process this. David Marcum had found the *Flor de la Mar*? Could it possibly be true? My head was spinning as I tried to think through the implications.

"They didn't tell you that, did they?" said Riker. "No. What did they tell you?"

"They didn't tell us anything. They withheld the information as ultra-sensitive under a protective order."

"Ultra-sensitive. I bet. Yeah, Marcum found it. Well, that's not exactly true. Gunthum and his outfit actually went out and located the wreck. It took some doing. But the information that led him there, I heard that was Marcum. That's why Marcum was involved with all of this in the first place, you see."

"How the hell did Marcum find it?"

"That's the billion-dollar question. Nobody knows. People have been looking for that ship for five hundred years. How some American college drop-out found it is a complete mystery."

Riker continued in a low voice. "The way I heard it, Marcum made a deal with Gunthum. Marcum had the information, you see. But he didn't have the money to search for and salvage something like that, much less deal with the fallout. He and Gunthum knew each other from somewhere. I think they worked on an oil rig together or something."

I nodded, thinking about their time in Colombia.

"Marcum contacted Gunthum, and persuaded him that the information was good. Gunthum agreed to mount a search. They went off to do it. And then they found it."

I nodded slowly. The pieces were all coming together.

"What did Marcum get out of this?" I asked.

Riker looked around and then leaned forward again. "I heard there was a contract."

"A contract?" My heart started thumping.

"Yeah. With a finder's fee. Marcum was going to get a piece of the action in exchange for telling Gunthum about it."

"You mean a percentage of the *Flor de la Mar*?"

Riker nodded.

"How much? What was the deal?"

"That I don't know. I never knew the particulars."

"Was any contract signed?"

"I don't know," said Riker, finishing the last of his beer. "Maybe. Marcum wasn't stupid, and you don't go around telling people information like that without some protection. But it's also something people don't like to put in writing. He may have trusted Gunthum."

"Why?"

Riker shrugged. "They were on the same wavelength. Friends, even. Gunthum is a hard guy, but he's not bad. He has honor. From the military. That creed, you know."

I nodded. "What happened to the deal?"

"I don't know," said Riker.

"And what happened to David Marcum?"

"That I don't know either. I wasn't there. It was all hush-hush."

"Could it have been a scuba diving accident?"

Riker shrugged. "Could have been. It's possible. But I heard Dave was a great diver."

"What are you saying?"

"There were rumors."

"What sort of rumors?"

"That's hearsay, ain't it?" he said with a grin.

"This isn't a court of law. What happened?"

Riker looked at me evenly. "What do *you* think happened?"

I looked at him. "Are you saying...?" I waited expectantly, but he said nothing more. "You think something happened?"

"I'm not saying that. I really don't know. But when you've got that much at stake, and something happens...you put two and two together, don't you?"

I flew back from London that night and delivered the explosive news to the team the next morning. Around noon, everyone gathered in the conference room to strategize. Kruckemeyer authorized lunch, and we ordered fajitas. Houston has its downsides, but one of the upsides is the best Tex-Mex in the United States.

The fajitas arrived within the hour, and we helped ourselves to sizzling plates of chicken, beef, and refried beans, piling stone-ground tortillas high with peppers and onions. While we ate, I recounted Riker's tale for the group.

Kruckemeyer was the first to pick up on the financial import of the news. "If Marcum had a deal," he mused, "then he might be owed a whole shitload of money. Shipload, excuse me."

"That's right," said Cindy, taking a bite of her third fajita. "He'd get a percentage of whatever the *Flor de la Mar* is worth."

"Hmm. What's the latest on that?" Kruckemeyer asked.

"Billions." I said.

"The news says a hundred billion," Harder added.

"Ye haw," said Kruckemeyer.

"It's not a hundred billion," I said, annoyed. "That's just a bunch of cranks bidding up the price."

"A hundred billion dollars," Kruckemeyer said dreamily. "Okay. Well look. Let's be realistic. Say it's ten billion, Jack. Even five. At a ten percent finder's fee. You're fast at math. What's that worth?"

I wondered if Kruckemeyer was aware that he was being anchored. But I didn't bring it up just then. "If that was the case—and it's a big if—then Marcum would be owed anywhere from half a billion to a billion dollars," I said. And then, because I knew what he was really after, I said "at a forty percent contingent fee, it would mean hundreds of millions for the firm."

"Hundreds of millions," said Kruckemeyer greedily. "That's real dough."

It was real dough indeed. Kruckemeyer was a successful attorney. He probably made a million dollars a year. That was a lot of money. Some of the top litigators in the country could pull down even more. But it was only the big plaintiff's lawyers—the ones who took a cut of the wins—who earned hundreds of millions. Those lawyers fought big corporations over catastrophic injuries, mass torts, or class actions, and reaped huge rewards. But it took a hell of a lot of luck to do that, and balls of steel. They were a different breed. The only practicing lawyer ever to make the billionaire's club was the infamous Texas trial lawyer Joe Jamail.

"That's a best-case scenario," I cautioned Kruckemeyer. "And that's not factoring in expenses. Cost of salvage. Percentage of the wreck that gets lost. Selling costs, time to market. Legal fees. It's not that simple." Schnizzel had explained all of this to me in detail.

"Right, right," said Kruckemeyer. "Legal fees. Gotta love 'em."

But even as I tried to urge caution, I was getting caught up in the mania too. Even if all of these figures were speculative, and there were expenses that went along with them, there was no doubt that the *Flor de la Mar* was worth a colossal sum of money. If we could prove a contract, Marcum's take would be astronomical. As would ours.

"What do you think, John?" Kruckemeyer asked, turning to Remington.

Remington had stayed quiet until then, listening to the discussion. "I don't know, Bob," he said. "I really don't. But aren't we putting the cart before the horse?"

"What do you mean?"

Remington pushed his plate away and leaned forward. "We've got a problem. Let's assume for the sake of argument that Riker is telling the truth. That David Marcum had a contract giving him some percentage of the *Flor de la Mar*. Here's the thing: because they filed the case in Florida, it doesn't matter. Even if there's a contract, we get diddly squat."

"Oh my God," said Cindy. "That's right. Sovereign immunity. Title to the wreck goes to Portugal under *Odyssey Marine*."

My mouth fell open. "That means no one else can get a piece of the wreck. The *Flor de la Mar* is Portugal's sovereign property. The only way Rockweiller gets it is through its deal with Portugal. But if we try to ask for Marcum's finder's fee..."

"...Rockweiller will say it never had rights to the property at all," Cindy finished. "And they can't give what they never had, so they can't give a percentage to Marcum. Any contract would be null and void."

Remington nodded. "That's right, kids."

"They screwed us," I said stupidly. "They totally screwed us. That's why they filed in Florida. So if we ever found out about the contract, we would have no way to enforce it."

"That may be one reason. But I suspect there are others. There are bigger players waiting in the wings," Remington said cryptically.

I didn't know what he meant by that, but just then I was too pissed off to care. "Those assholes," I seethed, imagining Bock's sneering face. "What are we going to do about it?"

"Good question," said Remington. "And while we're at it, there's another problem I should mention."

"What's that?"

"We don't have the contract."

I looked confused. "Yeah. But Riker can testify about it. At least he can prove it existed. Right?"

"How?" said Remington. "It's hearsay."

Hearsay is secondhand information. Something that you hear from someone else. You can't use hearsay to prove things in court. It's too unreliable. People would make up all kinds of things and try to pass them off as the truth. Because Riker hadn't seen or heard anything directly, his testimony would be hearsay and inadmissible in court.

"Even if it wasn't hearsay, I doubt Riker would volunteer to testify," Remington added. "And good luck subpoenaing him from across the Atlantic." I opened my mouth to argue with this but couldn't think of anything to say.

"Finally," concluded Remington, "we don't even know what the contract says. If there is one. The finder's fee could be one percent. It could be fifty percent. Or it could be nothing. We don't know the terms, and we don't know who signed it. In short, a hearsay statement about a contract that we don't have, that we're not sure even exists, isn't going to cut it."

We all looked down, pondering these seemingly intractable problems. "Do you believe Riker?" I asked Remington eventually. "Do you think there was a contract?"

"Yes."

Cindy looked surprised. "Why? Riker doesn't seem like the most trustworthy character. He may have just told us what we wanted to hear to get fifteen grand."

Remington nodded. "Maybe. But I've been wondering what David Marcum was doing mixed up with these guys. This explanation makes sense. And I'll tell you this: if there's a contract, I guarantee it was in writing, and Marcum kept a copy of it somewhere."

"What? How do you know that?"

"Think about it," he explained. "Everything we know about David Marcum suggests he's a smart cookie. He covers his tracks. He found, who the hell knows how, a five-hundred-year-old treasure, which has eluded the most experienced, well-informed treasure hunters for centuries. Even if Marcum trusts this Gunthum character, what are the odds that he gives out the location of the *Flor de la Mar* without a written contract to back it up?"

I sat back. "The odds are not good."

"So where is the contract?" Cindy interjected. "Shouldn't Rockweiller have given it to us in discovery?"

"They may be hiding it or withholding it in some clever scheme. But my guess is if there was a contract, only Gunthum had it. And he may not have given it to his bosses, or even told them about it at all."

We thought about that for a while. "Then we need to figure out where David Marcum would have kept the contract," I said. "But how?"

"I don't know."

"What do we do now?" Cindy asked.

"Three things," said Remington, ticking them off on his fingers. "First, we need to figure out some way around this *Odyssey Marine* ruling in Florida. If we don't do that, Marcum is never going to get his piece of the *Flor de la Mar*, whether there's a contract or no. Second, we need to find this contract, if it exists. And finally, we need to figure out how the hell David Marcum found the *Flor de la Mar*."

We all nodded thoughtfully as we considered the scope of these tasks.

Then, for some reason, I started to grin. "Is that it?" I asked Remington. He looked surprised, but then caught my attitude and grinned back at me. "All we have to do is find a way around the law, and beat out one of the biggest oil companies on the planet? Not to mention a sovereign nation of like, what, twenty million people?"

"Ten million!" Cindy interjected.

I scoffed. "Only ten? Piece of cake."

My energy was infectious, and pretty soon everyone else was grinning too. I could feel a fierce energy building around the table. We were going to do this, I thought. We were going to go for it.

"And don't forget," added Harder, "we also have to figure out how David Marcum solved one of the greatest mysteries of all time."

"Pshhaw!" said Kruckemeyer with a flamboyant wave of his hand. "No problem. Like taking Mongolian barbeque from a baby. Right, Jack?"

I laughed. "Exactly right!"

"A walk in the park," said Harder with bravado.

"And if we can do all that?" said Cindy. "Then what?"

"If we can do all of that," Remington answered, "then we've got a snowball's chance of hell at claiming David Marcum's share of the *Flor de la Mar*."

Over the next few weeks, we scrambled madly to answer Remington's questions. Cindy, Harder, and I pulled every Florida case for the last twenty years that had anything to do with shipwrecks. We pored over them, hoping to find some exception to the Eleventh Circuit's ruling in *Odyssey Marine*. We read every treatise about maritime law we could lay our hands on, determined to find something that would help. The rancor between Harder and me was gone now, and we worked together for the good of the case.

We also scoured the rules for procedural tactics. In the famous *Pennzoil v. Texaco* case, Joe Jamail's team had exploited a loophole to get the case out of Delaware, where they were sure to lose, and into Texas, where they eventually went on to win the biggest judgment of all time. To do that, they used an obscure procedural rule that allowed them to withdraw the lawsuit if the other side hadn't filed an answer, which is a routine pleading in a case. Texaco had neglected to file an answer in the rush of the litigation. So Jamail was able to yank the suit and re-file it in Texas. But I wasn't as brilliant as Jamail's brain trust, and I couldn't think of anything.

While we did all that, Ashley and I racked our brains trying to think where David Marcum might have kept the contract. The obvious answer was that he'd saved a copy in his email, or on his phone or computer. But we couldn't get access to those. And anyway, I doubted Marcum would put his faith in servers that could get hacked. Nor did I think he would leave a copy with a lawyer, like I might have. I suspected he would have used a more old-school method.

My most brilliant idea was to check Marcum's old room at the Aqua Ray dive resort with a magnetometer. We called Trevor Thompson and asked him to do it. I thought Marcum might have hidden more gold coins there, and maybe the contract as well. Thompson was happy to help. He rustled up Jared Diamond and they went in there while we stayed on the phone. I heard some shouting as Thompson evicted the occupant of the room, who sounded like a middle-aged white guy. The guy asked what the hell Thompson was doing in his room at 7:30 in the morning, and Thompson roared back that this was a dive shop and not a bed-and-breakfast, and that he ought to be out diving anyway instead of eating a ham soufflé. Another five-star review, no doubt. But although Thompson and Diamond searched every inch of the room, they found nothing.

Finally, we still had no idea how Marcum had located the *Flor de la Mar* in the first place. That was when I decided to study up on the matter.

TWENTY-ONE

I spread out a set of dusty old tomes in the firm library. No one used the library anymore now that legal research was online. The place was an anachronism. But it was quiet and spacious, and I liked to work there sometimes. The only inhabitant was Lyle, who waved at me as I walked in, and then silently returned to his work.

To figure out how David Marcum had found the *Flor de la Mar*, I resolved to learn everything I could about the ship myself. But real information about the wreck proved scarce. Online, I found little more than bits and pieces cobbled together in random articles and web pages. Some of it was consistent, and some of it was not.

To sort out truth from fiction, I turned to the source material. I had Lyle track down a copy of the *Commentaries of the Great Afonso Dalboquerque, Second Viceroy of India*. The *Commentaries* were Albuquerque's firsthand account of his exploits in Asia and the Orient, published in 1576 by his son, Braz. They were taken from Albuquerque's own letters and dispatches to King Don Manuel of Portugal. In them, Albuquerque described the capture of Malacca and the sinking of the *Flor de la Mar*. The *Commentaries* were the primary source for much of what was known about the ship, and Schnizzel had recommended I start there.

The following facts were known: Albuquerque had set sail on the *Flor de la Mar* in late 1511. With him were three other ships: the *Trinidad*, the *Enxobregas*, and an unnamed junk, a type of Chinese vessel. A few days into the voyage, on the night of November 20, a terrible typhoon struck the fleet. The ships made for the coast, hoping to find safe harbor. But the *Flor de la Mar* struck some dangerous underwater shoals and foundered. Her hull split in two, and she sank to the bottom. Albuquerque wrote of the sinking:

> ...the Pilots of Afonso Dalboquerque's ship not being on their guard concerning certain shallows which were situated off that part of the coast of Çamatra, just opposite to the kingdom of Darú, ran the ship *Flor-de-la-Mar* ashore upon them in the night, and the vessel, being by this time very old, broke up into two parts directly she struck. . . .
>
> Afonso Dalboquerque gave the order that a raft should be prepared with boards placed upon some timbers, and he got upon it, clad in a grey jacket, and lashed to the raft with a rope, lest the waves should sweep him off, and two mariners with him, who with oars improvised out of some pieces of boards, rowed the raft: and so in this plight, and by these means, and also by help of ropes which by Pero Dalpoem's orders were thrown out, tied to buckets, with infinite difficulty he reached the ship *Trindade*.
>
> The men who were left in the wreck of the *Flor-de-la-Mar*, seeing themselves already come to the last day of their lives, began with loud cries and complaints to

> shout after Afonso Dalboquerque, who was making way on the raft, and he, touched with profound pity at the sight of them in this sad state of misery, told them not to be alarmed, but to put all their trust in our Lord, for he would promise them that he would not desert them, even if he ventured to lose his own life and the other ship and all her company in saving them; and he desired them, in the meantime, to construct another raft, for he would come back without delay for them.[3]

Albuquerque never came back for the crew. Whether he was unable or unwilling, I couldn't say. The ship *Enxobregas* went down with the *Flor de la Mar*. As for the junk, the Javanese natives aboard mutinied and killed the Portuguese. The junk then sailed off to sea, never to be seen again.

The *Flor de la Mar* carried eighty tons of intricately worked golden objects taken from Malacca. These included gilded birds and animals, furniture, ingots, and coins worth millions upon millions of crowns. The ship also carried more than two hundred chests full of diamonds, emeralds, sapphires, rubies, pearls, and every kind of precious stone. Sadly, the *Flor de la Mar* had carried human cargo as well. As Albuquerque wrote:

> In this ship, *Flor-de-la-mar,* and in the junk which mutinied against us, there were lost the richest spoils that ever were seen since India had been discovered until that moment; and besides this, many women who were greatly skilled workers in embroidery, and many young girls and youths of noble family from

[3] *The Commentaries of the Great Afonso Dalboquerque, Second Viceroy of India, Volume III,* Translated from the Portuguese Edition of 1774, with notes and an introduction by Walter de Gray Birch, F.R.S.L.

> all those countries which extend from the Cape of Comorim to the eastward, whom Afonso Dalboquerque was carrying to the Queen D. Maria. They lost the castles of woodwork, ornamented with brocades, which the King of Malaca used to carry upon his elephants, and very rich palanquins for his personal use, all plated with gold, a marvellous thing to behold, and great store of jewellery of good and precious stones which he was carrying with him in order to send it as a present to the King D . Manuel. And they lost a table with its feet all overlaid with plates of gold, which Milrrhao presented to Afonso Dalboquerque for the king, when the lands of Goa were delivered up to him . . . . nothing was saved except the sword and crown of gold, and the ruby ring which the king of Sião sent to the King D. Manuel; but that which Afonso Dalboquerque grieved for most of all in this loss was the bracelet which had been found upon Naodabegea , for he brought it with great estimation in order to send it to the king, because the efficacy of it was so very admirable. So also he felt very much the loss of the lions, which he brought because they were found on certain ancient sepulchres of the kings of Malaca, and he took them with the intention of placing them on his own tomb in Goa as a memorial of the achievement of taking Malaca; and, of all the spoils which were then taken, he reserved only these two things (the bracelet and lions) for himself, for as they were of iron they were [not] of great value.

All of this was widely agreed upon. Where things started to get hazy was where the *Flor de la Mar* sank. All of the sources said that it went down in the Strait of Malacca. But just where in the Strait, no one was sure.

The *Commentaries* said that the ship ran aground on some shallows just opposite the Kingdom of Daru. Another source said the ship sank off Timia Point. The problem was that no one knew for certain where these places were anymore. Many of the countries and kingdoms that existed in 1511 no longer existed, and coastlines had moved over the centuries. In the early days of exploration, locations were approximate, and maps and accounts were often inaccurate. Although there were many theories about where the ship had gone down, no one had managed to find it.

The *Flor de la Mar* wasn't the only ship to have disappeared in the Strait of Malacca. There were some dark legends surrounding the place. One was the *SS Ourang Medan*, a Dutch vessel that disappeared in the Strait in the 1940s. The last message it sent was "all officers including the captain are dead, lying in chartroom and bridge. Possibly whole crew dead ... I die." A nearby ship responded to the distress call and found corpses everywhere on board the ship, with eyeballs popped out and eyes agape, but no sign of what caused it. An assistant to Director of the CIA at the time wrote that he felt "sure that the *SS Ourang Medan* holds the answer to many of these aeroplane accidents and unsolved mysteries of the sea."

It was easy to dismiss the *Ourang Medan* as a ghost story. But there had been modern disappearances in the Strait of Malacca too. Perhaps the most well known was Malaysia Airlines Flight 370, which disappeared in 2014. It was last caught on radar going north up the Strait before vanishing just past Sumatra. I remembered how it had boggled my mind that, in the modern era, with the whole world looking for something as big as an entire airplane that went down in a known area, it was never found. If Malaysia Flight 370 could be lost in the Strait, it seemed plausible that a ship as famous as the *Flor de la Mar* could be lost there as well.

People had searched for, and even claimed to have found, the *Flor de la Mar* many times. Including recently.

In 1989, Southeast Asia Salvage (SEAS) mounted an expedition to find the ship. They based their search on the sources saying that the ship was lost near the Kingdom of Daru, that survivors managed to reach the river Pacem (which did not exist on modern maps), and that the wreck sank within cannon-shot of the shore. Believing that they knew where these places where, SEAS spent several years and millions of dollars looking. But they didn't find it.

In 1992, a well-known American treasure hunter named Bob Marx announced that he had found the *Flor de la Mar* with the aid of an old nautical chart. But the find proved inconclusive, and little treasure was recovered. It was also rumored that the former President of Indonesia, Suharto, had spent millions of his own personal fortune to search for the ship. He didn't find it either.

We believed that Excel and Rockweiller paid SEAS and Suharto's foundation for their knowledge. That was what the consulting contracts were for. Anything that would help Rockweiller to find, verify, and salvage the *Flor de la Mar* would have been worth it to them.

After five hundred years, there had never been a confirmed find of the *Flor de la Mar*, and its whereabouts remained a mystery. The reasons for this were debated. Some said that the old maps were off, and that everyone was looking in the wrong place. Others said that the maps were right, but the ship was long since buried by the tides and sands. Still others maintained that the Sumatran natives had scavenged the treasure long ago, and nothing remained. I read a supposed eyewitness account that said the Flor de la Mar had sunk by the beach in four fathoms of water, which would have been within scavenging distance. Albuquerque himself thought this might have been the case, as he said in a letter to King Don Manuel after an attempted return to the wreck site. However, this didn't explain why there was no evidence that the ship sank there.

Some of the wildest theories about the *Flor de la Mar* were on internet message boards like Reddit. One user named Conquistador85 claimed that Alfonso de Albuquerque had faked the sinking of the *Flor de la Mar* and stolen the treasure for himself. Another user, ConspiracyOfFools, said this was hogwash, and that the *Flor de la Mar* was actually a ghost ship that had never really existed at all. Someone once told me that all the truths in the world can be found on Reddit. But apparently not this one.

Scholars said there might have been more information about the *Flor de la Mar* in the Portuguese Royal Archives. The Archives were a library in Lisbon that dated back to the fourteenth century. But the Archives had been destroyed in the Great Lisbon Earthquake of 1755. Many histories of the early Portuguese explorers were lost with them, and some said the truth of the Flor de la Mar was lost as well.

I had a theory of my own. I wondered if one of the many expeditions had been successful, but never told anyone. Knowing the way that these wrecks were fought over, why would they? Better to keep it quiet. Maybe even now someone was sitting atop eighty tons of gold on a private island in Indonesia, master of a great fortune the world thought lost long ago.

I took a break from my readings to eat lunch. I ordered a salad from the local deli. I was trying to watch my weight, especially with all the late nights and junk food. Unfortunately, I was hungry right after I finished the salad, and ended up raiding the vending machine for Fritos.

After finishing two bags of Fritos and the *Commentaries*, I stopped to learn a little about the author himself.

Alfonso de Albuquerque had been one of the great explorers and conquerors of the age. In those days, the line between navigator, general, and statesman was blurred. The King of Portugal granted Viceregal powers to his admirals, giving them *carte blanche* to sail the world and subjugate it in his name. Albuquerque gained fame for subduing Goa, India, which became the foundation of the Portuguese Empire in the East.

A painting of Albuquerque on Wikipedia showed an imperious-looking man with a gray beard that reached down to his waist. He was dressed in a rich robe and holding what might have been a baton or a telescope. He looked like a cross between a rabbi and a conquistador. To ancient Portugal he was a hero. But it wasn't hard to imagine that the people of Asia saw him as a murdering savage who took their wealth, their land, and even their young.

In life, Albuquerque had been a tremendously ambitious man. The *Commentaries* referred to him as "the Great," which was a clear reference to Alexander the Great, the ancient Greek warlord who had inspired so many copycat conquistadors. And the title of the *Commentaries* was an obvious parallel to Julius Caesar's famous *Commentaries of the Gallic War.* Caesar's *Commentaries* were his own personal account of his military exploits in Gaul (modern-day France), written in the same third-person style as Albuquerque's. Indeed, some called Albuquerque the "Portuguese Caesar," and the influence was hard to deny.

The reference also had a dark side. Caesar had returned to Rome a rebel, and after winning the civil war, he had usurped the power of the Senate, laying the foundation for the end of the Republic and the beginning of the Roman Empire. There had been similar whispers about Albuquerque toward the end of his life.

During his long absence from Portugal, Albuquerque's enemies convinced the King that Albuquerque planned to declare himself a sovereign in Asia. Fearing this, the King replaced Albuquerque as Viceroy with one of his rivals. This order was later countermanded, but Albuquerque died before he knew that. So his life ended on a bitter note. Posthumously, King Manuel was convinced of Albuquerque's loyalty, and gave his blessing to Albuquerque's son Braz, who later published the *Commentaries*.

I looked out the library window. It had grown dark. I closed the book and sat back in my chair to reflect.

I thought about what I knew for certain. First, the *Flor de la Mar* sank in the Strait of Malacca, somewhere off the coast of Sumatra. Second, it sank on a reef, close to the shore. Third, many well-prepared expeditions had set out to find the *Flor de la Mar*, and none had succeeded.

This begged the question: How did David Marcum and Lloyd Gunthum find the *Flor de la Mar* where so many others had failed? And how had the ship remained hidden for all these centuries in one of the busiest shipping lanes in the world?

The more I thought about it, the more I believed that Marcum must have stumbled upon new information. An old record, or a new piece of the puzzle. Something that no one else knew. Or maybe he put something together in a way no one else had before. But what was it?

Later that evening, back at my apartment, I cracked open a beer and plated a steaming hot carton of drunken noodles from my favorite Thai restaurant. According to an article I had read online, takeout tasted better if you put it on a plate. So I did that, and took my plated noodles to the TV for an episode of *The Dominator*. I found myself grinning with anticipation. Funny how little things will make your day.

The Dominator had been through some rough fights lately. His face was starting to look like a side of beef gone bad. I watched him flex his huge shoulders as he stepped into the ring. They were completely inked with old green tattoos. His opponent today was named The Vanquisher. I might have felt nervous, wondering if today would be the day The Dominator's reign would end. But I looked at his bald head and grim eyes and knew he couldn't lose. Not now, not ever.

Today's episode featured a sideshow about a court case The Dominator was involved in. He was being sued by The Subjugator, the guy he had knocked out in brutal and unscripted fashion in season two. The two wrestlers faced off in court, dressed in suits instead of speedos. "Dominant Jurisdiction," boomed the narrator, in a voice as heavy as molten lead. I smiled and settled in to watch the show.

Then I froze, and dropped my chopsticks to the floor.

That was it. That was the answer. In a flash, I knew how we were going to beat the *Odyssey Marine* ruling, do an end-run around Rockweiller, and get the hell back into the Marcum case.

I de-plated my drunken noodles, traded my beer for a Red Bull, and cracked open my laptop. It was going to be a long night.

TWENTY-TWO

The United States District Court for the Southern District of Florida was in a new building, made of blue glass with white trim. It was built to evoke a ship, and one side of the building crested higher than the other, like the prow of some great vessel. To me, it looked more like a giant blue wave about to crash down on my head. Modern art is all in the eye of the beholder, they say.

The courthouse looked considerably better, in my opinion, than its Galveston counterpart. But it lacked something. A certain solidity, maybe, that comes with age. The Galveston courthouse had withstood hurricanes that had levelled half of Texas. I doubted this courthouse had withstood anything stronger than a lawyer with yacht money.

Inside the courthouse, there was a great blue well of windows extending upward through a dozen floors into a great skylight. Somehow it reminded me of the wall of coral I had dived with Trevor Thompson, but reversed. This time, the void was up instead of down, toward the light instead of the darkness.

There was a fair amount of press at the hearing, which was the first to be convened in front of the Honorable Judge Jaclyn Merryweather, presiding. I saw Bock discussing the case with a reporter. I caught a snatch of his conversation as I walked by. He said he was "utterly confident" that the judge would award them possession of the wreck. The reporter seemed taken by his assuredness.

Remington ducked past all of this without a glance and walked into the courtroom. No one gave us a second look. The courtroom was spacious and paneled in warm wood. There were high-tech plasma monitors in front of the judge and the jury box, and a giant screen at the back of the room. They were part of some technological initiative that the court was testing.

The courtroom was filled with lawyers, reporters, and spectators. Bock & Co. were there, including the usual trio and others I didn't recognize. Lawyers for Portugal were there too, standing proudly toward the front. The Portuguese ambassador had flown down from Washington, D.C. for the occasion. There were also a number of well-dressed young men and women sitting toward the back, gossiping. I guessed they were law clerks for other judges in the building, come to watch the show.

Remington and I passed the bar in the courtroom and sat down. The bar is what divides the place where the judge, the jurors, and the lawyers sit from where the public sits. There's usually a swinging door that you have to pass through, like in an old saloon. In fact, the reason the lawyer's test is called the "bar examination" is because once you pass, you can literally "pass the bar" in the courtroom. Fun fact I picked up while I should have been studying for the bar.

Remington and I sat down quietly. After a while, the hubbub began to die down and everyone took their seats.

I had been up late the past couple of nights. Remington had immediately seized on my idea, saying it was a good one. He and Kruckemeyer told me to "research the shit out of it" and put together the best legal brief I could. I spent several days doing that, with Cindy and Harder's assistance. Then Remington had taken it over for a day and made it brilliant. We had filed it shortly before the hearing. I doubt that the Judge had read it yet, what with all of the heavy legal motions flying around.

The bailiff called "all rise" as Judge Merryweather entered the room. Everyone stood up. Bock was in front, thrumming with anticipation. Judge Merryweather ascended the bench in her black robes. She looked to be in her early fifties, with a handsome face and raven-black hair that fell mid-shoulder. Merryweather was a well-respected judge who was said to make sound decisions. She sat down and asked everyone to be seated as well.

"Good morning everyone," she said cordially.

"Good morning," chorused the assembled lawyers.

"I see we have people from a lot of different places here today." She looked around the courtroom. "Is counsel for Rockweiller Industries present?"

Bock sprang up and quickly assured her that he was. "And I believe we have lawyers for the nation of Portugal as well?" she asked. The lawyers for Portugal stood up and affirmed that this was so. "Welcome," Judge Merryweather said. "I am honored to have representatives from your great nation in our court today." The Portuguese ambassador looked pleased.

"The honor is all ours," he said with an accent and a courtly bow.

Judge Merryweather turned to another set of lawyers. They were young and serious-looking in dark suits and red ties. They were led by a handsome older man with a shock of gray hair. "I see that we are also graced with the presence of the Department of Justice, representing the interests of the Executive Branch of the United States."

The gray-haired man stood up. "I wouldn't go so far as to say graced, Your Honor," he said with a disarming smile. They seemed on familiar terms. "But you are correct."

"I presume you are here in *amicus* capacity only?" she queried. An *amicus curiae*, literally "friend of the court," meant someone who wasn't directly involved in the case, but had something to say. The United States would often submit amicus briefs in cases involving foreign nations. It was a way of expressing the views of the U.S. executive branch, which the court would consider, but was not bound by.

"Yes, Your Honor. *Amicus* only. The United States isn't seeking title to the *res*. Although I wish we were," he added.

"I think we all share that wish, counselor," the Judge said, and everyone laughed. One of the perks of being a judge, I guess.

"Very well," Judge Merryweather said. "Ladies and gentlemen, I have studied in detail all of the various motions and pleadings before the Court. I can see that this is a case of importance to everyone involved, including foreign sovereign nations.

"I understand that Rockweiller Industries and Portugal have reached an agreement regarding the disposition of the *res*, for which I commend them. However, we will nonetheless proceed with this admiralty action in the usual fashion. I would like to begin by setting a scheduling order, and then hearing everyone's views on the case. I anticipate that you all will want some hefty confidentiality protections in place, given the nature of the matter.

"For now, I'll allow each party thirty minutes to make a statement. We will do that now, unless anyone has anything to say first." She looked around perfunctorily. It was a formality. "Alright," she said. "Let's go ahead and..."

But before she could continue, Remington got up and made his way to the front of the courtroom. The heels of his boots clicked distinctively on the hardwood floors, and every eye turned toward him. Remington approached the front and then stood quietly, waiting for the Judge to acknowledge him.

"Yes, sir," Judge Merryweather said.

"Good afternoon, Your Honor," he said formally. "My name is John Remington. I represent the Estate of David Marcum in this matter. Respectfully, I do have something to say before we begin."

Judge Merryweather looked at him, puzzled. "David Marcum. Yes, I do recall seeing something..." she shuffled through her papers, and one of her clerks handed her a brief.

"I am sure that Your Honor has been receiving many filings, and this one may have slipped through the cracks," Remington said. "There are many illustrious lawyers and important nations here today, and I don't pretend to make that cut."

Judge Merryweather grinned at him. "You sound like you're from Texas, sir," she said. "How can you tell?" he replied in a deadpan drawl, and there was laughter all around.

"Welcome, Mr. Remington. We are pleased to have you. Please speak your piece."

"Thank you, Your Honor. I'll keep this short, because I know you have many things to hear today."

Remington clasped his hands behind his back and looked up at Judge Merryweather. "As you know, the threshold matter that any court must consider is jurisdiction."

Judge Merryweather nodded. Elementary stuff. I looked over at Bock. His eyes narrowed. I saw him almost sniff the air, as if he'd gotten a whiff of something he didn't like.

"As it happens," Remington said, "a case involving this very *res* was filed several months ago, and is currently pending in the United States District Court for the Southern District of Texas, Galveston division."

Judge Merryweather raised her eyebrows. "Galveston?" she asked.

"Correct, Your Honor."

"I was not aware of this."

"I don't believe that Rockweiller Industries mentioned it."

Bock rose to his feet and addressed the Judge. "Your Honor, the Texas lawsuit is a wrongful death case," he said dismissively. "It has nothing to do with this action."

"To the contrary," Remington responded, "it has everything to do with this action. It involves the same *res.* It involves the same parties. And we believe that the wrongful death happened around the same time, and in the same place, as the discovery of the *Flor de la Mar.*"

"Speculation and conjecture, Your Honor!" Bock said. "There's no proof of that. And even if there was, I fail to see the relevance to this admiralty action."

Judge Merryweather, who had been looking back and forth between them like a referee at a tennis match, turned to Remington. "Mr. Bock does have a point," she said. "Assuming all of this is true, what's it got to do with this case?"

"Why, that's simple, Your Honor. If the Texas action involves the same case and controversy, then the Texas court has dominant jurisdiction, and this Court must immediately transfer this action in its entirety to the Southern District of Texas, Galveston Division."

At this, the courtroom broke into commotion. The lawyers were all talking to each other, and the reporters were all talking to the lawyers, trying to figure out what was going on. Judge Merryweather had to bang her gavel a few times to settle everyone down.

This was the flash of insight that I'd had. Dominant jurisdiction was what stopped people from filing the same case in two different places. For example, if Al sues Bob in Houston, then Bob can't just file the same lawsuit against Al because he wanted to be in Dallas. The first-filed court usually has dominant jurisdiction. The same principle applied to cases that were related. The tricky part was how similar the cases had to be.

"Having two parallel cases would be a waste of time for everyone," Remington continued. "It would also risk conflicting decisions, if Your Honor and the Judge in Galveston saw things differently."

"This is ridiculous, Your Honor," protested Bock. "It's pure gamesmanship. This case has no business in Texas. There's nothing in the wrongful death suit that even mentions the *Flor de la Mar*. We have the right to file suit in the venue of our choosing."

Judge Merryweather regarded Remington. "Are the cases similar enough to warrant dominant jurisdiction?" she said doubtfully. "It seems a stretch." Bock nodded vigorously, as if she had got the right answer in Jeopardy.

"They are," replied Remington. "And as to what business this case has in Texas, there is another fact that Mr. Bock failed to mention."

"And what's that?"

"Rockweiller filed a TRO to get back a piece of this very *res* in Houston, Texas. Mr. Bock should know, since he filed the

TRO himself. Once a party intentionally invokes a court's jurisdiction, he can't very well claim that a suit over the same property doesn't belong in Texas."

Judge Merryweather turned to Bock, frowning. "Do you have a response to this, Mr. Bock?"

Bock spluttered, caught on the backfoot. "The TRO has nothing to do with this. It...that was state court. And the TRO has since been dissolved. Further," he added, grasping at something, "it would be inappropriate to have a case like this, involving sovereign nations, heard in some backwater court in Galveston, Texas. They don't have the capacity to handle it. The Florida courts have superior expertise in these matters."

"I take exception to the notion that this Court has superior expertise to the Galveston Court, Mr. Bock," Judge Merryweather said sharply. "Please watch your comments."

"Of course," said Bock, not looking sorry at all.

Judge Merryweather turned back to Remington and looked at him squarely. "Mr. Remington, does the case law really require a transfer in this situation?"

The truth was, probably not. I'd done the research, so I would know. We had enough to make a colorable argument. We could say it with a straight face. But dominant jurisdiction was a stretch here. Remington said it probably wouldn't fly, particularly with a judge as savvy as Merryweather. But we had a plan. Remington had drafted a pinch hitter, you see.

"I believe a transfer is warranted," said Remington. "However, Your Honor need not hear it from me. We took the liberty of filing our briefs in the Galveston court as well, so that the Judge there would have the benefit of the argument."

Judge Merryweather nodded. "When that Judge heard of

this hearing," Remington continued, "he thought it might be best to participate."

Judge Merryweather frowned. "I would certainly welcome the participation of a fellow judge. But I am not certain how he is planning to do so..."

Remington nodded to a clerk, who stood ready. On his signal, the clerk flipped a switch. We all felt a humming glow as the big screen behind us lit up in full color. Judge Merryweather looked up incredulously toward the back of the room, as did everyone else.

There, on the gigantic screen in the back of the courtroom, in full color and about three times life size, was Judge Nathaniel Graves, staring down at the courtroom occupants from his high bench in Galveston, Texas.

His voice boomed out, amplified by the excellent speakers at full volume. "Good afternoon, Judge Merryweather. Judge Nathaniel Graves, Southern District of Texas, Galveston Division. How do you do?"

Judge Merryweather was taken aback, but recovered her poise quickly. "How do you do, Judge Graves?"

"Very well, thank you. I hope you don't mind the intrusion. I was informed that we had a case of conflicting jurisdiction, and I thought the question might be best settled with my participation." He smiled slightly and cast his eye across the crowd, all of whom were staring up at him in awe.

Although I had helped engineer this, I still couldn't believe it. I had never seen, or even heard of, a judge attending a hearing in another judge's case, by video or in person. It was highly irregular. The older lawyers were speechless. The journalists were scribbling away gleefully, eating it up. I heard one of the young clerks whisper "awesome." Since the pandemic, videoconferencing technology had become more common in courtrooms. But this was something else. I looked over at Remington and saw that he was trying to suppress a grin.

"Not at all," said Judge Merryweather diplomatically. "The Middle District of Florida has great respect for its sister federal courts in Texas, and welcomes you to the hearing, in any capacity in which you choose to participate. Can I offer you anything?" she added with a faint smile. "Coffee? Tea?"

Graves' laughter boomed over the speakers, shaking the room with its heavy bass. "No, thank you," he said. "But I appreciate the offer, and the warm welcome. Now, would you mind if I addressed the attorneys?"

"By all means."

Graves took off his large reading glasses and peered at the attorneys through the camera. "Is Mr. Zachary Bock here?" asked Graves.

Bock looked around the room for some reason, as if looking for himself. "Yes, Your Honor. Hello. I am here."

"Hello, Mr. Bock. Do you remember me?"

"Yes, Your Honor," said Bock. I saw him swallow hard.

"Good. You filed this lawsuit, correct?"

"Yes, Your Honor. Although I will note that the lawsuit was joined by the Republic of Portugal, and—"

"Thank you for that note, Mr. Bock," said Graves, cutting him off. "I also thank you for your comments during this hearing, which I found edifying." Apparently, he had been listening in.

"Thank you, Your Honor, although some of the credit must go to my fine associates—"

"I particularly appreciated your argument regarding the 'superior expertise' of the Florida courts." Smiles began to slip off of faces at Bock's table.

"Your Honor, we didn't say that the courts here are superior, really—"

"You did not?" queried Graves. He put on his glasses again and eyed something in front of him. "A few moments ago, I believe you referred to the 'superior expertise of the Florida courts in these matters. Do you recall saying that, Mr. Bock? Am I reading that incorrectly?" He must have a transcript.

"No, Your Honor," said Bock, backtracking.

Graves' eyes bored into him. "Do you know where the Galveston courthouse is located, Mr. Bock?" he asked.

"Uh, yes, Your Honor. I recall from our hearing there."

"Mmhm. And did you know, Mr. Bock, that if you walk ten blocks in that direction," he pointed offscreen with a big finger, "you will reach the Port of Galveston?"

"I did not," said Bock.

"I assure you that it is so. Did you know that the Port of Galveston abuts the Atlantic Ocean? It is the very same ocean, in fact, that abuts the Southern District of Florida. And the very same one that, approximately four thousand and eight hundred miles away, abuts the Republic of Portugal as well."

"Of course, Your Honor. What I meant, is that this is a sensitive international matter with many implications beyond the United States' shores..."

"Do you not consider the Southern District of Texas, Galveston Division, politic enough to navigate a sensitive international matter, Mr. Bock?"

We were all wincing visibly at this point for Bock.

"Of course I do, Your Honor. But also, there's the matter of the location of the *res*, the availability of the parties and witnesses, and the greater ease of traveling to Middle District of

Florida, as opposed to flying into Houston and driving forty miles to Galveston, Texas..."

Graves whipped off his reading glasses and glared down Bock. "Mr. Bock," he said, "as one of my predecessors in this very courthouse once said, you should be assured that you are not embarking on a three-week-long trip via covered wagons when you travel to Galveston. Rather, you will be pleased to discover that the highway is paved and lighted all the way there, and the trip should be free of rustlers, hooligans, or vicious varmints of unsavory kind.4 You may be surprised to learn, in fact, that there are two major airports within approximately one hour's drive of Galveston, and I am told that one can book flights at either location easily. Even online." This drew a smile from Judge Merryweather, and some guffaws from the gallery.

"Further," continued Graves, "although we may not have the same day-to-day dealings with great foreign powers as our exalted brethren in the Southern District of Florida, you can be sure that we are more than capable of applying the law in an exact and even-handed fashion. Is that clear?"

"Yes it is, Your Honor. However, in the alternative, we also have a *forum non conveniens* argument—"

"I have read your briefs in full, Mr. Bock, including your alternative arguments. I am not persuaded. Unless the Fifth Circuit Court of Appeals, the United States Supreme Court, or the Lord our God—in that order—says differently, the case stays here. Are we clear?"

"We are clear, your Honor. Thank you." He wisely sat down.

---

[4] *Smith* v. Colonial Penn Ins. Co., 943 F. Supp. 782 (S.D. Tex. 1996).

Graves then turned back to Judge Merryweather. "Judge Merryweather," he said politely, "having reviewed the legal arguments in favor of each position, it is my considered opinion that this case belongs in Galveston, Texas. However, I am sensitive to the issue of jurisdiction between the federal courts. If you read the arguments and think differently than I do, I will of course consider your position."

Judge Merryweather nodded and thanked him for his opinion and said that she would consider it as well. Then Judge Graves bid us good day and signed off. The courtroom filled with the sound of excited whispering and chatting as Judge Graves disappeared from the screen. Bock stood there looking shell shocked.

"Other than the jurisdictional issue," Judge Merryweather said at last, after the hubbub had died down, "are there any other pressing issues that need to be resolved at this time?"

"Just one more thing, Your Honor," said Remington.

My stomach tensed up. I looked over at Remington. He hadn't told me about any one more thing.

Judge Merryweather smiled wryly at him. "And what is that, Mr. Remington?"

"Tonight, I intend to file a motion to join the nation of Malaysia as a required party to this action pursuant to Federal Rule of Civil Procedure Nineteen. Malaysia has an interest in the *Flor de la Mar*, and the Court cannot resolve this case without it. I don't know whether you or Judge Graves will be presiding over the case going forward. But I wanted to give you a heads up."

Bock made a choking sound that was lost amid the roar of lawyers, clerks, and reporters as everyone started yelling at each other at the same time trying to figure out what the hell was going on. Judge Merryweather banged her gavel, calling for order, as people rushed in and out of the courtroom, desperate to report this development to the outside world.

In the midst of all this, Remington quietly asked the Judge for permission to leave, which was granted. He walked out of a side door. I tried to follow him, but got caught up in the crowd of people, pressing in on me from all sides. By the time I reached the exit, he was already gone.

One week later, Judge Merryweather issued a brief opinion. She wrote that, having considered the arguments and the applicable law, she had determined that the Texas court had dominant jurisdiction. Accordingly, in the interests of justice, she would transfer the entire *Flor de la Mar* action to the Southern District of Texas, Galveston Division.

TWENTY-THREE

Since Remington had dragged Rockweiller, Portugal, and Malaysia kicking and screaming down to Texas, suddenly everyone wanted to talk to us. We were famous. I was getting half a dozen calls a day from news outlets, asking about the *Flor de la Mar* and David Marcum's death. Remington's response to all media inquiries was a brusque "no comment," so that's what we went with.

The legal gossip blogs had picked up the case too. One of them ran the headline "Big-Dick Federal Judge Reels Shipwreck Case Back To Texas." The article hit the high notes of the Florida hearing and chronicled some of the more colorful episodes in Judge Graves' career. My name was mentioned, and my lawyer friends texted me with such laudatory remarks as "dude, ur in the newz!" or "brah u famous!"

The press also ran segments about David Marcum, including some colorful vignettes from those who knew him. To my amusement, one of these segments featured none other than Trevor Thompson from the Aqua Ray dive resort in Key West, who appeared on MNN for an interview.

Rufus Rockaway, the anchor on MNN, was teasing an upcoming segment about piracy in Somalia. He planned to travel there, go undercover, and interview some pirates first-hand, thereby providing a glimpse to his viewers of life on the high seas. Co-anchor Katie Tyler was listening skeptically as he boasted about the dangers of the operation, and how journalists had been captured there before, when Rockaway interrupted the teaser to announce a special guest.

Rufus Rockaway and Trevor Thompson hit it off immediately. Rockaway spent the first five minutes of the interview lavishing praise on Thompson's moustache, his tattoos, and his "air of savvy seamanship."

Katie Tyler seemed jealous of this blossoming on-screen bromance. She flirted with Thompson aggressively, batting her eyelashes to get his attention.

"Eh?" he said in response to one of her questions about David Marcum's death.

"I said, surely a strong, savvy seaman such as yourself wouldn't have had any trouble excavating the *Flor de la Mar*. Am I right?"

"Are you daft, woman? Marcum was one of the best divers I knew. If he got caught down there somehow, I would have too. That's a fact."

"A fact," echoed Rockaway.

Tyler narrowed her eyes. "I see. I guess I assumed you were better than that."

"She assumed," said Rockaway, rolling his eyes theatrically. "You know what they say about assuming, right, Trev? It makes an *ass* out of *you* and *me*."

Thompson snorted with laughter. "You're damn right, Rufus. You know your stuff. A true journalist." Tyler huffed and gave it up as a lost cause.

"You know *your* stuff, my man," said Rockaway. "Before we sign off, is there anything you would say to David Marcum if you knew he was listening right now?"

"Just this. I hope you're resting in peace, son. If there was any foul play, and I find out about it, there's going to be a reckoning. I hope anyone who did it goes straight to hell."

"Amen, brother," said Rockaway. He and Thompson fist-bumped and signed off.

On a more sobering note, the case had made the international news as well. Malaysia was sharply critical of the *Flor de la Mar* lawsuit. Its bellicose Prime Minister denounced it, and the Minister of Foreign Affairs went even further, calling the *Flor de la Mar* a renegade ship that had sacked and raped the city of Malacca, and Alfonso de Albuquerque a pirate who should have got the hangman's noose.

Malaysia's state-owned media accused Portugal and Rockweiller of engaging in modern-day colonialism with the lawsuit. They said they were no better than the West of five centuries ago, which had killed and plundered and enslaved without regard for the lives of those they called heathens. It was hard to argue with this, and the narrative spread like wildfire across social media. There was a backlash against Rockweiller and Portugal as people learned more about what befell Malacca. A campaign began trending online in support of Malaysia. Whether it was organic or influenced by the government, I couldn't say.

As far as the lawsuit, Malaysia refused to participate in what it called a "sham proceeding" in Texas. It filed a parallel case in its own courts to adjudicate the rights to the *Flor de la Mar*. I had no doubt how that would turn out. There was also a case pending in the International Court of Justice at the Hague. But the Hague had no jurisdiction over the U.S., and little clout in international affairs. It was sort of like a court version of the U.N.

Judge Graves took heat as well. He was denounced as a rogue American judge who had no business interfering with nations thousands of miles away. Some of Graves' more controversial rulings percolated to the fore of the media's attention. I expect he paid about as much attention to this as a bull pays to Snapchat.

It was against this backdrop that Remington called a rare strategy conference in the case. Kruckemeyer, Cindy, Harder, Vijay, and I all gathered in his office. Ashley and Schnizzel had driven in for the occasion as well.

Once we were assembled, Remington wasted no time. "Well gang, we've grabbed the bear by the balls," he said in that colloquial way he had. "And we've stepped into a hot button geopolitical conflict. I called you all here to tell you where I see the case going from here." We waited expectantly as he began.

"We've put Malaysia in a tricky legal position," he explained, folding his arms across his chest. "On the one hand, they want nothing to do with this lawsuit. They will boycott it as a 'sham proceeding,' yada, yada. On the other hand, like it or not, this case is going to adjudicate the rights to the *Flor de la Mar*. And they don't want to be left out in the cold when that happens. So they're going to have to do a delicate little dance for the Court here."

"I have a question," said Cindy, raising her hand as if we were in class. "Why did we bring Malaysia into the case? It may hurt Rockweiller, but how does it help us?" I nodded. I had been wondering the same thing.

Federal Rule of Civil Procedure 19 governed the joinder of required parties in a lawsuit. Basically, there are some cases where you need to have everyone at the table to go the full monte. For example, if your uncle leaves a house to both you and your cousin, you might have to join both you and your cousin in a lawsuit about the house. That's where Rule 19 came in. It allowed you to join parties who were required for a full adjudication of the issue.

That's what Remington had done with Malaysia. Since the cargo of the *Flor de la Mar* had belonged to Malacca, that meant Malaysia needed to be part of the suit. Otherwise, there couldn't be a full adjudication of the rights to the wreck. We understood how Remington did it. Just not why.

Remington looked away for a while and thought about how to answer Cindy's question. "Because we needed a way to reframe the case," he said finally. "Let me see if I can explain.

"We were not in a good legal position in this case," he said. "Rockweiller and Portugal have a strong case for the *Flor de la Mar*. Stronger than us, no matter what some contract may or may not say. And even though we're out of Florida, sovereign immunity remains a tough hurdle to clear.

"By bringing Malaysia into the suit, we've changed the conversation. Now, you have two rival sovereigns seeking title to the *Flor de la Mar.* And Malaysia arguably has a better moral claim to it than Portugal. The two sovereigns' immunity cancels each other out, so to speak. That's a crude way to put it, but that's the practical effect. So now, it's anybody's ballgame.

"Besides giving us a shot at the *Flor de la Mar*, the joinder will also stop any deal-making that is going on behind the scenes. I suspect that Rockweiller, Portugal, and Malaysia are all talking. If they make a deal, I guarantee that Judge Graves will rubber-stamp it. And no one is going to care about David Marcum then. By dragging Malaysia into this, we've forced them to become adverse. You've seen the news out of Malaysia. The people are angry. It's going to be that much harder for them to make a deal." My jaw dropped at this master-level geopolitical strategy.

"The final reason," Remington concluded, "is to inflict pain. Like it or not, this is an ugly business. The more trouble we are, the more likely Rockweiller will give us what we want. As an added bonus, this will keep Badden & Bock off our backs. We've dragged all of these eight-hundred pound gorillas into the ring, and now they're going to go at each other instead of us. That takes some of the pressure off."

Remington surveyed the room. "Any questions?" he asked. We all just sat there and gaped at him.

"I don't know if this will play out the way I've said, mind you," he added. "But sometimes, when you've got a bad hand, it pays to shake the box. Create a little chaos. You never know what it might bring. Now. With that, let's talk about where this case is going. Jack, I'll turn it over to you for a legal analysis."

I nodded. This was my moment. Over the last week, I had been absorbed in research, trying to figure out what the law said about ownership of the *Flor de la Mar*. Unfortunately, there was no clear answer. One old treatise said it best:

> I believe that there is no branch of salvage law so little understood and free from misconception to proctors and laymen alike, as the question pertaining to ownership of distressed, abandoned, or wrecked property at sea.[5]

After fifty hours of research, I agreed wholeheartedly. But I did have some idea of what laws the judge might apply, and

[5] M. Norris, THE LAW OF SALVAGE § 157 (1958).

how the case would come out if he did. I wrote a memo about it. I was proud of it.

"Okay gang," I said, handing out copies of my memo and then standing to address the group. "Here's the deal. There are many different laws about ownership of shipwrecks. The outcome will depend on which law the court chooses to follow.

"First, the court could apply the law of salvage. That says whoever finds and salvages at least part of a wreck gets title to the rest. Rockweiller made a salvage claim based on the gold coins and bronze lions that they recovered from the *Flor de la Mar*. If Judge Graves applies the law of salvage, Rockweiller would win.

"Second, there's the law of sovereign immunity. That would mean whatever country owned the ship would win. In this case, that's Portugal, and by extension, its ally Rockweiller. But sovereign immunity is tricky here because of Malaysia. The court might find the ship's cargo to be the sovereign property of Malacca. Then, Malaysia would win.

"Third is the law of territorial jurisdiction. All countries have ownership rights over their territorial waters. They extend twelve miles out to sea. The *Flor de la Mar* sank off the coast of Sumatra, we believe, which is part of Indonesia. Although Indonesia isn't part of the case—yet—if the court applied the law of territorial jurisdiction, Indonesia would win.

"Fourth, you've got the law of equity. Equity is a fancy word for fairness. Whenever courts talk about equity, they basically do whatever they think is right. If the court did that, maybe it would award the *res* to Malaysia. Or split the baby. It's hard to say.

"Finally, there's the law of finds. Basically, that's a fancy way to say 'finders, keepers.' The law of finds only applies to property that is unowned or abandoned, though, where no one has stepped forward to claim it. Obviously, that doesn't apply to the *Flor de la Mar*. Courts almost never apply the law of finds, and I don't see it coming into play here.

"Our claim is derivative of Rockweiller's. It's based on contract. Our task is to prove that a contract existed between Rockweiller and Marcum. If we can do that, we may be able to get part ownership of the *Flor de la Mar.*

"There you have it," I said in conclusion. "Any questions?" Everyone stared at me, bewildered. Had I not explained it well?

"There's something I don't understand," said Harder, raising his hand at Remington. "About sovereign immunity. Didn't the Eleventh Circuit in the *Odyssey Marine* case already decide this issue? They said that the country which owned the ship gets title to the wreck and its cargo. And the company that found and salvaged it gets nothing. I get that Judge Graves isn't bound by *Odyssey Marine*, because it's a different court. But isn't this case basically the same thing? Doesn't the law dictate the same result?"

Harder made a good point. The *Odyssey Marine* case had said that the Spanish warship *Nuestra Señora de las Mercedes* belonged to Spain, including her cargo of silver, even though it had been found by Odyssey, and the silver came from Peru. Under the law of sovereign immunity, the court said that the ship and her cargo were one and the same. Here, we had the same situation. The *Flor de la Mar* was a Portuguese warship, found by Rockweiller, which was carrying gold from Malacca. Arguably, it was the same exact scenario, and should come out the same way.

"Pshaw," Kruckemeyer said dismissively. "The law? Law's so wishy washy here that the judge can do whatever the hell he wants. Then he'll dress it up in fancy language and call it the law. Like the U.S. Supreme Court does. The outcome of this will probably depend on what Graves eats for breakfast."

Remington smiled. "Bob makes a good point. As Jack ably explained, the laws governing this situation are so conflicted that there's no clear answer. That means Judge Graves has a lot of leeway.

"Some judges act like the law always dictates the result. As if foreordained. But that's not always true, especially in tough cases. Law isn't practiced in a vacuum. Judges think about the practical effects of their decisions. Even if they dress them up in the language of law. And every case is unique. For example, this case differs from the *Odyssey Marine* case in an important way."

"What's that?"

"Geography."

Remington picked up a globe from his desk and set it in front of us. "Where did Odyssey Marine Exploration find the wreck of the *Nuestra Señora de las Mercedes*?" he asked. His voice had taken on the Socratic tone.

"A hundred miles off the southern coast of Spain," Cindy answered.

"That's right," said Remington. He turned the globe toward Spain. "And where did the *Mercedes'* silver cargo come from?"

"Peru."

"Right." Remington turned the globe to South America. "Peru is on the west coast of South America. The silver was shipped overland to Uruguay, and then put on the *Mercedes*, bound for Spain. Now. How far is Spain from Peru?" We didn't know that, so he answered it himself. "Six thousand miles." He showed us the distance, spanning the Atlantic Ocean with his fingertips.

"Think about it," Remington said, putting down the globe. "You have two countries claiming rights to the *Mercedes.* On the one hand, you've got Spain, which is a hundred miles away. On the other hand, you've got Peru, which is six thousand miles away, across the Atlantic Ocean and an entire continent. Who do you think is going to win?"

"But why should distance matter to the law?" Cindy asked.

"Maybe it shouldn't. But it does. Just like in real estate, location matters. In our case, the *Flor de la Mar* is lying somewhere in the Strait of Malacca. Right in the backyards of Malaysia and Indonesia. Compare that to Portugal, which is seven thousand miles away. And Judge Graves, who is sitting in an American court, refereeing things from ten thousand miles away. Do you see how that matters?

"Also, you have to consider how these countries would react to a ruling," Remington explained. "Would Malaysia and Indonesia just sit there and take it if they lose this case? Would they respect the judgment of a U.S. court? What happens if they don't? I guarantee these are questions that Judge Graves is thinking about."

"I have another question," said Cindy. "Who's going to win?" Her blue eyes were guileless, as usual, as she looked at Remington. Kruckemeyer guffawed, and Remington smiled. "That's the billion-dollar question, isn't it?" Remington said. "I don't know who's going to win, Cindy. But if you want my best guess, here's what I think: if things stay the way they are now, my money would be on Judge Graves dismissing the case on sovereign immunity, and making no comment on who owns the wreck at all.

"That would be the most politic result. It would keep America from getting involved with a shipwreck hundreds of years old, and thousands of miles away, which involves difficult legal and moral questions about things that happened a long time ago. It would avoid pissing anyone off, which would be the inevitable result of awarding it to someone. And it would also avoid the tricky situation of whether a U.S. judgment would even be respected in this situation.

"But on the other hand, Rockweiller and Portugal have a strong case on the law. The Eleventh Circuit went their way in *Odyssey Marine*, and that is a very persuasive opinion. As Richard recognized, it's basically the same case, decided under the same law. Binding or not, it will be difficult to disregard.

"Judge Graves is a wildcard. He has strong beliefs. And he's not one to be intimidated. But he is also a realist. He will understand these things, and consider the ramifications in his decision. Ultimately, I don't know what he will do. Nor do I know what will happen on appeal. If the Fifth Circuit is of a different mind, they will reverse Graves. That's a whole different ballgame. There's even the possibility that the U.S. Supreme Court could get involved. I just don't know."

We all sat around and pondered the seemingly endless legal and political conundrums arising from the case. "Finally," said Remington, "all of that assumes everything stays the way it is now. Which it never does. So we will have to see how the case develops."

"Okay. What about us?" Cindy said. "What do we need to do?"

"We need to focus on our tasks: figure out what happened to David Marcum, figure out how he found the *Flor de la*

Mar, and figure out where he put that contract, if there is one."

"What if we don't find the contract?" Cindy asked.

"Then we are probably out of luck," Remington admitted. "At least with respect to the *Flor de la Mar*. There may be one more thing we can try. But I'd rather not go there." I opened my mouth to find out what it was, but then Kruckemeyer started talking, and the moment passed. Later, I would wish I had asked.

TWENTY-FOUR

It was 11 p.m. on a Tuesday night. Cindy, Harder, and I were all crammed into the war room.

Kruckemeyer said that we needed a war room if we were going to war. So we commandeered a conference room and put a sign on the door that said "Marcum War Room." We put up some décor as well. Schnizzel loaned us a bust of an ancient galleon. I brought my globe and TV. And Harder tacked up a picture of Alfonso de Albuquerque, that great conquistador, to give the room a more martial flavor. Cindy disapproved, but Harder outranked her, so the picture stayed. I looked up at him from time to time and wondered what he would think of all this. But he only glared down at me imperiously.

The war room was a mess of documents, laptops, and legal treatises strewn everywhere. Snack wrappers, diet cokes, and cartons of Chinese takeout littered the floor, testaments to our dedication.

We all looked up as Vijay walked in with a thick stack of papers. "Fourth motion to strike," he announced, slapping down copies in front of us. We had drafted Vijay to help on the case, because there was so much work to do. We also had several paralegals and assistants working on it full time.

"Another one?" Cindy groaned. "What are they trying to strike now?"

"They're moving to strike our objections to their last motion to strike."

"Seriously?"

"Serious as Quinto's hemorrhoids."

We laughed. At the last court hearing, we had noticed Quinto furiously scratching his behind. I maintained it was a simple case of swamp-ass from the Galveston humidity. Vijay and Harder thought it was more. We had a bet, although I didn't know how we'd resolve it. Serve interrogatories, maybe.

"Who wants to take this one?" said Vijay, brandishing the fourth motion to strike. "Harder?"

"Don't look at me. I'm handling the latest motion to quash Gunthum's deposition."

"Quash," Vijay repeated. "What a weird word."

"Quash," I echoed, chewing the word around in my mouth.

"What does it even mean?" asked Cindy.

"It's like squash without the 's,'" Vijay said unhelpfully.

Eventually, after some griping, Harder agreed to handle the fourth motion to strike. "Fine," he said. "But I want Taco Bell."

"You got it," I said. "Vijay, I think it's your turn to make a run." Vijay nodded and began jotting down orders for grilled stuffed waffle chalupas and other exotic fare from the late-night menu. I sat back for a moment to catch my breath.

Badden & Bock trying to bury us in legal motions. As the big hearing date approached, they had filed a motion to dismiss for lack of subject matter jurisdiction (saying the judge didn't have authority to hear our case); a motion to dismiss for failure to state a claim (saying that even if he did, we didn't have a case); a motion for summary judgment (saying that even we had a case, we should lose); five different motions to compel; two motions for sanctions; and a never-ending parade of motions to strike, motions for more definite statement, and objections to everything under the sun.

People dismissively refer to this stuff as "paperwork." But each of these motions had legal arguments that could hurt or even kill our case. Some of them were bullshit, but some of them were real. And even the bullshit ones were compelling, with arguments citing a dozen different cases that went their way. Remington thought the sheer amount of motions they were filing was going to piss off Judge Graves. But Graves was thorough, and he would read them all anyway. So we had to put our backs into it.

I felt outgunned. Frankly, Bock & Co. were better than us. Their writing was better. Their research was stronger. Their work ethic was greater. I couldn't imagine what it would have been like if Remington hadn't dragged Malaysia into the case. For all the ammunition that Badden & Bock was throwing at us, they were throwing ten times more at Malaysia. Marcum's death was important, but it was dwarfed by Malaysia's claim to the multibillion-dollar wreck.

As if all that weren't enough, Indonesia had intervened in the case too. The *Flor de la Mar* was thought to have sunk off the coast of Sumatra. That would put it squarely in Indonesia's territorial waters. So Indonesia had filed a claim to the *Flor de la Mar* as well. Malaysia and Indonesia had a love-hate relationship, I had learned. Sort of like a bad marriage. They usually got along fine, but there were scuffles. This had turned into one of them, and the countries traded increasingly harsh rhetoric as the case wore on. There were even rumors that India and Thailand might enter the fray. The *Flor de la Mar* wasn't only carrying the treasures of Malacca. It also carried the plunder from Alfonso de Albuquerque's conquest of Goa, India, and a treasure belonging to the King of Siam, now Thailand.

Finally, in a bizarre twist, no less than forty-four individuals had intervened in the case. Each of them claimed to have an interest in the *Flor de la Mar*. Some said they were descended from the people of Malacca. Others, from the Portuguese sailors. One man even said he was the direct descendent of Alfonso de Albuquerque himself. Each of these intervenors filed papers and hired lawyers and demanded to be heard. I imagined Bock's fury at having to deal with these small fry. The number of players in this game was becoming mind-boggling.

Meanwhile, Malaysia and Indonesia were moving mountains to find the *Flor de la Mar* themselves. They had reportedly mobilized their entire naval and intelligence apparatuses to the task. They were also filing repeated, heavy motions asking Judge Graves to make Rockweiller tell them where the *Flor de la Mar* was. So far, Graves had refused under the ultrasensitive order. But I wondered what Graves would do if Malaysia or Indonesia found the ship and tried to take it by force. What would happen then?

The U.S. Department of Justice had also expressed an opinion about the case. They filed an *amicus* brief urging the court to dismiss the whole thing. The government saw the case as a lose-lose proposition. No matter who won, the losers would hate America. There was no upside. The tone of the *amicus* brief was extremely respectful, though. They knew Judge Graves' temperament, and how he felt about interference in his cases. There was no mention of David Marcum in the brief. I guess we didn't rate the attention of the G-man.

As tiresome as all this motion practice was, it was the least of our tasks. Judge Graves had set an accelerated scheduling order, and discovery was in full swing. The number of documents being produced was mind-boggling. Terabytes of data flew across file transfer sites every day, and armies of contract reviewers pored through them at a breakneck pace. Although we had a war room, we didn't have an army, so we made do with targeted keyword searches here and there. Other than that, we didn't even try to dam the river of electronic information.

The deposition schedule was like a death march. All of the expert witnesses had to be deposed in the space of a month. Between all of the historians, archaeologists, numismatists, oceanographers, and others—Schnizzel among them—the timetable was insane. Sometimes there were several depositions in one day. A firm like Badden & Bock could cover that much ground, although I suspected it was taxing even for them. But we couldn't. We tried our best, and Cindy, Harder, Vijay, and I split up the important ones and attended as many as we could.

The depositions were savage. The lawyers tried to make mincemeat out of each other's expert witnesses. Badden & Bock questioned how bad the sack of Malacca really was, and tried to bully the Malaysian experts into admitting that the Sultan of Malacca was basically asking for it. Many of the experts weren't used to being deposed. They were hoary old historians, used to teaching lectures at Princeton, now getting lit up by rabid litigators who tore apart everything they said. One poor guy even broke down crying.

I saw Loudamire at some of the depositions. She looked exhausted. Like she was edging the line between sanity and madness. I also saw Cornelius Adipose, one of the associates I'd met at the Judicial Honors Gala. He sneered at me once, but otherwise we had little contact. Lucius Quinto, he of the lacrosse captain vibes, was nowhere to be found. I looked him up online and saw that he had left the firm. So had the other associates I'd met at the gala, Chad Waller and Derek Doniger. I gathered that Zachary Bock was not an easy man to work for. But there were plenty of new Badden & Bock associates to fill the breach, including one tool named Lucas Windsor, who I don't think ever stopped billing. I didn't bother to keep track of all their names.

Every day it seemed there was another hearing in front of Judge Graves over some discovery matter or other. Graves refereed squabbles over everything from what documents had to be produced, to how many depositions could happen in a day, to whether a historian could be deposed again after he was cut short because Bock literally gave him a heart attack.

Amidst all this, we needed to depose Lloyd Gunthum too. At first, Loudamire gave me the runaround. She said they were too busy and there were much more important issues at stake. But I threatened to go to Judge Graves, and she caved and agreed to a date.

The media attention to the case was unrelenting. There was a feeling of high drama to it all; the grand treasure, the ancient history, the rival claimants, the powerful lawyers, the domineering judge, the breakneck pace. Consistent with the gladiatorial sensibilities of American litigation, it had the feeling of a contest, where many would fight but only one would win.

And in the midst of all this, as we tried to keep our heads above water, we also had to keep our eye on the ball: Marcum's death, the contract, and the *Flor de la Mar.*

A half hour after he left, Vijay came back with Taco Bell. He passed out handfuls of Doritos locos tacos, grilled stuffed black jack enchiritos, and double decker supreme jalapeno popper quaesaritos to everyone.

I turned on the small TV and put on MNN, and we all took a little break to eat and watch the latest. Katie Tyler was reporting, as she did nearly every day lately.

"Where's Rufus Rockaway?" Harder asked, his voice muffled by enchirito.

It was a good question. We hadn't seen Rufus Rockaway on MNN for a while. Only Katie Tyler. I found myself missing Rockaway's flamboyant reporting and mannerisms. "I've been wondering that myself," I admitted.

"Maybe he got canned," Vijay said.

"I hope not."

"Maybe Katie will say something about it," Harder suggested. We continued to watch, but Tyler made no mention of Rockaway or where he might be.

"Guys?" said Cindy, interrupting us. She was frowning at her computer screen.

"Cindy," said Vijay in a long-suffering voice. "We've talked about this. It's taco time."

"I know. But Rockweiller filed another motion."

I groaned. "What is it this time? A fifth motion to strike?" I was resigned to the fact that we would be here all night.

"No," said Cindy. "It's a motion to disqualify."

That made me go cold. I put down my food and went to look over her shoulder.

"And there's something else too," she added. "I just got a case notification. Of a new lawsuit, filed by Rockweiller Industries. The subject is legal malpractice."

"Who's the defendant?"

Cindy looked up at me.

"We are."

TWENTY-FIVE

The motion to disqualify hit like a hammer. Rockweiller accused us of gleaning confidential insights into the company's strategy from our past work for them. Then, we had betrayed that confidence and weaponized it against Rockweiller. A conflict of interest.

The lawsuit said the same thing—and also demanded fifty million dollars in damages. The law firm of HH&K itself was the defendant. David Wurlheiser and Bob Kruckemeyer were personally named too.

It was total bullshit. We hadn't used any "confidential insights" from Rockweiller to our advantage. I would know, as I'd been on the case from day one. But as Cindy printed out copies and we began to read, I grew more concerned. Wurlheiser's work was more closely related to the case than I knew. He had drafted the partnership agreement between Rockweiller and Excel Resources. He had also drafted the employment agreements for Lloyd Gunthum and his crew, and the insurance policies that covered them. Finally, he had drafted some settlement agreements for Rockweiller in the past.

We hadn't actually used any of this information. I hadn't even known about it until now. But it looked bad. In theory, knowing that stuff could give us an advantage in the case. And conflicts were as much about appearance as reality. The motion and the lawsuit both had a lot of detail, including a description of the conflicts meeting we'd had. I wondered how they knew all this stuff.

And then I saw it. Rockweiller had gotten their information from a source inside HH&K. And they named him: Richard T. Harder III.

One by one, as we reached that part of the brief, we looked up at Harder. No one said anything. We just stared at him. Harder flipped through the pages, white-faced. Eventually, he got up stiffly and left the room.

The next day, Harder and I were summoned to an emergency meeting of the partners. Copies of the disqualification motion and the lawsuit littered the table. The mood was ugly. Kruckemeyer was reading the lawsuit with a worried look on his face. David Wurlheiser was pacing the room, shaking his head and talking to himself.

Remington looked up at us as we walked in. "Sit down," he said grimly. Harder sat down rigidly in a chair. I sat next to him. "You want to tell us what's going on?" he asked Harder.

Harder nodded. He took a few moments to collect himself. Then he spoke in a wooden voice, his eyes never leaving the table.

"A few months ago, I had dinner with some Badden & Bock associates. Lucius Quinto and Cornelius Adipose. I met them at the Judicial Honors Gala a while back. One day, they called me and asked if I wanted to join them for dinner at Oichi Omakase. I said yes." Oichi Omakase was the fancy

Japanese restaurant I'd seen Harder at, the night I had dinner with Ashley.

"I thought it was just dinner," Harder said. "I didn't see a reason not to go. They seemed like okay people. We didn't talk about the case or anything, at first. Just law school, and work. Life in Houston and New York. That sort of thing."

Harder cleared his throat. "We drank a lot. They kept buying. The conversation started to touch on the case. I tried to stay clear of it. But then they brought up this conflicts thing. They asked whether it was true that HH&K had done some work for Rockweiller in the past. And if it wasn't a problem that we were working against them now."

Harder cleared his throat. "I said yeah, we had done work for them before. But I told them there was no conflict of interest. We had done a thorough conflicts check, I said. And even had a partnership meeting about it." The partners murmured and shook their heads at this revelation. That wasn't good.

"What else did you tell them?" said Remington.

Harder reddened. "I told them about the work that Wurlheiser had done. On partnership agreements, and other stuff. Kruckemeyer asked me to pull those files after the conflicts meeting. So I knew about them."

"Goddamn it!" yelled Wurlheiser, slamming his fist down on the table. "Why did you tell them that?"

"I was trying to show them there was no conflict," Harder said miserably. "That we did the right thing. And it's true. None of this stuff is a real conflict of interest. I wanted them to see that." He was pleading.

Kruckemeyer sighed. "You're right. It's not a real conflict. But it doesn't have to be real to start a lawsuit. You don't need lemons to make lemonade."

"Anything else?" prompted Remington.

"I told them about the conflicts vote. That some of the partners were against it." Wurlheiser cursed.

"That was it," concluded Harder. "I realized I'd said too much. I stopped drinking. I excused myself and left soon after. I haven't heard from them since."

"Why did you go to dinner with them in the first place?" Wurlheiser demanded.

Harder looked embarrassed. But he owned up to it. "I thought I'd made a good impression at the gala. I thought…I thought they might offer me a job."

Wurlheiser shook his head disgustedly. "After dinner," Harder said, "I went to Bob and told him everything."

Wurlheiser whirled on Kruckemeyer. "You knew about this? Why didn't you tell us?"

Kruckemeyer looked uncomfortable. "It's a sticky situation, David. I was trying to think before I brought it to the full partnership. I didn't know if anything would come of it."

"Well, something has," said Wurlheiser. He pointed a finger at Harder, as if charging him with a crime. "This associate disclosed confidential information to an opposing attorney. I want him fired."

Harder's face paled. So did mine. As much as I had my issues with Harder, this was a bridge too far. "Hang on now," I said. "Isn't that a little much? Richard wasn't trying to do any harm. He barely told them anything they didn't already know. They had all the bills and records already. We gave them to them in the first place!"

Wurlheiser rounded on me. "You don't have a say in this. If I had my way, you'd be fired too!" Then he turned back to the partners. "Rockweiller would never have put this together without help. Their old general counsel left. The one

I worked for. You think this new lawyer, Stephanie Rivera, had any fucking idea where those files were? Or what kind of work I did for the company back then? I bet those files were buried at the bottom of a file cabinet somewhere. They never would have seen the light of day!

"I told all of you!" Wurlheiser screamed at the assembled partners. "I told you we shouldn't have taken this case!"

"Calm down, David," said Kruckemeyer, trying to placate him. But Wurlheiser exploded at him.

"Don't tell me to calm down!" he yelled. "They're suing us for fifty million dollars. They've named me personally. *Me!* I'm the one that did the work. They want to take my deposition. All our depositions. It's going to be a nightmare. Lawyers don't make good witnesses. We're going to get screwed!"

"Well, David," Kruckemeyer said gently, "to be fair, you didn't tell us exactly the work you'd done for Rockweiller. You said it was just some general contracts and drafting stuff. We didn't know—"

"You're blaming me for this?" Wurlheiser shrieked.

Kruckemeyer made calming motions with his hands. "No one's blaming anyone, David. We're all in this together."

"And we need to get out of this together. I vote we recuse from the Marcum case immediately. Withdraw and see if Rockweiller will drop the lawsuit."

Remington shook his head. "That's not going to work. They're not just going to drop the lawsuit because we ask nicely. Just the opposite. We show weakness, they smell blood."

Kruckemeyer nodded reluctantly. "John's right," he said. "They're playing hardball now. Rockweiller's mad, and they've got deep pockets."

"Then what are we going to do?" asked Wurlheiser.

Kruckemeyer cleared his throat. "We may have a way out," he said. "Zachary Bock called me this morning and made a settlement offer. For the Marcum case. The offer was two million dollars. He hinted they would drop the lawsuit if we took it. I think we could negotiate that up to three, and make everything go away."

I saw from Remington's slight reaction that he hadn't known about this. Bock had gone behind his back. Bock probably hoped to get a better deal that way, and sow dissension among the partners. I thought about what Remington had said about inflicting pain. It seemed that could go both ways.

"Of course," cautioned Kruckemeyer, "we can't let this new lawsuit affect our decision to settle or not settle the Marcum case. We have a duty to our client. This pressure tactic can't cloud that duty, and it won't." Kruckemeyer looked uncomfortable. "But nonetheless."

Wurlheiser seized on this and voiced his immediate assent. "I say we do it. That's a good deal. Hell, they started out at a quarter million dollars. It's a win and an easy out. Let's take it."

"It is one way out," Kruckemeyer said. "But ultimately, it's got to be the client's decision." He looked at me now. He knew I was in a unique position here because Ashley trusted me.

"Our client is the Estate," said Wurlheiser, "not Ashley Marcum. Tell her she takes the deal, or we drop her."

"She's the executor of the estate," I argued. "That makes her the client. And I'm not going to tell her to take a deal at gunpoint or we'll toss her to the curb."

"You'll tell her whatever we damn well say!" said Wurlheiser.

"No, I won't," I spat back, not caring that I was overstepping my bounds. "This lawsuit is bullshit. And Bock is a bully. I'm not going to fold as soon as they put some pressure on. There's no real basis for disqualification."

"And you know that from what, your five minutes practicing law?" Wurlheiser retorted.

Kruckemeyer agreed. "Jack, you haven't been in this business long enough make that judgment call."

"He hasn't, but I have," said Remington, breaking into the discussion. "And he's right. This is a bullshit lawsuit. They're not going to get fifty million dollars, or even one million dollars. I've handled enough conflicts suits to know this.

"All of this stuff," he said, hefting the lawsuit, "is just fluff. These partnership agreements, settlement agreements, employment agreements—they're just boilerplate documents that Rockweiller uses in a hundred different situations. We didn't 'weaponize' anything against Rockweiller. There's no case here."

"Even if that's true, we'll still have to defend it," argued Wurlheiser. "They've sent deposition notices to me, to Richard, to Bob, to half a dozen other partners. They're going to make this ugly."

"Yes, they will make it ugly. That's the way this works. But it's not easy to get attorney depositions. They're privileged."

"Not always," said Wurlheiser."

"No. Not always."

Another partner spoke up. "Denton's got hit with a thirty-million-dollar malpractice verdict over a conflict a few years back." Denton's was a well-known law firm, one of the biggest in the world. There were murmurs around the table. People remembered it.

"That's true," Kruckemeyer said. "That was a different situation, though. Nothing like here. But still." Kruckemeyer looked troubled. "And there's something else to think about," he added. "This case hasn't exactly been profitable for us. We're putting up a lot of money, and a lot of time, and we don't have much to show for it. And to be honest, John, it doesn't seem like the case is trending our way."

"He's right," said Wurlheiser. "Marcum's death isn't worth that much money. It was a scuba diving accident. Where's the blame for that? You think the Judge is going to come down hard on Rockweiller? If they're offering a good settlement to get rid of us because of this *Flor de la Mar* mess, then let's take advantage. Let's get out while the getting's good."

"As I've explained," said Remington patiently, "I don't think this was a simple scuba diving accident. I suspect there's more to it. It's also possible that David Marcum may have had a deal with Rockweiller Industries, which could entitle him to a portion of the *Flor de la Mar*."

"Suspect," Wurlheiser said dismissively. "May have. It's all speculation. Words!"

"Come on now, John," said Kruckemeyer. "We've turned up no evidence for any of that. It's just not realistic. We did a good job on the case. Maybe it's time we put it down." Many of the partners murmured their agreement.

But Remington was unmoved. "There are ups and downs in every case, Bob. You knew this was a contingency fee case when we took it. Our money comes at the end. And I am convinced that we can get significantly more than two or three million dollars if we stay the course."

"Maybe so," said Wurlheiser, "but it's not worth all of this collateral litigation. I say we take the money, write this off as a win, and move on. Let's vote."

At the first conflicts meeting nearly a year ago, most of the partners had voted to take the case. But now the tide had turned. Wurlheiser's fear was infectious. Bock's pressure tactics were working.

Wurlheiser raised his hand to vote for recusal. Other partners reluctantly followed. The vote had a herd-like feel, as the partners looked around to gauge what everyone else was doing. Eventually, it became clear that more than half the room was in favor. At that point, more hands started to go up.

Kruckemeyer still had his hand down, along with a few others. He looked guiltily at Remington. But it was clear which way the wind was blowing.

Wurlheiser began to tally the vote. All he needed was a simple majority, and he had it. I didn't know what I was going to do. I could tell Ashley not to take the offer, but the firm would probably drop her anyway. They might even drop me too. I didn't have any power here. Hands continued to go up. Harder and I exchanged desperate glances, and I began to despair. How was I going to break this to Ashley? Was this the end of the line?

Then John Remington slowly stood up from the table. Everyone turned to him.

"We're not doing it," he said quietly.

"John," said Kruckemeyer, "Be reasonable. This is a firm decision. We have to make it together. You know that."

"No, it's not a firm decision. I'm lead counsel on the Marcum case. That means the only one that settles or recuses is me. And I say no."

"This is outrageous!" said Wurlheiser. "You have to abide by the vote of the partners. It's in the bylaws. You know that damn well. We can go to the court on behalf of the firm if we have to and withdraw from the case." The other partners nodded. It was true.

"Go ahead," Remington told him evenly. "I'll oppose. Judge Graves would have to approve any withdrawal under Rule 74. We'll see how that circus plays out."

This comment sparked general outrage at Remington, as the other partners spoke up in favor of Wurlheiser, or at least in favor of consensus in decision making. Even I was a little shocked at this display of brinksmanship.

But Remington didn't move a muscle. When the hubbub died down, he spoke. "Like I said, we're not withdrawing, and we're not going to get pressured into any lowball settlement. We have a duty to zealously represent our client, and that's exactly what we're going to do." Then he leaned forward. "And if you all don't like it, you can go to hell."

With this, Remington got up and stalked out of the room, ignoring the storm of shouts and recriminations thrown at his departing back.

I ran after him and caught him in the hallway. "Strong move," I said as we walked down the hall, in awe of what he had done.

"Yes. But I was bluffing."

My face registered surprise. "But aren't you lead counsel?"

"I am. But if the partners force a withdrawal, we'll have to recuse. Wurlheiser is right about the bylaws. And I won't go against the partners like that, no matter how strongly I feel. I'm not going to air the firm's dirty laundry in public." He smiled wearily. "But they don't know that. Which will buy us some time."

"Time to do what?"

"Time to win the goddamn case, Jack."

TWENTY-SIX

The trial in Galveston, Texas was the legal event of the year. Maybe ever.

The old courtroom was packed wall-to-wall with lawyers, reporters, and others who had come to see the action. The lobby had turned into an overflow room, jammed with people trying to get in. Judge Graves had put up a big screen there to broadcast the proceedings.

But all of that was dwarfed by the size of the crowd outside. Thousands of people thronged the courthouse steps, chanting and waving signs like "Stop the Slay," "Finders Keepers," "America First," or "Albuquerque ó Grande," depending on their persuasion. There was even a sign that said, "Save the Whales." Vintage.

The *Flor de la Mar* case had become a lightning rod for criticism from every angle. Anti-corporate groups called Rockweiller a gang of capitalist pigs trying to profit from the heritage of nations. Human rights activists decried Portugal and the West's cruel history of murder, pillage, and slavery in their former colonies. Malaysia had become something of a cause célèbre, and seemed to have the moral high ground. For now. But corruption allegations swirled, and ordinary

Malaysians asked where the money would go. The 1MDB scandal, in which the Malaysian prime minister had been accused of funneling hundreds of millions of dollars in state funds into his personal bank account, was still fresh, and the people remembered the way their money had been squandered.

We arrived at the courthouse dressed to the nines and ready for day one. The whole team was there. Remington, Kruckemeyer, Ashley, Schnizzel, Harder, Cindy, Vijay, Lyle, and me. Our paralegals and support staff were there too.

Behind the scenes, the HH&K partners bordered on a state of open war over the Marcum case. Half of the partners wanted us to recuse immediately, even if it meant Remington leaving the firm, as he had threatened to do. Wurlheiser was trying to force another vote, and was stirring up the partnership against us. Despite some misgivings, Kruckemeyer had come down firmly on our side. He was fighting a rearguard action to block any further votes. But there was only so long he could delay, and the pressure mounted every day.

I glanced over at Harder as we walked toward the courthouse door. He was subdued, as he had been for the last few weeks. The firm hadn't fired him. He hadn't intentionally done anything wrong, and Remington and Kruckemeyer spoke up for him. Ashley and I had forgiven him. But he hadn't forgiven himself. He had stayed apart lately, doing what work he was given and not talking much. I was glad he was with us, though. We needed all the help we could get.

The U.S. Marshals were at the courthouse in force. They had pulled extra personnel from Houston and Dallas for the trial. I waved to the lead Marshal as we arrived. I had gotten to know him during the discovery hearings. His name was Butch. An aptronym if I ever heard one. With his shaved head and huge bulk, he reminded me of no one so much as The Dominator, the star of my beloved TV show. Butch nodded to me and lifted a black cordon. He escorted us inside like VIPs.

Inside the courtroom, Judge Graves sat on his high bench, surveying the multitudes before him. He was dressed in his best black robes and seemed to be enjoying the situation immensely.

The case was going to be a bench trial. That meant that Judge Graves would hear the case and make the ultimate decision himself. There were no jury trials in admiralty, I had learned.

The Seventh Amendment guarantees a right to trial by jury. But not for every kind of case. The way courts decided whether a particular case gets a jury depends on whether that type of case got a jury when the Seventh Amendment was adopted in 1791. If it did, you got your jury. If not, you didn't. Admiralty cases didn't get jury trials in 1791. So we wouldn't get one today. This didn't make a whole lot of sense. But it was consistent, at least.

Graves banged his gavel vigorously as the hour approached nine. It had no effect on the mob, and people continued talking unabated. Graves' bushy eyebrows drew down in a frown. I suppressed a grin, knowing what was coming.

There was a particularly garrulous lawyer standing up front, just a few yards from Judge Graves. One of the intervenors' lawyers. He was arguing animatedly with his associate and paying no attention to Judge Graves' calls for order. Graves beckoned over one of the Marshals.

"Seize him," ordered Graves. The lawyer looked up in surprise as the Marshal approached. He put his hands up. "Okay, okay," I heard him mutter as he sat down. "Yeesh. Relax, guy."

But the Marshal jerked the lawyer to his feet, turned him around, and cuffed him. The lawyer started yelling about due process and his rights under the First, Sixth, and Fourteenth Amendments to the Constitution. "You can't do this!" he shouted. "You can't just arrest me in the courtroom. I demand a stay of this order until I can appeal!"

"Denied," said Graves. "Good luck with your appeal. The Fifth Circuit is sitting in New Orleans this week. Address any postage thereabouts." The Marshal dragged him away. This had the effect of finally quieting the courtroom.

"That's better," said Graves, his good humor restored. "Now, I believe we are ready to begin.

"Ladies and gentlemen," he said in a sonorous voice. "I welcome you to the United States District Court for the Southern District of Texas, Galveston Division. Our little town is pleased to be the site of such a great international event. For those of you who have not been here before, I would recommend visiting the pier for lunch. Try the Gulf oysters. They are excellent."

Judge Graves turned his attention to the attorneys. "To the litigants: I appreciate the gravity of the case to you all. I recognize that I am an American judge sitting in a small beach town in Texas, being asked to rule on events that happened thousands of miles away, and hundreds of years ago, in a time and place far remote from our own.

"I also recognize that a number of sovereign nations are here today. Be assured that I have the utmost respect for you and your people. I will hear your arguments with the keenest of attentions. But I also have respect for the rights of individuals and companies to challenge such great powers, which is the foundation of our republic. Finally, I have the greatest respect for the law itself, and you can be assured I will follow it in my rulings."

Graves smiled broadly. "As those of you who know me can attest, I am a cantankerous old judge. I hope you will indulge me if I make the occasional jab or witticism. But notwithstanding my at-times sarcastic commentary, you can be assured that I and my staff will give your presentations our fullest attention, and after hearing the arguments, the evidence, and the law, I will come to the best conclusion that I can. Thank you."

It was a good speech. I was impressed. The Portuguese, Malaysian, and Indonesian contingents looked pleasantly surprised. The way the media covered the case, they might have expected a provincial old man who spoke in tongues and didn't even know where Malaysia was. But instead, they found an attentive, if iconoclastic, judge who promised to hear them fairly.

"We will now hear opening statements," Graves declared. "Would Malaysia like to begin?" There was a shuffle up front as the attorney for Malaysia stepped forward. His name was Aquil Jafaar.

Jafaar was a small, unassuming man. He wore a scruffy suit that didn't fit him very well. He looked more like an aged schoolteacher than a lawyer. In fact, I thought he looked like a villager who might have lived in the ancient city of Malacca. Jafaar had a patient smile on his face and radiated good humor. There was a marked contrast between him and the high-powered lawyers at Badden & Bock.

But this was all for show. In reality, Jafaar was a well-known trial lawyer in Washington D.C. He was Malaysian-born and educated at Harvard Law. He graduated near the top of his class, and went on to clerk for the U.S. Supreme Court. Now, he was a sought-after litigator in big international cases. Jafaar had represented Fortune 500 companies and sovereigns like Saudi Arabia and China in the U.S. courts. Beneath his humble manner, Jafaar was a killer, and his simple charm had pulled the wool over some bad things his clients had done.

So far, our relations with Jafaar had been cordial. Malaysia was unhappy that we had dragged them into the case. But they were also the biggest winners from the transfer to Texas. Frankly, I thought they ought to thank us. In any case, Remington said we ought to watch Jafaar as carefully as we did Bock.

The courtroom went quiet as Jafaar approached the podium. "Good morning, Judge," he said with a beatific smile. "I am Aquil Jafaar. I represent the good nation of Malaysia. If you will indulge me, I would like to begin with a small anecdote about the ancient city of Malacca. I hope this will give you a flavor of how our city came to be."

Judge Graves nodded and bid him continue. "Malacca was founded in 1400 A.D. by a Sumatran prince named Parameswara," said Jafaar. "According to our legends, Parameswara was out hunting one day, and stopped to rest in the shade of a Melaka tree. There, Parameswara saw a small white animal called a mouse-deer. His hunting dog went after it, and Parameswara thought that would be the end of the little creature. But the mouse-deer kicked the dog in the nose, sending it tumbling into the river, and escaped.

"Impressed by the animal's courage, Parameswara said, 'It is best that we establish a kingdom here; even the mouse-deer is formidable.' And so he did, and named the city after the Melaka tree that had given him shade." Jafaar smiled. "Of course, this is most likely a fable. But it is an old tale, and I hope you do not mind me relating it."

"Not at all," said Graves, bemused.

"During the century that followed," Jafaar continued, "Malacca became a great trading port, and the richest city in all Asia. It had a fine natural harbor and commanded the Strait that bears its name. Malacca means 'to meet,' and indeed the city became the meeting point between traders of the East and the West."

Jafaar flicked on the courtroom's screen, displaying a painting of an old, exotic city by the sea. "Every sort of silk and spice could be found in ancient Malacca," he told us. "Merchants would trade porcelain from China, sandalwood from Timor, fragrant resins from Saudi Arabia, and metals, stones, and artifacts of every kind. The Sultans of Malacca, the first of whom was Parameswara, presided over a thriving, cosmopolitan city in which Malays, Arabs, Persians, and Chinese all lived in peace together. This was the golden age of Malacca, which is remembered still.

"This state of affairs lasted until the early sixteenth century. Then, Malacca was discovered by the Portuguese." The screen flashed to another picture, of the Portuguese arriving at the city. It was notably darker. "Seeing its riches, the Portuguese craved dominion over Malacca, as they did all Asia. In 1511, a Portuguese Admiral named Alfonso de Albuquerque arrived at Malacca with a fleet. He demanded an extraordinary tribute from the Sultan. When the Sultan refused, Albuquerque attacked the city."

Jafaar's expression sobered. "The Portuguese bombarded the city from dawn to dusk with cannon, setting it ablaze. Then they made their assault. Thousands perished, and the city burned. No quarter was given. The people were mercilessly put to death in the streets. In his own memoirs, Albuquerque writes that of the Moors, one ethnic group in Malacca, 'women and children, there died by the sword an infinite number, for no quarter was given to any of them.'

"After subduing the city, the Portuguese stole everything they could carry, and stowed it in their great ships. They took the treasures that belonged to the Sultan of Malacca, and the gold from the wealthiest merchants. They also took hundreds of young Malay boys and girls, ripping them from the arms of their mothers and fathers, to become slaves in a faraway land. These youths never made it to Portugal. They perished, to a boy and girl, during the sinking of the *Flor de la Mar*.

"Your Honor," Jafaar said somberly, "the Portuguese burned down the city of Malacca and slaughtered its people. They took its wealth and its sons and daughters for their own, on the pirate ship known as the *Flor de la Mar*. These treasures rightly belong to the people of Malacca, which is today part of the proud nation of Malaysia. I humbly request that the Court honor their memory, vindicate their rights, and grant Malaysia title to the treasures of the *Flor de la Mar*." There was a resounding silence in the courtroom as Jafaar finished his tale. Judge Graves' expression was unreadable.

After that, Jafaar launched into his legal argument. It was impressive. He talked about sovereign immunity, and pointed to cases that went his way. He distinguished the *Odyssey Marine* case, explaining why it was different and the court should not follow it. In all, he talked for about an hour before thanking Judge Graves and sitting down.

After Jafaar, it was Bock's turn. I had watched him during Jafaar's presentation. He sat like a racehorse, barely able to contain himself from bursting out the gate. When his moment came, he sprung up from his seat and buttoned the jacket of his best dark suit and tie. Then he stood proudly and faced Judge Graves.

Bock had a difficult road to walk. He didn't have the moral high ground like Malaysia did. Rockweiller's claim to the *Flor de la Mar* hinged on Portugal. And Portugal had sacked the city of Malacca and taken its treasures for her own. I saw the lawyer for Portugal watching from the sidelines. He was an older man with a bushy gray moustache. He deferred to Bock on everything, and I could never remember his name.

Kruckemeyer once told me that if you don't have the facts, you hammer on the law. And that's what Bock did. "Good morning, Your Honor," Bock began. "I stand before you as the representative of Rockweiller Industries, a great American company. I also stand before you on behalf of the nation of Portugal, a proud country with maritime roots over a thousand years old.

"Let me first tell you what we are *not* here to do." Bock clasped his hands behind his back and paced across the courtroom. "We are not here to re-fight old wars. We are not here to air old grievances. We are not here to judge who was right and who was wrong centuries past.

"Instead, this case presents a straightforward question of law: does sovereign immunity apply to a Portuguese warship that sank five hundred years ago? The answer is yes."

Bock drew his remote control like a pistol and switched on his presentation. He displayed a brilliant picture of the *Flor de la Mar*. The ship was beautiful, with high forecastles and blooming white sails full of the wind.

"Last year, Rockweiller Industries discovered the wreck of an ancient Portuguese carrack deep in the Indian Ocean. The *Flor de la Mar*. The vessel was the flagship of Admiral Alfonso de Albuquerque, one of the great Portuguese navigators of the day. At great cost, the men and women of Rockweiller Industries located this wreck and salvaged it.

"Under the law of sovereign immunity, the *Flor de la Mar* rightly belongs to Portugal, the nation that owned it. Sometimes, disputes arise between the owner and the finder of an ancient vessel. But not here. There is no daylight between Rockweiller and Portugal in this case. They have joined together to bring the *Flor de la Mar* back to the world. Together, they intend to honor Portugal's right to its national heritage, and reward Rockweiller's hard work and ingenuity in recovering the vessel. Today, I ask that the Court honor those rights."

Bock then launched into his own legal argument, relying heavily on the *Odyssey Marine* case, and citing other cases that had followed it. Bock used up about an hour as well before sitting down.

After these presentations, Judge Graves banged his gavel and we adjourned for lunch. There was a loud buzz as everyone began talking at once. People filed out of the courtroom, no doubt making for the pier and the bountiful lunch options that were said to be available there.

We made our way through the crowd and stepped outside. The day was muggy and warm. We left the courthouse and walked the mile to our hotel. On the way, we coalesced into pairs and talked excitedly about the hearing; how the arguments had gone, what Judge Graves was thinking, who wore the best tie, and all of the important things. The tension of the conflict lawsuit had faded for now, amid the excitement of trial.

We had booked rooms at a Galveston hotel for the duration of the trial. There wasn't time to commute back and forth to Houston every day. When you're in trial, it's a sixteen-hour-a-day business, all day, every day. The outside world fades into irrelevance. It feels like going underwater. I had been to trial twice before, including a week-long one in state court. It was both exhilarating and exhausting. Afterward, I had slept for two days straight.

We were staying at the Hotel Galvez, one of Galveston's oldest and most famous hotels, built in 1911. It was said to be haunted, and ghost tours could be had amongst its chandeliered ballrooms and dimly lit corridors. Remington knew the owner, so we got a deal. Bock & Co. were staying there too, no doubt paying full price.

In a stroke of bad luck, Loudamire had the room just next to mine. I wondered if some sadistic clerk had done that on purpose, or whether Loudamire had requested it to try and eavesdrop on our legal strategy. I wouldn't put it past her. We ran into each other in the hallway on the first night. She stopped and seemed about to say something. Some condescending remark, no doubt. I ignored her and went straight into my room. It was only later that I reflected on this, and realized she might have just been trying to talk to me.

After the lunch break, the trial continued with more opening statements. Indonesia went next. The Indonesian lawyer was not as impressive as the others. But he didn't need to be. He made a simple argument: Since the *Flor de la Mar* had sunk just off the coast of Sumatra, it was within Indonesian waters. The United Nations Convention for the Law of the Sea (UNCLOS) recognized the territorial jurisdiction of every state up to twelve miles from its coast. Ergo, the ship belonged to Indonesia. It was a solid argument. I wondered for a moment whether this dark horse might win the day.

After Indonesia, Judge Graves let some of the lawyers for the intervenors speak. All forty-four of them wanted an hour for opening statements. Judge Graves refused. Instead, he let two or three of them speak for the group. The lead lawyer was a fat old man with a heavy Texas accent and the loudest voice I had ever heard. He rambled on about the importance of family and insisted that the people, not the states or the corporations, should get the money. He jimmied up some kind of genealogical chart and displayed it on a PowerPoint, and proceeded to trace his client's lineage all the way back to the sixteenth century. Judge Graves looked bored.

We didn't make an opening statement for David Marcum. This phase of the case was not about Marcum's death. That would come later. We had amended our papers to say that Marcum had found the *Flor de la Mar*, so the Judge knew about our claim. But we didn't yet have any proof, and Remington said we needed to bide our time before we entered the fray.

After that, the trial began in earnest. Over the days that followed, witnesses testified about the history of ancient Malacca; about the *Flor de la Mar*; about the sack of the city; and about the value of the ship. Evidence was presented. Legal argument was made. Countless objections were ruled upon. Expert witnesses were cross-examined. A typical exchange went like this:

"May I cross-examine, your Honor?" (Bock speaking).

"You may." (Graves).

"Thank you for your testimony, Professor."

"You are welcome, sir." (Malaysian historian whom Bock had given a heart attack. Not looking well).

"Did you leave anything out of your story today?"

"No doubt. The history of Malacca is long. And I didn't want to go past lunch." (scattered laughter from the gallery).

"Did you leave out, in particular, the reason for Albuquerque's ah...action?"

"The sack of Malacca, you mean?"

(Ignoring this) "Isn't it true, Professor, that before Albuquerque's expedition, a Portuguese admiral named Sequeira sought to establish a peaceful Portuguese trading post in Malacca?"

"I would dispute that was his intent."

"And isn't it true that the Sultan of Malacca agreed to this, but then reneged on his promise, ambushed the Portuguese, and took them hostage?"

"True." (Murmurs from the crowd).

"And isn't it also true that Alfonso de Albuquerque sailed to Malacca to remedy this situation, and rescue the Portuguese who were being held by the Sultan?"

"I don't think that's the primary reason why he sailed to Malacca, no."

"Right. And isn't it true that, before attacking the city, Albuquerque tried to negotiate the return of those hostages, and only after that failed, did he take the city by force?"

"There were negotiations. They were unsuccessful."

"Uh huh. So isn't it true, Professor, that the Sultan of Malacca brought the attack upon himself?" (triumphantly).

"For the hostages, perhaps there was cause. But for the extortionary ransom demands, no. The Portuguese were there to conquer. This can be seen from the history of their empire's colonization of India, the Middle East, Africa, and South America—"

(Bock, interrupting) "But you're not an expert on the Portuguese Empire, are you?"

"No. I am not." "Move to strike."

"Sustained." (Graves, yawning).

"Back to my question, Professor. Speaking just of Malacca—your area of expertise—wouldn't you agree there was justification for the attack?"

"No. I don't think that the taking of twenty hostages justifies the burning of a city, the wholesale slaughter and subjugation of its inhabitants, the theft of all of its wealth, and its conquest and colonization for the next hundred years."

(long pause) "Nothing further."

I talked to Remington and Kruckemeyer about this one evening after trial. We were sitting in the hotel lobby, waiting on Cindy to print out the day's briefing from the business center.

"How can they justify all that?" I asked. "What Portugal did, I mean."

"They can't," said Remington. "It was wrong. No question about it. But you also have to be careful about going back in time like that. You might open up a can of worms. Take where we are now, for example. Texas used to be part of Mexico. So did California, until the U.S. annexed it in the Mexican-American war."

"But there was cause for that," I argued.

"Was there? Read President Ulysses S. Grant's memoirs. He served in the war. See what he says about it."

I thought about that. "And there's also the question of how far back to go," Remington added. "Before Mexico's independence, it was a colony of Spain. And before that, it was part of the Aztec Empire. The Aztecs practiced human sacrifice. Should we give the country back to them?" I didn't know what to say to that.

"Hell," remarked Kruckemeyer, "right or wrong, I'd rather be in the good ol' U.S. of A. Mexico's run by the drug cartels. They got no law. Government's corrupt. Good people that try and stop it, the cartels kill 'em. The police all have to wear masks just to do their job, and the judges don't last long enough to hear a motion. You think we'd be better off if Texas was part of Mexico?" he grunted. "Then why is everyone trying to cross the border?"

I was troubled by this, but didn't have a good answer.

The trial went from nine to six each day. We settled into a kind of all-consuming routine. During the day, we would attend court and listen to everything that was said, sitting in the back and working on our laptops. After the day's hearings, we would walk back to the Galvez, gather for dinner at the restaurant, and discuss how things went.

Over the evening meal, Remington and Kruckemeyer would hold forth and explain what the lawyers were doing, why they were doing it, and reveal all the subtle tricks they played to try to influence the outcome. They talked about how the experts were holding up, and how Judge Graves was taking it. They would also tell war stories of cases past, and we would listen, spellbound, sometimes in awe, sometimes with laughter. Both of them were fantastic storytellers, and it was a rare opportunity. You can bond with people in a trial like in almost nothing else. After dinner, the evening's work began. We would read and respond to the legal filings that came in at all hours of the day. Time started to blend together.

At night, after the day's hearings and the evening's motions, Ashley, Vijay, Cindy, and I took to gathering for a glass of wine by the pool. The pool was closed by that hour, so we had it all to ourselves. Each night, we would hop the fence, take off our shoes, dip our toes in the water, and unwind for a little while. Vijay would smoke cigarettes, and Cindy would bring a pad and pencil to sketch. I caught her sketching me once. In the black and white hash, I looked tired, and older than I wanted to. Harder didn't join us at first. But then he gradually started coming. We didn't talk about the disqualification motion or give him a hard time about it. We all bonded in these quiet nights together by the pool, the dimly lit lamps and the sound of the ocean soothing our tired minds.

One night, we were gossiping about Loudamire and Quinto, and I mentioned that Loudamire looked like she was cracking up. I told the others how I had seen her sobbing after the settlement meeting a few months ago. Cindy shared that she knew someone who had gone to law school with Loudamire, and said she was very smart but had issues.

Harder nodded. "Apparently everyone at Badden & Bock hates her. Quinto and Adipose told me so at dinner. She's really smart, no doubt. She was first in her class at Yale. But she's not well adjusted. The firm puts up with her because she's really good and bills crazy hours. But she doesn't have a lot of friends. I feel kind of bad for her, really." I nodded soberly.

Mental health problems were common in the legal field. Attorneys often look put together on the surface. But a lot of times, they're not. Depression, anxiety, and substance abuse rates were all high. Many people came into law school with big dreams but left broken, with bad jobs and a jaded outlook on life.

Part of this was because of the realities of the job market. A lot of people want to be lawyers, but there aren't that many good legal jobs. Competition for the best positions is fierce. Most get stuck with mediocre or bad jobs, dead-end gigs that don't fulfill them and don't pay a lot of money, either. And even the good jobs are often stressful and require sixty or eighty-hour workweeks.

The stress is at its peak in my line of work. As a litigator, you fight with everyone all the time. Opposing counsel tries to screw you like it's their job. Which it is. The Judge waits for you to slip up. Your own side will turn on you if you make a mistake. The client won't be happy if you lose, which will happen sometimes.

Contracts and deal work looked less stressful to me. But on the other hand, those lawyers spent their time copy-pasting forms from old deals to new ones, taking flak from the bankers and executives who were actually running the show. When people asked me whether they should go to law school, I usually tried to talk them out of it.

As the courtroom drama continued unabated, we continued to work feverishly on our own case. We needed to find a way to prove that Rockweiller's witnesses were lying. We needed to figure out what happened to Marcum. We needed to figure out where the contract was, and how Marcum had found the *Flor de la Mar*. These questions consumed me night after night. We continued to scour the documents, including the new ones produced every day, looking for anything that would help. I tried calling Riker again, to see if he knew more. But he didn't return my calls.

We needed to find something soon. The case was moving quickly. Judge Graves was pushing hard, conscious of the mounting international pressure. There had been reports of an isolated clash between the Malaysian and Indonesian navies in the Strait of Malacca. Graves was not one to be deterred by that or anything else, but he was certainly aware of the ramifications of the case, and wanted to get it over with one way or another. Meanwhile, Wurlheiser was waiting in the wings, trying to sabotage us and force us out of the case.

Finally, about three weeks into the trial, we caught our break. It came from an unexpected source.

One of the interesting parts about litigating a world-famous case in the modern era was the sheer number of people who speculated about it. They ranged from news anchors, to experts, to law professors, to random posters on the internet. They all dissected the arguments and court filings in the case—which were public—and boldly opined on what was going on, whether they had a clue or not.

Among the random posters on the internet, one of the most active was a Reddit subgroup called r/FlorDeLaMar. Reddit was an internet message board. The favorite topic of this subgroup was the location of the *Flor de la Mar*. They treated it like a puzzle, or a TV show, analyzing clues scattered throughout the case to try and predict the ending. The collective minds of Reddit were remarkably successful in TV show predictions. And in the same way, they proved successful in uncovering an important secret in the case. One that all of the lawyers and experts had missed.

Bock and Jafaar had been sparring for weeks over what Rockweiller had to disclose about the *Flor de la Mar*. Judge Graves had mostly let Bock keep things under wraps with the ultrasensitive order. But Graves did make Bock produce a report that Gunthum had made—the formal record documenting the details of the *Flor de la Mar* find. Naturally, the report was more blacked out than a CIA memo. All of the location information, or stuff that anybody actually wanted to see, was redacted.

But one particular version of this report, attached to one particular court filing, among hundreds of exhibits, contained a page where certain information was not blacked out. Specifically, it was a measurement taken at the *Flor de la*

Mar site, which yielded this set of numbers: 2043.82, 20.44, 296.43.

If any of the attorneys or experts actually saw this version of the report, they did not make anything of it. I certainly didn't. But some of the Reddit posters found it, and started to analyze the numbers, trying to figure out what they meant.

It was finally a poster named Barre83, a geologist-turned-barre-instructor with too much time on his or her hands, who figured it out: they were pressure measurements. Barre83 knew this because each of these numbers was actually a different way to express the same value. 2043.82 kilopascals equals 20.44 bar, which equals 296.43 pounds per square inch. Barre83 realized that this must be the water pressure at the *Flor de la Mar* site.

Even more interesting was this: Pressure underwater increases linearly with depth. That means if you know the pressure under saltwater, then you also know the depth. By reversing the calculations, Barre83 was able to figure out the depth at which Lloyd Gunthum had found the *Flor de la Mar*: 668 feet below sea level. And just like that, Reddit had solved one of the three geospatial coordinates that represented the final resting place of the *Flor de la Mar*.

Once the internet got wind of this, it spread like wildfire across social media, and then regular media. The news admiringly reported on how a bunch of Redditors had solved a problem that all of the lawyers, experts, and great minds could not. "How many lawyers does it take to find the *Flor de la Mar*?" went the ensuing meme. "r/1."

Once this became public, Malaysia and Portugal immediately shot interrogatories and requests for admission off to Rockweiller, forcing Bock to admit it under oath. Bock didn't try to deny it, and pretty soon the secret was out. I expected Malaysia and Indonesia were even now modifying their searches, and were scouring the Strait of Malacca at a depth of 668 feet below sea level for the *Flor de la Mar.*

It also turned out that this information would have particular importance to us. It was the single piece of the puzzle that we needed to put the lie to Rockweiller's coverup, and finally reveal what had happened to David Marcum.

It was some days after the news came out that Remington sauntered into my office and sat down. I looked up at him quizzically. He was holding a copy of the redacted report and had a smile on his face. A big, cat-got-the-cream smile.

"What's up?" I asked him.

"I found their mistake," he said.

TWENTY-SEVEN

Two and a half weeks into the trial, Judge Graves declared a Friday off. We used the day to finally take Lloyd Gunthum's deposition in a conference room at the Hotel Galvez.

The conference room was packed. A dozen lawyers from Badden & Bock were there, with another half-dozen apiece for Malaysia, Portugal, and Indonesia. Adding paralegals, assistants, and IT, there were almost fifty people in the room. Laptops, iPads, and extension cords littered the space, making it look like a wired jungle. I half expected the fire marshal to burst in and break up the party.

Lloyd Gunthum sat in the pole position. Gunthum was fifty years old and looked every inch the former military man. His silver hair was cropped short, and he wore slacks and a dark polo shirt that exposed his bulging biceps and pectoral muscles. Zachary Bock sat on his right, whispering some last-minute advice in his ear. Our eyes met once, and he turned away contemptuously.

Remington sat on Gunthum's left, in his usual quiet manner, as if carved out of wood. I sat next to him, with Cindy, Harder, and Ashley next to me.

I was as tense as a steel spring. We needed to get something done here. Wurlheiser had finally succeeded in scheduling another vote of the partners. Most of them wanted out, and Kruckemeyer couldn't stall any longer. Remington said they were going to force the issue with or without him. Without bringing home some kind of win, we wouldn't be able to continue much longer. I had been candid with Ashley about this, and she understood.

The appointed hour struck. The videographer switched on the camera, and the court reporter made everyone state their names for the record. This took nearly twenty minutes because of the sheer number of lawyers present. Finally, Gunthum was sworn in, and Remington began.

"Would you please state your name for the record, sir?" Remington asked, with the air of someone who has asked a question a thousand times.

"Lloyd Gunthum."

"What is your date of birth?"

"November 7, 1968."

"What is your occupation?"

"Diver and salvor."

"When you say diver, you mean scuba diver, is that correct?"

"That's correct."

"And when you say salvor, you mean that you specialize in the search for, and the recovery of, items from the deep oceans, is that correct?"

"Yes."

"How long have you been working as a diver and a salvor?"

"Over twenty years."

"And prior to that, you served with the U.S. Navy SEALs?"

"I did."

"How many years did you serve with the SEALs?"
"Fifteen years."
"Did you see any combat?"
"Yes," Gunthum said warily. I could tell it was a sensitive subject.
"Do you carry a firearm?"
"Sometimes."
"What type?"
"A SIG Sauer P938. I have some others."
"Were you carrying a firearm aboard the Excelsior?"
"I uh...I don't recall. No wait, yes, I was. I had it." I waited for more, but Remington just nodded and moved on.
"Who is your current employer, Mr. Gunthum?"
"Excel Resources, LLC."
"And you own a stake in the company?"
"Yes."
"Excel Resources, LLC is majority-owned by Rockweiller Industries, is it not?"
"Yes, it is."
"Would you say you effectively work for Rockweiller Industries?"
"No. I would say I effectively work for Excel Resources, LLC." There was just a hint of self-satisfaction in his response.
After that, Remington went through an exhaustive history of Gunthum's background, followed by point-by-point questioning of his work for Rockweiller Industries, founding of Excel Resources, past salvage & recovery operations, hiring and employment practices, revenues and tax records, and other such details. He also asked about Gunthum's safety record, disputes with employees, lawsuits he'd been involved in, and more. This went on for hours. I grew bored, as did everyone else. The air in the room was stifling.

Eventually, Remington reached the subject of Marcum's death. I listened closely. But Gunthum told the same tale that his crew had. Marcum had disappeared on a dive and was presumed dead. The story sounded rehearsed, which I knew it was. But that didn't mean it wasn't true.

Gunthum added a few more details now that the *Flor de la Mar* was public. He said that Marcum was in the water full time, examining the wreck site and salvaging its contents. With that amount of bottom time, Gunthum said it was no surprise, although it was regrettable, that something had happened.

Gunthum was cool and collected under questioning. We were about five hours into the deposition when Remington finally asked the question I had been waiting for.

"Did you have any type of contract with David Marcum?" Remington said. He asked it casually, like it was no big deal. But he tensed up as he asked the question. As did Gunthum. As did I.

None of that tension showed in Gunthum's voice. "No," he said simply.

"What about Excel Resources, LLC? Did the company have a contract with David Marcum?"

"Yes."

I looked up sharply. What?

"Pardon?" Remington said. He looked nonplussed, and I could tell he hadn't expected that answer either. Did Gunthum really just come out and say it? I leaned forward intently, waiting on his next answer.

"I said yes," Gunthum repeated. "Excel Resources had a contract with David Marcum. An independent contractor agreement. I believe you have the relevant records."

"Oh," said Remington. "Yes. That's right. We do." Remington fumbled with his notes for a moment. He looked unusually disconcerted. He recovered himself and turned back to Gunthum. "Did you, Excel Resources, Rockweiller Industries, or any of their agents, employees, affiliates, or subsidiaries, have any agreement with David Marcum, whether oral or written, which would have awarded Mr. Marcum a share of the *Flor de la Mar*?" he asked, looking Gunthum directly in the eye as he asked the question.

"No," said Gunthum. As if he had been born to answer.

"Any contracts related to the *Flor de la Mar* at all?"

"No."

"What about any agreements with David Marcum, of any kind, aside from the one you just mentioned?"

"Well," said Gunthum, finally cracking a smile, "we played poker a few times. I owed him a hundred bucks. Don't tell anyone, though."

This drew some laughter from the lawyers, and eased the tension in the room. The atmosphere that Remington had slowly been building broke. And from that moment, I saw Gunthum relax. He leaned back imperceptibly, his arms folded across his chest, with just the hint of a smile on his face. This was a contest, and it seemed like he had won. This was our shot, and we had whiffed.

After that, Remington took him through the aftermath of Marcum's death, and cleaned up a few other details. Gunthum answered everything easily and with growing confidence. Then Remington switched tracks.

"What type of scuba diving certification do you have, Mr. Gunthum?" he asked.

"A few. PADI Master Scuba Diver. IDC Staff Instructor. ADCI commercial diving certification. Some others. You have a copy of my resume. I'd be happy to go over it with you."

"That's fine, thank you. You also received scuba training during your time with the Navy SEALs, correct?"

"That's correct."

"How many dives have you done?"

"Over my whole career?"

"Yes." Gunthum sat back and thought for a moment. "I couldn't really say. Too many to count."

"Hundreds?"

"Definitely."

"Would it be fair to say that you are an expert in scuba diving?"

"Yes," Gunthum said with a hint of pride.

Remington nodded and flipped through his notepad. He took his time, unconcerned by the expectant faces waiting on his words.

"Mr. Gunthum," he said at last, "what is technical diving?"

"Technical diving?" Gunthum looked at Bock, who shrugged, not knowing where this was going. "Technical diving involves diving past the normal depth limits."

"What are the normal depth limits?"

"For recreational diving, about a hundred feet."

"Why is that?"

"The deeper you go, the more things can go wrong." There was a stir as this piqued interest around the table.

"What sort of things?"

"For one, a hundred feet is about the depth where nitrogen narcosis begins to set in."

"What is nitrogen narcosis?"

"It's like being drunk underwater. It causes impaired judgment and coordination. At greater depths, it can cause hallucinations, loss of vision and hearing, and in some cases, even unconsciousness and death."

"I see. What else can go wrong underwater?"

"The bends." There were murmurs around the table from those who knew what this was.

"What's that?"

"The bends happens when you come up from depth too fast. When you're deep underwater, the nitrogen in the air forms bubbles in your bloodstream and tissues. If you come up too fast, those bubbles expand, resulting in decompression sickness. Better known as the bends. Milder symptoms include joint pain, fever, and nausea. In severe cases, it can lead to tissue expansion or even rupture. If you come up from a great depth too fast, and you don't get to a hyperbaric chamber, you're a dead man. I've seen it happen."

I didn't know where Remington was going with this. But everyone was fully absorbed in the testimony now. Bock nodded along subconsciously as he listened. Typically, a witness is supposed to answer narrowly during a deposition. Gunthum had been doing a good job of that. But now he was talking more freely. He felt that the game had been won, and seemed to be relishing his role as storyteller of the dangers of the deep.

"What measures can divers take to mitigate the effects of nitrogen on deeper dives?" Remington asked.

"You change the gas mix," Gunthum explained. "Both nitrogen narcosis and the bends are caused by nitrogen. Air is made up of twenty percent oxygen and eighty percent nitrogen. Under pressure, the nitrogen starts to cause these side effects. So you use an air mixture with less nitrogen."

"What kind of air mixtures are available?"

"The most common is nitrox. Nitrox has more oxygen and less nitrogen than regular air. It helps divers resist the effects of the nitrogen longer. On nitrox, a diver can go to a hundred fifty, maybe two hundred feet safely."

"I see. Why not lower than that?"

"Because once you reach that depth, oxygen toxicity begins to set in. Compressed oxygen has its own problems. It affects the central nervous system. This can cause spasms, twitching, and convulsions. At extreme depths people experience seizures, which are fatal if you're underwater."

"What do divers do at depths even lower than that?"

"At the lowest depths, divers will use trimix. This contains oxygen, nitrogen, and helium. Helium is an inert gas that doesn't have the ill effects of the other two. So you can go to still greater depths."

My breathing slowed as I imagined being deep under the ocean, breathing a mixture of artificial gasses. I wondered how cold it was down there.

"What kind of depths can you reach with trimix?" Remington's voice was almost hypnotic by this point.

"Hundreds of feet. Three, four, maybe even five hundred. But at those depths, everything is dangerous. And eventually, helium shows its own side effects. It can induce high-pressure nervous syndrome. I don't know much about that. I've never been to that depth in scuba gear."

"Are there any gas mixtures that can take you deeper than that?"

Gunthum shook his head. "I've heard of an experimental mixture called hydrox. It uses hydrogen, the only gas lighter than helium. But I don't know much about it. There are other ways to go deeper. Atmospheric pressures suits. Saturation diving. But as far as scuba, several hundred feet is basically the limit."

"There were no atmospheric pressure suits or saturation diving equipment aboard the Excelsior, were there?" Remington asked the question casually. But I felt a twinge, as if someone had played a sharp note on a violin.

Gunthum frowned. "No," he answered.

"Thank you," said Remington, turning the page on his legal pad. "Now, I am going to hand you a document that was produced by Rockweiller Industries. It is an inventory of the equipment aboard the Excelsior."

Gunthum took the document, taking his time to flip through it.

"I'll direct your attention to page eleven, which contains records of scuba diving equipment. It lists eight scuba tanks, an air compressor, twelve masks, ten sets of fins, nine wetsuits of varying size, eleven weight-belts of varying weight, and a number of additional items. Do you see that?"

"Yes."

"All of these tanks were filled with air, correct?"

"Correct."

"There was no nitrox gas on board the Excelsior, was there?"

A distinct pang rippled across the room as the listeners caught their first glimmer of where Remington was going with this.

"No. There was no nitrox."

"There was no trimix gas, either, was there?"

"No." I saw the faintest hint of sweat break out on Gunthum's forehead.

"The only gas mixture available was air?"

"That's right." Gunthum's voice was calm. But he was breathing faster now.

"Objection," muttered Bock. "Uh...objection. Relevance."

Remington ignored him. He reached into his briefcase and took out a copy of Gunthum's report on the *Flor de la Mar*, the one with the pressure measurements. He handed a copy to Gunthum.

"You prepared this report, did you not?"

"Yes."

"And this is your signature on the last page?"

"Yes."

"According to the information in this report, later confirmed by Rockweiller Industries, you found the *Flor de la Mar* at a depth of six hundred and sixty-eight feet below sea level. Is that correct?"

"Objection," repeated Bock. But it lacked conviction.

"Uh...six hundred and sixty-eight feet. Yes. Part of it."

"What part of the *Flor de la Mar* was not found at six hundred and sixty-eight feet?"

"Parts we haven't found...I don't know."

"But the part that you did find—the main body of the wreck—was at a depth of six hundred and sixty-eight feet below sea level, correct?"

"I guess."

"You guess? That is what you recorded, is it not?"

"Yes."

"And you testified that items in the wreck were recovered by scuba divers, including David Marcum, correct?"

"Yes." Gunthum was twitching now.

"And that these divers spent time on the bottom to salvage these items?"

"Yes...that's right."

Remington nodded and flipped a page in his notes. "You say that David Marcum died in a scuba diving accident while recovering the remains of the *Flor de la Mar*. Right?"

"Right."

"And your crew testified to the same?"

"He did. They did. Yes."

Remington nodded. Then he paused, dropped his notes and looked directly at Lloyd Gunthum.

"Mr. Gunthum, are you telling me that Mr. Marcum dove to depth of six hundred and sixty-eight feet in scuba gear, on pure air, to recover the remains of the *Flor de la Mar*?"

Gunthum didn't answer.

"Based on your testimony today, that would be virtually impossible, wouldn't it?"

Gunthum just sat there, frozen.

"Would you, Mr. Gunthum, a scuba diving expert of twenty years' experience, with master diver and technical diver certifications, and with training in the U.S. Navy SEALs, ever undertake a scuba dive at six hundred and sixty-eight feet on pure air?"

No answer.

"Would you even undertake such a dive at all, even with an enhanced gas mixture such as nitrox or trimix?"

No answer. The silence was deafening.

Remington waited for a while. But no answer was forthcoming. He asked the next question quietly, almost gently.

"Isn't it true, Mr. Gunthum, that David Marcum never dived to recover the treasures of the *Flor de la Mar*?"

No answer.

"Isn't it true that, because of the depth, you used the remotely operated vehicle that was on board the Excelsior?"

No answer.

"Isn't it true, Mr. Gunthum, that David Marcum never died in a scuba diving accident at all?"

The silence was thunderous. Every eye in the room was fixed on Lloyd Gunthum. He didn't say a word. But everyone, from Zachary Bock right down to the twenty-two-year-old paralegal in the back, knew the answer to the question.

After a few moments, Gunthum recovered himself. He got up from his chair and ripped the microphone off his shirt. Then he glared at Bock and marched out of the room. He slammed the door behind him, shaking the glass. Everyone turned to Remington and looked at him as if he had just invented fire.

But Remington just spoke to Bock in his usual understated manner. "It seems that your witness would like a recess. Shall we reconvene after a break?"

The room slowly woke up, as if from a trance. People started to talk amongst themselves, and type on their computers. Some of the lawyers placed calls, probably to report back about what had happened.

Bock spoke loudly as people left the room. "We are designating everything at this deposition as confidential and attorney's eyes only pursuant to the protective order. The information cannot leave this room without court approval..." Everyone filed out, barely paying attention to him.

Remington walked outside the conference room. Cindy, Harder, Ashley, and I followed him. We walked away from the crowd, and huddled in a corner. No one said anything for a minute. I felt stunned.

"So that's why you wanted all of those scuba records," I said finally.

"Yes," said Remington. "I knew they were lying. Something in those records was bound to trip them up. And it did. It's all in the details, Jack."

"What happens now?" Ashley asked. She seemed dazed. "Are you going to make him tell us what really happened?"

"We can't make him tell us anything," said Remington. "But we can do one better.

"There's something called the crime-fraud exception to the attorney-client privilege," he explained. "Lawyer-client conversations are not privileged if made with the intent of committing or covering up a crime. It's not easy to invoke, but this is just what it was made for.

"Gunthum is lying to cover up your brother's death. Either Bock didn't know, which I find hard to believe, or he knew and suborned perjury, which is worse. So tomorrow, we're going to file a motion with the court to strip Rockweiller's attorney-client privilege under the crime-fraud exception. We're going to ask for unrestricted access to the death memo and all of Rockweiller's privileged communications. And after what just happened in there, we'll get it. And then, I hope, we'll finally know what happened to your brother."

We stood for a while to let that all sink in. "Was this your plan all along?" I asked him.

"One of them."

"What about the deposition?" Cindy asked. "Are you going to continue?"

"With Gunthum? No. He's done. I just wiped the floor with him. No way he's coming back for another round today."

Sure enough, after we reconvened, Bock notified everyone that Gunthum could not continue with the deposition. He didn't specify a reason, but everybody knew.

All the rest of that afternoon and into the evening, Cindy, Harder, and I began drafting a motion to pierce the attorney-client privilege. Cindy did the research, Harder wrote the facts, and I wrote the legal argument. There was no bickering about who did what, and we all worked together late into the night, revising drafts, pulling case law, and trading ideas about the best way to address this or that legal point, or the best way to frame this fact. We re-convened early the next morning. After working feverishly all through that day and the one after, we filed the motion with the court.

A new settlement offer came in soon after that. Badden & Bock had responded to our privilege brief with their customary skill, and put up a formidable opposition. It cited a wealth of case law, characterized our request as outrageous, and framed Lloyd Gunthum's testimony as nothing out of the ordinary.

But the settlement offer betrayed how desperate they really were. Badden & Bock was offering us eight million dollars to settle the case confidentially, today, without further disclosures. Remington said their real number was likely higher.

The offer went a long way to quieting the acrimony among the partners. Just a few weeks ago, they were jumping at the opportunity to take two or three million dollars. Now, by holding firm and staying the course, Remington had about tripled that. Kruckemeyer was thrilled, and even Wurlheiser was pleased. He apologized for doubting Remington. The partners wanted to take this offer too, but they didn't push Remington this time, and deferred to his judgment.

We put the offer to Ashley. She didn't even think about taking it. She was determined to know what happened to her brother. And it seemed that we were finally on the verge of finding that out.

TWENTY-EIGHT

Dear Mr. Carver:

I am in receipt of your request for David Marcum's flight records. I apologize for the delay. Our office has been occupied with other matters.

Having considered the interests of privacy versus the need for full and fair disclosure, the government has elected to provide you with the information you seek. Please find enclosed copies of Mr. David Marcum's flight records for the last five years.

Best,

S. Patrick Oggenbotham

I blinked. It was an email from the TSA. A response to the subpoena we had served months ago.

I hadn't actually expected the government to write back. The best I had hoped for was that they would tell us to pound sand, rather than ignore us completely. But here was a scrupulously polite letter from one S. Patrick Oggenbotham, Senior Counsel for the Transportation Security Administration, giving us everything we had asked for. I reflected that it was good to live in a country of laws.

Unfortunately, the records came late. By now, we had received everything from the airlines already. Between that and the bank statements, we knew where David Marcum had gone during the last five years. But I clicked open the records anyway.

It was Saturday, and I was sitting in my favorite coffee shop in Houston. It was a long weekend, and we had Monday off. For Columbus Day, ironically. No one took Columbus Day off anymore, except the courts. But for the time being, that included us, so we traveled back to Houston for the weekend. We ended up working the whole time, anyway. But at least we got a change of venue.

The coffee shop I was at was called Mykonos. It was a quaint Greek establishment in the Montrose neighborhood. The same area that David Marcum had lived in. Mykonos had two floors. The interior was paneled in dark wood and scattered with antique furniture. It was near a college campus, and there was a bohemian mix of students reading textbooks, freelance artist-types on their MacBooks, and businesspeople quietly meeting over espresso. And there was me, sitting in a cozy room on the second floor and drinking Turkish coffee.

I took a sip of coffee and scrolled through the TSA records. As I thought, they lined up with what we already knew. There were the ski trips to Colorado, the surf trips to California, the weekend jaunt to Mexico. The two flights to Malaysia. I saw no flights after that.

I was about to close the records when I saw it.

A month before David Marcum's first trip to Malaysia, he had taken another flight. I had never seen this one before.

I pulled up the airline records, but I couldn't match up the dates with any of them. This was new.

My heart started beating faster. The flight was on an airline called TAP. I didn't recognize it. I checked the airport codes. The flight was from MIA to LIS. MIA was the code for Miami International Airport, I knew. LIS was unknown to me. I looked it up. When I saw what it was, my jaw fell open.

LIS was the code for the airport in Lisbon, Portugal.

I ripped out my phone and called Cindy.

The phone rang a few times, and she answered with a yawn. "Hello?"

"You're not going to believe this," I said urgently.
"Let me guess. Seventh motion to strike? I thought this was our day off."

"I just got flight records from the government. David Marcum flew to Lisbon three months before he died."

There was a pause at the other end of the line as Cindy stopped whatever the hell she was doing and paid attention. I heard her lean closer into the phone.

"Did you say Lisbon? Like Lisbon, Portugal?"

"Yes. I'm sending the records now." I forwarded her the documents from the TSA and then waited impatiently while she looked through them.

"Oh my God," she whispered. "You're right."

I clasped my hands together fixedly, trying to think. "Why didn't we see this in the banking records?" Cindy wondered. "TAP is the Portuguese national airline. We could have subpoenaed them like you did with American Airlines. Under the Hague Convention for...what is it again?"

"Service Abroad of Judicial and Extrajudicial Documents in Civil or Commercial Matters," I said absently.

"Right. Always forget that one."

"I suspect we didn't see this flight in the bank records because David Marcum bought it with cash. That way no one could trace where he'd gone." I smiled. "Except for the deep state," I said, thinking of Jared Diamond.

"I can't believe they actually sent us the records," Cindy marveled. "The TSA subpoena was Harder's idea. Remember? You said it would never work."

"Yeah, yeah," I muttered. Harder was going to lord it over me for this.

"What does this mean? What was David Marcum doing in Lisbon?"

I ran my hand through my hair, thinking about it. "It's got to be connected," I decided. "It can't be a coincidence that David Marcum flew to Portugal months before he found an ancient Portuguese shipwreck and died, right?"

"When you put it that way...no."

I got up and started pacing around the small room. "This is how he found the information," I said with growing excitement. "It must be. This is how he figured out where the *Flor de la Mar* was. We suspected that Marcum must have found new information about the ship. Something that no one else knew. That's how he was able to locate it. Right?"

"Right. I'm following you so far. And you think he found that information in Portugal?"

"What else could it be?"

"I don't know. But what did he find there? And how do we figure out what it was?"

Three hours later, the door to my little Greek war room opened, and Ashley walked in. "Cool spot," she said, looking around in approval. "Way better than Starbucks."

"Agree," I said. "Plus Starbucks coffee tastes burnt."

"Ha! My brother had a conspiracy theory about that. He said that Starbucks burned their coffee on purpose so people have to buy those bougie, five-dollar lattes instead of the two-dollar drip."

I laughed. "Brilliant. The more I learn about your brother, the more I like him." She smiled.

"So. Any luck figuring out what David might have been doing in Portugal?" she asked, sitting down next to me.

"No," blared the voice of Jacob Schnizzel from my speakerphone. He was so loud that the phone vibrated when he spoke. Ashley jumped, not realizing he was there.

"Hello, Professor," she said, recovering quickly.

"Hello," he said loudly. I grimaced apologetically and turned the volume down a few notches. "Your brother has outsmarted all of us maritime archaeologists, as far as I can tell. But I don't know how he did it."

It was true. We had been racking our brains, but couldn't figure out what David Marcum had been doing in Portugal. It was sheer luck that we got his flight records. Beyond that, we had nothing. I guessed that Marcum had kept a low profile and only used cash during his time there. That's why his bank records didn't show any charges.

I had read every recent article I could find about the *Flor de la Mar*, hoping that some new detail would emerge and lead me to the truth. There were a lot of articles. But most were just clickbait that parroted information from other sources. That was the state of the news business these days, unfortunately. There were a few in-depth articles by real journalists, including one by John Carreyrou at the Wall Street Journal, but they didn't tell me anything that I didn't already know. I also kept a close eye on Reddit, to see if it would answer the question for us. It did not.

Schnizzel and I filled Ashley in on our progress. "My first thought was that your brother went to the Torre do Tombo National Archives in Portugal," said Schnizzel. "That's where I'd go. It's a huge library with a lot of original information about that era. But if the answers were there, someone would have found them already. The library is old. And when I say old, I mean it was built in 1378."

"Wow."

"Right. If there was more information about the *Flor de la Mar* there, someone would have found it a few hundred years ago."

"What if it was something new?"

"New? It's a library. Nothing new happens at libraries. They only record old things that happen."

"Maybe a new publication? A book collection?"

"We tried that. I keep tabs on that stuff. We checked their website and catalog, and I even reached out to some people I know. Nothing."

Ashley went downstairs to order a coffee. I recommended the Turkish, and she came back with two of them. I thanked her as she sat down and opened her laptop. The two of us and Schnizzel worked silently at our computers, tracing threads of thought through the interwebs.

"What about this?" said Ashley after a while.

She showed me her screen. It was a news article that said, "newly discovered documents at the Portuguese Royal Archives."

I was dumbfounded. "How did we not see that?" I tried to pull it up on my computer, but it didn't appear.

"What is it?" yelled Schnizzel.

"An article about new documents in the Archives. It's dated six months ago."

"Are you kidding me? Why don't I see this?"

"I bet I know why," said Ashley. "I'm using the Portuguese version of Google. Google.pt. So I'm getting Portuguese results, which you wouldn't see."

"Duh," said Schnizzel. We heard an audible *thwack* as he hit himself on the head. "How could I be so thick? Well go on, what does it say?"

Ashley clicked through the link, which lead to the Archives' website. The entry was in Portuguese. She translated it for us.

> Newly discovered documents at the Portuguese National Archives.
>
> Portuguese archivists have stumbled upon a trove of new documents at the Torre do Tombo National Archives. These documents were found during a reconstruction project in the Archives' east wing. A construction worker put his foot through a weakened floor, revealing a large cellar in which many old books and manuscripts had been stored.
>
> The cellar is thought to be very old. A curator said that it was likely buried in the Great Lisbon Earthquake of 1755, when a fire consumed the Archives. Amidst the collapse, the rubble, and the later rebuilding, the cellar was forgotten.
>
> The cellar was discovered approximately two years ago. But due to budget cuts and other priorities, the Archives' staff have not been able to review the documents until recently. The documents are thought to be mostly old merchant records from the days of the Portuguese Empire.

> The curators have not yet reviewed all of the new documents. But they are being made available to the public on a strictly on-site basis, due to their age and sensitivity.

I stared at the article for a while. Then I plugged it into Google translate so I could read it for myself. Then I read it again. Was this what David Marcum had gone to Portugal for? Was this how he had found the *Flor de la Mar*?

Schnizzel was ranting. "It took them two years to tell anyone about this?" he yelled. "And they didn't even post it in English? What kind third-rate library is this? Manuel de Maia would roll over in his grave."

I didn't know who Manuel de Maia was, or much care. "Check the catalog," I said to Ashley. "Let's see if they have more information."

We browsed around the Archives' website but found nothing more. The new materials were not online. Evidently they were only available in person, like the press release said. "What do you think?" Ashley asked me.

"I think this is where your brother got his information." Over the past few months, I had developed growing confidence in my instincts. They had led me in the right direction, even when others thought I was wrong. Now, my instincts told me this was it. This was how Marcum had found the *Flor de la Mar.* I was sure of it.

It felt like things were finally starting to turn. First, there was the revelation at Gunthum's deposition, and the desperate settlement offer from Badden & Bock. Our crime-fraud motion was pending a decision, and I was certain that we would get the death memo soon. And now, we had a real lead on how Marcum had found the *Flor de la Mar*. If we could just find the contract, we might be able to win everything. But I was getting ahead of myself.

"I definitely think it's worth investigating," said Schnizzel. "But how are you going to do it?"

I smiled, though he couldn't see it through the phone. "Well that's obvious, isn't it?"

Ashley and I took the next flight to Lisbon.

The rest of the team could have easily been upset about this. We were in the midst of a trial, and I was going on an all-expenses-paid trip to Portugal while they were stuck holding the bag. But there was not a word of complaint. Everyone knew how important this was. If I could find something in Portugal, we would have a shot at bringing it all home. Remington said to find out what I could in Lisbon and get back as quickly as possible. We didn't have a lot of time.

We landed in Lisbon in the early afternoon, and took a cab straight from the airport to the National Archives.

The Torre do Tombo National Archives were housed in a building that looked like two blocks supported by giant concrete T's. It was modern, like all architecture seemed to be these days. The building reminded me of the Houston federal courthouse, albeit without the bomb shelter chic-style windows. The Archives were fronted by palm trees and an inviting green lawn. The day was sunny, and we crossed the warm grass and entered the building.

The lobby was dark and cool. Few people were there. Our footsteps echoed loudly on the marble floor, the way they do in empty museums. Ashley walked up to the main desk to inquire about the new materials. I hung back and idly walked around the entrance room.

I stopped at an old painting that showed a city being destroyed by some virulent natural calamity. It depicted buildings falling at crazy angles, and almost had the feel of a Van Gogh. Fire and smoke blotted out the sky. The plaque next to it read: Great Lisbon Earthquake of 1755.

The rest of the plaque was in Portuguese, so I pulled out my phone and looked it up. I found an article called *Recovery Amid Destruction: Manoel de Maya and the Lisbon Earthquake of 1755*, by Luciana Lima and Russell Craig.

> In 1755, a massive earthquake and ensuing fire and tsunami consumed the Portuguese capital, Lisbon. The earthquake was one of the most powerful in history, estimated at between 8.6 and 9.0 on the Richter scale. It is alleged to have been the "first modern disaster...localized to a specific place and time...and international event." In the aftermath of the earthquake, the actions of a remarkable eighty-three-year-old archivist, Manoel de Maya (later spelled Maia), were instrumental in preserving many of the archival and library records of Portugal. Maya's actions made the task of developing a well-informed understanding of Portugal's economic, commercial, social, and cultural history prior to 1755 a less complicated one.

Lisbon had a population of nearly three hundred thousand people during the time of the earthquake. A third of them died in the disaster. It happened on the morning of All Saint's Day, while people were attending mass. The seismic shock collapsed churches and cathedrals, killing the worshippers within. I imagined they must have believed it was divine retribution.

The Archives were badly damaged by the quake. Many historical documents were lost. This included accounts of Vasco da Gama and other early navigators, and records of the Portuguese East India Company. And perhaps, records about the *Flor de la Mar.*

Ashley finished her inquiries and walked toward me quickly. Her eyes were blazing. I could tell she had found out something.

"He was here," she whispered excitedly. She motioned me to follow, and began walking across the lobby toward a large stairwell.

"Your brother?"

"Yes. Well, I don't know for sure. But the receptionist remembered a handsome American man who matched his description. Said he'd asked about the same records. They're in a special room, and you have to ask for a key to see them. Only about a dozen people have. She remembered."

"And you think it was him?"

"How many handsome American men would be looking through newly discovered documents in the Portuguese Archives recently?"

"Present company excluded?"

She rolled her eyes at me. "Let's go."

We descended three levels of stairs and walked through a hallway. Then we entered an older area of the Archives.

This area didn't have the modern flair of the lobby. It looked more like the old libraries I was used to in the U.S. Greenish fluorescent lighting, shelves crammed together uncomfortably, and a musty smell to the air. We passed an old man with a long white beard who was quietly reading a book. He looked up, seeming surprised to see anyone down there.

We navigated our way between the narrow shelves. At the end of the aisles, along the far wall, we came to the room we were looking for. It was a simple space with a glass door. The interior was dark. Ashley took out the key that the librarian had given her. She unlocked the door and we walked in. The only things in the room were a desk, two wooden chairs, an old computer, and a projector. A single naked light bulb hung from the ceiling.

"What's this?" I asked, looking around in confusion.

"The records."

"Huh. I was expecting they'd be out there," I said, gesturing toward the shelves.

"They're on microfiche," she explained. "The documents are too old to flip through by hand. They'd probably turn to dust. The Archives scanned them, basically taking snapshots of each page and putting them in a repository here."

"Microfiche?" I said. "What is this, the eighties?" She shrugged.

"Why didn't they just digitize them? That way they could have put them online too."

"I asked. The librarian seemed offended. She said something about Portugal's national heritage not being available to any Juan, Dick, or Harry with an internet connection." I imagined what Schnizzel would have to say about that.

We pulled up the chairs and sat down in front of the projector. Ashley read the instructions and turned it on. The screen warmed up slowly, and I watched as Ashley adjusted some knobs and made it come into focus. The display showed some kind of index. It was all in Portuguese, and illegible to me. I sat quietly while Ashley looked through the index and pulled up various documents.

After a while, she stopped and turned to me, looking frustrated. "There are tens of thousands of pages here. At least. I don't know how we're going to do this."

I pursed my lips thoughtfully. I didn't know Portuguese. But I did know how to wade through thousands of pages of documents. If that was the challenge, I was the man of the hour. "What kind of records are they?" I asked.

"They vary. I see bills of sale for old merchant expeditions. Property deeds from the 1600s. A book about topography in ancient Brazil. It seems random. It's going to take a long time to go through all of it."

"Are they in any particular order?"

"They seem to be ordered by date. I think whoever compiled these in the first place did that." I imagined some ancient librarian going through these records in centuries past, sorting them by the light of a candle.

"Why don't you start with records soon after the *Flor de la Mar* sank in 1511?" I suggested. "If there's something useful, it would probably be from that time."

"Yes! That's a good idea. I'll do it." She leaned forward and got to it.

I wasn't much use on this project, so I left Ashley and got up to wander the Archives. The quiet was a relief, and I savored the feeling of being far away from everything going on Stateside. The last several months had been a blur of work. I was bone tired. I had promised to log on remotely and do what I could to help Harder, Cindy, and Vijay with the case. But first, I needed some time to myself. I roamed the Archives, taking in the paintings and books and statues and busts, admiring strange artifacts and works from centuries ago.

After sundown, when the Archives closed for the day, we left to check into a hotel. I hadn't expected to find anything on the first day, so I wasn't disappointed. Neither was Ashley. If anything, she looked energized as we walked out of the building. There was an electricity in the air that we both felt.

We were sure that we would find something at the Archives. We ate some dinner at the hotel and discussed the records Ashley had seen. Then we went to sleep. The next morning, we were back at the Archives as soon as they opened.

We repeated this routine the next day. We arrived at the Archives early. Ashley studied the records while I sat nearby and worked on the case. Our only company down there was the white-bearded old man and a few visitors who meandered through now and then. When the library closed, we had an early dinner, went back to the hotel, and slept.

It was on the third day that she found it.

I was working on a legal brief when I saw Ashley walking over to me. She looked dazed. As if she couldn't quite believe what she had seen. I knew immediately that she had found something. I slammed my laptop shut and jumped to my feet. "What is it?" I said urgently.

She just shook her head at me, seemingly unable to answer. She glanced over at the white-bearded old man who was reading a couple of tables down. Then she gestured with her chin toward the new materials room. Once inside, she sat me down and pointed at the screen.

"This," she said. I looked at it blankly. It was a document written in Portuguese, which to me looked the same as all the others.

"What is it?"

"A confession."

"A confession?" I said, confused. "Like to a priest?"

"Sort of. It was given by a Portuguese sailor."

"Who?"

"His name was Manuel Roberto. He sailed with Alfonso de Albuquerque aboard the *Flor de la Mar*."

I felt goosebumps prickle all over my body, and my hair stood on end. "What?" I whispered.

"I found it in a set of church records," she continued. "It was recorded by a priest, who doesn't leave his name. I don't think it was an actual confession. A priest wouldn't have broken the seal. It seems like something that the man needed to get out before he died. To atone."

"To atone for what?" I asked. Ashley just shook her head, unable to come up with the words. "What does it say?" I asked breathlessly. "Does it say where the *Flor de la Mar* sank? Does it have more information? Is this what your brother found?"

She nodded absently. "This is definitely what he found." Then she took a deep breath, steadied herself, and then translated the confession for me in full. This is what it said:

> My name is Manuel Roberto. I served Afonso Dalboquerque the Great, Captain-Major of the Seas of Arabia, Governor of Portuguese India, aboard the ship *Flor de la Mar*. In 1511 A.D., we set sail from Malacca, to return to King Manuel, and to present him with the treasures of Malacca, the greatest that had ever been taken in all the history of the Empire.
>
> It is known that the *Flor de la Mar* sunk in a storm, on some shoals near the Kingdom of Daru in Sumatra. It is known that the bold and intrepid Afonso Dalboquerque and some others escaped on a raft, and that they barely missed drowning in the sea, and that the rest of the ship, and the six hundred souls aboard, sank to the bottom of the seas, never to be heard from again.
>
> By my name, this is not true.

Before the voyage from Malacca, Dalboquerque the Great gathered me and the other trusted captains, and told us that the *Flor de la Mar* was not to be taken to King Manuel, but was to be sailed to Goa, the Indian province which Dalboquerque the Great was to rule. Dalboquerque said that this was on the orders of the King.

We knew it was not, as we were not fools; but we loved him, this conqueror who had led us through the nations of the East, who had given us great victories and treasures, and who had promised us undreamed of rewards if we obeyed. Who was the King but a man in a faraway land, who would never know our Christian names?

In the storm of November 1511, the ships of the fleet became separated, and Dalboquerque the Great seized the moment. He abandoned *Flor de la Mar* on a raft with some few trusted men. But the greatest trust he placed in those of us that remained, and we, hidden by the storm, steered a course toward Goa. We killed the natives, so that they would not talk, and kept only a skeleton crew to sail the ship. Anyone whose loyalty we felt doubtful were put overboard.

But the hand of providence was against us. We never reached Goa. Although we escaped unscathed the great storm of November 1511, days later, another, greater storm caught us at sea, in sight of some uncharted land. There the *Flor de la Mar* foundered and sank. Most everyone was lost. I and some others managed to swim to nearby rocks, where we clung to life as waves washed over us ceaselessly. Death seemed assured. But miraculously, we were able to swim to a small vegetated island of less than a mile, to the east of the wreck, and took shelter among the trees.

In time, the storm passed, and some days later, by the grace of God, we were found by some native fishermen and taken to a bigger island nearby. They tended and fed us, and I am eternally grateful to these peoples, and wish upon their descendants the blessings of Christ. After we were well, and with the help of the natives, we made our way back to Sumatra, and then to Malacca, there to return to the Portuguese garrison. We vowed never to speak a word of the treason of Dalboquerque the Great, and what transpired on the *Flor de la Mar*.

I have the sickness now. I make this confession on my deathbed. It has hung over me these last years. I pray to God for forgiveness of our sins. I go with God now, may he save my soul.

Manuel Roberto, 1513 A.D.

We sat in silence for a while after she finished. Reading it had exhausted her. And hearing it had exhausted me. I didn't know what to make of this fantastic tale.

"This is from 1513," I said absently. "Two years after the *Flor de la Mar* sank. And two years before Albuquerque died." Ashley nodded.

At first, the whole idea seemed insane to me. The notion that Alfonso de Albuquerque had betrayed the King, diverted the greatest treasure ship in history for his own ends, and lost it far from the place that everyone believed—I could scarcely conceive of it. It seemed impossible that a piece of history writ so large could have been subverted in this way, and happened so differently than anyone had imagined. There was no inkling of this in any of the other accounts. I wasn't a big believer in conspiracy theories. The idea that such a one as this could have happened five hundred years ago, and never been discovered, seemed impossible.

But the more I thought about it, the more plausible it seemed. I remembered what I had learned about Albuquerque. There was no doubt that he was a tremendously ambitious man. In life, he had been one of the great explorers and conquerors of the age. He had attained the rank of Viceroy, a step below the King himself. He had styled himself "the Great," after Alexander, and his *Commentaries* were modeled on Caesar's.

Was it so far-fetched that Albuquerque had been megalomaniacal enough to try and seize power in Asia for himself? Or that he had diverted the *Flor de la Mar* for that purpose? Wasn't that what Caesar and Alexander had done? Albuquerque's enemies at court had been whispering just these accusations in the King's ear in the years before Albuquerque's death, which caused his fall from grace. What if they were true?

The thoughts raced through my mind, one after the other. Wasn't it true, after all, that there were only a handful of supposed eyewitnesses to the sinking of the *Flor de la Mar*? That it had happened five hundred years ago, long outside of living memory? That there were no accurate records of where it had gone down, and that the wreck of the *Flor de la Mar* had never been definitively found, even though it supposedly sank in the shallows of one of the most well-trafficked waterways in the world?

What if that was because it never sank there in the first place?

"What are you thinking?" Ashley said at last.

"I think it fits," I said slowly.

But she looked doubtful. "How do we know this document is real?" she asked.

"Real?" I said, puzzled. "It's a five-hundred-year-old record in the Portuguese Archives."

"Yeah. But just because it's old doesn't mean it's authentic."

"What do you mean?"

Ashely ran a hand through her hair, looking frustrated. "I don't know. It just feels off somehow. Who is this guy, Manuel Roberto? Who took this confession? Why is it in Portugal, instead of Malacca? Why have we never heard any of this before? I just...how can you keep a secret this big for this long? Is it even possible?"

We decided to call Schnizzel to help us puzzle through it. He might have a good idea of whether it could be true, and what to do with the information. I opened up the Signal app on my phone and dialed him.

We had all downloaded Signal, as well as another messaging app called Telegram. Remington had instructed us not to talk or text about the case on the phone. There was too much at stake, and there were too many big players involved, to risk talking on an unencrypted line. Unless we were at the office, all of our communications went through these apps. Just like David Marcum had done.

When I told Schnizzel what we'd found, I had to turn him down to the lowest volume setting to avoid alerting the entire Portuguese Archives about the discovery. Then I had to spend about ten minutes calming him down before we could get anything out of him. He was so jubilant that I thought he might choke up and die right there on the phone.

"It's incredible," he said over and over. "Incredible. To think that a treasure of that magnitude, a twist of history like that... it's unbelievable."

"Isn't it?" Ashley asked. The skepticism in her voice was plain.

"Ashley has doubts," I explained. "About whether the source is authentic."

"Well. That's only natural," said Schnizzel.

"Why would it not be authentic?" I interjected. "I mean, this is a centuries-old document in the Portuguese Archives. Isn't it?"

"Yes. But it could be wrong. Or it could be something else. A forgery, for instance."

"A forgery?" I said, startled by the idea. The possibility hadn't occurred to me. Ashley nodded. This was the type of thing she'd been thinking about. "But why would someone forge a confession like that?" I asked. "And how could they even do it?"

I could almost hear Schnizzel shrug over the phone. "Who knows. People forge records for all sorts of reasons. Albuquerque had a lot of enemies in Portugal. Enemies who tried to discredit him with the King. Maybe this was a false confession. Placed in the historical record to do just that. Forged confessions are not unheard of."

"That seems a little far-fetched, doesn't it?"

"Perhaps. But so does what you've found." That was true enough.

"However," Schnizzel said, "I think there is a logical proof here." There was an undercurrent of excitement in his voice.

"How so?"

"Think about it," Schnizzel said. "We know that Rockweiller found *Flor de la Mar*, right?"

"Right."

"And we know David Marcum led them to it."

"Right."

"And we suspect that Marcum found his information there, at the Archives. This is what led him there. Right?"

"Yes," Ashley said. "This must be what my brother found."

"Then don't you see?" Schnizzel said triumphantly. "The proof is in the pudding. If David Marcum gave this information to Rockweiller, and Rockweiller used it to find the ship, then it follows that the information must be true!"

"Of course," I breathed. I should have seen it immediately. I was supposed to be the logical lawyer, after all. I saw Ashley turn the concept over in her mind. "I can't say that it doesn't make sense," she said finally, unable to find fault with Schnizzel's logic. "But it just feels off, somehow."

But I ignored her, because something else had just occurred to me. A flash of inspiration. Perhaps the strongest one I'd ever had. "I'll tell you what else, Professor," I said. "Now we know where the ship is."

"What?" Ashley exclaimed.

"*What?*" Schnizzel yelled.

I ran outside of the room, grabbed my laptop, and dashed back in. Breathlessly, I opened the laptop and pulled up Google Earth. The internet was slow, and it took forever for Google to load its 3D rendering of the world. I tapped my foot nervously, ignoring repeated questions from Ashley and Schnizzel. Once the image loaded, I clicked the globe and zoomed in toward Malaysia.

"Everyone believes that the *Flor de la Mar* sank somewhere around here," I said, indicating the Strait of Malacca. "That's where Albuquerque escaped the ship, and where all the other witnesses said it went down."

"Right."

"Now. Let's extrapolate from Manuel Roberto's account. He said they were making for Goa." I zoomed out and traced my finger northwest, up through the Strait of Malacca, across the Bay of Bengal, and to the far side of the Indian subcontinent, where the province of Goa was located.

"Yes."

"But they never made it to Goa. Roberto says that they wrecked in a storm not long after departure, in sight of some uncharted land. After that, they were rescued by natives, and convalesced at a nearby tropical island. Right?"

"Right. That's all in the account."

"Okay. Now. What place matches that description?"

I leaned forward and looked at the empty blue ocean north of Indonesia, northwest of Sumatra. I was almost feverish with anticipation, hoping against hope that I would find what I was looking for. I checked the map scale, and thought about how fast ships travelled in those days. I zoomed closer and closer, deeper into the image, deeper into the ocean.

And then, at nearly the maximum zoom range, in just the right place, at exactly the right distance, I saw a small flash of green appear, northwest of Indonesia. Just where I knew it had to be.

"Look," I whispered to Ashley, pointing at it.

"What is it?" Schnizzel veritably screamed, unable to contain himself anymore. "I can't see!"

"I'll call you back," I said, hanging up amidst his shrieks of anguish.

I was looking at a small chain of islands, just a few hundred kilometers northwest of Sumatra. The islands were barely visible against the great expanse of the ocean. The southernmost island was the biggest, and then they dropped off in size as they went up the chain. They looked almost like an inverted version of the Florida Keys, on the other side of the world. The legend on the map named them the Nicobar Islands.

"Here," I breathed. Ashley looked over my shoulder, spellbound. We looked up the islands online and read about them in more detail. The Nicobar Islands were a tiny archipelagic chain in the Indian Ocean. According to Wikipedia, the larger ones were sparsely inhabited, and drew some tourists for scuba diving and other watersports. The smaller ones were mostly empty.

I quickly skimmed through the history of the islands. There was no Western presence on the Nicobar Islands until the later colonial period, when the Danish East India Company occupied them in the late 18th century. The Dutch then sold the rights to the British in the 19th century. Eventually, after World War Two, the islands became union territories of India. But in the sixteenth century, the islands would have been virtually unknown.

"It fits," I whispered. "A set of uncharted islands on the way to Goa. That's what Roberto wrote. These wouldn't have been on any maps in 1511."

"But how do you know that's the spot he's talking about?"

"Where else could it be?" I said impatiently. "Roberto's account speaks of a primitive tropical island on which they were nursed back to health. It would have been lightly inhabited. There's nowhere else that fits the description." We swept across the map, zooming around and looking for other possible locations. "Do you see anywhere else?"

"No," she admitted. "But...there's no way," she said.

"Why not?"

"I just...you can't just draw a line on a map and find some islands and then theorize that an ancient ship sank there!"

"But that's exactly what your brother did. And he was right."

Ashley and I spent the rest of the day going through the records to see if there was anything else. There wasn't. We weren't supposed to take copies or pictures of the records, so Ashley copied out Manuel Roberto's account by hand.

We emerged from the Archives in the late afternoon. It was sunny outside. I squinted, unused to the bright light after spending all day underground. I heard birds chirping. The world seemed somehow ethereal just then. I felt that we had uncovered this great secret, hidden away deep in the bowels of history. We alone knew something significant, the location of this great treasure, which held the whole world in its thrall.

I pulled out my phone. I had missed calls from Cindy and Harder. They must have tried to reach me earlier. We didn't always get good reception underground in the Archives.

I also checked my email. I hadn't looked at it in a while, engrossed as I was with the confession. I scrolled through a couple dozen emails about the case and various other things. Then I noticed that two court orders had been entered just a few hours ago, involving our claims. I frowned and clicked through the link to download them.

My stomach tightened into a knot when I read the title of the first order. It was called "order regarding motion for crime-fraud exception to attorney-client privilege."

A thrill went through me as I opened it, and my heart began to pound. Here it was. The order we had been waiting for. The order that was going to reveal the death memo and blow the case wide open. I could barely stand it. I eagerly began to read.

> Before the Court is the Estate of David Marcum's Motion to Compel Production of Attorney-Client Privileged Information Pursuant to the Crime-Fraud Exception. The Court has reviewed the motion, as well as any responses and replies thereto.
>
> The attorney-client privilege is one of the bedrock principles of our legal system. It facilitates the free flow of information between attorney and client, which is essential to effective representation. It is not to be taken lightly. Without the privilege, the client would be unable to freely recount the facts of a case with the lawyer, which would damage the right to a fair defense.
>
> Therefore, exceptions to the attorney-client privilege are narrow. In this instance, the Marcum Estate has presented evidence that Rockweiller's witnesses have lied under oath, and argue that the crime-fraud exception should be applied. This evidence comes in the form of deposition testimony and equipment records, which the Court has reviewed at length.
>
> Having considered the evidence, the Court concludes it is not sufficient to invoke the crime-fraud exception. Although it is a close case, and the Court has serious questions regarding the truthfulness of Lloyd Gunthum and others, the evidence does not warrant the wholesale abrogation of the attorney-client privilege. Although some privileged documents may have tantalizing names such as "death memo-

> randum," that is not sufficient reason to lose the sacred shield of privilege.
>
> The Marcum Estate will have every opportunity to cast doubt on the veracity of Mr. Gunthum and other Rockweiller witnesses during trial. The Court has no doubt that the Estate will ably do so. Accordingly, the Marcum Estate's motion is DENIED.

It was signed by Judge Graves.

I felt faint. Like I was about to fall. I needed to sit down. "What's wrong?" Ashley said, concerned. I didn't answer her. I cast about for somewhere to sit. I saw a bench on the grass a few yards away. I made my way there unsteadily and sat down.

I didn't know how to tell Ashley. I just handed her my phone. Then I sat silently while she read the order. I felt numb.

"I don't understand," she said after she finished reading. Then she read it again, as if it might say something different, or make more sense the second time around. "I thought we had this. It was so obvious that Gunthum was lying. Everyone in the room knew it. How could the Judge not see that?"

I shook my head. I had no words to answer.

Maybe it was the transcript, I thought. Things sometimes appear differently on paper than they do in real life. We had attached the video, but Graves might not have watched it. Maybe it was our brief. Maybe it wasn't good enough. Maybe Badden & Bock's was just better. Maybe it was what Judge Graves ate for breakfast. I didn't know.

I saw my phone vibrating in Ashley's hand. I was getting a call. It was Remington. She handed it to me. Exhilaration and sorrow vied for control of my emotions as I answered it.

"Jack," said Remington.

"John. I just read the order. On the memo. It's terrible. I can't believe it. But I'll get to that in a minute. Listen. You're not going to believe this. We found it." The words were coming out faster than I could stop them, faster than I could reasonably explain. "We figured it out how Marcum found the *Flor de la Mar*. And more than that. You're not going to believe this. I know where it is. It was all in the Archives."

"Jack," he said again. "Hang on."

"Alfonso de Albuquerque never intended that the *Flor de la Mar* reach Portugal," I said, talking over him. "He—"

Remington cut me off sharply. "Jack, stop before you say another word. You need to listen to me."

I stopped, confused. "What is it?" I asked, finally paying attention.

"Have you seen the other order that came down today?"

"No. I just read the first one. The privilege order. I can't believe he denied our motion. It's total bullshit. I—"

"You need to read the second order."

"Okay. I'll download it in a minute. I've just been caught up in the—"

"We lost the disqualification motion. The court has disqualified us from further work on the case."

"I'm sorry, what?"

"We've been disqualified."

I couldn't comprehend what he was saying. It just didn't register. "What do you mean? I don't...the disqualification motion? But we filed a response to that."

"We did."

"Do you mean Wurlheiser? Did they...but Kruckemeyer was blocking the vote, right? I thought we had more time."

"No. I'm not talking about the firm. I'm talking about the court. Rockweiller won their motion to disqualify. It's Judge Graves that disqualified us, not David Wurlheiser."

"But..." my head spun as I tried to wrap my head around this. How could this have possibly happened? "There's no way," I said. "It was a bullshit motion. You know that. We put up a great response. I just..."

"I know," Remington said heavily. "It shouldn't have happened. I think it was the wrong decision. By a mile. But unfortunately, that's the way it came down. A judge doesn't always see things the way you would like, or even see clearly sometimes. This is why I was concerned about taking the case from the get-go."

"But we're on the verge of...we're so close. I just, I..." I stuttered on for a few more sentences. "After all this?" I said wrenchingly.

"After all this."

Ashley caught the look on my face and knew something was wrong. Something worse than having our motion for a crime-fraud exception denied.

I turned away. I couldn't face her just then. I was gripped with a sense of unreality.

"I...what do we do now? Are we going to file an emergency appeal? A motion for reconsideration?" I said to Remington.

"We've been discussing it. But it's unlikely that we would win."

"Surely there's something we can do. Some procedural tactic..."

"No," said Remington with finality. "I'm afraid we need to steel ourselves for the reality. Whatever information you found may be great for Ashley, but some other lawyer is going to have to run with it."

I cupped my hand over the phone and turned farther away. "How am I going to break this to her?" I asked.

"Do it now. Don't keep her in the dark."

I didn't say anything for a few beats.

"We've got forty-eight hours to transition off the case," Remington told me. "We need to collect all of our files from the hotel by then and give them to Ashley. Then it's pencils down."

TWENTY-NINE

It was in a state of shock and unreality that I sat on the bed in my Galveston hotel room. There were papers and binders everywhere, making the place look like a recycling facility. I tried to bring myself to start the cleanup. But I couldn't do it. I couldn't come to terms with what had happened.

We'd been on the case for nearly a year now. I thought back to the little pro bono clinic in Houston where it all started. I thought about how far we'd come. How much I'd learned about David Marcum. About Rockweiller Industries. About the *Flor de la Mar*, and the unimaginable riches buried deep beneath the ocean. About Ashley. And now, at the zenith of the case, after holding our own against all of the countries and corporations ranged against us, with the whole world watching, we had been disqualified. I couldn't believe it.

Harder and Ashley were sitting with me in the hotel room. We had spent the day going over the nuances of the case, so Ashley would be prepared to take it forward with her new lawyers. Remington and Kruckemeyer had spent the last two days on the phone, talking to lawyers they knew who could take it over. There was no shortage of good ones for Ashley to choose from. Better than us, probably. Because of the high profile of the case, attorneys were beating down our door trying to get a piece of the action. Some of them had even been calling Ashley directly. I promised her that we would find her someone great.

But when I said that, she just shook her head and looked me straight in the eye and said "I don't want any other lawyer but you." It made my heart jump near out of my chest to hear that. I tried to come up with something to say, but I couldn't, and so we just gazed at each other for a while. Harder looked away uncomfortably and began picking up binders.

Harder was deeply miserable. He blamed himself for the disqualification, I knew. But it wasn't really his fault. Badden & Bock would have filed their motion anyway, with or without Harder's information. Part of the blame lay with the firm. We knew the risks going in and chose to accept them. But mostly, I blamed Judge Graves. It was a bad decision. No two ways about it. There was no conflict, and I couldn't understand how he had gotten it so wrong.

Ironically, I knew that a state court judge like Gleeson never would have disqualified us from the case. He would have been too conscious of the blowback. Disqualify a whole law firm, and every lawyer in it would hold a grudge against you for years. Gleeson would have denied the motion to disqualify and let the case play out. Oh well. Roads not taken.

The rest of the team had said their goodbyes earlier. I ran into Loudamire in the hall. I could swear she almost seemed sad to see me go. "Bye, Jack," was all she said, in a quiet voice.

We finished cleaning out the hotel room at 11:30 p.m. We had until midnight to exit the case. We stood up to say our goodbyes.

"Well, I guess this is it," I told Ashley, struggling to hold back my emotions. I saw her fighting back tears. "I hope we can be friends," I said. "Even if I can't give you legal advice anymore." She nodded, her lips pressed together tightly. We embraced and held each other for a long time. Then we stepped apart.

"At least you can get back to your contract work now, Jack," Harder joked, trying to ease the tension. I shook my head. He had the worst timing.

"What?" said Ashley, confused.

"Never mind," said Harder, reddening.

"It's an old joke," I explained. "Technically, I'm an independent contractor for the firm. Like your brother was for Rockweiller. I get paid on a 1099 form, is all it means. Harder likes to give me grief about it."

"Sorry," said Harder, embarrassed. "I don't always have the best timing. I'm just kidding, though. You know that I think you're a great lawyer, Jack. Really. You're basically a member of the firm."

"Thanks buddy," I said, touched.

I expected the firm would bring me on as a full-time employee after this. Disqualification or no, I'd done good work on this case. Kruckemeyer and Remington knew it. The other partners knew it too. No more 1099 for me. I was basically a member of the firm.

But then I froze as something occurred to me. *Basically a member of the firm*. But not a member of the firm. *Of course*, I thought, realization dawning. I remembered the ethics seminar I had taken months ago. About imputation of conflicts. I dropped the binder I was carrying.

"I'm not a member of the firm," I whispered. "I'm a contractor. That's it."

"What are you talking about?" said Ashley.

I turned to her. "Do you still want me on this case?" I asked urgently.

"Of course," she said.

"Even without the rest of the firm?"

"Yes! You know I do. But I thought you've been disqualified."

"The firm has," I said. "But I'm not a member of the firm."

I could see Harder catching on. "I'm an independent contractor for HH&K," I explained. "Practically, it makes no difference. I work full time. I get paid the same. I'm a regular employee in all but name. But if you want to get technical, I'm not actually part of the law firm. Harder, quick, pull up the ethics rules."

Harder whipped out his laptop and looked up the rule on imputation of conflicts. An imputed conflict was when the conflict of one lawyer carried over to the rest of the firm. It was Rule 1.10. Harder read the rule aloud: "While lawyers are associated in a firm, none of them shall knowingly represent a client when any one of them practicing alone would be prohibited from doing so...."

"While lawyers are associated *in a firm*," I repeated. "I'm not in the firm. That means that whatever conflict the firm has doesn't involve me! I can continue on the case!"

Harder squinted at the text of the rule. "Are you sure about that?" he said. "You're still associated *with* the firm, right? Even if you're not in it. I feel like the spirit of the rules might bar you. And these are the American Bar Association rules. The Texas rules may be a little stricter—"

"Fuck the spirit of the rules," I said savagely. "We go by the letter. And the rules say *in* a firm, not *with* a firm. Hell, I wasn't even at the firm when Wurlheiser did the Rockweiller work."

"That's true," he said, nodding. "It's colorable."

"What are you going to do?" Ashley asked. "Are you going to ask the judge if you can stay on?"

"No," I decided. I had a good argument. Maybe it was a winner, maybe it wasn't. But either way, it was enough to me give legal cover for what I had to do. I didn't trust Graves to make the right decision, and it would be better to ask for forgiveness than for permission. Let him ream me over it later if he wanted to.

I stood up straighter, and my voice took on more formal tone. "Judge Graves has disqualified the law firm of HH&K from representing you in this case," I told Ashley. "He has not disqualified me. I have concluded, based on the ethics rules and the applicable law, that the conflict and the disqualification order does not apply to me. So pursuant to my duties as an advocate, I will continue to zealously represent you to the best of my ability. If you want me to, that is," I added, feeling a little abashed.

"Yes!" she said to me, tears streaming down her face. I smiled and drew her in for a hug. Then out of the blue, she leaned forward and kissed me full on the lips. My eyes widened.

"I..." I stammered after she pulled back.

"Don't say another word, Jack, about the ethics rules right now," she warned. "Just shut up and kiss me." Harder looked away, but I caught him smiling.

It was sound legal advice, and I acted on it.

By the time the clock struck midnight, we had everything packed up and ready to go. I felt ablaze with new energy. We had debated whether to tell the firm what I was doing, but decided not to. They couldn't help with it anyway, and I didn't see the point.

Just as we were getting ready to leave, we heard a sound from next door. A crash and a thump. Like something had broken and fallen. We froze for a minute, listening. But we didn't hear anything further. I exchanged worried glances with Harder. The sound had come from Loudamire's room. What if she had been listening to us?

"She probably dropped one of those huge deposition binders she's always lugging around," I guessed.

"I don't know," Harder said doubtfully. "That definitely sounded like something breaking."

I put my ear against the wall. I still heard no sound from Loudamire's room. It was dead silent. Harder and I looked at each other, wondering what to do. But Ashley didn't hesitate. She marched straight out into the hallway and up to Loudamire's door. Harder and I followed reluctantly.

The door was propped open a fraction. The light in the room was on. I could see it spilling out from the cracks around the door. The hinge must not have closed all the way. We still couldn't hear anything from inside.

Ashley knocked loudly on the door. "Hello?" she said. "Kathleen?" She knocked a few more times, but there was no answer. "Kathleen? This is Ashley Marcum. Is everything okay?"

"Why wouldn't she be answering?" Harder whispered. "Beats me."

"We should go there and make sure she's alright," Ashley decided.

"That's asking for trouble," I warned. "Don't you know Loudamire by now? She'll probably sue us for trespass."

"Come off the lawyer bullshit for a minute," she said sharply. "She's a person." I backed off, stung.

"Have it your way," I said.

"Kathleen?" Ashley called. "We're coming in."

Ashley pushed open the door slowly and walked into the entryway. I followed carefully, as if walking into a booby-trapped temple. I half-expected hidden snakes to fall from the ceiling, or knives to stab from the walls. Or the legal equivalent.

"Kathleen?" Still hearing no answer, Ashley walked into the bedroom. Then she stopped. I heard her gasp.

Harder and I rushed in. There, by the bed, we saw a broken bottle of vodka on the floor, leaking cold liquid across the carpet. Next to it was a large bottle of pills, opened, with the contents spilling out.

And next to the bottle was the immobile form of Kathleen Loudamire.

"Shit!" I said, rushing over to her.

"Is she okay?" said Harder.

I kneeled and shook her gently. "Kathleen!" I said urgently. I tried to check her pulse, but didn't know how. Ashley pushed me aside and put two fingers to her throat. "She's breathing." Loudamire mumbled something. I couldn't make out what it was. "Call 9-11," Ashley instructed. Harder ran to the phone and dialed. He gave them the room number. They said someone was on their way. Then Harder called the hotel operator too.

"What the hell happened?" Ashley whispered, stepping back. She was in shock. "Why would she do this?" I shook my head wordlessly.

"She was under a lot of stress," Harder said. "I guess it finally got to her."

I thought back to Loudamire's behavior. She had always acted pretty oddly. I thought about the fatigue. The mental health issues. Harder's comments about her reputation at Badden & Bock. When I reframed things, I could see it. But until now, I hadn't. I had always seen Loudamie as a successful, if unpleasant, attorney. A suicide attempt was just not on my radar.

I looked around the room as we waited for the paramedics to arrive. It was neater than mine, but there was even more stuff. I saw two laptops, an iPad, and a library's worth of legal briefs and binders stacked up in the corners. I glanced at the desk. There were a couple of papers she must have been working on.

And then I saw it. On the edge of the desk. Half-flipped open, with the cover page visible. It was no more than a handful of pages, stapled together.

Memorandum Regarding the Legality of Death in Extraterritorial Jurisdiction – Privileged & Confidential.

"Look," I whispered, pointing. Ashley and Harder stopped dead in their tracks when they saw it.

I stood stock still as the situation flashed through my mind. It was the death memo. The one they had kept from us. The one Judge Graves had refused to give us, even in the face of Gunthum's blatant lies. I knew that document told exactly what had happened to David Marcum.

But it was heavily privileged. We couldn't take it. It would be a serious ethical violation even to look at it. We could get disbarred. Doubly, ten times so in this situation. The girl had just tried to commit suicide, for God's sake. I didn't even yet know whether she would turn out to have been successful.

But I also knew deep in my bones that they were lying about David Marcum. And I knew the truth was in there.

How could I close my eyes and remain willfully ignorant while it was staring me in the face?

"We can't," said Harder in an agonized voice, reading my thoughts. "Think about what Remington would say."

"I know." I thought about the ethics exam I took before the bar, with all of its easy bullshit questions that we had laughed at. I thought about what I had gone to law school for. I thought about when I was sworn in as a lawyer. I thought about my parents.

"If we don't look now, we'll never see it again," I said. "We'll never find out what happened."

"Maybe not," said Harder, his face contorted. "But we're members of the bar. We've got to uphold the attorney-client privilege. Right?"

You think you know the answer to this question when you see it on an ethics exam. It's easy. Circle A, move on. But when it's real life, and there's a real client standing behind you, and her brother is dead, and they're lying about it, it's different.

We stood there, frozen in time. I knew we had minutes, at most, before the paramedics showed up. Before it would be too late. Before it would be impossible to get the memo, now or ever.

In the midst of our indecision, as Harder and I agonized over the choice, Ashley didn't. She stepped forward and deliberately took the memo from Loudamire's desk. "Fuck the attorney-client privilege," she said evenly. Then she folded up the memo and stuffed it into her pocket.

We gazed at her in shock. "What?" she said defiantly. "I'm not a lawyer. I'm not bound by your rules. And what's ethical about letting Rockweiller lie and cover up the death of my brother? The right and wrong of this situation are crystal clear to me."

I opened my mouth, maybe to argue with her, maybe not, I wasn't sure. But it didn't matter. Because at that moment, the door burst open, and a crowd of paramedics and firefighters ran in, brushing past us without a glance, unaware of the terrible ethical dilemma that we had confronted, and the path that we had chosen, as they rushed in to try and save Kathleen's life.

Hours later, I was in the hospital, sitting in Kathleen's room. She was unconscious but stable. After the paramedics had arrived, they asked if one of us would go with her to the hospital, and so I rode with them in the ambulance.

Once at the hospital, I called Bock's office to let him know what had happened. Then I found Kathleen's emergency contact info in her phone and called her parents. They sounded like nice people. They were worried sick, and thanked me profusely for telling them. They said they would be on the next flight out there.

After that, I just sat there with Kathleen, feeling numb. It almost felt like my mind was switched off. There were no thoughts running through it. A few hours passed by like they were nothing at all.

At around 3 a.m., Zachary Bock showed up. He was wearing his usual dark suit, but looked disheveled for once. He stiffened reflexively when he saw me, assuming his adversarial expression for a moment. But then he looked at Loudamire, and his face softened. He stood for a few beats and then sat down across from me in a chair by the bed.

"Hello Jack," he said quietly.

"Hey Bock."

There was a long silence. I didn't know what to say to him, if anything. Eventually, I told him what happened, leaving out the part about the death memo. I wondered if Ashley and Harder had read it already, and what it said.

Bock thanked me for calling the ambulance and taking Kathleen to the hospital. I nodded, and then decided it was time to go. I was beginning to get up when Bock spoke again.

"Do you have children, Jack?" he said suddenly.

"No," I said.

He nodded absently. "You're young. I do. A boy and a girl. They're twelve and fourteen. They want to go to law school when they grow up. Like me." His mouth twisted a little, with some feeling I couldn't place.

"Kathleen has always been hard on herself," Bock continued. He was looking at Loudamire, but seemed to be talking more to himself than to either of us. "And I've always been hard on her. I'm hard on everyone. But there's a reason for that. This is a tough business. You have to be able to take the pressure. It's not a game for the weak of heart. I always impress that on people. If you're soft, if you're nice, you're going to lose. Your client's going to lose." There was a certain amount of self-reflection in Bock's voice. But no regret.

"People come to us for the best legal advice money can buy," Bock said. It wasn't arrogant or prideful for him to say it, because I knew that it was true. "They come to us when they're backed into a corner. When the stakes are high, and the pressure is on.

"Life is hard, Jack. That's the way it is. I'm not doing anyone any favors by being easy on them." He finally turned and looked at me directly.

"Go. I'll take it from here. Thank you for what you did. Sincerely. I know I've been tough on you in this case. I won't pretend otherwise. But you could take it. You were a worthy opponent, Jack."

He extended his hand. Our eyes met. For the first time, he really looked at me, and there was no condescension in his face. We shook hands solemnly, and then I took my leave.

Ashley, Harder, and I sat silently on the bed in my hotel room. We were all cross-legged, forming a triangle on the bed with the death memo in the middle. Ashley and Harder had not read it yet. They were waiting for me to come back from the hospital.

From the cover page, I observed that the document was written in the typical style of a law firm memorandum. There would be a facts section, followed by a legal analysis, and then an ultimate conclusion. It was customary to write memoranda in the third person, which gave them a certain objectivity, or impersonality. Or at least the appearance of it.

The three of us looked at each other. It was past midnight. Harder was technically supposed to be off the case. But he didn't look like he was going anywhere, and I wasn't about to say anything.

Eventually, Ashley took a deep breath and picked up the memo. She paused for a moment, as if weighing it in her hands. Then she held it out to me. I took it, flipped to the second page, and began to read aloud. The acoustics were strange in the small hotel room, and my voice sounded almost muffled as I spoke.

From: Kathleen Loudamire

To: Zachary Bock

Re: Memorandum Regarding the Legality of Death in Extraterritorial Jurisdiction

PRIVILEGED AND CONFIDENTIAL

Question Presented: Under what circumstances may a corporation be held vicariously liable for negligent homicide or murder on the high seas, outside of the jurisdiction of any state or country?

Facts: These facts were relayed during a confidential witness interview with Thomas Barber, a crew member on the ship Excelsior on the date in question.

On [redacted], the Excelsior was anchored at [redacted] in the Indian Ocean. The Excelsior is a vessel owned by Excel Resources, Inc. ("Excel Resources"), which is a majority-owned subsidiary of Rockweiller Industries. The Excelsior was engaged in search and recovery operations for the wreck of what is believed to be the Portuguese carrack *Flor de la Mar*, which sank in 1511 in that area.

Aboard the Excelsior were Captain Lloyd Gunthum, seamen Thomas Barber, Michelle Kauller, and Richard Layes, and equipment operators Carl Ruthers and Jason Dubino. Also aboard the Excelsior was David Marcum. Marcum had been on the voyage during the discovery of the *Flor de la Mar*. Marcum then flew back to the United States, but returned some weeks later due to a dispute with Gunthum.

Marcum and Gunthum engaged in a series of heated arguments on the date of [redacted]. According to Mr. Barber, he heard "shouting and angry voices" from Gunthum's cabin during the morning. The arguments continued throughout the day. The subject of these arguments was the contents of the shipwreck that the Excelsior had located, and Marcum's demand for compensation for purportedly locating the shipwreck.

On the afternoon of [redacted], Marcum threatened to leave the Excelsior and publicly report the find of the *Flor de la Mar*, along with its coordinates, to the Malaysian, Indonesian, and Portuguese authorities, as well as to the international news media, unless Gunthum agreed to honor an alleged contract.

Subsequently, Marcum attempted to leave the ship on a small, motorized lifeboat. Gunthum refused to let him go, citing safety concerns for the crew without a lifeboat as well as the confidential information that Marcum had threatened to reveal. In the ensuing confrontation, Marcum became violent, and Gunthum instructed Barber and Leyes to subdue and confine him. This was carried out, although not without injury. Marcum broke Barber's nose and arm and gave Leyes a concussion. With the further assistance of Gunthum, Ruthers, and Dubino, the crew was able to tie Marcum to a heavy metal pole on deck using a length of rope, with all due care to ensure Marcum's safety. Marcum continued to struggle violently and hurled insults and abuse at Gunthum and the crew. Gunthum ordered a guard to be placed on Marcum at all times while he sought advice regarding the situation.

At approximately 10:45 p.m., Marcum broke free of the restraints with the artifice of a small knife that he had concealed on his person. Michelle Kauller was guarding him at the time. Marcum immediately started for the lifeboat, at which point Kauller aimed a Glock 19 handgun at him and fired several warning shots. One shot hit Marcum in the leg. Marcum turned on Kauller and stabbed her in the stomach with his knife, disarming her and taking her gun.

Shortly thereafter, Barber, Gunthum, Ruthers, and Dubino arrived on deck, having been alerted by the sound of gunfire. Gunthum was carrying a firearm. Marcum pointed Kauller's weapon at Gunthum, Ruthers, and Dubino, and told them to stop. Marcum stated that he was leaving in the lifeboat and they should not try to stop him. Gunthum, however, told him to stay put, and pointed his own firearm, a SIG Sauer P938, at Marcum.

After some additional verbal exchanges, Gunthum fired his weapon twice, hitting Marcum in the chest and killing him. After this, Gunthum stated to the crew that "he was about to fire on me. You all saw it." Barber states that he saw Marcum edging toward the boat, but was unable to confirm whether he believed Marcum was going to fire. Kauller was unconscious by this time due to loss of blood. She was later revived and her wounds staunched with first aid. Thereafter, David Marcum's body was weighed down with scuba weight belts and put overboard.

Legal Conclusion: Rockweiller Industries could be held liable for the death of David Marcum in international waters.

Analysis: Jurisdiction: A United States federal district court would have jurisdiction over Marcum's death. The Death On The High Seas Act ("DOHSA") governs the death of a person that is caused by wrongful act, neglect, or default occurring on the high seas beyond a marine league from the shore of any State. 46 U.S.C. § 30302. In addition, the Jones Act provides an additional remedy if the deceased is a seaman. 46 U.S.C. § 30104.

Here, Marcum's death occurred in international waters beyond a marine league from the shore of any State. Therefore, DOHSA would grant a federal court sitting in admiralty jurisdiction over a claim for Marcum's wrongful death.

A corporation may be held vicariously liable for the acts of its agents if the agent is acting in the scope of employment. *Painter v. Amerimex Drilling I, Ltd.*, 561 S.W.3d 125 (Tex. 2018). However, a parent corporation will not generally be held liable for the torts of its subsidiaries. *Lucas v. Texas Indus.*, 696 S.W.2d 372, 374 (Tex. 1984).

Here, Excel Resources could be held vicariously liable for Lloyd Gunthum's killing of David Marcum under the doctrine of *respondeat superior* if Gunthum was considered to be acting in the scope of his employment. *Painter*, 561 S.W.3d 125. Since Gunthum was captain of the Excelsior during a voyage, and was also compensated as a direct employee of Rockweiller Industries, that finding is likely.

On a more promising note, it should be observed that both DOHSA and the Jones Act preclude the application of punitive damages in cases of wrongful death. In addition, jury trials are typically not available in admiralty cases, which are instead tried before a judge. *See, e.g., Dunham v. Expro Americas*, 423 F. Supp. 2d 664 (S.D. Tex. 2003); *McBride v. Estis Well Service*, 768 F.3d 382 (5th Cir. 2014). Both of these factors would likely reduce the amount of a damages awarded against Excel Resources or Rockweiller Industries.

However, should the plaintiff discover the above-described facts and circumstances surrounding Marcum's death, this analysis could change. If Gunthum's killing of Marcum was determined to be intentional, rather than negligent, Rockweiller could face additional liability. It is possible that Lloyd Gunthum and/or Rockweiller Industries could be held criminally liable if such a determination were made. Accordingly, it is recommended that the company use all available means at its disposal to prevent the disclosure of these facts to any outside parties. This will have the effect of limiting legal exposure, and will also reduce the risk that the location of the *Flor de la Mar* is discovered.

/s/ Kathleen Loudamire

It took me ten minutes to read through the whole thing. We all sat in silence after I finished.

So that was it, I thought numbly. That was how David Marcum had died. He found the *Flor de la Mar*. He made a deal with Rockweiller Industries. And then Lloyd Gunthum shot him. They tossed his body over the side into the ocean somewhere, weighted down by the belts.

"They killed him," Ashley said dully. Her voice was hollow somehow, as if she couldn't really feel it.

"Why would Loudamire put that in a memo?" I wondered, more to have something to say than anything else.

"I bet it was a mistake," guessed Harder. "Loudamire must have interviewed Barber before they all got their story straight. She got the truth. Bock probably didn't want to hear it. But once she wrote it down, he couldn't destroy it. So they buried it with privilege." Harder shifted uncomfortably. "I made that kind of mistake once," he confessed. "Kruckemeyer asked me whether it was legal for a client to dump chemicals somewhere. It was my first week on the job. I wanted to impress Kruckemeyer, so I wrote a whole memo on it. Spent a week getting it perfect."

"And you concluded that it wasn't legal," I guessed.

"Right," Harder said. "Kruckemeyer reamed me for it. He said he just wanted to know the answer, not get a whole formal legal opinion about it. Said now he'd have to share it with the client, and the memo might be discoverable in litigation, if the issue ever came up. Like this."

I nodded. I could well imagine.

"Kruckemeyer explained that you have to know when to put something in writing, and when not to. It wasn't that the client was actually going to dump anything there—that's why they asked, and they never did. But some questions, you'd rather not have a record they were ever asked."

I nodded. "Bock must have been furious at Loudamire," I realized. "And then she let slip the memo title in the privilege log...the pressure measurement report...Gunthum shitting the bed at deposition...God. I bet Bock took it all out on her. That's why..." Harder nodded soberly.

"What are you going to do, Jack?" Harder said finally. He was looking at me. So was Ashley. I was suddenly reminded that I was lead counsel now. Harder couldn't help me. Nor could Remington or Kruckemeyer. I was on my own. I wondered for a moment whether I was in over my head. Whether I should have given the case to another lawyer. A more experienced one. But there was no turning back now.

I thought about what to do. The death memo was the key, I knew. It showed that Lloyd Gunthum had killed David Marcum, and that Rockweiller Industries had covered it up. Their witnesses had deliberately lied under oath, and Bock had suborned perjury. This would blow the case wide open. They could face criminal charges for it.

But we weren't supposed to have the memo. Taking it was unethical, and maybe illegal. Especially after what happened to Loudamire. Graves wouldn't care that it was Ashley that took it, not me. He would skin me alive. Very likely he would sanction me, strip me of my legal license, and maybe even throw me in jail. In front of the whole world.

But that wasn't what worried me the most just then. The worst possibility was that Graves might refuse to consider the evidence at all. If the memo was illegally obtained, Graves might exclude it. Fruit of the poisonous tree. That would be a disaster. I knew Bock & Co. would do everything in their power to try and cover it up. They would have to. They might say the memo was fabricated. Or that Kathleen had been out of her mind when she wrote it. I didn't know how far Rockweiller would go if we pushed them into a corner.

How could I prove that Rockweiller had killed David Marcum without the memo? Was there a way?

I also thought about the contract. We still didn't have proof that it existed. The memo hinted at it, but only in vague terms like "purported" and "alleged." Those were lawyer weasel words. It wouldn't be enough for Judge Graves, I knew. We still didn't have any solid evidence that there was a deal. But that was secondary just then. First, we had to figure out how to prove that the death memo was true. That Gunthum and Rockweiller had killed Marcum.

Time was short. Soon, Bock would find out that we had taken the memo. Assuming that Kathleen survived, she would go back to her hotel room and find that it was gone. There was no way to put that cat back in the bag. I tried to think of what Remington would do.

"We need proof," I said at last. "Proof of what happened to David. Proof that he found the *Flor de la Mar*. Proof that he was killed for it."

"But how do we get it?" Ashley asked.

I looked at Harder. He was going to have to leave the room for this. Now that he was off the case, we couldn't rely on his attorney-client privilege anymore. They could subpoena him and force him to give up everything we said. Harder nodded at me, understanding.

"Good luck," he said resolutely. Then he walked out and shut the door.

I turned to Ashley. "Here's what we're going to do," I said.

THIRTY

We flew to Malaysia on Singapore Airlines. The food and service were surprisingly good. Much better than the U.S. airlines I usually flew. The flight took almost twenty-four hours. I tried to get some rest on the plane, but didn't sleep a wink. Instead, I passed the time in feverish contemplation of what we were about to attempt.

The night before, I had received a call from Remington. The conversation was short, since he couldn't give me legal advice about the case. But he said he'd heard where we were going (never mind how) and wished me luck. He said whatever I was looking for, he hoped I would find.

We arrived in Kuala Lumpur in the late morning. The weather was overcast, and we were greeted with a sweltering, tropical heat. It made Houston and Florida feel dry by comparison. This was the true jungle.

As we took a cab into the city, I gazed around in wonder. It felt like a different world. Kuala Lumpur was ultra-modern, with glass and steel skyscrapers everywhere, lit up in brilliant colors that were visible even during the cloudy day. The Petronas Towers dominated the city, standing like twin sentinels, their gaze reaching all the way to the sea. Everything about the place felt exotic. It was like a strange mirror image of New York, on the opposite side of the world. The deep, lush green of the jungle loomed in the background. It felt forbidding. As if it couldn't be extinguished, but only kept at bay. It bided its time, waiting to reclaim its territory in a day when this city of man no longer reigned.

We arrived at our hotel, checked in, and killed a couple of hours in the lobby. One by one, the team I had assembled began to arrive.

Vijay was the first. He wore a short-sleeved button-down shirt, a pair of Ray Ban sunglasses, and a grin that stretched across half his face. We locked hands and embraced. Vijay was an independent contractor like me. That meant he could still work the case. We hit a stroke of luck in that. Vijay's father was from India, but his mother was from Malaysia, so he spoke the language fluently. That made him indispensable for this trip. Vijay relayed to me that Cindy and Harder were insanely jealous. He taunted them over text, promising that he would send them plenty of selfies of him on the beach digging up buried treasure with his bare hands. I tried to smile, but I couldn't share his excitement. I was too preoccupied with the dangers of what we were about to do.

The next to arrive was Trevor Thompson, from the Aqua Ray dive resort in Key West. He was dressed in a faded old fishing shirt and cheap gas station sunglasses that made him look even more suspicious than he already was. Thompson had brought Jared Diamond too. Diamond looked even shadier than Thompson did, if that was possible. But at least he wasn't high. I hoped.

I had called Thompson two days ago about the trip. The conversation had gone something like this:

"Hello. Trevor Thompson? Jack Carver here. Lawyer for David Marcum. Remember?"

"Eh?"

"The lawyer with Ashley Marcum. Ashley, say hello."

(Ashley, "Hi Trevor!")

"Hey, girl! And lawyer. What is it?"

"I've got a business proposition for you," I said. "How'd you like to fly down to Malaysia and help us find the greatest treasure of all time?"

After convincing Trevor that no, I was not mocking him, and no, I was not a "wingtip-wearing, ass-puckering, horse-shit eating lawyer" trying to screw him, he agreed to come, on the condition that I buy his flight and give him cold, hard cash up front. I persuaded him that a wire transfer later would do just as well, and he said yes, and that he would bring Jared Diamond too. Initially I balked at Diamond, not wanting to widen the circle more than I had to. But Thompson was adamant. Diamond was a Gulf War veteran, he said, who would die before he disclosed anything, or kill someone, and that it wouldn't be the first time. I reluctantly agreed.

When he arrived at the hotel, Trevor set down his luggage and gave Ashley a big hug. Then he greeted me with a non-committal grunt. Diamond followed suit.

The last to arrive was Professor Jacob Schnizzel, dressed in a Hawaiian shirt and carrying an oversized suitcase. He was veritably jumping with excitement. I greeted him and made introductions all around.

"Hello," Schnizzel said to Thompson, reaching out and pumping his hand enthusiastically. "Professor Jacob Schnizzel. Pleased to make your acquaintance."

Thompson eyed him warily. "Eh?"

"Schnizzel."

"Schnitzel? I don't like Germans," he spat.

"Neither do I," Schnizzel muttered.

"Eh?"

With everyone there, it was time to begin. My plan was this: we were going to rent a boat and equip it with sonar, a magnetometer, and an ROV. Then we would follow the directions in Manuel Roberto's confession—the same directions that had led Marcum and Gunthum to the *Flor de la Mar*. Once there, we would use the equipment to locate the ship, and, if the death memo could be believed, Marcum's body as well. In one fell swoop, we would verify our theory about the *Flor de la Mar*, locate the treasure, and find David Marcum's remains. Then we would return to Galveston as heroes and win the case.

I was well aware that the plan bordered on insane. It assumed that we could actually locate the supposed site of the *Flor de la Mar* based on the confession, which had taken an expert team on the Excelsior I didn't know how long to do. The plan also assumed that Marcum's body was still at the wreck site, and that we'd be able to find it at the bottom of the ocean. Finally, it assumed that the *Flor de la Mar* was actually there, and wasn't some fantasy cooked up in my imagination.

I knew the odds against us were long. But I didn't know what else to do. Back in Galveston, the case was reaching its zenith, and we still had no claim. We had no proof that Marcum had found the *Flor de la Mar*, or that he had a contract with Gunthum. And although we knew now what had happened to David Marcum, our only proof of that was a privileged memorandum that would as likely get me excommunicated from the legal profession as win the case.

As long as I knew my plan was insane, I rationalized, that very fact made the plan sane. This was perhaps questionable logic. But I didn't have any other options. What Remington would think of this plan, I couldn't guess.

I didn't know how to do any of the sailing or the plotting or the finding of the *Flor de la Mar* myself. But I knew people who did. Trevor Thompson and Jared Diamond knew how to sail, dive, and work a sonar and magnetometer. Jacob Schnizzel knew enough about the *Flor de la Mar*, and about wreck search theory, to hatch a plan to find it, and identify it if we did. And Vijay spoke the local language, which would allow us to navigate an unfamiliar country. With this team, I felt that I had a fighting chance.

I had tried to convince Ashley that it would be dangerous, and that she didn't need to come. You can guess how that turned out. I didn't have access to firm funds anymore, so Ashley and I opened up a dozen new credit cards between us and maxed them all out, barely scraping together enough money for the boat and equipment we needed. I told the team I would pay them later. The trial was going on even now, and there wasn't a moment to lose.

After rendezvousing at the hotel, we set out on separate errands. Vijay, Thompson, and Diamond went to check out the boat that we had arranged. On the way back, they would pick up supplies for the voyage. Schnizzel, Ashley, and I went up to my room and unrolled a set of detailed nautical charts of the Nicobar Islands. We studied them against Roberto's confession from the Lisbon archives. Schnizzel had plotted out the possible coordinates of the wreck and the route we would take, one that would maximize our chances of finding the *Flor de la Mar* in the least amount of time. If it was there.

That night, Ashley and I had dinner together at the hotel restaurant. We sat in a quiet corner and discussed plans for the voyage. Ashley also brought some records that she wanted to talk about. She spread them out on the table. I recognized them as her brother's banking records, which we had been through some time ago.

"I've been going back through these over and over again," she told me. "I kept getting the feeling that we missed something. There's one charge that I keep coming back to."

She showed me a statement dating six months before Marcum's disappearance, and another one a year before that. "Look here," she said. She pointed to a charge for seventy-five dollars from six months ago. The description simply read "box."

"What's your first reaction to that?" she asked.

I shrugged. "One of those subscription boxes, maybe? You know, the ones that send you food or shaving cream or whatever once a month." I had signed up for a cooking box one time, but quickly grew bored with it. It seemed that you could find niche box subscriptions for anything these days. I'd even seen ones for animal skulls and vegan jerky. I wondered with vague disquiet why those particular ones had appeared in my ad feed.

"But see how there's no merchant name?" Ashley said, showing me the entry. I saw what she meant. Most of the charges had more detail. At a minimum, you could see the seller's name and address. This entry didn't have any of that. "The charge recurred exactly one year before," she said, showing me another statement.

"Okay," I said. "Some type of yearly subscription box, then. I am a little curious about it. But I have to confess, I don't see why it's important."

"Look at this." She pulled up Bank of America's website on her phone. Then she went to the products and services section. One of the things listed were safety deposit boxes. She clicked on pricing. The smallest one available cost seventy-five dollars per year.

It dawned on me. "You think the charge was for a safety deposit box."

"Yes. That's why there's no further detail about the merchant. Because the merchant is Bank of America itself. They probably just say "box" to keep it discreet. Like how they send you credit cards in unmarked envelopes."

"Right. And you think there's something in that box."

She nodded. "I think that's where he put the contract."

Later that night, Vijay and I sat down at the hotel bar, ordered a couple of beers, and wrote a scathing letter to Travis Scott at Bank of America demanding immediate access to the safety deposit box. It was more of a manifesto, really. We berated Scott for failing to disclose the existence of the box and accused him of violating the discovery rules by not doing so. If he didn't give us access, we threatened to subpoena the entire Bank of America leadership team down to Galveston, Texas, haul them in front of Judge Graves in what was now the most famous case in the world, and move to sanction them for hiding key evidence about David Marcum's death.

We had a grand time writing the letter. Scott would not have as much fun reading it. After we finished, we put the letter in a sealed envelope and left it with the hotel clerk, with instructions to send it via the fastest available mail the next day.

The next morning, we took a car to the nearby harbor of Port Klang. We picked our way through a crowded fish market, with all sorts of sounds and smells and people yelling in languages I didn't understand. There were live prawns and lobsters and fish of all kinds in big water tanks. I watched as shopkeepers plucked them straight out of the tanks and into a bag or a frying pan on request.

Once through the market, we reached the docks. After some searching, we came to a medium-sized boat, rigged up with equipment and gear. Vijay talked business with the owner while Thompson and Diamond stomped around on board, checking this line and that chain.

Schnizzel climbed aboard excitedly, looking around at everything like a curious child. "Is this a 5900 side scan sonar?" he asked Thompson, pointing at a long machine on the deck.

"Huh. It is," said Thompson, seeming surprised that Schnizzel knew this.

"Fantastic," said Schnizzel. "I've read so much about these. But I've never seen one in person. It's bigger than I thought." Schnizzel ooh-ed and ahh-ed over the magnetometer and the small ROV that was attached to the vessel. The ROV would be able to dive down to where the *Flor de la Mar* was, like Excel Resources had, and even retrieve a piece of it. It had cost me about three maxed credit cards by itself.

We set sail on the Strait of Malacca at noon. Thompson took the helm, and Diamond sat beside him, chain-smoking cigarettes in a silence as perfect as Zen. Schnizzel sat with them, asking questions about the gear and how they planned to use it. Once Thompson realized how knowledgeable Schnizzel was, he was awed, and hung onto Schnizzel's every word as he described the location and contents of treasures both known and unknown.

Vijay, Ashley, and I lay on the deck, enjoying the ocean breeze and the calm blue waters. I checked my email during the first few hours, anxious about developments in the case. But reception soon faded to zero, and I gave it up. Vijay tried to send a selfie to Harder and Cindy, but he had no coverage either. Ashley, Vijay, and I gave up on the electronic world and traded it for the real one. We looked up at the sky and talked about anything and everything but the case.

The Strait of Malacca felt like a superhighway. Oil tankers and cargo ships dotted the blue waters in every direction, calmly steaming toward their destinations. The Strait was so crowded it looked almost like a festival, a gathering of yachts somewhere in the Mediterranean. But instead of beautiful white sails scattered across the horizon, the ships were massive, blocky cargo vessels, sedately trundling along to bring oil or food or machinery to wherever they needed to go.

That evening, Vijay cooked a gourmet dinner for us under the stars. Most of what we had packed was canned beans, frozen food, pasta, and other things you bring on a sea voyage. It was intended to last, not to taste great. I had made the mistake of letting Jared Diamond buy some of the food, and he came back with something called pemmican, which was a paste of dried meat, fat, and berries that had been invented by indigenous peoples of North America and probably last used by European explorers in the Arctic at the turn of the nineteenth century. I guess they were out of Cliff bars.

But for tonight, Vijay had picked out some fresh seafood from the Port Klang market. Using a boiler and a small grill on deck, he cooked us a feast of mackerel, shrimp, and red snapper. He seasoned it with lemongrass, coconut milk, and chili paste, and passed around cans of cold Tiger beer to wash it down, a favorite from nearby Singapore. We ate and drank and were merry under the stars. It was an evening to remember.

Later on, I sat on deck with Ashley, and we talked late into the night. It was dark, and the ship skimmed serenely along the ocean. We watched the black water pass us by, pleasantly drained from the long day in the sun. The coastlines were barely visible, just a mesh of dark mangrove trees from end to end, with little river inlets here and there. Jared sat silently at the helm, guiding us. The rest of the group were below deck, sleeping.

The Strait felt spookier at night. The dark waters and the endless mangrove trees seemed to be hiding secrets that I hadn't felt in the light of the day. I remembered the dark legend of the *SS Ourang Medan* and the disappearance of Malaysia Flight 370. With sudden disquiet, I realized that Flight 370 had been flying north up the Strait of Malacca when it disappeared just past the island of Sumatra. The very same place we were going.

The next morning, it was time to focus on our destination: the Nicobar Islands. I pulled out the maps and consulted with Schnizzel and Diamond about our progress. The closest of the Nicobar Islands was a thousand kilometers from Kuala Lumpur. They had looked a lot closer on the map, just half an inch away, measured by my fingers. But the ocean was bigger than it looked on Google, and it took us two full days and nights to get there. Thompson and Diamond took turns manning the helm, with whoever was not on duty drinking, playing solitaire, and smoking Benson & Hedges cigarettes, of which we'd procured two cartons.

During the leadup to our voyage, I had read everything I could get my hands on about the Nicobar Islands. There were about one or two dozen islands in the chain, depending on how you counted. The biggest of them were Great Nicobar and Little Nicobar, which were a hundred miles off the northern coast of Sumatra. Both were inhabited. The other islands were much smaller, and many were empty. There was another island chain nearby called the Andaman Islands, one of which had an active volcano on it, making me think of a Bond villain's secret lair. But I didn't think Roberto and the *Flor de la Mar* could have gotten that far.

I had read through Roberto's account many times. He said that the *Flor de la Mar* sunk just west of some uncharted islands. Roberto and the others had escaped on a makeshift raft to a "small vegetated island of less than a mile," he wrote. There, they had been marooned for several days before being rescued by some natives, who took them to a larger, inhabited island to convalesce.

In looking at the Nicobar Islands, there was only one island in the chain that fit that description perfectly: Meroe Island.

Meroe was a tiny island just north of Little Nicobar. Its total area was only half a square mile. It was uninhabited and overgrown with trees and brush. This fit Roberto's account. Schnizzel and I believed that the *Flor de la Mar* must have sunk off the coast of Meroe Island. Roberto and the others reached its shores and sheltered there for a few days. Then, the natives had probably taken them to Little Nicobar or Great Nicobar, the larger islands that might have been inhabited in the sixteenth century.

We also had another crucial piece of information, which made this less of a fool's errand: the depth of the ship. Lloyd Gunthum had recorded the *Flor de la Mar* at a depth of 668 feet below sea level. Our maps contained detailed depth charts of the ocean, and our equipment would tell us the depth of the ocean floor at any given point. By searching off the west coast of Meroe Island, at a depth of 668 feet, we hoped to find the ship, and find it more quickly than Gunthum had.

My excitement grew by the hour as we made steady progress toward the Nicobar Islands. Finally, late in the afternoon on the third day, we arrived.

"Land ho," Diamond called laconically. We all ran to the bow and looked ahead. I squinted, trying to make out the coastline.

It took a few moments to come into focus, but then I saw it. "There it is!" I said, pointing excitedly. We could just make out the edge of the southernmost island, Great Nicobar, on the horizon.

Diamond took the speed of the ship down a notch, and we cruised along the western coast of Great Nicobar and past Little Nicobar. Then, just as the sun was setting, I got my first glimpse of Meroe Island.

I stared at it, fascinated. Great Nicobar and Little Nicobar were real islands, measuring three hundred square miles and fifty square miles, respectively. They were substantial pieces of land, inhabited by people with all sorts of businesses and lives and families.

Meroe was different. It was deserted, the type of island you imagine yourself getting stranded on. It was less than a mile long, and only half a mile wide. It seemed a mysterious, miniature tropical paradise in the remotest part of the ocean. I was reminded of Rockweiller's man-made island off the coast of Cartagena. Over the past few days, I had stared at maps and satellite images of Meroe Island so many times that I felt like I knew the place. Last night I had even dreamed of it, although I couldn't remember what the dream was about.

Meroe Island had three beaches: Anuradha to the north, Taranga to the east, and Serene to the west. I imagined Manuel Roberto crawling ashore on the shifting sands of Serene Beach, over five hundred years ago, in the teeth of a lashing storm, far from civilization. Then, against all odds, he had been saved, and lived to tell the tale.

The next morning, we rose at dawn and began our search. Schnizzel's plan called for us to "mow the lawn" in the area to find the ship. This was a basic technique used by treasure hunters. We would methodically sweep a predetermined area in stripes until all of it had been covered. It looked a little like mowing the lawn, hence the name. Often, this type of search could take weeks or months, depending on the area plotted. But we had an advantage in knowing the depth and the location of nearby Meroe Island. This was good, since we didn't have weeks or months to spare. Schnizzel had calculated our search parameters, and expanded the area to cover possible discrepancies in Roberto's account. All told, we expected to cover the search area within a few days.

The tools we used were the side-scan sonar and the magnetometer. The sonar was attached to the ship, and the magnetometer was towed behind, on a long cable that stretched all the way down to the ocean floor, trailing just a few dozen feet above the bottom. That way it would pick up whatever was down there clearly. Once or twice we had some trouble with its positioning, and Vijay and I had to jump into the water to rejigger it. I wondered uneasily if there were any sharks in the area. But we didn't see any, and I have to say I enjoyed the swimming.

Thompson and Diamond moved us slowly along the search area, watching the displays for any signs of a shipwreck. We were looking for anything metal, ideally the cannon that so often marked a wreck to the treasure hunter's enhanced eye. Thompson, Diamond, and Schnizzel all took turns monitoring the equipment, looking for the slightest pings that could indicate the presence of metal below the surface.

Sometimes, when the equipment registered something, we would stop to get a better look. Once we even sent the small ROV down to the bottom. We found an old ship's anchor that way, which caused tremendous excitement for a few minutes until we realized it was of modern design, not more than a few decades old. We also found scraps of metal and pieces of what might have been ships, or anything else, as we searched the depths.

The excitement aboard for the first few days was palpable. We were far from civilization, out in the open ocean, seeking fame and fortune and a treasure that had been lost for centuries. It felt like high adventure, and there was a certain romance about it that was hard to come by in modern life. Everything in today's world had already been discovered, indexed, and catalogued *ad nauseum*. It felt like there was no more to explore on this planet, except perhaps the depths of the oceans.

But the excitement started to fade as the days passed and we didn't find anything. We had covered almost the entire search area already. The sea west of Meroe Island, at the right depth, wasn't that big, and we had combed it thoroughly. In another half day, we would be done. Sometimes, I caught myself gazing at Meroe Island as if it were alive, willing it to reveal its secrets.

But it did not. The third day came and went, and still there was nothing. I looked at Schnizzel. He shrugged at my unasked question, not having any answers.

I was at a loss as to what to do. I had been sure that the *Flor de la Mar* was here. From the account, we knew that the ship had wrecked a few hundred kilometers off the coast of Sumatra. And we knew that Roberto and the others had been stranded on a tiny, uncharted island, and were later taken to a larger, inhabited one. This was the only place in the sea that perfectly matched that description. What were we missing? Was there a broken link in our logic? Was there a problem with our search? I didn't know.

There was one other possibility that Schnizzel and I had considered: that the *Flor de la Mar* had actually sunk near one of northern Nicobar Islands. Up until now, I had assumed that Roberto must have been talking about Meroe Island, because Meroe was the right size, it was on the Goa route, and it was close to Great Nicobar and Little Nicobar.

But there were also some bigger islands in the northern part of the Nicobar archipelago. Two in particular, Katchall and Camorta, just might have been inhabited in the sixteenth century. A narrow waterway ran between them, almost like a miniature version of the Strait of Malacca. Both islands had people living on them today. North of Katchall and Camorta was Teressa Island, and then north of that was a small island called Chowra. Like Meroe, Chowra was tiny, just larger than a mile in area, and uninhabited. Perhaps Chowra was the island that Roberto had swam to, later to be taken to Katchall or Camorta. The chances of this were small, but it was possible.

Schnizzel had prepared a contingency search plan for the northern islands just in case. After some discussion amongst the team, and lacking any alternatives, we decided to go for it. We raised anchor and headed north. Before long, we reached the western coast of Chowra Island, and began another search.

But one day wore into two, and we found nothing. The cloudless sky, reflected in the calm blue waters, seemed to mock us, staring down from above without a care in the world. The sky had been there when the *Flor de la Mar* sank five hundred years ago, and it would be there five hundred years from now, when all of us were long dead and gone. My efforts felt somehow futile beneath it, and I wondered what I was doing scrambling for treasure at the edge of the world for a dead man I'd never met. The only thing we saw during those days were a few fishing boats, whose occupants stared at us with mild curiosity. Once I thought that one of them might be following us, but it disappeared soon after.

By the end of the second day at Chowra, our enthusiasm was gone. As the search wore into its sixth day, the mood darkened, and tempers began to fray. I had warned everyone that searches usually took weeks or months, and even with our more precise measurements, it could take longer than anticipated. But it didn't help.

I had read books about deep-sea expeditions. In all of them, mutinous grumblings by the crew were part of the game. Although this was far from the months-long voyages that the early navigators had endured, it seemed that the same principles applied.

Thompson started blaming Schnizzel for our failure, calling him an armchair archaeologist who'd never got his dick wet. Schnizzel retorted that Thompson was an incompetent buffoon who couldn't work a magnetometer to save his life. They almost came to blows one day, and Vijay had to step in and calm them down. We were also running low on good food, and started eating the pemmican. It didn't help.

"Damn fool of a search plan, if you ask me," muttered Trevor Thompson for at least the fifth time that day. Schnizzel glared at him.

"If you have a better idea, be my guest," he snapped. "I'd love to hear you double check my calculations."

"Shut up!" I told them both. "This is my plan. And we're sticking with it."

They sullenly obeyed, and Thompson got back to steering the ship.

But although I tried to project confidence to the team (which I have no doubt they all saw right through), I was beginning to feel the edge of desperation. We were running out of time. I had only rented the ship for a week, and we were already going beyond that. There was no money for anything more. We also faced diminishing returns. The longer we stayed, the less likely we were to find anything. Most of the probable spots had been searched by now.

We hadn't had internet reception in days. Back home, I imagined the case was moving on without us. I wondered what was happening in Judge Graves' court. In the world. It all felt so remote here, far out in the Indian Ocean.

Thompson, Diamond, and Schnizzel were no longer optimistic about finding anything. I could see it in their faces. Vijay appeared to have given up too. He just spent the time larking around, taking shirtless selfies when he thought no one was looking. It was no skin off his back if we didn't succeed. Only Ashley and I remained committed.

Maybe the *Flor de la Mar* wasn't here. Maybe this had all been a fool's errand. But if we went back emptyhanded, I didn't know what we would do. During the past few days, I had resolved to reveal the truth of the death memo and throw myself on Judge Graves' mercy if it came to that. I might lose my legal license, or even face jail time.

I hoped that Graves would agree to hear the evidence, and that we would have a shot at proving our case. But if Bock persuaded him that it was all fabricated, we would lose everything. Without that memo, we still had no evidence that Gunthum killed David Marcum. And without the contract, or the wreck itself, we had no evidence that Marcum played any part in finding the *Flor de la Mar*. Maybe Remington could have come up with some genius plan to save the day. But Remington wasn't here, and I didn't have one.

That evening, over some pemmican and the last of our boxed wine, we had a candid discussion about our options. There was one last possibility left: Batti Malv Island.

Batti Malv was a tiny island, one of the northernmost in the Nicobar chain. Like Meroe, it was less than one square mile in size. No one lived there, and the only structure on the island was an old lighthouse that rose two hundred feet above the sea.

Batti Malv was fifty miles north of Chowra, and even farther from the bigger islands. We had excluded it early on because we didn't see how the *Flor de la Mar* could have gone that far north on the way to Goa, or how Roberto could have been rescued so far from the bigger islands. But we decided to try anyway. Perhaps the storm had blown them off course. Or the maps were off. We had nothing to lose. If we didn't find anything, we would give it up and go home.

The team reluctantly agreed to give Batti Malv a shot. Thompson and Diamond didn't mind another day or two per diem, and Vijay didn't much care either way. Professor Schnizzel was interested, but even he didn't seem to think we would find anything. He dutifully took out his maps and charts and began plotting out search parameters for Batti Malv, which would only take one day. Diamond took the helm, and said he would get us there by morning.

In the deepest part of the night, I awoke to the insistent voices of Trevor Thompson and Jared Diamond. They were whispering excitedly about something. I sat up in bed. I felt lucid and wide-awake despite the hour. I got up made my way on deck. I checked the clock. It said 2 a.m. The weather was as clear and balmy as ever.

The tone of Jared's voice alone made me think that something was up. He wasn't an excitable guy, and I'd never heard this much vigor from him before. I made my way toward the steering wheel where they were sitting.

"What's going on?" I asked.

"Look here," said Diamond. There was a cigarette hanging from his mouth, half-lit and smoking. He pointed toward a large blip on one of the displays.

"There's something there," said Thompson. By the tension in his voice, I knew he meant something real. We had been through enough fakes by now to know the difference.

I went inside and roused Schnizzel. He groaned and cursed at me in what I thought was Yiddish. Then he got up and joined us on deck, blearily rubbing the sleep from his eyes. But when he saw the reading on the magnetometer, his eyes snapped open at once, and all traces of tiredness disappeared.

"Oh my God," he whispered.

"What is it?" I asked impatiently. Schnizzel leaned forward and examined the readouts more closely. He fiddled with a few dials as Thompson and Diamond watched intently.

"It's consistent," he muttered. "Let's make a bigger circuit of the area," he said. Thompson agreed, and in a nod to the gravity of the moment, he didn't even bother to take offense at the instruction. Diamond held the wheel as we slowly moved the ship forward. On the surface, the ocean looked the same as it did every night. The moonlight shined down on us placidly.

I checked our location on the GPS. I frowned in puzzlement when I saw it. We weren't near Batti Malv Island yet. In fact, we were only halfway there, somewhere in the open ocean. But we were on the 668-foot depth line. We had decided to straddle it on the way there, just in case. I looked around, but didn't see any land in sight. It was dark, though, with only the moon and our small headlight shining against the vast darkness.

We trawled around the area for about thirty minutes, carefully taking readings. By this time it was 3 a.m., and Ashley and Vijay had joined us on deck. Vijay made hot coffee for everyone. We drank it together, our eyes glued to the images.

I had always had my doubts about Thompson and Diamond, and whether they were keeping track of whatever floated across the sonar and the magnetometer. But now, as Diamond softly pointed out what he was seeing to Schnizzel, who was viewing it with increasing excitement, I realized that all of them knew exactly what they were doing.

Our eyes were now fixed on a particularly big set of images underwater. They stood out in bright relief on the screen. The sonar and the magnetometer were registering large metal objects directly underneath us.

"What are we looking at?" I asked.

"Well," said Schnizzel, "I would say that, given the size, shape, and metallurgical signatures being emitted, the logical conclusion is that, well—"

Diamond interrupted him. "Cannon," he said with a rare grin. Schnizzel nodded his agreement, smiling from ear to ear.

We spent the next hour in breathless anticipation. Thompson, Diamond, and Schnizzel carefully maneuvered around the area and took readings. They confirmed multiple signatures consistent with cannon, though they cautioned us that we couldn't yet be sure.

At about 4 a.m., as the first hint of the sun blushed the sky, Thompson and Diamond engaged the ROV. We lowered it down over the side and into the water. This was difficult to do in the darkness, but none of us could stand to wait another moment, so we all pitched in to get it done. Once the ROV was at the bottom, there would be no difference between day and night.

The ROV descended slowly, and we looked through its eyes on our monitors. The moonlight quickly faded, and we were left with a grainy blue-green feed from the ROV's floodlamps, which illuminated the ocean as it went deeper. A few startled fish passed through the ROV's field of vision. After their initial surprise, they ignored it entirely and continued with their strange, deep ocean lives.

"One hundred feet," called Diamond, guiding the ROV inexorably toward the ocean floor.

"That's thirty meters," added Schnizzel, for the benefit of the audio record we were making. It was a measure of our preoccupation that Thompson didn't even glower at him.

"Two hundred feet," said Diamond after another minute.

"Visibility good," Schnizzel said. "Current low. ROV functioning within normal parameters."

We watched in absolute silence, as deep as the ocean floor, as the ROV continued down into the depths. Diamond quietly counted out three hundred feet, four hundred feet, and then five hundred feet, with no change to the grainy blue-green screen in front of us. We waited breathlessly, our anticipation growing with each foot the ROV descended.

At about six hundred feet, the view began to change. Particles flitted across the monitors. The ROV kicked up silt as it reached the end of its journey. It looked like a swirling sandstorm down there.

"ROV approaching bottom," Diamond said. "Visibility obscured. Stand by."

We leaned closer to the monitors to try and make out the view. Jared moved the ROV carefully. He didn't want to hit anything. Slowly, the swirling particles relaxed.

Suddenly, the bottom loomed into view, and we had a clear view of what was in front of us. This was the spot that the magnetometer had highlighted. Diamond set the ROV down gently on the bottom. And as we craned our necks forward, even my untrained eyes could see what was right in front of them. It was covered in mud or sand or barnacles or whatever else. But it was unmistakable.

"We have cannon," Diamond said laconically.

"Yes!" I screamed. My voice was shockingly loud in the soundless, open ocean, and I thought for a moment that the entire Nicobar Island chain must have heard me. But Ashley and Vijay were yelling at the top of their lungs too. "We're rich!" Vijay yelled. "We're rich!" Schnizzel whooped and cheered and broke into some kind of crazy Yiddish dance, and then Thompson started dancing a sailor's shanty, and all of this was so infectious that we all started jumping and dancing and flailing around the deck, screaming at the top of our lungs at this magnificent thing that had just happened.

"By God, Schnitzel," roared Thompson, clapping him on the back. "You did it! Your plan wasn't half bad after all!"

"No, no," Schnizzel protested. "It was your sonar skills. And Jared! Brilliant!" Jared was grinning along with all the rest of us, lighting a victory cigarette with a silver Zippo.

We continued to scan the ocean bottom with the ROV. It remained sandy, and the screen's vision was murky. But we began to make out what looked like wooden beams, or a corroded hulk, through the grainy lens. Schnizzel, Thompson, and Diamond agreed there was no question that we had found a wreck. They also saw signs that things had been moved around or unearthed recently. Lloyd Gunthum and his crew, I thought.

Soon after that, Diamond spotted a glint on the ROV's camera. It was something buried in the sand. It had been partially unearthed. I didn't even notice it. But Jared's sharp eyes seemed to miss nothing. "Look," he said. "I think that's a coin."

And sure enough, as he gently worked the ROV's robotic arms in the sand, we saw what looked like coins scattered within a three-foot circumference on the ocean floor.

"Oh my god," I said breathlessly. "Can we bring them up?" My heart was pounding.

Diamond nodded. He had been reluctant to bring up any piece of the cannon, because it was too big and we risked damaging it. But with the coins he smiled and obliged. He maneuvered the ROV's robotic arms under the coins. It reminded me of one of those claw machine games at an arcade, where you try to grab a prize like a stuffed teddy bear or a nerf gun. Except here we were grabbing at the beginning of what might be several billion dollars' worth of solid gold. Diamond was skilled, and he carefully coaxed a few coins into a bowl-shaped panning device on the end of the robot's arms.

Then he slowly brought the ROV up. A few minutes later, it broke the surface.

We dashed over to it. The ROV was dripping, seeming like it had returned from an alien world. I still didn't quite believe that what we had seen on the screen was real.

But there in the ROV's claws sat the three coins that Jared had brought up. Even though they were dirty and caked in mud, I saw the unmistakable glint of gold.

Jared stepped aside and extended his hand toward Ashley with a flourish. She grinned and stepped forward do the honors. Ignoring Schnizzel's protestations, she took the coins and rubbed one of them clean on her shirt, holding it out for us to see.

There, on the surface of the coin, were the very same markings that we now knew represented the rich and proud city of Malacca, conquered by the Portuguese some five hundred years ago.

After that, we yelled and screamed and cheered until our throats were raw. Vijay broke out our last case of Tiger beers to celebrate the occasion. I hesitated, since it was not quite 5 a.m., but Ashley cracked one open, and the rest of us followed. Thompson got the ship's radio working and managed to find some music on a Malaysian nautical channel. Incongruously, they were playing old 50s or 60s American swing, and we started dancing around the deck, singing and yelling wildly as dawn broke over the horizon.

I couldn't believe it. Here we were, in the middle of the open ocean, and sitting precisely 668 feet below us was a treasure almost beyond what the human mind could conceive. I imagined Alfonso de Albuquerque's great hoard, eighty tons of worked gold and two hundred chests of sparkling gems, sitting right there beneath us, just waiting to be claimed.

As the sun started to come up, I became aware of a noise in the distance. It sounded like a buzzing or humming. As it grew louder, I recognized it as a motor, and then multiple motors. I glanced over at the others and saw that they heard it too. Jared walked toward the other side of the boat, where it was coming from. We followed him, and craned our necks to try and see what it was.

There, in the distance, was a cluster of small boats, rapidly headed our way.

THIRTY-ONE

This was the first time we had seen anything like this before. For the most part, the only watercraft we had seen were some isolated fishing boats. This was different. The boats were making straight for us. I felt a malevolent intention from them, whether real or imagined. Trevor Thompson grunted something. Jared Diamond was silent, but he looked concerned, which worried me more than anything else.

The boats closed in on us quickly. One of them turned on a floodlight, suddenly blinding us. I heard shouts, and then the staccato burst of an automatic rifle. I had fired one on a range once, and I knew the sound. The burst came again, closer, and this time I thought I heard the whine of a bullet flying past my ear. I crouched down and threw a hand across my eyes, straining to see against the harsh light. I could vaguely make out the outline of a figure, poised high in the bow of the lead boat, a rifle raised defiantly toward the sky.

In moments, one of the boats was alongside us. Up close, I saw it was a small wooden craft fitted with a heavy outboard motor. Two hooks sailed out from the boat and caught on our railing. The hooks were lashed to long bamboo poles, and before we could blink, two men shimmied up like squirrels and leapt onto our deck. They didn't have guns, but were brandishing some type of primitive machete. The weapons looked sharp, and they glistened with oil.

More followed, and soon men from all four boats were aboard. One of them carried an AK-47 rifle. A few more carried old handguns. The rest were armed with machetes. There were maybe a dozen of them altogether, all of them screaming and shouting as we put our hands up in the air and yelled back at them in English, trying to figure out what the hell was going on.

There was a crescendo of shouting from behind me, and I spun around to see that five of them had surrounded Jared. Their machetes were raised, and the AK-47 rifle was pointed directly at him. Jared had a hand in the back of his waistband, and I saw he was fingering a pistol. I saw the set of his face. He looked ready to pull the thing and send everyone to hell.

"Don't!" I yelled. "Jared, don't do it! There are too many of them!" Ashley started screaming at him, and then Trevor Thompson did too, and Jared slowly took his hand off the gun and came back from the brink. He spat over the side of the rail, and then the men jumped on him and took the gun and forced him to the deck.

Vijay was speaking to the men in Malay. Gradually, amid the clangor, they realized this. The men seemed surprised that he spoke the language. They went back and forth with him in harsh voices. I couldn't understand a thing. One of the men pointed a finger firmly at his own chest a few times and said something that sounded like "noon." Eventually, Vijay and the men seemed to reach an understanding.

"What are they saying?" I asked Vijay during a lull in the conversation, as the men talked amongst themselves.

"They're telling us to surrender. That we should put up our hands and nothing bad will happen."

"And what the hell is 'noon'?" They kept jabbering that. Or something like it.

"*Lanun*," Vijay said. "They are saying that they are *lanun*."

"*Lanun?* What does that mean?"

"Pirates," he said grimly.

We spent the next day below deck in our own boat, our hands bound behind us. Two of the *lanun* guarded us at all times.

Up close, and in the daytime, the *lanun* were not as fearsome as they had first appeared. One of the two men guarding us couldn't have been more than seventeen. The other was older, maybe in his forties, with sparse grey hair and missing teeth. His skin was weathered and wrinkled, and he wore ripped jeans and a threadbare Armani shirt. Neither of the men could have been much more than five feet tall.

The leader of the gang was different. He was taller and well-muscled. He carried the rifle, and the few times that I glimpsed him, I noticed what looked like other equipment on his belt too.

When they first captured us, the *lanun* had searched us thoroughly. They threw our cell phones, computers, and other electronics overboard. So no one could trace us, I guessed. When they threw my firm laptop away, I had the absurd thought that IT had just issued it to me, that they were going to kill me when I didn't come back with it. The *lanun* took our money, credit cards, passports, and everything else of value. They also took the gold coins we'd found at the *Flor de la Mar*, which I saw the leader put into a pouch at his belt.

After the raid, the pirates were pretty lax, and not altogether unfriendly. They fed us and offered cigarettes and coffee from time to time. But we weren't allowed to talk amongst ourselves. I tried once and almost got a machete butt in the face for my trouble.

Vijay, charmer that he was, got on well with the guards. He got them to redo our bindings in front of us after we complained they hurt. One of the guards, the old man who often watched us, spoke a smattering of English. With a gap-toothed smile that was oddly endearing, he told us that his name was Ricky Tang and that he loved American movies. All fraternizing stopped, though, when the leader was around.

As far as our destination, we couldn't tell where we were going. All we could discern was that were going south through the Strait, back the way we had come. It was hard to get a sense of direction from the brief glimpses of the outside that we got. I saw nothing more than blue waters and the endless mangrove trees that dotted the edges of the Strait.

Eventually, we arrived at our destination. I heard the *lanun* yelling and jumping off the boat, and guessed we had tied off somewhere. The *lanun* ushered us out of the hold and onto the deck. Our hands were still bound. I looked around.

We weren't in the Strait anymore. We were in the jungle, floating on a narrow river. I guessed the *lanun* had steered us into one of the innumerable rivers and inlets that ran off the main waterway. They led off the boat and marched down a well-trodden path that ended in a large clearing. There was a ramshackle collection of rough wooden buildings there, an outpost in the middle of the jungle. We stopped outside the largest building.

"Where are we?" I muttered to no one in particular. Ricky Tang heard and grinned at me with his missing teeth. "Coffee shop," he said, gesturing at the crude building. The others laughed uproariously.

The *lanun* ushered us inside. The place was smoky and dimly lit. There were half a dozen men already there. They greeted us with hearty cheers and applause. I saw a bar on one side of the room, lit with old neon signs. One said "Singapore" and displayed a glowing rendition of the skyline in screaming green. Another looked like it had been stolen from a dive bar in the American Midwest. Beer and liquor bottles littered the room, and there was an acrid aroma of chemicals in the air. It smelled like burning plastic, or nail polish, mixed with something rotten.

The men inside got up to greet us. They spoke quickly in Malay and slapped our captors on the back with enthusiasm. Then they greeted us the same way. I felt more like a celebrity than a prisoner. "Happy happy!" One of the men said to me, laughing and pointing at us.

After that, the *lanun* split us up and led us to small rooms adjoining the main one. They put Thompson and Diamond in one room, and Vijay, Ashley, Schnizzel, and me in the other. They must have figured that Thompson and Diamond were doubly as dangerous as the rest of us, which was probably true. They closed the door, and I heard the lock turn. The room was dark.

When my eyes came into focus, I saw a dirty floor and bare, grimy walls. And then the figure of a man, sitting on the floor, his hands bound like ours. Another captive. To my shock, I recognized him.

"Rufus Rockaway?"

Rufus Rockaway looked up at me blearily through grimy strands of hair. "You know me?" he said, sounding surprised.

"Of course. I..." I stuttered out a few more words and then trailed off. I was hardly able to believe the surreal situation I now found myself in.

Vijay grinned. "Don't mind him. He's a little star struck. Aren't you, Jackie? You're our favorite show, Rockaway. MNN. We watch it all the time."

"Oh," said Rockaway, sounding flattered. "Why thank you. I'm always pleased to meet a fan. Even under the circumstances."

"What are you doing here?" I managed to ask.

"That's a bit of a tale," Rockaway said, easing himself back against the filthy wall to tell it.

"Ironically, I came here to report on pirates. The maritime news business has been slow of late. Doubtless it looks all flash and glamor from the outside. But to be honest, it's kind of a niche market."

"You don't say," said Ashley.

"Yes. Ahem. Anyway, I decided I'd run a little story on modern day piracy. Everyone likes that, right? Excitement, a little danger. A bit of knowledge, delivered in serialized, thirty-minute segments. Some bang for the old buck. I began doing the research. I wanted to talk to real live pirates. I traveled to Batam, as other distinguished journalists have done before me, in the hopes of speaking with some of them, and telling their story. Hope, desperation, and perhaps a bit of derring-do."

"How'd that go?" asked Vijay.

"As you see," he said, indicating his fetters. "I met some pirates. But they kidnapped me to ransom me back to the network. I guess they decided that money was worth more than fame." Rockaway shook his head sorrowfully.

"I thought pirates were in Somalia," Vijay remarked.

"There too," Rockaway said, nodding. "In fact, I had originally planned to go to Somalia. But some of the pirates there are a little more hardline. And I'd rather be ransomed than beheaded."

"Good choice," said Vijay. "But this is a pirate hotspot as well?"

"Yes. The Strait of Malacca is one of the highest-risk areas for piracy in the world. In fact, there was a brief time in the early 2000s where Lloyd's of London classified it as a war zone for insurance purposes."

"Why is piracy so big here?" I asked.

"Myriad factors. Malaysia and Indonesia are poor countries. Large parts of them are lawless. And the Strait of Malacca is one of the busiest shipping lanes in the world. A hundred thousand ships pass through here every year. At some points, the Strait is only miles wide. To either side of the Strait is dense jungle, which serves as a haven for the *lanun* to operate from, and escape to.

"The political situation is conducive to piracy as well. There's historically been a lack of trust between the powers of Indonesia, Singapore, and Malaysia. They don't always work together to coordinate a robust response. With all of these ingredients, it's not surprising that you have a lot of piracy here."

I blinked a few times. I looked at Ashley, and saw her mouth hanging open. Clearly, she hadn't expected to hear this level of analysis from Rufus Rockaway, either.

"Damn, dude," said Vijay. "You know your stuff."

"Thank you," said Rockaway, flipping his grimy hair in an attempt to capture the signature flair with which he did it on MNN. "Anyway. To pursue the story, I journeyed to Batam."

"Where's Batam?" I said.

"Batam is a small island, a part of Indonesia. Just opposite Singapore. It is a slum and a notorious haven for pirates and cutthroats and criminals of all types."

"Is that where we are now?"

"No. I was taken from there and smuggled to this place. Doubtless they believed that a journalist of my caliber would attract too much attention there. It would be much too easy for the authorities to find me."

"Doubtless. So where are we then?"

"As best I can tell, we are somewhere in Sumatra, off the Strait of Malacca. This place has just the type of environment I mentioned earlier. It's a sparsely populated, almost uninhabited jungle. It would be difficult, if not impossible, to track anyone here. A perfect place to hold hostages. Indeed, I daresay there's virtually no chance that anyone will be able to find us.

"I've been here for about a month. They treat me well. I play dice with them, and they're pretty generous with their drink, and their women. Not a bad life, really. But MNN has not paid the ransom. Apparently their highest offer was ten thousand dollars, which Ricky Tang refused. He says that a television personality such as myself should command a higher value. I can't say I disagree.

"Katie Tyler has taken over my broadcasts on MNN. They let me watch from time to time. But I try not to. It hurts. I'm not sure they even miss me over there." He shook his head sadly. "I suspect that Katie is not unhappy to have the whole show to herself. She's not such a great person, to be honest." I sensed an undercurrent of emotion there, and thought there was more to the story.

"You're right about that," muttered Schnizzel, breaking into the conversation. "I ought to know."

"What do you mean?" Rockaway asked.

"Katie is my ex-wife."

We all looked at Schnizzel incredulously. I thought back to his tale of marrying the big-haired blonde from Texas. And the football coach who stole her away. Mentally, I juxtaposed the image I had of Schnizzel's wife with Katie Tyler. It fit.

"You're *that* Jacob?" Rockaway asked in disbelief. "She's talked about you." "I am. Nothing good, I'm sure."

"Some good," Rockway said. "But lots bad. Very bad." He shook his head and shivered at the remembrance of it.

"Why didn't you tell us?" I demanded.

Schnizzel shrugged. "What would have been the point? It still hurts. But I'm not the first guy she's played. And I won't be the last. This new guy, Cal, he's not going to last. I'll tell you that. Anyway. I wouldn't be surprised if she's the one holding up your ransom, Rockaway."

"Katie...You think her and Cal won't work out?" Rockaway said, sounding intrigued.

"Is that really what you took out of that statement?" Schnizzel said dryly. "But hey. Go for it."

"You mean it?" said Rockaway. As if we weren't being held captive in a pirate's den thousands of miles away.

"Knock yourself out. If we ever get out of here alive, that is. Just don't say I didn't warn you."

After that, we all peppered Schnizzel with questions about Katie. He answered readily enough, seeming resigned to the whole thing.

At length, we switched subjects. We introduced ourselves properly to Rockaway, and told him how we had been captured, although I was cagey on exactly what we were doing in the area. Rockaway was impressed to find out that we were the lawyers on the *Flor de la Mar* case. He said he was secretly rooting for David Marcum, whom he considered to be the underdog. This made Ashley smile. He was also thrilled to learn that Trevor Thompson was here too, albeit in another room. He said he looked forward to the opportunity to bro out with him later.

After we told him our story, Rockaway frowned. "That's odd," he said.

"What is?" I asked.

"The entire tale. It doesn't add up."

"Why not?"

Rockaway shifted around in his corner and leaned back against the wall. "I've learned a little bit about the *lanun*. Prior to, and during, my stay here. I can tell you that the circumstances of your capture are quite unusual.

"Most people think of pirates as boarding ships and taking people hostage, like they did with you. But in reality, that type of attack is rare. The *lanun* usually stick to simple robbery. They'll board a boat that's tied down for the night and steal everything on it. They call it a "shopping trip." Sort of like stopping at the old Walgreens, but without paying. Sometimes they'll rob the ship's crew too, but there's rarely any violence involved. It's small-time stuff.

"More rarely, the *lanun* will pirate oil tankers that sail through the Strait. They board these ships on their fast *pancung* boats, tie up the crew, and siphon off the oil into a waiting vessel. Then they mix the stolen oil with legally purchased stuff, and sell it off with no one the wiser. They can make good money that way.

"Hostage incidents are the rarest of all. They are high risk for the *lanun*, who can be captured or even killed. They also draw a lot of attention, including from powerful foreign actors. When hostage incidents do happen, as often as not, they're carried out with someone on the inside. A crewmember might give information about a ship to the *lanun*, for instance. In return, they get a piece of the action.

"Which brings us to you," Rockaway said finally. "The details of your capture don't add up."

"How so?" I asked.

"For one, you said that the leader of this attack was carrying an automatic rifle, and that several of the *lanun* had guns."

"Right."

"That's unusual. Most of the *lanun* don't have firearms. Just knives and *parangs*, a type of primitive machete that they carry." I nodded remembering the weapons that they had.

"Another thing is where you were taken," Rockaway continued. "Most pirate attacks happen to the south, near Singapore, or to the northeast, off the coast of Malaysia. They don't happen as much near this part of the Strait."

Ashley and I glanced at each other. We hadn't told Rockaway exactly where we had been. But I suspected that piracy would be even more unlikely near the Nicobar Islands.

"Finally," said Rockaway, "the oddest thing about the attack are the odds themselves. Piracy gets a lot of media attention. Witness myself. Hello. But in reality, there are only a couple of dozen pirate attacks each year, out of a hundred thousand ships that pass through the Strait. Even if you assume that many more attacks go unreported, it's still a rounding error."

My brow creased in thought as I considered all of this. "What are you saying?"

"What I'm saying is this: what are the chances that you, an American lawyer on the *Flor de la Mar* case, happen to be captured in a random pirate attack, using an assault rifle, in an area where attacks are known to be rare, and where only about one in a thousand ships gets attacked by *lanun* to begin with?"

We all sat back and thought about that.

"Remember what I said earlier?" said Rockaway. "A lot of the big pirate attacks here have someone on the inside."

Just then, our conversation was interrupted as the door kicked open with a bang. Ricky Tang stood in the doorway, a cigarette hanging from his gap-toothed grin. "Time to play," he said.

Ricky Tang led us out into the main room. Thompson and Diamond were already there. Rockaway seemed to know all of the *lanun*, and they greeted him with hearty hellos and backslaps. Someone brought him a beer, which he cracked open and chugged. There was a crude stage in the center of the room, and one of the *lanun* was up there singing bad karaoke. Scantily clad young women were now scattered around the place, sitting on the men's laps. It reminded me of a low-rent strip club. The smell of drugs and tobacco assaulted my nostrils.

Our arrival drew applause from the crowd. "Happy happy in the coffee shop, neh?" one old man said to me with a wink and a nudge.

"Why do they keep calling this a coffee shop?" I whispered to Rockaway.

"Coffee shop is slang for a den of gambling, drugs, and prostitution," Rockaway explained. "You find them in poor, lawless places like Batam. I guess they set up one here, wherever we are, to give them something to do."

"Better than Starbucks, at least," I muttered. "And 'happy happy'?"

"That's a celebration, often thrown after a successful piracy attempt. Traditionally, it involves hookers and crystal meth."

"So that's what that smell is," I said, wrinkling my nose. Rockaway nodded.

The *lanun* all seemed thrilled with our attendance. They left our hands bound in front of us, but offered us seats, and cold beers and cigarettes were passed around. I guess a bunch of American hostages was good news for them. We could mean a big payday.

Ashley and I looked at each other as they handed us the goods. She accepted a cigarette, and I shrugged and popped open a Bintang beer. I clinked bottles with Ricky Tang, which drew a rousing cheer. They also offered me crystal meth, which I politely declined. Rockaway took a hit, though. When I looked at him, he shrugged. "When in Rome," he said, lighting up again. Jared Diamond smoked some too.

Thereafter unfolded one of the most bizarre experiences I had ever had in my life. The *lanun* turned up the music and took turns singing karaoke on stage. They seemed to love old American songs. One guy drew applause for an awful rendition of "I Love Rock 'n Roll", and then another did "I Want it That Way" by the Backstreet Boys. One of the prostitutes sat on my lap, high on crystal meth and giggling.

At length, the *lanun* managed to get Rufus Rockaway on stage, and to everyone's surprise, he belted out a lusty performance of the Korean K-Pop phenomenon "Gangnam Style," complete with a drugged-out breakdance. This was too much, and we all cheered and collapsed in gales of laughter along with the pirates. The whole situation was so absurd I wasn't even sure whether it was real. But there was nothing to do but go along with it.

The evening continued in this fashion for some hours. At one point, I even had a heart-to-heart with Ricky Tang. He sat next to me, a beer in his hand and a prostitute in his lap. He pointed drunkenly at the Singapore skyline, lit in flickering green neon above the bar.

"You know the difference, Singapore and Batam?" he said, slurring his words. I told him that I didn't. He grinned crookedly at me. A bent cigarette stuck out from between his yellowed teeth. He leaned close, and his breath smelled terrible.

"Singapore," he said. "Big business. Big money. No crime. Batam, no business, no money, all crime. You know why?" I shook my head mutely.

"You know how far away, Singapore and Batam?" I said that I did not.

"This far," he said, putting his fingers an inch apart in front of my face. "Forty kilometers. That it. Why so different? You know why?"

"I don't know."

"Difference is you," he said, poking me hard in the chest.

I was confused. "What?"

"Difference is you," he repeated. "Lawyer. Law and order. What you have in Singapore. What you have in United States. Without law, everything—" he waved around to indicate the coffee shop, the islands, the world— "shit. Nothing. Law and order." I nodded at him uncertainly. I thought about that a lot later on. I wasn't expecting to hear a defense of the Western legal system in an Indonesian drug den. But there it was.

After some hours of this bizarre celebration, the main door to the coffee shop opened, and a man walked in. I recognized him as the leader of the *lanun* who had captured us. He was carrying his rifle, and towered over the other scrawny men.

A hush swept over the room as he walked in. The man singing karaoke, drugged out and belting "Party in the U.S.A." with feverish abandon, was dragged off the stage and silenced. The leader issued some brusque instructions, and most of the *lanun* cleared out of the room, grumbling. A few remained.

The leader approached Vijay, and said something in Malay. Vijay answered him readily, but I could tell it wasn't satisfactory. The two of them went back and forth as the leader continued to question Vijay in increasingly harsh tones. I didn't know what was being said, but I could tell that the leader was not getting the answers that he wanted. He shouted at Vijay, and then all of a sudden, his hand snaked back and hit Vijay across the face, sending him sprawling to the floor. Vijay lay there, stunned.

Trevor Thompson, Jared Diamond, and I all rose to our feet, shouting for him to stop. The leader barked a command at Ricky Tang and the other *lanun*, who drew handguns and machetes and bared them at us. I sensed a certain reluctance from them. Ricky Tang said something that might have been backtalk. But maybe that was all in my head. The leader shouted angrily at him, and he obeyed, his face grimly set.

The leader left Vijay on the floor and then stalked over to me. He stood in front of me and said something I couldn't understand. Ricky Tang translated haltingly.

"He ask what you are doing here," Tang said.

"We're tourists," I told him. "Here on vacation. We were planning to visit Malaysia, Singapore, and Thailand." This was the cover story we had agreed on earlier in the adjoining room, in case anyone should ask. I hoped Vijay had stuck to it.

Ricky Tang translated this back. But I felt that the leader wasn't listening. His eyes were fixed on me. I got the feeling that he understood everything I said. He hissed something back to Ricky Tang in Malay. Tang looked troubled.

"He says you are lying," Tang said. "He not stupid. He see your identification cards. You are lawyers from America. You here for big ship that everyone after." The leader said something else, sharply. "You lie to him, it go very bad for you," Ricky Tang said nervously. He didn't seem to like what was going on.

I shrugged and spread my hands, as if to say, I don't know what to tell you, but as I opened my mouth to speak, the leader stepped toward me. His arm blurred and suddenly his fist smashed straight into my jaw.

I toppled to the floor, stunned. I could feel blood coming out of my mouth. I pressed a hand to it. There was no pain. It just felt numb. I dimly heard Ashley screaming something in the background. There was a ringing in my ears.

Slowly, I picked myself up from the floor and put my hand up, trying to call for calm. The leader said something in Malay again and Ricky Tang translated. He had to say it again before I grasped it. "He say he know the kind of equipment you have on the boat. Deep-sea equipment. He know what you have found. We know it. He ask, how you find it." Tang looked outright frightened now.

I spat out some blood and I decided it was pointless to hide who we were. They knew that already. "Yes, we're American lawyers," I said. "We're here on a case. But I'm afraid I can't reveal any more than that. Attorney-client privilege, you understand."

Even as the words came out of my mouth, I couldn't believe what I had just said, or what I was doing. What possessed me to stand on the attorney-client privilege in an Indonesian drug den with a gun pointed at my head I didn't know. It didn't make any sense. None.

The leader grabbed me by the collar, dragging me fully to my feet. Then he *slammed* me bodily against the wall. The breath whooshed out of me. I took short, shallow breaths as I tried to get my wind back. He yelled something. "How did you find it?" Ricky Tang repeated.

"As I said," I repeated thickly, the blood running hot out of my mouth, "I'm afraid that's privileged."

The leader relaxed his grip on me, and then I saw him smile for the first time. It was a scary sight. His eyes were full of malevolence, and his voice was cruel. Then he spoke to me himself, in accented but perfectly intelligible English. "There is no attorney-client privilege here," he said.

Then he turned to Ricky Tang and the others and barked some commands. There was some back-and-forth, as if Tang wasn't happy with the instructions, but eventually they relented and did what they were told.

Two of the *lanun* grabbed me and slammed me into a chair, holding me in place. A third brought over a scarred wooden table and placed it in front of me. Then a fourth man grabbed my arm and bent it out before me on the table. I struggled feebly but to no effect.

The leader stepped back and unsheathed a wickedly sharp *parang* from his belt. He tested the edge with his finger. I saw blood well out of a small cut. Then he advanced toward me as the others held me down.

"Hey. Hey!" I screamed at them. "What the hell are you doing? We're hostages. American lawyers. You hurt me, you're going to be fucked." I continued to struggle and fight but they were holding me down, and I couldn't do anything. I felt more helpless than I ever had in my life.

Dimly I realized that Vijay and Ashley and Schnizzel were all screaming at the top of their lungs. Rockaway was yelling something at Ricky Tang in bad Malay, trying to intercede. The leader barked something else to Tang.

"Hold still and you lose the finger," Tang translated, his face pale. "Otherwise, you lose the hand. Up to you." I struggled madly to free myself. But there were four of them holding me down and I couldn't move.

The leader stepped forward brought the *parang* up carefully over my struggling and screaming form. I started gibbering something, and I heard Rockaway shouting "Wait, wait, let's talk about this, he'll tell you what you want to know, just—"

And then at that moment, I saw the figure of Jared Diamond come barreling out of nowhere, slamming into the leader, knocking him over and making him drop his *parang*. Somehow, Diamond had gotten free of his bonds, and now he and the leader were wrestling viciously on the floor. Then Trevor Thompson, his hands still bound, yelled something and rammed into the *lanun* who were now trying to stop Diamond, taking two of them down in a heap.

Everything was chaos as Diamond and the leader wrestled on the floor right in front of me. Diamond's teeth were barred like a wild animal. But moments later, the leader freed his hand and reached for his belt. He grabbed a handgun, placed it against Diamond's stomach, and triggered two shots at point blank range. The sound was deafeningly loud in the enclosed space. Ashley screamed.

I saw Diamond choke right in front of me, and blood spurted out of his mouth. But then his face contorted into a terrible grin, and somehow he got his hands on the leader's *parang*, and he plunged it right into the man's stomach, once, twice, a third time, blood gushing out all the while. I saw the leader's face twist in agony. Then Diamond brought his hands up to the leader's face and in a snapping movement darted his fingers forward. There was a bloody scream and I saw, with horrified fascination, that Diamond had gouged out one of his eyes. The leader lay back, screaming in pain, blood welling out of the socket.

Ricky Tang struggled to bring his rifle to bear over Trevor Thompson, who was stronger than the three skinny *lanun* trying to hold him down put together, but Thompson was shoving them and Tang couldn't get a clear shot.

Diamond managed to pull himself to his feet, leaving the leader screaming bloody murder on the floor, and went for the gun. But then Tang finally got the rifle free and popped off a half a dozen rounds straight into Diamond's back. Diamond fell forward and crashed to the ground in a tangled heap. Then he twitched and was still.

In the midst of all of this, I saw that Ashley had grabbed something from the leader's belt. A phone. It was an old flip phone, from times past. I saw her grit her teeth and flip it open. Then she just stared.

"What the hell do I dial?" she yelled.

"Shit. What's 9-11 in Malaysia?" I said.

"I have no fucking idea!"

"Google it?" Vijay suggested.

"You want me to fucking Google it?" she screamed. Everyone was fast getting to their feet, and I could tell the situation was about to turn against us.

"Call the American consulate!" yelled Schnizzel. "+60 3-9212 6000!"

"Why in God's name do you have that phone number memorized?" I said, amazed.

"In case I get kidnapped in a foreign country and have a chance to use the phone! Katie used to call me paranoid. But look who's laughing now!"

I was momentarily nonplussed, but Ashley didn't hesitate. She dialed the number. Apparently she connected with someone, because she started screaming into the phone about being a U.S. citizen, with a bunch of other U.S. citizens, and her name was Ashley Marcum, and they had all been kidnapped by pirates, or *lanun* or whatever, and that we were probably in Sumatra off the Strait of Malacca and we were in some building they called a coffee shop and that someone had just been shot and they—

Then the phone was snatched away from her by Ricky Tang. He dashed it to the floor, where it broke into pieces. By then, more *lanun* had rushed into the coffee shop. They forced Trevor Thompson down and soon had the rest of us on the floor as well. Jared Diamond was bleeding out, dying or dead already. The *lanun* herded us into the middle of the room with the rifle, pistols, and *parangs*, and started yelling at us, which I couldn't understand, but I got the gist. We all lay face down on the floor and put our hands behind our heads, praying that we wouldn't get shot. Vijay tried to get medical attention for Diamond, and for Thompson, who looked to be in bad shape, but they kicked him in the face, splattering his nose with blood, and then he just lay there and shut up.

From my position on the floor, I heard the *lanun* making frantic phone calls. Maybe to more senior people. I didn't know what would happen. Maybe they would try to ransom us. Or maybe they would just kill us outright, for the trouble we'd caused.

We lay that way, frozen, face down on the floor, for some hours, through the remainder of the night and into the early hours of the morning. The time passed without sensation. My mind was numb, and my thoughts refused to connect. My jaw was pounding, and I was dimly aware of cramps in my stomach. I was in desperate need of water.

Some unknown number of hours into this ordeal, probably soon after dawn, judging by the light leaking in through the cracks, I began to hear noises outside. At first, I thought I was hearing things. But the noises steadily grew louder and louder. Mechanical noises. I heard the faint whir of machinery, coming closer. I figured it must be more *lanun* arriving in their *pancung* boats. But when I snuck a glance at the *lanun*, I saw that they looked troubled.

As the noises grew closer and closer, and louder and louder, I began to realize that they must coming from heavy equipment. Heavier than anything the *lanun* would have. I heard the *lanun* talking to each other animatedly. Some of them ran outside.

The sounds had sharpened into focus, and I could hear them clearly. They weren't coming from boats at all. The whirring noises were unmistakably coming from the blades of a helicopter. More than one helicopter, I soon realized.

I felt a spark of hope in my chest. There was no way that the *lanun* would have a helicopter. It had to be someone else. The Malaysian authorities, maybe. But how would they know where we were? I looked over at Ashley. Could her phone call have possibly worked? Was someone able to trace us just from that? It seemed too fast to be possible.

The helicopter noises were almost overwhelmingly loud now. The *lanun* had lost interest in us. They shouted at each other frantically as they tried to figure out what was going on. I heard the sounds of yelling and heavy movement outside.

Suddenly, we heard the bursts of gunfire. Pistols, firing scattered shots. Then the sound of heavy, sustained automatic return fire. Big holes broke out in the plywood walls of the coffee shop as bullets slammed into them. I kept my head down and screamed something.

I heard more shouting and gunfire outside, and then the rush of booted feet. "Go, go, go!" came the shouts. It took me a few moments to process that they were speaking English, and I could understand their words. They weren't Malaysian. They were American!

In that moment, a big black combat boot slammed through the door to the coffee shop, bursting it clear out of its frame. Silhouetted in the doorway stood a bulky soldier in full camo gear, wearing a Kevlar vest, night-vision goggles, and holding a huge black rifle in front of him. He loomed in the entrance, looking like a veritable giant compared to the scrawny *lanun*. The soldier advanced inside with his weapon raised and yelled something in badly accented Malay. A prepared phrase. More soldiers followed him in a rush, their booted feet shaking the crude wooden floor of the coffee shop.

The soldiers were shouting, and the *lanun* were shouting back, including Ricky Tang, and the soldiers had their rifles up, and then one of our guards raised his pistol and shot a round into the lead soldier's chest, punching into his vest and knocking him back a step.

The return fire came from half a dozen automatic rifles at once. It was so loud that I went momentarily deaf, and couldn't hear my own screaming as the bullets passed over our heads and tore the poor *lanun* to shreds. Ricky Tang and the other guards immediately dropped their weapons and put their hands up, gibbering. They were quickly forced to the floor and taken captive. In the confusion, I saw Ashley lunge toward the leader's still form, open the pouch at his waist, and pocket the gold coins that they'd taken from us.

The soldiers fanned out across the coffee shop and quickly searched the adjoining rooms. They called out "clear!" as they swept each one. More booted feet stamped around outside. Eventually, after all threats had been neutralized, one of the soldiers took off his night-vision goggles and approached us. He stopped in front of Ashley.

"Ms. Ashley Marcum?" he inquired politely.

After the soldiers finished mopping up the *lanun* and securing the area, they untied us, and a medic tended to our injuries. Thompson was pretty badly beat up, but he would be okay. Vijay had a broken nose. I had a loose tooth and a busted lip. There was nothing the soldiers could do for Jared Diamond, who was long dead.

The pre-dawn raid had been a full-scale military operation. There were two combat helicopters parked in the clearing outside. Dozens of soldiers were roaming the area. I recognized their insignia. They were Navy SEALs. About a dozen *lanun* were lying face down in the clearing with their hands tied behind their backs. The leader was among them. He was badly injured, but still alive. About a half a dozen more of the *lanun* were dead, their bodies resting under white shrouds.

"How did you find us?" Ashley asked the soldiers after we had thanked them profusely and things had settled down. "I didn't think I'd reached the consulate for long enough to say anything useful."

"Yes ma'am. Someone must have received orders about you beforehand, because we were on alert when the call came in.

When you called the consulate, we were able to trace it to right here."

"Who put you on alert?" I asked.

"Don't know, sir. Above my pay grade."

They gave us food and water, which we accepted gratefully. After they received the okay from mission control, the soldiers escorted us onto a helicopter. It took off with a roar, and the jungle faded away below us as we made our way over the ocean and through the sky.

THIRTY-TWO

I stood on the deck of the USS Pickney. It was high noon, and I was looking out at the blue waters of the Strait.

The ship felt ominous here. The USS Pickney was an Independence-class littoral combat ship in the U.S. Seventh Fleet. It looked futuristic from the front, with concave, layered steel walls designed to repel water or radar or whatever else. The rear looked more like a station wagon, with a fat helicopter deck jutting out the back. The littoral combat ship was a jack of all trades, capable of anti-submarine warfare, intelligence, reconnaissance, and special operations. It was armed with Mk 110 57 mm guns and RIM-116 rolling airframe missiles. It housed two Seahawk SH-60 helicopters, as well as autonomous surface and underwater vehicles.

All of this was being relayed to me in great detail by Petty Officer Third Class Connery, who had been assigned to guard me. Apparently, the Navy was considering decommissioning the littoral (a fancy word for coastal) combat ships. Connery thought this was a grave mistake. I half-listened to him as I tried to think through my situation.

During our absence, the world had gone insane. The story of our capture by, and subsequent rescue from, pirates in the Strait of Malacca was getting wall-to-wall coverage in the media. It was a sensational story. Two American lawyers and their compatriots, working on the hottest case of the day, seized by pirates, and then rescued in dramatic fashion by Navy SEALs. We even made the *Wall Street Journal*, albeit on the third page, after an article about a two percent correction in the Dow Jones Industrial Average.

I felt for my cell phone before I remembered that it was gone. I imagined it must be ablaze with calls and texts from everyone I knew. The first thing I did was use the ship's communications system to call my mom and tell her I was okay. After that I put in a call to HH&K. Then I read the news to try and figure out what was going on.

The world was dancing perilously close to an international incident over the *Flor de la Mar*. The news was reporting military build-up from countries in the area. Malaysia had put its Navy on high alert. Indonesia had bulked up its presence in the area. So had India, which controlled the waters near the Nicobar Islands. Portugal was also reportedly sending a squadron of ships, although they would take some time to arrive. The world had somehow found out that *Flor de la Mar* was near the Nicobar Islands, though I didn't know how. The exact location was still unknown. Air footage of the sea near the islands showed destroyers and heavy cruisers everywhere.

The U.S. also had a prodigious presence in the region. The USS Pickney was part of the Seventh Fleet, which was the largest forward-deployed fleet in the world, operating primarily in the Pacific. The Seventh Fleet was based in Japan, and had sixty to seventy warships, including nuclear-powered submarines, an aircraft carrier strike group, and tens of thousands of Navy and Marine personnel at the ready.

I thought about all the force all these ships could bring to bear in a mere moment. The seas by the Nicobar Islands were fast becoming a powder keg. The situation could be set alight by the slightest wrong move by anyone.

But as earthshaking as all of that was, there was even bigger news. To me, at least. It was about the case. Someone had filed the death memo in Judge Graves' court, and its contents were being widely reported in the press. The dramatic story of David Marcum's death and Rockweiller's coverup was all over the news, with details that could only have come from the memo. I couldn't believe it.

It must have been Harder, I thought. He was the only other person who knew. We had given him a copy of the memo for safekeeping in case anything happened to us. Maybe he had felt the need to do something to atone for the disqualification. To balance the scales. I didn't know. I wondered what Judge Graves would do to him.

I didn't have to wonder what Judge Graves was going to do to Rockweiller. According to news reports, Graves had hauled Rockweiller's top executives and the entire Badden & Bock team down to Galveston, Texas, and was stretching them out on the rack in a week-long sanctions hearing. Graves had threatened to throw the lot of them into federal prison if they didn't come clean. Rockweiller's stock had tanked, and the board of directors was resigning en masse. Word was that the CEO was going to be forced out. I had a dozen unread emails from Zachary Bock and John Cartwright, begging me to settle the case for ever-increasing sums of money. I couldn't believe it.

On deck, an officer approached me, interrupting my train of thought and Connery's soliloquy about the littoral combat ship. Connery saluted and stood at attention.

"Sir," the officer said to me. "I've spoken to the U.S. consulate as well as Seventh Fleet Command. They've determined that there's no further danger to you at this time. I have orders to escort you safely to a local airfield. A plane has been chartered to take you back to the United States."

The Navy flew us back in a transport plane. The aircraft was huge, the cavernous interior big enough to hold a hundred people and their gear. Today, it was only the five of us and Jared's casket. On another day I might have been awed, but today I barely noticed. During the flight, we didn't speak much. I sat quietly and thought about our capture and rescue. About Jared's death. About the memo. About the case, and what was going to happen next.

Before going back to Texas, we landed in Florida. To drop off Rufus Rockaway, and to attend Jared's funeral. The military respectfully agreed to stop there and ferry us back to Texas afterward.

The funeral was a simple affair at the Aqua Ray dive resort. Jared's kin were there. I met his mother, a hard-bitten woman of eighty years. I also met his brother Jacob, who was his spitting image.

I told them what had happened, and how Jared had saved us in Sumatra. That we wouldn't have escaped without him. His mother nodded proudly. That was just like him, she said. He was never one to take it lying down. His brother said that was how Jared would have wanted to go, if he had a choice.

Trevor Thompson said a few words on the beach, and then we took Jared's ashes out on a boat. Jared had wanted his remains scattered at his favorite dive site. It was the sheer wall of coral that Thompson had taken us to on our first visit to Key West. I watched Jared's ashes disappear beneath the surface, and imagined them drifting down to the bottom, like a deep well. Thompson broke down and shed tears, weeping unashamedly for his friend. Jared's brother, mother, and I remained grim-faced. I felt sad for the role I had played in causing Jared's death. But there were people more responsible than I was. And they were going to pay.

After that, there was just one last thing we had to do in Florida.

At 9 a.m. the next morning, Ashley and I walked into the Key West branch of Bank of America.

Travis Scott had been frantically trying to reach me ever since we'd sent the demand letter about the safety deposit box. When he finally got ahold of me, he apologized profusely, and said he hadn't known about the box. He agreed to give us access if we would forego sanctions against Bank of America. I said yes, and we went to go see the box.

The bank was quiet. No one else was there. The branch was a standard retail office of the chain, with regulation desks, regulation teller stands, and a few artificial plants placed here and there. Some bland elevator music was playing. It was all so ordinary that it felt surreal.

The bank manager hurried up to greet us. He was nervous. No doubt Scott had told him who we were and not to mess around with us. The manager led us back to the safety deposit area. Then he gave Ashley a key and a box number and left us alone. Ashley and I looked at each other.

This was our last shot at the contract, I knew. The wrongful death lawsuit had basically been won. The death memo had done them in, and Rockweiller was desperate to settle. It was just a question of how much. That seemed crazy to say, after we had been pursuing the case with everything we had for the last year. It was stunning to see the mighty Rockweiller Industries and Badden & Bock fall so quickly, and so unexpectedly, while we hadn't even been there to witness it.

But although the death case was won, David Marcum's share of the *Flor de la Mar* was still in play. It wasn't just about the money. It was about David's rights. If Marcum had a deal, I wasn't about to let Rockweiller screw him out of it in the grave. Marcum's estate was my client, and I meant to collect, come hell or high water. All we needed was the contract.

The case was almost at its end. Judge Graves had gotten sidetracked with the sanctions hearings. But when those were done, Graves was going to finish the trial and render a decision on the *Flor de la Mar*. If we didn't have the contract by then, I knew we wouldn't get another chance.

So it was with a tingling sense of anticipation that I looked at the cold, gleaming rows of metal boxes in front of us, wondering if one of them held the answer that we sought.

Ashley consulted the piece of paper that the manager had given her. Then she slowly walked up to box number 352. David Marcum's box. It was the size of a small mailbox, nothing more. I stepped back to give her some privacy.

I watched Ashley slip the small key into the lock and turn it. She opened the box slowly. Then she stopped and blinked. There was a surprised expression on her face.

"What is it?" I asked, barely able to contain myself. She beckoned me forward. I walked up to the box and looked inside.

It was empty.

Back in Texas, Cindy and Harder were waiting for us at the military airbase.

Cindy ran up and hugged me. "Jack!" she shouted. There were tears in her eyes. "You're okay!" I hugged her back, patting her shoulder awkwardly. Then she ran up to Vijay, Ashley, and Schnizzel, embracing each of them in turn. They all warmly returned her affection.

Harder stepped forward self-consciously. I smiled and clapped him in a rough embrace. "Never thought I'd be so glad to see you," I told him. He grinned at me unsteadily. "What the hell happened?" I demanded. "With the death memo? Did you really leak it?"

"Are you really asking *him* what happened?" Cindy said incredulously. "Don't you think we should get to ask that first?"

"Fair enough," I said with a laugh.

"But as long as we're on the subject," said Harder. "It wasn't me that leaked it. It was actually Kathleen."

"Kathleen *Loudamire*?" I said, shocked.

"Yep. She blew the whistle. A few days after you left for Malaysia. She filed the death memo with the court. She also filed an affidavit explaining what happened," Harder said.

"What did happen?" I asked.

"It was as we suspected. Loudamire interviewed Thomas Barber before they got a chance to get their story straight. Barber told the truth. But nobody wanted to hear it. Later, Gunthum pressured Barber to change his tune. He threatened him, and said they would all go to prison if he didn't. So it wasn't Bock, for what that's worth. But Bock didn't question the discrepancy either. The new story was convenient for him. Loudamire had already written the memo by then, though. Bock was furious, but he couldn't destroy it. That would have been spoliation of evidence."

I found it ironic that Bock would adhere to the ethics rules about spoliation, given everything else his firm had done. But I guess his actions always had a thin veneer of legality.

"After Kathleen's…attempt," Harder said uncomfortably, "she spent some time in the hospital. I visited her. She said she had started to think about everything, and it didn't sit well with her. She decided to say something, and told Judge Graves what had happened."

"Wow. That took some guts. What's going on in court?"

"Oh, man," said Harder, shaking his head. "You can't imagine. Graves is on a warpath. He ordered everyone involved in the case down to Galveston. I heard he threatened to send the U.S. Marshals to arrest the CEO after he refused to come. The guy backed down and showed up. There's a big sanctions hearing going on right now. Graves is deciding how bad he's going to give it to them.

"And that's not all," Harder continued. "The U.S. Attorney's office is investigating too. After Loudamire's confession, Thomas Barber recanted and told the truth about what happened. Got some kind of plea deal, maybe. Others might have flipped too. It's all coming crashing down. Word is the feds are going to bring criminal charges. Gunthum and his crew have already been arrested."

Ashley was speechless. I could see tears in the corner of her eyes.

"They really got arrested?" she whispered.

"Yep," Harder confirmed. "I heard Gunthum fought it, and five guys had to kick his ass."

"Good," Ashley said fiercely. I laughed. Then she stepped toward me, snaking her arm around my waist and beckoning me to pull her into a hug. I did, and we stood that way for a long time. Cindy shot a questioning glance at Harder, but he didn't say anything. I saw Vijay and Schnizzel standing in the background, smiling faintly.

Finally, I broke away from Ashley and turned back to Harder, although I wasn't sure I wanted to hear the answer to my next question. "What about us?" I asked. "Are we..." I trailed off and looked at him carefully.

Harder's face turned grim. "Judge Graves knows about what we did. Loudamire didn't out us, actually. Not at first. But when Judge Graves called her to testify, he got it out of her. She said she was sorry. That we did the right thing. But I'm due for a sanctions hearing myself after Graves is done flaying Bock & Co." I saw Harder's haggard expression and tired eyes and understood. "You'll be in for it too," he said. I nodded. It was inevitable.

But right then I found it hard to care. We'd just escaped capture and maybe death by pirates in Malaysia. Rockweiller had gone belly up, and the case had been blown wide open. The wind was at our backs, and right then I couldn't feel too down about sanctions. Let them string me up to high heaven tomorrow. Today was mine. My worries melted away as I smiled. Ashley caught on, and then everyone else did too. It felt glorious.

"Did you find it?" Cindy exclaimed, unable to hold it in any longer.

I smiled at her. "I'm afraid that's privileged information, miss." Her mouth described an "O", but then I laughed and nodded, and she jumped up and down in circles, cheering. Then we all piled into Harder's SUV, and Ashley, Vijay, Schnizzel, and I filled the others in on our crazy adventure as we drove home to Houston.

It was past dark when Harder dropped me off at my apartment. We had already dropped off Cindy, Ashley, and Vijay, and taken Schnizzel to a hotel.

"What now?" Harder asked, as he helped me unload my stuff. "I guess you'll be able to settle the case. They'll pay anything you want. Ten million, easy. They're going to beg for it." I nodded, and told him that they already had.

"Did you ever find the contract?" Harder asked. "Was there any sign of it?"

I shook my head. Harder nodded thoughtfully.

He didn't have to say more. Though we might have won the death case, without the contract, we had no way to enforce Marcum's share of the *Flor de la Mar*.

But I had a plan.

THIRTY-THREE

The press outside the federal courthouse in Galveston was insanity. Vijay and I walked toward the entrance, dressed in our best suits and ties, our shoes shined to mirror brightness. Ashley was with us, as was Jared's brother Jacob.

It seemed like every news outlet in the world was there to cover our return. Reporters yelled questions at us faster than I could register, let alone answer them, even if I'd tried. There were so many camera flashes that I felt like I was in an old black-and-white movie. Our arrival galvanized the protestors around the courthouse, who started pushing and shoving and chanting their causes, whatever they might be.

I walked through the crush with my eyes fixed straight ahead, looking neither left nor right. Strangely, I barely felt the tension. After the kidnapping and Jared's death in Sumatra, everything else felt like it had the volume turned down. Maybe I was walking into the hangman's noose with Judge Graves. But I couldn't bring myself to care. The presence of Jacob, grim-faced and silent just like Jared would have been, reminded me of what had happened, and how lucky we were to be there at all.

But gradually, through my stoicism, I noticed that the tone of the chants had changed. None of the protestors were yelling slogans about Malaysia or the West or Portugal anymore. Instead, they were cheering. It took me a split second to realize it. They were cheering *us*.

A funny thing had happened during our absence. Somehow, David Marcum had become the hero of this story. The press had gradually picked up on it, abetted by subtle hints that Remington had dropped here and there in court filings.

The rumor was out that Marcum might have found the *Flor de la Mar*. The story was irresistible. A dashing, handsome young American adventurer, college dropout turned amateur treasure hunter, who had somehow found the greatest shipwreck in the world and was then killed for it by agents of a giant corporation on the high seas—it was too much. Our recent capture by and escape from the hands of pirates drove the story to a fever pitch. The media was boiling over, and so was the public. The newspapers wrote and speculated and conjectured about it freely, to the utmost of the wildest blogger's imagination, although the accounts varied and most of them were dead wrong.

The loudest voice was Rufus Rockaway, who talked about the case non-stop on MNN, and alternated between interviewer and interviewee as everyone wanted to hear his story. Rockaway had abandoned all sense of journalistic objectivity, and he was David Marcum's staunchest champion. The pirate ordeal had also given him a certain glamor, which I could see from the interest with which Katie Tyler now regarded him on their split-screens.

Bock & Co.'s public relations people tried to change the narrative. They highlighted Marcum's criminal past, like Bock would try to do in court. But it didn't work. The media brushed it off as youthful indiscretion, or adversity overcome. And once the death memo went public, all of Rockweiller's deflections imploded under a tidal wave of public anger that swept over them.

All of this came with a flood of emotion for Ashley. "They're cheering us," she said in wonder. "They're cheering my brother." People cried out to us as we passed, and reached out to touch us and wish us luck. I saw tears streaming down Ashley's cheeks as we pressed through. I knew she was crying because the world was finally able to see her brother for who he was. To see that he meant something to the world. That he mattered. The people had heard her story, and they believed her.

I was less sanguine. I knew that the media was fickle, and the narrative could change in a heartbeat. And more importantly, I knew that none of this would sway Judge Graves, who was the one who mattered. For that, we needed a different tactic.

Ashley said thank you to as many people as she could as we made our way through the crowd. In the end, Butch and the Marshals had to hustle us through, muscling people aside so we could get past.

Eventually, we made our way inside the courthouse and then into the courtroom itself. The courtroom was nearly empty. Judge Graves had sealed it for the hearing. Only the court staff, the marshals, and the primary attorneys were allowed in. The courtroom felt cool and quiet after the press of the crowd outside.

The mood in the courtroom was grim. Bock was sitting at the right-side counsel table, his customary arrogance gone. He looked like a man who had been beaten within an inch of his life. Cornelius Adipose and some other associates were with him, looking like so many lost boys dressed up in their fathers' ties. Loudamire was absent. The lawyers and ambassadors for Malaysia, Indonesia, and Portugal were there, waiting.

Judge Graves himself sat on his high bench, wearing black robes and his blackest expression. He glared at me balefully as I walked in. His eyes swept the room, daring anyone to speak. No one did.

Everyone stood up as the clerk called the case. Then Judge Graves began. "Never in my thirty years on the bench have I seen conduct like this," he said scathingly. "Never. And I have seen a lot." He waited for anyone to say something, but no one answered.

Graves pointed a thick finger at Bock. "Your star witness murdered David Marcum. And lied about it under oath. I don't know the full extent if your involvement yet. Or whether you suborned perjury. But believe me, I intend to find out." His voice was chilling.

"Your Honor," Bock said weakly, "I dispute the characterization of Mr. Gunthum's actions as murder. Further, I had no definitive knowledge that he was being untruthful. I took Mr. Gunthum at his word—"

"*Shut up!*" thundered Graves. "If I hear another word out of you, I will have you arrested on the spot. I will personally call the U.S. Attorney for the Southern District of Texas and make sure you are charged tomorrow morning. Do you understand?" Bock nodded. There was no color in his face anymore.

"And you!" said Graves, turning his wrath on me. "You stole privileged materials from a woman dying by her own hand, to gain advantage in this litigation. That it has revealed Rockweiller Industries' own sins does not elevate your act. I am certainly going to recommend ethics charges, and God knows what else." I looked back at him neutrally and didn't say a word. It was no more than I expected.

Graves then eyed the lawyers for Malaysia, Portugal, and Indonesia, looking for an excuse to rip into them too. But they only stood quietly. Jafaar was smart enough to know when to shut up. Graves turned back to Bock and me.

"I will deal with the both of you in due course," he said ominously. "Count on that. But for the time being, I am going to adjourn to consider what to do with this royal mess that I have inherited from the sixteenth century, colloquially known as the *Flor de la Mar*. Does anyone have any last words before I do?" The question was obviously rhetorical, and Graves' gavel was half raised, ready to bang down and make an end.

I stepped forward. "I do." Everyone turned toward me, wondering what the hell I was doing.

Judge Graves' eyes bored into me. "Do you indeed, Mr. Carver?" he said. I could see the hangman's rope coiling in his gaze.

"Yes."

"Is it a choice of prisons?" Graves said acidly. "If so, I would recommend Galveston County. Good Yelp reviews. If it is anything else, I would suggest you hold your tongue."

"No. It's a legal motion. I am moving to amend our complaint to add a claim regarding the *Flor de la Mar*."

Some muttering broke out in Bock & Co.'s section, but Judge Graves silenced them with a look. Jafaar snapped out of his penitent pose and eyed me sharply.

"A claim regarding the *Flor de la Mar*?" Graves repeated, his eyes narrowing. "Do tell."

"David Marcum found it," I said simply.

"I am aware of that allegation, Mr. Carver. But insofar as I have seen, there is no proof."

"There is now."

With that, I reached into my pocket and drew out one of the gold coins we had recovered from the Nicobar Islands. I tossed it to Judge Graves, as casually as if I were flipping a quarter. Graves caught it with a start. He turned it over in his hands, bemused by its strange markings and golden glow.

"I recovered this coin from *Flor de la Mar*," I said. "Personally." This caused another round of muttering from the attorneys, louder this time. There were plenty of rumors flying around about what we had been doing in Malaysia. But this was the first time I'd confirmed it.

"I found the coin using David Marcum's information," I continued. "The same information that he gave Lloyd Gunthum and Rockweiller Industries. The same information he was later killed for."

"And your evidence of this?" demanded Judge Graves.

"Is the coin itself."

Judge Graves frowned in puzzlement. "Think about it, Your Honor," I said with all the persuasiveness I could muster. "I was able to find the *Flor de la Mar* in a matter of weeks, using the same information that David Marcum did. What are the chances I could have done it if his information was wrong? When every one of the sophisticated, well-capitalized expeditions before me have failed? When all of the expeditions for the last five hundred years, for that matter, have come up empty handed? If I was able to find the *Flor de la Mar* with Marcum's information, then that information must be true. I stand ready to provide the source of this information to the court *in camera* upon request." *In camera* meant for the court's eyes only. I wasn't about to tell Bock and Jafaar about Manuel Roberto's confession if they didn't already know.

This made an impression. I could see Graves turning it over in his mind. "And how do I know this coin is from the *Flor de la Mar*?" Graves said absently, staring at the coin with fascination, his anger forgotten for a moment in the light of the gold.

I was ready for this. I opened my briefcase and pulled out some papers. "I have here an affidavit from Professor Jacob Schnizzel, maritime archaeology expert, attesting that everything I say is true. Professor Schnizzel has examined the coin and determined that it is nearly identical to the ones in the possession of David Marcum, Rockweiller Industries, and now this Court."

I handed the affidavit to Judge Graves, and Vijay passed out copies to the other lawyers. "Professor Schnizzel is ready and able to testify to this. I can also provide the coins to the opposing experts for analysis."

Judge Graves nodded slowly. "I see." Graves remained silent for a while, thinking. I resisted the temptation to talk further, and just waited. "Tell me," Graves said at last. "Supposing for a moment that this is all true. That this coin is in fact from the *Flor de la Mar*. And that David Marcum uncovered the information leading to the wreck. What right does that give Mr. Marcum to the ship?"

Graves leaned forward. "I know you say there was a contract, Mr. Carver. A contract which gave Mr. Marcum some type of finder's fee. Rockweiller denies it. Although I am not inclined to believe anything they say." He glared at Bock, who didn't meet his eye. "I am certainly sympathetic to Mr. Marcum, given what I now know happened to him. You were right about that. I give you due credit. And believe me, the wrongdoers will be punished to the fullest extent of the law.

"Nonetheless, the fact remains that I have no hard evidence of any contract. Without one, I cannot entertain the Marcum estate's claim regarding the *Flor de la Mar*. I simply have no legal basis by which to award Mr. Marcum any part of the *res* over the likes of Malaysia or Portugal, which claim sovereign rights to it, or Rockweiller, which claims the right of salvage."

"I'm not making claim based on contract, Your Honor," I said.

"No?" he asked, puzzled.

"No. Nor am I asking for a piece of the *Flor de la Mar.*"

"Well, what then?" Graves asked impatiently.

I looked at Judge Graves calmly and said, "On behalf of the estate of David Marcum, I am making a claim for the entire *res* of the *Flor de la Mar* pursuant to the law of finds."

At this, all of the lawyers erupted in a cacophony of shouting. I couldn't have caused more uproar if I'd set off a bomb. Bock forgot his ignominy amid his outrage. The lawyers for Malaysia and Portugal were yelling at me in languages I didn't understand. The Portuguese ambassador was jumping up and down, his face red. Everyone was screaming at the same time, heedless of Judge Graves' calls for order. I weathered it all calmly.

This had been Remington's backup plan all along, you see. If we couldn't find the contract. That's what he had meant by his cryptic last remark to me. "Whatever you're looking for, I hope you'll find."

I had known about the law of finds for a long time now. I also knew it was virtually impossible to win on it. The law of finds only applied to property that was unowned or abandoned, where no one came forward to claim it. Here, there was no shortage of people claiming it. But I had done more research. And I'd found a handful of cases. Old ones, where courts had said ancient shipwrecks could be lost so long they were considered abandoned. It was a hell of a long shot. A fingernail on a ledge. The skin of a tooth. But that's all I needed, for what I was going to do next. I wasn't really trying to get the whole *Flor de la Mar*, you see. It was like Kruckemeyer said. Sometimes, if you ask for the whole store, maybe you get a piece of it.

After Judge Graves finally restored order, I stood calmly and made my legal argument. I explained that the law of finds was an ancient principle that long predated sovereign immunity, the law of salvage, or any other nation-made law. The *Flor de la Mar* was over five hundred years old, I said, and no one had found it until now. David Marcum had discovered it. If not for him, the treasure might not have seen the light of day for centuries more. If ever.

Who better to get the *Flor de la Mar* than the one who actually found it? Wouldn't that encourage people to find more ancient ships, and bring up more wonders of the world? Wouldn't that incentivize people to report their finds, instead of hiding them? Wouldn't that be the best thing for everyone? Wouldn't it be the right thing to do?

Judge Graves listened to all of this thoughtfully, giving no hint as to his intentions. I knew how tenuous my argument was. But I made it with a perfectly straight face. Sometimes, the best way to make the most outlandish claim is to do it so casually that it doesn't seem crazy at all.

After that, Judge Graves heard some counterargument from Bock and Jafaar. Bock was so angry he was spitting, and could barely form coherent sentences. He and Jafaar both said they were going to file hundred-page briefs explaining why I was dead wrong. I had no doubt they would.

After hearing argument for about an hour, Judge Graves banged his gavel and adjourned the hearing, giving no hint as to his feelings. He just said he would take the matter under advisement and retired without further word. But as he disappeared into chambers with his law clerks and his staff, I thought I saw the ghost of a smile flicker across his face.

THIRTY-FOUR

Judge Graves' jury room was a simple space. The table was brown and the walls were white. The only decoration was a plaque that said, "In God we trust."

Around the table were Zachary Bock, John Cartwright, Aquil Jafaar, the Malaysian ambassador, the lawyer and ambassador for Portugal, and myself.

It was one week after our last hearing in front of Judge Graves. The previous day, Graves had issued an order. After deliberating, he said that, as much as he would like to throw the lot of us in prison and award the *Flor de la Mar* to someone actually worthy of it, he was going to have to render a decision.

But before he did, Graves was offering us one chance, and one chance only, to resolve the matter amongst ourselves. "This chance is not for your sake," he wrote in a short order. "But for the sake of comity among nations, and respect between fellow men. A mutual agreement regarding the *Flor de la Mar* would best serve the interests of justice, and perhaps serve as an example in future cases."

So Graves was going to give us one day, from 9 a.m. until 5 p.m., to try and reach an agreement. If we didn't, he would do it for us, and issue his ruling directly thereafter.

That morning, we appeared at the courthouse. Butch greeted us in silence and escorted us to the jury room. We were to deliberate, as a jury might, until we reached an agreement, or until the clock struck five, whichever came first. Stale bagels had been provided, that we might break bread with one another. No one touched them.

This was how things stood, at the lunch hour of the last day:

Rockweiller was desperate to settle the case. They had offered me steadily increasing sums for the death claim. And there was more. Incredibly, after my stunt with the law of finds, they were now offering a ten percent share of the *Flor de la Mar* as well. With how much Graves hated Rockweiller right now, they couldn't take the risk that Graves would go my way, however unlikely it was. So Bock made the offer, through gritted teeth. This was exactly what I'd hoped for. Ten percent was more than reasonable. In fact, it was everything we could have dreamed of at the beginning of the case.

But I refused. All morning, I sat there with my arms crossed and unwaveringly demanded a full twenty-five percent share of the *Flor de la Mar*. Bock almost choked with rage when he heard this demand. Jafaar called it ludicrous. Which it was. Realistically, the chances of Judge Graves going our way on the law of finds was small. But I did my best Hubert Thung impression and stubbornly refused to budge.

The biggest obstacle to a deal, though, was Malaysia. Rockweiller's offer was contingent on Malaysia agreeing to something. And so far, they had no interest in doing so. Jafaar believed he was in a strong position, and with good reason. I suspected he was only attending the settlement conference to show Judge Graves that he was a reasonable man, and open to compromise. But he wasn't. Yet.

But there was one more card to play.

The clock struck one, and the door opened. John Remington walked in. A sudden wave of relief washed over me. As if everything was going to be alright. I grinned at him. He didn't return my smile, but just sat down and assumed his typical expression, looking as if he were carved out of wood.

"Gentlemen," he said, putting his battered old briefcase on the table. "Where are we on the negotiations?"

Bock sputtered to life. "Excuse me," he said with a hint of his old vim, "you've been disqualified from representing the Marcum estate in this case. You can't be here."

"I'm not here representing the Marcum estate," Remington said calmly. "I'm here on behalf of the estate of Jared Diamond." Bock stared at him in disbelief.

After Jared Diamond's funeral, I had spoken to the family about retaining a lawyer. I said I knew a good one. They took my advice and hired John Remington.

"That is immaterial," argued Bock. I could see him start to wind up like an old motor. "The Marcum conflict is obviously imputed to any other—"

"Shut up, Zachary," a voice said sharply. I turned around. Surprisingly, it was John Cartwright. "We need to get a deal done," he said. "If John can help, so much the better. Maybe he can talk some sense into this kid." Meaning me. "We'll waive conflict for the purposes of this negotiation," he said, waving his hand, thus waiving away the conflict that had so bedeviled us and nearly sunk our entire case. Bock looked apoplectic, but Cartwright was the client, and he had no choice but to do what he said. Jafaar studied Remington carefully, but didn't object.

We sat in silence for a while after that. Remington didn't move a muscle, and waited for someone to speak. But for once, Bock didn't seem interested in opening the proceedings.

Eventually, Jafaar did. "I hate to be a stick in the mud," he said apologetically. "But I am not optimistic about reaching any deal. I firmly believe that the *Flor de la Mar's* cargo belongs to Malaysia. Moreover, I believe that, based on the trial and on...recent developments," he said, looking at Bock, who sank lower in his chair, "that we will prevail, and Judge Graves will award the entirety of the *res* to Malaysia.

"While I appreciate the Marcum estate's creative arguments, you can't seriously believe that Judge Graves will award title to the *Flor de la Mar* based on the law of finds." Jafaar spread his hands. "That's the way I see things. With that in mind, and with the numbers I have heard here today, I don't think a compromise is possible."

It was a remarkably honest assessment. And to all appearances, Jafaar was right. He had the upper hand. We all knew it. Rockweiller was in the dog box, and we had a slim to zero chance of prevailing under the law of finds. Malaysia looked like the presumptive winner.

Except for one thing.

"Is that your final position?" Remington asked.

"It is," said Jafaar politely. But his lip curled ever so slightly.

Remington nodded. "Fair enough. That's reasonable. But there's one thing I'd like you to know first. So you have all the facts before you make a decision. I'd like you to step outside with me for a moment. Don't worry, no fisticuffs. Just a conversation that I think you will find edifying."

Remington got up and opened the door. Waiting in the hallway were several grim-faced men in dark suits and crew cuts. G-men. Jafaar got up unsteadily and followed Remington outside.

You see, after the Diamond family had retained Remington to represent Jared's interests, we had been paid a little visit by the U.S. government. Officials from the CIA, the State Department, and the Navy had informed us about certain details regarding our kidnapping and Jared's death.

It turned out that Malaysia was behind it.

We couldn't prove it. Not perfectly. But the evidence was damning.

After Rufus Rockaway's observation that our capture might have been an inside job, I had suspected that Rockweiller was behind it. They had the motive. And after the way they covered up Marcum's death, I didn't think there was anything they wouldn't stoop to.

But the government said it wasn't them. Rockweiller didn't have the sort of deep connections among the *lanun* to pull something like that off, they said. Only Southeast Asian governments did.

Malaysia had been watching us for a long time now. U.S. intelligence suspected they had been tapping our phones for months, ever since we dragged them into the case. We had certainly been tracked from the moment we landed in Kuala Lumpur. Every step of our journey was surveilled by satellite, cell phone interception networks, and covert government operatives. By the time we arrived at the Nicobar Islands, Malaysia was all over us. There were shadow ships just miles away, out of sight, waiting for the order to pounce.

It was scary to think of the resources a whole country can bring to bear, especially when that country is not bound by the same laws as the United States. I thought about David Marcum and his conspiracy theories. His shunning of phone calls, his reliance on cash. It turned out he had been right all along. I felt like an idiot for not realizing it.

We led Malaysia right to the *Flor de la Mar*, of course, which was what they had wanted. And once we found it and salvaged some treasure, they couldn't risk letting us leave. If we had taken it back to the U.S., they feared we would lay claim to it and broadcast its location to the whole world. So they made a move.

They didn't do it directly. Malaysia was afraid of provoking the U.S. and wanted to minimize the risk of an international incident.

So they used a proxy. The Malaysian government had long been rumored to have secret links with the *lanun* who plied the Strait of Malacca. It could be useful. When an incident happened, there was a backchannel. A way to get a hostage back, or an important cargo returned. For a price. Some even said the Malaysian government had secret operatives embedded within the *lanun*.

The leader of the *lanun* was believed to be one of these. The CIA and military people couldn't confirm this. But they strongly suspected it. The man's name was Haziq Lim. Lim was a former agent with a secretive intelligence agency called Meio, a sort of Malaysian counterpart to the CIA.

But the CIA didn't think Lim was a former agent at all. They believed he was a current one, working off the grid, taking on assignments that official agents could not. U.S. intelligence had interrogated Lim after his capture. We weren't privy to exactly how they did it, or what he said. But the result was that they strongly believed he was operating under the orders of the Malaysian government.

U.S. intelligence believed that the Malaysian government had secretly ordered the *lanun* to capture us, through Lim. Lim and the *lanun* were to take the treasure and hold us in a secure location until the *Flor de la Mar* business had wound down. Then we would have been ransomed back as ordinary hostages, with no one the wiser.

But the thing had turned into a colossal fuck-up. The *lanun* were not the most reliable of agents. Most of them had no connection to the government, or any idea that it was involved. They just wanted money and hostages. Doubtless they were aware of the *Flor de la Mar*, and perhaps they had hoped for a taste.

Remington must have had a sixth sense that something like this might happen. When he'd learned we were going to Malaysia, he called someone in the Governor's office, who called someone in Washington, who put someone in Malaysia on notice to look out for us. So by the time Ashley made her desperate phone call to the consulate, they were already on high alert. They were able to trace the cell phone signal and send an extraction team immediately.

Incidentally, when I asked Remington about his last, cryptic comment, "whatever you're looking for, I hope you'll find," he asked me what the hell I was talking about, and said he hadn't meant anything remotely like the law of finds, and that he couldn't believe I'd tried something so harebrained as to try and claim ownership of the entire *Flor de la Mar* that way.

The U.S. pressed Malaysia for answers on our kidnapping, officially and through other channels. Malaysia vehemently denied any involvement. Probably many Malaysian officials thought they were telling the truth. It was unclear who had ordered the operation, or how high up it went. I wondered if Jafaar knew. Somehow, I suspected not.

After laying out their information, the U.S. officials offered their sincere condolences to the Diamond family, and to us, and asked us what we wanted to do. The President had been briefed, and to a large extent, what happened next depended on us. If we wanted to go public, they wouldn't keep us from doing that. If we wanted to resolve this quietly, they wouldn't interfere with that either.

Jafaar and the Malaysian ambassador were gone for nearly two hours with Remington and the G-men. They returned sometime after 3 p.m., their faces ashen. Remington closed the door after them. Then he sat down, waited until he had everyone's full attention, and addressed the room. "Let's recount the facts," he said quietly.

First, he turned to Bock and Cartwright. "You are dead meat," he said matter-of-factly. "Your client killed David Marcum. And you covered up his death. Rockweiller's stock is in the tank, and half the board of directors has resigned. The U.S. attorney is investigating, and everyone aboard the Excelsior is going to face charges. You will too, if I have anything to say about it. All of that's done. I can't change it."

His voice took on a bleaker tone. "But I can make it worse. The *Flor de la Mar* case is over. But the death case is just beginning. You're at the start of a long, ugly road. Do you remember what you said in your letter, back at the beginning of this case? Allow me to retort."

Remington leaned forward and looked John Cartwright dead in the eye. "I will depose every one of your executives. I will interrogate your CEO and the entire board of directors. Think they can get out of this by resigning? Think again. I'll nail them to the wall no matter where they go. I will also go after each and every one of the lawyers, including both of you, personally. I will find out exactly what you knew, and exactly when you knew it. Judge Graves will give me all of this and more.

"Your attorney-client privilege is dead. I will pull the truth out of you, inch by inch. It will take years. And at the end of it, Judge Graves is going to be standing there with an ax, waiting to hit you with a big, fat verdict the likes of which you've never seen. Think you can't kill a corporation? Watch me."

I was shocked by the violence in his voice. This wasn't just posturing. This was real anger. I had never seen him so coldly furious before. Bock and Cartwright looked scared half to death. As they should have been. Remington paused for a beat to assess the effect he'd had on them. Then he nodded, satisfied, and turned to Jafaar.

"As for you," he said, "the CIA has credible evidence that Malaysia aided and abetted the capture, kidnapping, and killing of a U.S. citizen to further its interests in this legal dispute. What do you suppose will happen if I walk out of here and tell Judge Graves that? Do you have any idea?"

Jafaar looked like he was about to throw up. "And forget about what Judge Graves will do," Remington continued. "He's the least of your worries. Start thinking about what the U.S. government will do. Oh, yeah. If we don't walk out of here with a deal, I will go public tomorrow morning across every news and radio station in the country. If you're lucky, Malaysia will be looking at billions of dollars' worth of sanctions from the United States. Want to see what a trade war looks like? Go ahead. And if you're unlucky, you're looking at an actual war with the U.S. Seventh Fleet."

Jafaar and the ambassador were shocked speechless as Remington continued. "You are fortunate in one thing, and one thing only. Mr. Jared Diamond's family is not interested in making a public spectacle out of this. They would rather deal with this quietly and move on.

"Gentlemen, I suggest that we make a deal. You're going to pay blood money, and we are going to divvy up the *Flor de la Mar* between us. Right here, right now. Because if we don't, I am going to walk out of here and take my chances with the Judge, and with the public. I don't really care either way. It's up to you."

Having put it all out there, Remington crossed his hands behind his head, kicked his boots up on the table, and stared them down.

Bock, Cartwright, and Jafaar looked at each other. And then all at once, they caved.

"Very well," Jafaar said wearily. "I see the wisdom in what you have said. Let us begin negotiations. I don't know if we will reach a conclusion this day. But perhaps if the Judge sees we are on the way, he will give us more time to—"

"There's not going to be any more time," Remington said flatly. "And there's not going to be any negotiation. I'm not interested in building an elephant by committee. I'm going to give terms. Either you take them, or you don't. These are my terms."

Remington bulled over their vigorous protests and stated his terms. "Malaysia gets forty-five percent of the *Flor de la Mar*. Portugal gets twenty-five percent, including rights to the ship itself. Rockweiller Industries gets twenty percent. The Estate of David Marcum gets ten percent. Any remains of soldiers, seamen, or passengers will go to the country of their nationality. That's the deal."

The lawyers were ready to protest anything that came out of Remington's mouth. But when they heard his terms, they stopped. They actually sounded reasonable. Fair, even. Bock and Jafaar exchanged glances.

In fact, the one who came closest to protesting was me. Ten percent was already on the table. And after what Remington had just unloaded on them, I felt sure we could do better. But I trusted him, and kept my mouth shut.

"What about the death claims?" Bock asked.

"Rockweiller pays fifty million to David Marcum's estate. Malaysia pays fifty million to Jared Diamond's estate. And we're done."

That was high but reasonable, given the circumstances. Bock frowned, trying to figure out how he was getting screwed. Attorneys are used to playing games and dragging out negotiations as long possible. To have a fair deal presented at the outset was deeply unsettling to them. And yet, they couldn't find fault with it.

"There's just one thing," said Remington. Everyone's hackles went up. "The percentage of the *Flor de la Mar* allocated to David Marcum's estate will be paid in cash, today, from the collective funds of Malaysia, Portugal, and Rockweiller Industries."

This drew spirited protests from Bock and Jafaar, who vetoed it immediately. No way they could do that, they said. No one even knew for certain what the *Flor de la Mar* was really worth. Or how long it would take to salvage. Or the cost. Or a hundred other things.

Remington cut them off. "It seems to me that you all have experts who pegged the value of the wreck pretty precisely. I don't see what the issue is. But in any case, payment up front is non-negotiable. I am not going to put the estates of Marcum and Diamond in some jackpot that could take years to resolve, if ever. You want to settle this, those are the terms. Else we walk."

Bock and Jafaar looked at each other sourly. And then the haggling began.

Remington gave ground steadily on the finder's fee and the death payments as the time neared four o'clock. Over the course of an hour, Bock and Jafaar negotiated him down to a five percent finder's fee instead of ten, and thirty-five million to each estate instead of fifty. But all of the money would be payable immediately, like Remington demanded.

We also had to agree on a value for the *Flor de la Mar* for the sake of the deal. Expert testimony put the figure anywhere from three to thirty billion dollars. We agreed on five billion, which was decidedly toward the low end of the range. I thought we could have done better. Much better. But I still didn't question Remington, and that was the value we used. There were also some details to be worked out regarding India and Thailand, which were making noises about rights to the wreck. It was agreed that Rockweiller, Malaysia, and Portugal would have to deal with that, and any other issues that came up. The estates were out.

Under the deal, the total sum payable to the Marcum estate was 285 million dollars. Cash. Somehow, this didn't make any more impression on me than a set of twenty-dollar bills coming out of the ATM. The sum was so staggeringly huge that it didn't register in any way that made sense.

Remington reached into his briefcase and took out a settlement agreement which, to my amazement, he had already drafted. He filled in the numbers and handed out copies to everyone for signature. The collective attorneys hesitated with their pens in hand, almost constitutionally incapable of committing to something like this so fast. But the clock was fast approaching five, and Remington just stared them all down until they signed.

After that, we left the jury room and announced the settlement to Judge Graves. He pronounced himself well pleased with us, signed off on it, and declared the case resolved. And that was that.

THIRTY-FIVE

The settlement agreements were signed, the monies were paid, and the lawsuit was over.

The newspapers loved the ending. Rockweiller, Portugal, and Malaysia chose to announce the settlement as a great victory for them and all mankind. The death settlements were confidential, and no word of the leverage Remington and I had exerted to force this outcome was spoken. All the news saw was a grand bargain between nations, companies, and individuals, which fairly allocated the treasures of the *Flor de la Mar* among everyone involved. Marcum was hailed as hero for finding it, Rockweiller commended for salvaging it, Portugal praised for sailing it, and Malaysia celebrated for creating it. All of the fights and the lies and the deaths were swept away in a tide of good feeling. Governments extolled the agreement as a model for future disputes over treasure wrecks, and several international treaties were proposed based on its terms.

The first thing we did afterward was sleep for about a week. The second thing we did was pay out bonuses.

After our contingency fee, David Marcum's estate took 171 million dollars all in. Jared Diamond's estate took 21 million.

And HH&K itself took a cool 128 million. The numbers were so big that they felt like the distance between the stars.

Of the firm's share, Kruckemeyer got the biggest slice as originating partner. Remington got the next biggest as lead counsel. I got a big bonus too. A huge bonus. Enough that I might never have to practice law again if I didn't want to. I suspected Ashley had insisted on it. The rest of the money was shared out among the partners, with generous bonuses to Harder, Cindy, Vijay, Lyle, and everyone else who had played a part in the case.

I could have pushed for more money. Technically, I was Ashley's lawyer when we won. Not the firm. If I had been a real asshole, I might have asked for the whole store. A lot of lawyers were sharp enough to do just that. But not me. The whole firm had won the case, and there was more than enough money to go around.

The third thing we did was throw a huge party.

Kruckemeyer booked the baddest country club in town, the same one that hosted the Judicial Honors Gala, and we threw a massive bash the likes of which the Houston legal community had never seen. We invited almost every attorney in town, and everyone who was anyone showed up.

The centerpiece of the party was a huge ice sculpture of the *Flor de la Mar*, mapped out in meticulous detail by Jacob Schnizzel, and brought to life by a famous ice sculpturist. Its frozen white sails sparkled like diamonds, reaching nearly to the roof of the grand ballroom. Kruckemeyer got some maritime artifacts on loan from the Houston museums, and we scattered them around the room, displayed under crystal cases for guests to marvel at. As a party favor, each guest received an actual silver coin from a shipwreck, with a plaque explaining where it came from, curated by Dr. Richard Avoulay. For the guests we really liked, the coins were gold.

The food at the party was incredible. We had six different food stations. Five-star chefs cranked out delicacies from Malaysia, Portugal, Colombia, and Spain, with an ice sculpture of a famous shipwreck to match each one. The *Mercedes* was there, as were the *San Jose* and the *Atocha*. Schnizzel also rustled up some lesser known ships, the *Santa Margarita* and the *Madre de Deus*, which sank near Mexico and Japan, because Kruckemeyer wanted to serve sushi and fajitas. There was also a desert station, complete with a chocolatier and whatever the equivalent of that was for ice cream.

Waiters walked around, offering mountains of crab cakes, bacon-wrapped scallops, stuffed dates, and caviar to all and sundry. Kruckemeyer had wanted the waiters to dress in pirate costumes. But Harder took him aside and convinced him that might be insensitive after our near-death experience in Malaysia. Kruckemeyer grumbled but relented. No pemmican was served.

The amount of alcohol on tap was outrageous. Glasses of champagne and wine flowed around the room, and the chefs created a signature cocktail for each food station. Vijay requested Tiger beer in honor of our Malaysian voyage, and I added the Singapore Sling, a bright pink drink I had tasted on the flight to Kuala Lumpur. There was top-shelf liquor of every kind, everywhere, and the bartenders were pouring doubles without even being asked.

All of the HH&K partners attended, and congratulated me on a job well done. They were dressed in black tuxedos, and so was I, having finally got one for the occasion. David Wurlheiser approached me toward the middle of the night and pumped my hand for all he was worth, his glasses skewed and his skinny face red with drink. I heard he'd asked Stephanie Rivera to be his date to the party, but that she had declined on grounds of a conflict of interest.

Kruckemeyer was there, of course. He clapped me on the back and told me that I'd better be in by 9 a.m. the next day to start billing. I wasn't sure if he was joking.

Rufus Rockaway and Katie Tyler came too. Rockaway wore his best green turtleneck and a rust-red coat. The colors clashed horribly, and I loved it.

At some point in the evening, Tyler ran into Schnizzel. I was close by and watched the encounter with interest.

"Hello, Jacob," she said in a sultry voice.

"Katie," Schnizzel said with a curt nod.

"You seem to have gotten famous lately," she said nonchalantly. It was obvious she'd had a lot to drink. It was also obvious that she was flirting with him.

"Happens to the best of us," Schnizzel said with disinterest.

Her delicate eyebrows furrowed in a frown. "Don't pretend that you're not happy to see me."

Schnizzel grunted. "Where's Cal?"

She curled her lip. "Cal? Cal and I are taking a break. The guy fell for me way too fast. Asked me to marry him three months in. But you know all about what that's like, don't you?"

Schnizzel ignored this. "Taking a break huh?" he said.

"Yes." She waited expectantly for him to say something else. But he didn't. "I miss you," she said at last.

"I miss you too," said Schnizzel. "Like the bubonic plague. Enjoy the party." Then he spun on his heel in a fabulous pair of black cherry-colored cowboy boots and walked off rudely, leaving Tyler to gape at his back. She turned to Rufus Rockaway to make some scathing comment, but found that he had deserted her too. Rockaway was over by the bar getting blasted with Trevor Thompson and unashamedly flirting with Ashley, who couldn't stop laughing.

The most formidable guest at the party was undoubtedly the Honorable Nathaniel L. Graves of the Southern District of Texas, Galveston Division. We had invited him to be polite, and hadn't expected him to come. But to everyone's surprise, he did. This was edgy, since he had presided over the case. But the lawsuit was over, and technically there was no bar to him socializing with us now. Graves scared the hell out of everybody, especially the younger attorneys, until about ten o'clock, by which time he was roaring drunk, as was everyone else. By eleven, Graves' booming laugh could be heard from across the ballroom.

He and I crossed paths at one point. I was on edge. The disciplinary proceedings against Harder and me were still ongoing, and I didn't know how he would punish us. But Graves seemed in perfectly good humor. He asked about my Malaysian adventures, and said he thought he'd warned me against swashbuckling. I told him I was a slow learner, at which he roared with laughter, and we got on alright after that. Judge Gleeson was there too, and he warmly shook my hand, complimenting me on my performance at the TRO hearing, which seemed so long ago.

Cindy, Harder, Vijay, Ashley, and I all got wasted and had a fantastic time. Incredibly, Vijay had taken a selfie with the Ricky Tang in the drug-fueled environs of the Sumatran coffee shop. He had made Tang text him the photo, and he showed it to us. I was astonished, and wondered if the text had played any role in our being found and rescued. After midnight, Vijay started texting Tang, asking "Where are you bro?? Come 2 party," at which we all collapsed in gales of hysterical laughter. Poor guy was probably locked up in a CIA black site somewhere.

Toward the end of the night, Vijay and Harder reprised their eye patches and paper mache swords and went at me. I took an actual pirate sword from one of the display cases, and to the museum custodian's horror, started swinging it at them. This play-fight got so raucous that we eventually smashed into the giant ice sculpture of the *Flor de la Mar*, shattering the beautiful thing to pieces. This drew a standing ovation, and was taken as the signal to wind down what was generally acknowledged to be the legal party of the century so far.

Over the next few days, I took it easy. I came into the office but didn't do much. I kept Rockaway and MNN on in the background, feeling like I was watching an old friend. I had little motivation to get back to billing. Instead, I lounged around and enjoyed the aftermath of our great victory.

Eventually, Cindy, Harder, Vijay, and I went upstairs to track down Remington. He had been away at some hearing for a few days. We stomped into his office with big smiles on our faces, and plopped down in his big leather chairs without so much as a by-your-leave.

"Well, well," Remington said, smiling at us. "Look who showed up to work."

"Come on," I said. "You have to admit we deserve some time off after that."

"Jack and I do, at least," said Vijay. "I'm not sure about these two." He crooked a thumb toward Cindy and Harder. "They just sat around in the office all day while we got ransomed by pirates."

"That's not fair!" said Cindy. "I would have been ransomed by pirates too, if I could have."

Remington chuckled. "I'm sure you would have." He kicked his black cowboy boots up on the desk. He spat, and I noticed he was chewing tobacco.

"So. Case turn out the way you expected?" he asked me.

I shook my head, not able to find the words to answer. I thought back to the day I had first met Ashley Marcum at the pro bono clinic. It seemed like a lifetime ago. We chatted for a while about the case, and the party, and Judge Graves, and all that. Eventually, I asked the question we had come for.

"I have to know something," I said. I'd been thinking about this ever since we settled the case. I had tried to find Remington afterward, but he was gone from the courthouse. Then I'd tried to ask him at the party, but he left early.

"Why did you make that deal?" I asked. "We could have gotten more. I'm sure of it. You started at ten percent, and went down to five. But they were already at ten when you walked in. With what we had on them, we could have asked for twenty. Maybe more."

"Twenty percent," mused Remington. "Perhaps. I don't know about that."

"And why the all-cash deal?" I persisted. "Why didn't we just take a percentage? It would have been a lot more money. You know that. Was it a risk calculation? Did you think they wouldn't pay, or the case would continue for that much longer?"

Cindy, Harder, Vijay, and I all looked at him expectantly, waiting for an answer. We had discussed this at length. We all felt the same way, and wanted to understand. "I know we got a huge settlement," I said. "Don't get me wrong. It's a big win. But I can't help feeling like we left money on the table," I said frankly.

Remington sat quietly for a while. He looked thoughtful. "Well," he said finally. "I guess that depends on how much you think the wreck is worth."

"All of the experts agree it's worth billions," Cindy said. "Including Professor Schnizzel."

"And those were just the reasonable ones," Harder said. "Remember the TV experts? They could still be right."

Remington nodded slowly. "Let me ask a different question, then," he said. "How sure are you that the wreck we found is that of the *Flor de la Mar*?"

A flicker of uncertainty went through me. It was a bizarre feeling. What was he talking about? I waited, thinking it was a rhetorical question. But Remington just gazed back at us steadily. Back to the Socratic method, then.

"We're sure," I said confidently. "The ship was carrying coins from the ancient city of Malacca, dated five hundred years ago."

"And bronze lions were found at the site," said Cindy. "That's consistent with the known cargo of the *Flor de la Mar*."

"So what?" Remington said with a shrug. "You could have found those coins on any ship sailing in that day and age. And lions are hardly rare. They were a symbol of strength in the ancient world, as they are today."

Vijay and Harder exchanged glances. "Fine," I said impatiently. "Manuel Roberto's confession, then. That's what led David Marcum, Lloyd Gunthum—and eventually, us—to the wreck. That proves beyond a doubt that the wreck is the *Flor de la Mar*." Cindy nodded her agreement.

"And how do you know that Roberto's confession is true?" Remington challenged.

"Because we found the ship!" Cindy said, exasperated. "It's like Jack said. Roberto's confession led us directly to the wreck. Ergo, it must be the *Flor de la Mar*. Plain and simple."

I nodded. Exactly right.

"It led us to *a* wreck," Remington corrected. "A wreck that no one had found before."

I was tired of the riddles. "I don't get it," I said, irritated. "Are you really saying that despite what everyone thinks, we didn't find the *Flor de la Mar*?"

Remington didn't answer right away. Instead, he reached into his desk and took out a small tin. He opened it and withdrew some chewing tobacco, which he carefully placed into his mouth. Then he sat back and addressed us.

"What do we know for certain?" he asked. This time, he answered his own question. "We know that a newly uncovered historical source claims that Alfonso de Albuquerque secretly diverted the *Flor de la Mar* for his own ends. This source claims that the ship didn't really sink in the Strait of Malacca. Instead, it sank somewhere else, northwest of Sumatra. This story is contradicted by Albuquerque's own account, as well as that of other eyewitnesses. What makes you so sure that it's true?"

"Because it is!" Cindy shouted. "Because we found the ship! And it's not just us that thinks so. David Marcum thought so. Lloyd Gunthum thought so. Rockweiller Industries, Portugal, Malaysia, and all their experts think so. These are smart people, and they spent a lot of money on this. Why would they do that if they weren't sure? Oh, and the whole global media is sure of it too. How do you explain that?" I was taken aback by her intensity. She seemed almost angry.

Remington just gazed back at her calmly. Then he looked out the window for a little while. Finally, he turned back to us.

"You know, I studied psychology as an undergraduate," he said. "Before it was fashionable, like it is today." Him and Kruckemeyer both, I thought. I didn't know what that had to do with the *Flor de la Mar*, but I wasn't about to interrupt him.

"I decided it was mostly hogwash," he continued, "and went into law instead. But I continue to use and apply some basic psychological principles in my work today."

"Like what?"

"Like confirmation bias. That's the tendency to search for, interpret, and process information in a way that confirms one's own existing beliefs. Put another way, people believe what they want to believe."

I frowned but didn't say anything.

"Another psychological principle is social proof. That means when everyone else believes a thing, you are more likely to believe it too."

Cindy, Harder, Vijay, and I all looked at each other uncertainly. These principles sounded vaguely familiar. I had probably learned and forgotten them in psych 101.

"Now," said Remington, "apply those principles to our present situation. Rockweiller isn't stupid. Not by any means. Nor are their lawyers, or their experts. But once this case took off, and the publicity began to spiral, they lost control.

"The financial markets loved the find. Rockweiller's stock price shot up as a result. Their CEO looked like a genius. The media loved it too. The sunken treasure. The deal with Portugal. The international intrigue. Rockweiller started to get swept along by the tide. They may have had doubts about what they had found. In fact, I'm sure they did. But who was going to air them? It was in everyone's best interest for this wreck to be the *Flor de la Mar.*"

"What about the lawyers?" I said. "Shouldn't they have said something? Isn't that their job?"

Remington waved his hand dismissively. "Badden and Bock? Please. They were just as captive as Rockweiller was. Bock and all of his fancy experts were happy to egg this case on. They made a killing. Millions, at least. And as the case got bigger, it began to feed more people, and generate more bills. Other countries joined the fray, worried they were going to be left out. And it snowballed."

"What about the press?" Harder said. "They don't have a vested interest."

"Don't they?" Remington countered. "The press wants a story. They always have. Holy grail of treasures found, billions in gold at stake, that's a story. No-name wreck stumbled upon by accident? Not so much. You know what old newspapermen say about the news? It's just the hole between where the ads go. How many advertisements do you think the *Flor de la Mar* sold?"

I stared at him. "What are you saying?" I asked. "Are you really telling us that this has all been a wild goose chase? That we never found the *Flor de la Mar* at all? You don't believe that, surely?"

"But why didn't you say anything?" Cindy cried. "Have you thought this all along? Why didn't you tell us?"

I answered this time. "Because we have a vested interest too," I said softly. "The more Rockweiller, Portugal, and Malaysia thought the ship was worth, the more they would pay to settle the case."

Remington nodded. "That's right."

Then I seized on something. "But if that's true...then how did we find the wreck from Roberto's account? How do you explain that?" I said it challengingly, as if daring him to answer.

"My guess is it was just a lucky coincidence," said Remington. "Gunthum and Marcum searched a wide swath of ocean near the Nicobar Islands, on a well-traveled trade route between Malaysia and India. A lot of ships sank there. The chances of finding one, if you looked long enough, were relatively good.

"Did you ever wonder why you didn't find the ship near an island?" he continued. "Like Manuel Roberto's account said? The wreck was halfway between Chowra and Batti Malv Islands. I checked the nautical charts. There was no land within sight of the wreck. So how could Roberto have made it to shore?"

"Maybe the account was off," said Cindy. "Or the maps were wrong. Or he got carried away by the storm."

"Maybe," said Remington. "And of course, it's unlikely that you would stumble across a ship with the particular cargo that this one had. But that is far more likely, in my opinion, than the possibility that this wreck is the long-lost *Flor de la Mar.*"

"And the confession itself?" I heard myself ask.

Remington shrugged. "I'd say it was a fake. Somebody forged it to discredit Albuquerque. He had no shortage of enemies. Or it could have been a sailor, or a priest. I really don't know, and it's a good question. But a deathbed confession, buried in the archives of Portugal? That no one has seen before, let alone corroborated? I don't buy it. I'm not a big believer in conspiracy theories.

"Mind you," Remington said, "this is all just speculation on my part. Maybe the wreck really is that of the *Flor de la Mar*, and I'm wrong and everyone else is right. But you asked me what I think, and there it is."

After that, we sat there in dead silence for the longest time. I couldn't think of what to say. Was it really possible that the wreck wasn't the *Flor de la Mar?* That none of this had been real? I felt a sense of vertigo. As if the floor was shifting under my feet. As if the basic foundations of what I believed were suddenly being called into question. What had this all been about, then?

Eventually, Cindy broke the silence. "If this isn't the *Flor de la Mar*," she asked in a small voice, "then what happened to it?"

Instead of answering immediately, Remington got up and walked over to his bookshelf. He carefully thumbed through a few volumes. Then he withdrew a book I knew well. It was the *Commentaries of the Great Afonso Dalboquerque, Second Viceroy of India*. Remington sat down again, and opened the book to a place he had marked. Then he took out a slip of paper, which I recognized as a translation of one of the few other purported eyewitness accounts to the *Flor de la Mar's* sinking.

"I don't know what happened to the *Flor de la Mar*," Remington said. "That's a question that has vexed archaeologists and treasure hunters for centuries. And I don't pretend some country lawyer like me has the answer. But if you'd like, I can give you my best guess."

Remington then read aloud from the eyewitness account of the ship's sinking. "The *Flor de la Mar,*r sunk in four fathoms of water. The ship had very high fore and aft castles. It is likely that the wreck was visible on the surface and that the locals could reach it easily. A hundred people were left on board, and most of the precious cargo was able to be saved. Everything that the water did not spoil was recovered..."

Remington closed the book with the heavy sound of finality. "My guess is that what happened to the *Flor de la Mar* is exactly what Albuquerque and the other eyewitnesses said: it sank by the shore in the Strait of Malacca, in four fathoms of water.

"Four fathoms of water is about twenty feet. What do you think happens when a billion dollars' worth of gold and gems washes up under twenty feet of water by the beach? And the Portuguese all leave and sail home? I bet it took the locals a couple of weeks to recover most of it. The rest would have washed up over the years that followed."

"And the ship itself?" I asked.

"You know the answer to that, Jack. The *Flor de la Mar* sank in the shallows. Not the deep ocean, like the *Mercedes* or the *San Jose*, where ships can be preserved for centuries. The *Flor de la Mar* was made of wood. It probably broke up in the time and tides a long time ago."

"Occam's razor," I said dully. "The simplest explanation is usually right." Remington nodded.

"So my best guess about what happened to the treasure of the *Flor de la Mar*?" Remington said, kicking his black cowboy boots on the table. "It was all salvaged and divvied up about five hundred years ago."

EPILOGUE

We held a funeral for David Marcum in Houston. A lot of people turned out. Ashley didn't know half of them. But they all knew her brother. It seemed that David had left a mark with his life, however short.

Ashley donated a big part of her settlement proceeds to charity. One of the biggest recipients was the Houston Legal Aid clinic. With the new funds, the clinic was able to hire more attorneys and move to nicer offices downtown. Ashley herself went back to school at the university in San Marcos. To study psychology.

Two of the new attorneys hired by the legal aid clinic were Harder and myself. Judge Graves held a disciplinary hearing on our conduct. He didn't disbar us, but he suspended us from practicing law for pay for one year. He also ordered us to do no less than one thousand hours of community service each. In his order, Graves wrote that while our actions had uncovered a far greater crime, that didn't change the law. Graves said he had a duty to punish us to uphold the ethics rules and deter such conduct in the future. But the sentence was lenient, and less than I'd feared. It could have been worse.

I was happy to have some time off from corporate work. Harder and I set up shop in adjacent offices at the legal aid clinic and gave legal advice every day to those who needed it. The new offices that Ashley had financed were bright, airy, and (of course) modern, and we enjoyed a prime view of the Houston skyline. Cindy and Vijay would come down to the clinic on Fridays to help out, followed by what became a traditional weekly happy hour at Sushi King. Cindy and Vijay both stayed on at HH&K, and regaled us with the latest stories about Kruckemeyer, who was as crotchety as ever.

John Remington continued to practice law unabated. His next case was a massive trade secret trial involving the alleged theft of intellectual property from U.S. technology companies by China. Remington's expert witness in the case was Professor Jacob Schnizzel.

Lloyd Gunthum was charged with murder by federal prosecutors. They charged the crew too, as accessories or for lying under oath. Most pled guilty. Lloyd Gunthum fought it and went to trial, maintaining that he had acted in self-defense. A jury of his peers disagreed, and Gunthum was unanimously convicted of murder and sentenced to life in prison.

Kathleen Loudamire resigned from Badden & Bock and became an ethics professor at a small law school in Florida. She wrote a textbook and won some teaching awards, and eventually got tenure. I didn't keep track of what happened to Quinto, Adipose or the other Badden & Bock associates.

Zachary Bock avoided disbarment or any criminal charges for his role in covering up Marcum's death. He mounted a no-holds-barred legal defense, arguing that he had acted properly under the ethics rules. Bock hired a former federal judge in New York and a respected ethics professor from Harvard to represent him, and got off by the skin of his teeth.

But he was forced out of Badden & Bock by the scandal. He landed at some other New York megafirm the next day.

We never found David Marcum's contract for the *Flor de la Mar*. I thought about it sometimes, and wondered where he had kept it, and whether it had existed at all.

Two years after the lawsuit ended, Rockweiller Industries still had no definitive proof that the wreck found near the Nicobar Islands was that of the *Flor de la Mar*. In a short press release, Rockweiller announced that it was temporarily suspending salvage operations due to "various factors." The statement did not disclose the value of what was recovered, or say when operations would resume.

Rockweiller later instituted a private arbitration proceeding to try and claw back the money it paid to David Marcum's estate. It charged fraud, misrepresentation, and tortious interference with contract. The arbitrator threw out the case under the anti-claw back provision that Remington had inserted into the settlement agreement. The arbitrator further ordered Rockweiller to pay all of the Marcum estate's attorney's fees for defending the claw back action.

As for me, I bought a new car, and finally furnished my apartment. Otherwise, I haven't spent much of my money. I'm dating Ashley Marcum, and I haven't fucked it up yet.

Jacob Schnizzel gave me the model of the *Flor de la Mar* that he had in his office. He added a gold plaque, which the whole team from HH&K signed as a parting gift. I keep it on a shelf at the clinic.

Sometimes I look up at it, and my mind drifts across the seas and the centuries. I think about Alfonso de Albuquerque, scion of the Portuguese Empire. About Malacca, and the blood and treasure that was taken when it fell. I think of the modern-day battle waged in the Texas courts, a more civilized kind of warfare, but fought by warriors no less fierce.

Most of all, I think about the ship itself. About the many people that sought it over the years, and those who claimed to have found it. Remington was probably right about the *Flor de la Mar*, I knew. That it had broken up in the sea, and that its contents were scavenged long ago. It was the most logical explanation.

But a splinter of doubt remains in my mind. I think about all of the wild theories out there. The inaccuracies of the old charts, with their ancient rivers and lost kingdoms. The vastness of the ocean, and the unexplained disappearances in the Strait of Malacca. I think about whether someone might find the wreck one day. Or whether someone already had. And so from time to time I look up at the model and wonder. What really happened to the *Flor de la Mar?*

THE END